AFTER THE WASPS

A NOVEL BY T. LLOYD WINETSKY

Legacy Book Press LLC

Camanche, Iowa

The author was originally going to donate a portion of book sales to charity. However, the manuscript of After the Wasps was concluded following the author's diagnosis of Lewy Body Dementia. Please include any support you can offer to the Michael J. Fox Foundation.

TABLE OF CONTENTS

Part I:
SUB-ORDER APOCRITA

CHAPTER 1
Rudy Lanier

On his way across the high school grounds to meet his friends, Rudy was startled by loud buzzing near his ear. He cursed the small garbage bee, swung at it twice, then some guy walking by mocked him with a laugh. *Asshole*, Rudy thought, then hurried off, peeking back twice to check for the jerk or the bee.

He had come to dread his daily five-mile trek from Truman High School in East Los Angeles to his neighborhood, La Plata. Every September, the long walks left Rudy with blisters, sore calves, and chafed thighs until he gradually adjusted and healed. On this day in October, however, his anxiety wasn't related to physical discomfort.

Rudy was regularly accompanied by three of his childhood friends—Noah Korman, Artie Mata, and Jonny Wilson—all four of them in their second month of eleventh grade. They shared one physical attribute, sturdy calves from years of so much walking.

Back when they started junior high, Noah and Artie wanted to commute to school on their bikes, but Jonny, short for Jonathan, wasn't allowed and Rudy didn't ride a bike, so they continued to walk both ways. When they graduated to Truman, even more distant, they began taking the bus to school, then walking home. Bicycles weren't "in" at high school, so Rudy didn't worry as much about his humiliation for never riding a bike. He easily secured his driver's permit and practiced with his father. Rudy hoped his bicycle phobia was over, but he didn't want to find out.

About five-ten and well over two hundred pounds, Rudy was the heaviest of the four as well as the youngest, about to turn sixteen.

Below the neck, Rudy's body was roughly the shape of an upper-case R, and he typically wore an extra-large shirt tucked into "husky" jeans. His size 7¾ California Angels baseball hat was so tight that he kept his dark-blond hair relatively short, or the cap wouldn't fit at all. Back when he started at Truman, Rudy felt good about the JV football coach recruiting him for the offensive line, but he eventually lied to the coach and some of the kids that his dad wouldn't allow it.

Approaching the student store, his peripheral vision picked up two guys, one bulky and the other lanky, walking toward him. *Shit, Harry and Sikes.* Rudy watched them nervously; he could even see Harry's snarling grin. Most Truman students knew that Harry's name was short for Harrier—a monicker blessed upon him by his hawk-inspired hippie parents.

*Second time he's followed me. What the hell did **I** do?* Rudy considered himself fortunate that he had managed to make it relatively unscathed through junior high into his third year of high school by bluffing bullies or avoiding them. *Get inside, idiot.* As soon as he entered the small store, Rudy immediately looked outside; Harry and Sikes were gone. *Where?* He heaved a sigh. Four or five students were milling around while Noah and Artie bought their baseball cards.

Physically, those two defined polar opposites. Noah, six-six and still growing, had a narrow face, reedy limbs, light-brown skin, curly dun hair, and he was expecting to make varsity basketball after a year on JV. He wore a hand-me-down business shirt with long slacks sewn by his father, a struggling tailor in the more standardized economy. Noah's sweat-stained ballcap had faded from its original Dodger blue.

Artie had his full growth but was only about five-four. He was wiry strong and the number-two miler on the track team. His straight, tar-black hair fell to his neck around a small, round, very dark face. He had a downward-curved pre-Columbian nose and brilliant black eyes. Artie wore a shrunken, faded green t-shirt that hinted of his prematurely developed biceps, and he was in patched blue jeans with sneakers, his only new apparel.

Noah turned to Rudy. "How come your face is so white, Casper?" *What? Ignore him.*

Noah sloughed off Rudy's silence. "What took you? Me and the midget already got our cards."

Rudy glowered back. "When are you going to get over calling him that?"

"Forget it, Rudy," Artie said. The other students in the store paid no mind to them.

"Ha!" Noah applauded himself. "Midgets can't even drive; can't reach the pedals."

Rudy snarled. "And you're the only one on earth who can hide behind a flagpole."

"That's old as the hills."

Jonny came in, his books stowed in a new polyester red rucksack over his shoulder. Chubby and not three inches taller than Artie, Jonny was towheaded with a feathered haircut, a few light strands stuck to his neck. A grill of shiny braces covered his food-pocked but even teeth, still not straight enough for his mother. Rudy knew she also insisted on nothing less for Jonny than the most stylish clothes, like his already rumpled corduroy bell-bottoms and untucked madras shirt. Rudy saw that his new thick-heeled brown oxfords were scuffed. *She'll have a cow.*

Jonny looked down his pug nose at Artie's cards. "No wonder you're always broke."

No wonder there's a silver spoon up your ass. "Who pays for your coin albums, Jonny?"

"My mom says they're educational."

Rudy scoffed a short raspberry, then quickly bought his cards and walked out with Artie—Noah and Jonny behind. When they were well away from other students, the three with card packs took them out to sneak a peek at the ballplayers, then they pocketed them right away.

"Mine are crap," Rudy groused to no one in particular. *Theirs must suck too.*

Taking the warm Thursday afternoon for granted, the boys moved along at Rudy's steady pace. He always led the group to their part of L.A., although the others probably couldn't explain why. Across the street, six clamorous diesel-belching yellow buses idled in their own lane near a tall, long hedge of dusty cedar. The sidewalk narrowed, then Jonny hurried away from Artie to walk with Rudy, who nervously watched the kids lining up for the buses. *Thank god, no Harry.*

"Anybody hear the Dodgers cream the Yankees yesterday?" Noah was loudly referring to the 1977 World Series.

"I heard they were lucky," Rudy stated. "Parker confiscated my radio."

Noah rolled his eyes. "*Confiscated*—Jesus. Can't you just say she took it?"

"It's more accurate." Rudy checked the students near the buses again. *Damn, there he is.* Harry was standing with Sikes near the next-to-last bus, facing Rudy, who lowered the brim of his Angels cap and increased their pace.

Noah smirked. "What's the big hurry, Rudy?"

"No hurry. Shut up." He paused on the sidewalk where a mature poplar in the home's parkway partly obscured them from the bus students. Rudy walked on, his eyes straight ahead.

"He saw you." Noah switched to baby talk. "Who pwotec widdow Wudolf fwom mean ol' Hair-we?"

Artie had ignored the squabble, but Jonny was giggling over the baby talk.

"Not you," Rudy said, "that's for sure."

"So what?" Noah looked away. "Oh, you wucked out, Wudolf; he's gone."

What? They don't load up this early.

Chewing the stale gum from his card pack, Noah blew a grapefruit-sized bubble. It popped, but he inhaled most of the pink gossamer goo, then faced Jonny. "Think you could beat that, metal mouth?"

"Funny." Jonny sucked noisily at Noah through his braces, the only retort he dared to use since sixth grade when Noah beat him up and Jonny became his servile follower.

Rudy hardly paid attention to them. *Where the hell is Harry?* He sighed, then gazed up at the second story of a light-yellow gabled house, likely the largest home in the modest neighborhood.

"Do you see something up there, Rudy?" Artie asked, craning his neck.

Rudy snapped out of his brief reverie. "Uh, no, Artie."

"Wu-dy, Wu-dy, Wu-dy." Noah was mimicking hackneyed TV impressions of Cary Grant. "Fess up, man. You wondered if Queen Elizabeth was up there." He horse-laughed. "She's not bad for a big girl named after a boat."

"Yeah, the James Bond ship," Jonny added dully.

Idiots. Rudy and Libby had often been in the same classes since seventh grade. He had noticed her, even thought about her a little, but it was only the previous year when Rudy was taken by her long, dark-red hair, unusual green eyes, and her affable but serious demeanor. "She's not so big." *Shut up, Rudy.* His head ached above his brow as he walked on.

"So, Wudy, you saw she lost weight? You've had your eye on her for a long time."

"Noah, your stupidity and hostility are showing again."

"Ooo, *hostility*, Professor Lanier—good one. I talk to her every day in homeroom; you're too chicken-shit to talk to her at all."

"We talk, just not in homeroom." *Yeah, a couple times in the lunch line.*

"Bullshit, gramma's boy, like your sister says." He sniggered.

"So says Romeo, who took his sister to the dance."

"At least I went." Noah blew a small bubble and popped it. "My dad would croak if I dated *goyim*—he doesn't give a rip that Jewish girls here are so stuck-up."

"And with black fuzz on their lips," Jonny said, avenging Noah's crack about his teeth.

"What is fuzz?" Artie asked as they walked on.

Jonny just sneered. With Artie in honors science and math, and Rudy in high-track English, the only classes they all had in common were P.E. and Spanish II, where Jonny and Noah regularly depended on Artie's homework.

"It's like fuzzy," Rudy told Artie.

"Oh." Artie turned to Noah. "Then fuzz is a noun—so Jonny said Jewish girls have hair on their faces." Artie shook his head. "Another insult."

"Except it's usually true." Noah chortled, then turned to Jonny. "No sweat, man."

"Yeah. Hey, you guys, Atari has this new computer thing you plug into your TV. Costs a lot, but Dad called and said he'd get me one for Christmas—we could play it at my house."

Noah nodded. "Sounds cool."

Rudy looked askance at Noah and Jonny. "I read that it has *Pong* and *Fun with Numbers*. I'd rather watch pavement dry."

"I like the arcade anyway," Artie said.

"You both suck," Jonny grumbled, then wandered off.

"That computer thing sounds rad to me," Noah told them. "You guys pissed him off."

"Tough shit," Rudy said in a flat tone.

Jonny was almost a block ahead when the rest of them approached a fenced-in yard, one of few with foliage in bloom—especially a showy bougainvillea with lacy, magenta flowers. Some of its branches reached across a pastel-yellow picket fence where three or four kinds of late-season pollinators buzzed from stamen to stamen as if politely taking turns with the bounty.

Rudy detoured to the curb to avoid the tall plant. He waved his cap at a hovering black and yellow bumble bee, its thorax about the diameter of a nickel. Escaping Rudy's attack, the bee remained over his head. Rudy flailed again, losing his hat and books as he dashed into the street. From the sidewalk, Artie gaped while Noah guffawed and stuffed Rudy's hat into a back pocket. Rudy joined them under a tree on the other side of the bush. His headache had returned.

"That was very foolish," Artie said quietly as he handed Rudy his books.

"My mom says I'm allergic to bees."

"More like scared shitless," Noah hissed.

"Shut up. I need to sit down a sec."

"Jonny's waiting for you up there," Artie told Noah, who walked off in that direction.

Rudy waited until Noah was gone. "Thanks for getting rid of him, Artie. I'm a little dizzy." They sat down on the curb; Rudy scanned the street. "What happened to my damn hat?"

"Noah has it."

Rudy, sighing, hand-dusted his books. "I'm sick of being scared of everything, Artie."

"I think that's an exaggeration. Are you scared of Noah?"

"He thinks I am, even if I don't show it." *Say it.* "He's right, I guess. When I act like I'm not afraid, that's when I usually am."

"Yes, I think that is very common, and it's also true of Noah."

"How do you know?"

"I can see it. Noah is afraid of me because he knows I'm stronger than he is."

Rudy and Artie stood, then dawdled toward Noah and Jonny, two blocks away. They silently approached them at the end of the second block.

Noah horse-laughed again. "You two aren't turning fag, are you?"

Tittering, Jonny picked up his pack. He and Noah started off.

"You can both stick it, especially you, Ichabod," Rudy nettled from a few feet behind.

Noah turned. "Whatever that means."

"Enough insults," Artie said, bluntly for him.

Noah smiled. "*Suh-len-ci-owe, Are-TOO-row. My es-pan-yoll estaw be-yen*—right?"

"You know it's terrible. You don't even try."

"Yeah, not like *San-toe-roo-dole-full*."

"Rudy teaches me correct English, and he tries to speak Spanish right."

Artie's English, his third language, neared perfection over the years, and he still knew Zapoteco, his indigenous tongue, as well as Spanish. Rudy's tutoring had mostly been in English conversation, especially idioms and contractions that Artie asked about. Their Argentinian Spanish teacher, Mrs. León, told Artie he needed to refine his Spanish from "Mexican dialect." Artie ignored that, and she still criticized him but was obliged to give Artie the top grade in the class.

Artie saw Rudy touch his temple again. "What's wrong, Rudy?"

"Nothing's wrong," Noah broke in, then faced them, holding Rudy's bent cap. "Rudy talks a big game, but he's still a big chicken-shit." He taunted Rudy by dangling the cap.

"Not scared of you." *That's telling him.* "Give it, jerk."

"What would you do lard-butt, sit on me?" Noah sniggered again. "Wudy, your fairy hat with the halo is all RF'd."

Rudy snatched the hat from Noah, slapped it on his knee, then put down his books. He rounded the bill of the cap and put it on.

Noah pointed at Rudy's hat. "Hell, the Angels'll never even *get* to a World Series."

Rudy picked up his books without responding.

"Geez, enough baseball," Jonny called back, starting toward the street where the neighborhood transitioned from residential to light industrial.

Halfway to the corner, Rudy stopped. "Jesus." Harry was walking toward them on the sidewalk, his follower at his side. Jonny crossed the street and ran to the corner.

Noah chuckled. "Uh, oh, Wudy, here comes twubble."

In a white t-shirt and jeans, Harry's stout orangutan-shaped frame swayed side-to-side with each step, the taps of his infamous steel-toed boots clicking on the pavement, getting louder as he approached with Sikes, who was spindly, maybe six-two, and suffering from rampant acne.

Rudy's lower jaw quivered a little. He saw Harry's wrist and right arm were encased in a soiled white cast all the way up to his bicep. *Artie hasn't moved. If we run, they can't catch him, but Sikes can catch me, and Harry kicks my ass. Bluff him. What else can you do?*

Harry chortled to Sikes. "See, man, the smart-ass has boys: Noah the kike, Farty the spic, and Jonny the pussy, who don't even count."

Sikes, in a white tee and jeans like Harry, eyed Noah. "Yeah, the kike lives on my block."

Noah stepped back and ran off, stopping about twenty yards away on the sidewalk near the last house before the corner. Artie still hadn't moved.

Harry shouted, "Boo!" at Noah, who ran off around the corner. Harry scowled at Rudy. "Some boys you got. I didn't want stick-man anyway. Now it's two against two."

Shaking slightly, Rudy nevertheless glared at him. "What the hell do you want, Harry?"

Rudy's tone made the bully half-grin. "You know what I want, smart-ass. This is the end of *you* makin' fun a' *me* in P.E."

What? "Yesterday? That wasn't about you. You were laughing too."

"Liar." Harry got right in Rudy's face, speaking to Sikes without looking at him. "See if you can hold onto the spic."

"No problem," Sikes said, smirking. He tried to clamp his large hands onto Artie's shoulders, but Artie easily slipped away and started to land rabbit punches to the guy's nape. "Harry, I can't get hold a' the little shit."

"Big baby, I told you he boxed before. Just keep him back."

Bastards, leave him alone. Rudy's heart raced as Sikes finally got his arms around Artie. "Cops come by here all the time, Harry."

Harry chortled. "When they see we got us a wetback, they'll just laugh it off. Can't bullshit me, fat boy."

"Listen, Harry—"

"Shut up, smart-ass."

A man in his forties with black hair and dark eyes came out onto his porch in a white shift that didn't hide his tall, sturdy frame. In a thick foreign accent, he shouted, "Stop—stop what you are doing!"

Harry scoffed. "Mind your own business, raghead."

The man leaped over his porch steps and practically race-walked toward Harry. An angry frown on his face and a red-and-white hound's tooth scarf around his neck, he stopped a few feet shy of Harry and Sikes, pointing at them. "You are a disgrace. All my life I work to bring my family to this country, and now I see kids like you do this."

"So what? Nobody wants you here anyway," Harry mocked.

The man stepped forward, face-to-face with Harry, who backed off a couple of inches.

"I ain't scared a' you." Harry's retort sounded unconvincing to Rudy.

"Better you should be scared. Do not move." The man turned to Rudy. "What is the direction you go?"

What? Rudy nodded toward the end of the block.

"What will happen is this. You two will go that way." The man pointed to the arterial, then turned to Harry. "You two stay with me a few minutes, then you will go another way."

Harry shook his head. "That's like kidnapping. I know my rights."

The man sneered. "You know nothing of rights." He turned to Rudy and Artie. "Walk away proud—you tried to stop them."

Yeah, Artie did. Rudy and Artie started off.

"I ain't done with you two," Harry called out.

"He means it, Artie."

"Yeah."

Continuing toward the corner, they heard the man scold Harry and Sikes again. On Garner Drive, Rudy exhaled in relief, then he ambled with Artie onto the wide sidewalk, passing mostly repair and parts shops while rush-hour traffic rumbled along nearby.

"Maybe we should walk faster, Artie."

"That's what he expects us to do."

Great. "Aren't you worried they'll be waiting up there?"

"They could run up Ash Street all the way. If Harry is waiting long, he might get tired and go."

And maybe he won't. Along with a mild headache, Rudy's teeth chattered slightly.

"Are you cold, Rudy?"

"Still scared, I guess."

"Try not to worry about it. Let's take our time. Give them a chance to get bored if they are up there somewhere."

"Yeah." They passed a quiet machine shop, then approached an alley. Rudy peeked around the corner of the building. *Nothing.*

"Rudy, they won't hide where a lot of people can see them."

Rudy's shoulders relaxed a little. They walked on; Rudy was thinking about the foreigner. *…he saved our skin.* "Artie, why do you think Harry backed off from that man?"

"Fighting a full-grown adult isn't Harry's game. He knows the guys at school, so he never has to take a chance. He didn't know what to expect from the man."

After they came to a main cross-street and waited for a red light, Rudy stared at the traffic, noticing a shiny hubcap rolling in the road, somehow avoiding all the cracks and potholes. He watched it go into a spin, fall over, then get flattened by a bread truck. *Functioning seconds ago—now it's nothing. Write it later.*

Rudy and Artie approached Freddy's Freeze, where the four boys sometimes stopped for soft ice cream. *Doesn't sound good, but it'll waste some time.* "It's on me." Rudy had meager but regular income from his allowance and the English tutoring he did once a week.

Artie practically strutted beside him. "Rudy, the ice cream is on top of me."

On top? Just let it go.

"My dad let me keep ten dollars instead of saving all of my salary for me." His father was *jefe* of a Mexican crew at a large tree nursery in Hollywood. The eldest of five, Artie worked with him there on Saturday mornings.

"Thanks, Artie, but I just want a small cone—not feeling great."

After Artie paid, he and Rudy walked toward the corner, licking their treats. They were coming to La Plata Avenue, where Noah and Artie usually waited for Rudy and the morning bus. Artie now had to walk ten blocks south to what remained of the old Mexican-American neighborhood known to many Whites as Flytown. More than half of the area had been displaced by freeway construction when Artie was in fourth grade. He and the other kids from the severed northern blocks had been allowed to continue attending La Plata Avenue Elementary.

Another damn headache—must be brain freeze—get rid of the ice cream. "Artie, I appreciate the ice cream, but I'll have to ditch the rest."

"You ate it too fast?"

"I guess so." He walked back to the trash can, then returned to

Artie, not far from the corner, where they looked around.

"It looks like the coast is clear, Artie."

"No. It isn't." He pointed up La Plata Avenue.

What the hell?

CHAPTER 2
Ambush

Artie and Rudy gaped toward La Plata Avenue's slight upgrade. "What did you see, Artie?"

"Where does Sikes live?"

"Between here and Noah's." *Shit.* "I should've thought of that before."

"I saw Sikes peek out up there. They are waiting for you; they think I'm going home."

Now what, Rudy? He sighed. "Okay, I think you *should* go home. I'll go with you and call my mom to pick me up."

"Rudy, if we take off, Harry will wait for us tomorrow or the next day. I have an idea."

"You mean just go up there? Why would we do that when we have a way out?"

"I think that is what Reed would say. I don't want to worry about a *pendejo* like Harry."

"I don't know how to fight."

"Just listen to my idea. If you don't want to do it, that's okay."

Rudy sighed. "Alright, let's hear it."

"See that alley?" He pointed across to a narrow lane of gravel and weeds between a house on the corner and its neighbor. "I think it runs behind all of the houses on that side. So, we…"

Artie explained his plan, Rudy reluctantly agreed to it, then they scrambled quietly up the alley past mostly stick-built one-car garages. They came to the Sikes' open and empty garage.

"Remember what Jonny said about Sikes's father?" Artie asked quietly.

"Yeah, he never comes home until late. We don't have to worry about him being here."

"Right." Artie stealthily checked the path that went from the garage to the front yard. After he checked the porch, Artie started back to Rudy.

What am I doing here? Shit, you can't leave Artie.

"Okay, Rudy, Sikes is hiding on the porch; I saw Harry go inside. Remember, after I go, then you come out when—"

"Yeah, I know." He took a deep breath.

"Scared?"

Harry's going to—damn. "Absolutely."

"So am I, but it's a good plan. Like I said before, Sikes will probably run in."

That's what I'd do. "Right, two on one—except the *one* is Harry."

"With a broken arm. We will be okay. Let's go."

They started on the path, staying close to the small cinder-block house until Artie stopped, then stole into a hedge out front to peek through the branches. He turned back to Rudy. "Perfect," Artie said under his breath. "Here goes."

Rudy attempted to take Artie's spot, but it was too small for him. Hardly able to see out, he watched Artie walk into the front yard.

"Hey, Sikes," Artie said quietly.

Sikes stood up from behind the porch rail. "What are *you* doing here? I'm gonna' call Harry. He'll kick the crap outta' you this time."

"What about you, *cabrón*, do I tell everyone you are afraid of a little Mexican?"

Just like Artie planned.

"Bullshit." Sikes took every other stair down to Artie, who waited on the concrete path that divided a scruffy yellowing lawn. Sikes took two wild swings; Artie easily dodged them, then jabbed Sikes repeatedly in the gut until he nearly doubled over. Artie stopped punching.

Rudy saw Harry come out onto the porch, dropping his donut when he saw Artie. He lumbered down the stairs, laughed and said, "You're a pussy, Sikes."

"I didn't want to do this anyway." Sikes pulled himself up the banister to the porch. "Get off my property, alla' you!" he screamed, then the front door slammed.

Damn, get out there like you're supposed to. Rudy left the bushes.

Harry turned to him and laughed. "Good, you're next, smart-ass."

With Harry distracted, Artie had launched a jab up toward his face. It hit Harry's neck, but not full-on. "That all you got, spic?" Another punch brushed his ear. "Ha! Mosquito bite!"

Artie landed a right jab to his chin, faked, then tried a roundhouse blow with his left. Harry caught the fist with his good hand and forced Artie to the sidewalk, twisting his left arm at a radical angle.

"*¡Hijo de la puta!*" Artie spat out, then scooted away and tried to get up.

"What's 'at mean, beaner?" Harry, chuckling, moved closer to Artie.

Goddammit. "Hey, Harrier—harrier than anybody. Try someone your own size."

"Don't make me laugh, fat-ass." He turned back to Artie and began to cock his leg.

Go! Adrenaline kicking in, Rudy took two long strides and dove for Harry's legs. The bully's black boot missed Artie's ribcage and his leg swung overhead, making him lose his balance and fall back on the dry grass.

"Bastard!" Harry bellowed.

Shit, what now? Pro wrestling hokum flashed through his mind before Rudy thrust his full weight down on Harry's chest; an *oof* escaped the bully's mouth. Grunting, Harry's face was flush as he attempted to push Rudy off with his left arm. He soon succeeded, then Rudy tried to stand, but Harry was up, leaning over to kick Rudy hard twice in the rear end.

"Shit!" Rudy bawled, squirming in pain. *What the hell? Something extra was on his toe.*

Through a few tears, Rudy saw that Artie was back up in a boxer's shuffle, jabbing Harry's head, face, and cast with his right fist only. Now breathing hard, Harry flailed at Artie with his good arm, then he made a surprising move by swinging his injured arm. Harry's cast struck Artie in the neck. The blow propelled him several feet away, but Harry had lost his balance again and fell directly onto the hard path, the bad arm beneath his massive frame.

Harry got up slowly and lifted the loose, cracked cast. "Son of a bitch!" he cried out. "Arm's broke again, you goddam little spic!"

Rudy got to his feet as Harry lurched towards Artie, who was struggling to stand. *He'll kick Artie for sure.* Rudy hobbled over, wiping his eyes. "Hey, Harrier."

Harry turned, snarling. "You're dead meat, smart-ass."

What the hell—hit him. Never having used his fists in a fight, Rudy opened his right hand and attempted to strike Harry with the boney part of his palm.

Harry easily avoided Rudy's poor attempt, laughed at him, then cringed and wailed from jostling his broken arm. Raising his good arm like a charging fullback, Harry straight-armed Rudy hard in the sternum and watched him fall. "Ha!" he blared.

Rudy had fallen on his side and thought his skull bounced once on the sidewalk like a playground ball. He groaned, then a couple of tears smeared his vision. *Damn, can I get up?*

Harry stumbled over to Rudy. "One last shot, smart-ass." Harry started to size up a kick to Rudy's ribs, then he stopped and cringed, his arm writhing in pain again. "Shit, you pricks tell anyone you broke my arm, I'll break your damn legs." He meandered off, cussing at his dangling appendage.

Rudy still hadn't moved much. "Artie, he's gone, right?" he asked quietly.

"Yes." Artie knelt down to Rudy. "Are you okay?" Artie sat nearby on the path.

"I guess." Rudy leaned gingerly onto the prickly grass and sat there, touching the abrasion on the side of his head. "It's not bleeding much—guess it didn't hit as hard as it felt." He pressed the thumb and forefinger of his right hand to his breast bone. "Chest is just a little sore—it's my butt that hurts."

"*Sí*, he really got you."

"There was something on his toe."

"Yes, they were tied on there. My dad said they are ball, um—"

"Ball-bearings?" *Damn, could've been worse—* "What about your neck, Artie?"

"It's pretty sore." He shook his head. "I think my arm is dislocated."

"Jesus."

"Yes, no use trying to hide it, my mom always knows if I'm hurt." He paused. "Rudy, use my handkerchief for your head."

"The blood will ruin it." His body stiff, Rudy stood, folding his cap into a back pocket.

"I can wash it later." Artie handed him the small, embroidered square cloth.

Rudy dabbed the wound. "Thanks, Artie."

"*Seguro.*"

They walked haltingly on the path, then stopped at the sidewalk near the street. Rudy faced him. "I didn't know your boxing was that good, Artie."

"*Sí*, the one-armed boxer."

"Reed's advice helped you come up with that plan, right?"

"Yes, I think Harry was confused until he got in that lucky shot."

Rudy released a long sigh. "When Reed gave me that advice last year, I shrugged it off."

"The last part is to defend yourself with whatever works. After my brilliant plan failed, you tried to defend yourself. That's the hardest part. You even tried to hit him."

"I had no clue what I was doing."

"Rudy, defending yourself and helping me took some guts. Maybe I can teach you some boxing. One punch stops a lot of them."

"Not Harry."

"Yes, I learned today that he's stronger and quicker than I thought, and he's not all talk like most bullies—like Noah or Sikes. But he's also stupid like a beast that sees only what it wants to kill. Even worse, he likes how it feels to hurt people. Harry *está bien cascado, es un maníaco*, um, maniac. Before he's twenty, I think he will kill somebody." Artie paused.

"Our ribs would be broken now if his arm didn't hurt him so much. We are lucky to still be walking." Artie sighed. "Reed said it isn't a coward who stays away from *locos* like Harry, or a gang. I'm thinking now that he's right, and *you* were right; we had a chance to avoid all of it. I'm sorry my foolish pride got you into this."

"No need to apologize, Artie. At least now I know what it's like."

"Yes, I think that's the first step with anything you are afraid of."

A first step. "I think I'm ready to try out some other first steps." *Sounds good, but can you do it?* "Maybe I should start with those boxing lessons."

"Any time," Artie said with a smile. "Rudy, I'm very late." He paused. "I have to, um, face all the music. Did I say that right?"

"Close enough. You gave me a lot to think about. Maybe we can talk tonight."

"Yes, if I'm not in trouble." Rudy gave him the handkerchief; they exchanged *see-yas*, then Artie started down La Plata Avenue. Rudy hobbled off the opposite way. His rear end stiffened again, and it took more time than usual to get to Noah's block.

The homes here were also small, chiefly stucco or cinder-block, some with fenced-in dirt yards or postage-stamp front lawns. Tall, venerable palms grew two to a parkway, but one or two on each block had dry fronds and seemed to be failing.

Rudy walked slowly by the Kormans' simple, well-maintained frame house, a small garage in back like the others. The palm fronds out front cast insufficient shade over the home. Its small, neat front yard was rocked-in around prickly-pear, stonecrop, cholla, and other drought-tolerant flora behind a chain-link fence. Rudy glared at their small front porch. *You there, dickhead? What if he **did** come out? I wish he would. Bullshit—no you don't.*

Rudy walked on, biting a fingernail as he covered several blocks to upper La Plata. He crossed at a four-way stop on Palm Street, which had no palms left or right, nor were there any more ahead. Rudy started to pass the corner Italian grocery, which was more of a butcher shop with a few basic necessities and plenty of sweets.

Jonny came out, eating the last of a multicolored popsicle, dribbling it all over his new sport shirt. *Jesus, he's a worse slob than Si.* Besides a mild headache and his sore butt, Rudy felt a pang in his stomach.

"Noah and me waited a while at Freddy's. I felt like a popsicle anyway."

"Oh, how does a popsicle feel, Jonny?"

"What?"

God. "Nothing. Did you kipe it?"

"I have plenty of money. Why would I?"

Because you like to, and you're a cheapskate.

When they started walking, Jonny eyed Rudy's dirty clothes. "Noah said you and Artie were going to get it. You're just limping a little— doesn't look like Harry got you very bad."

Ignore him. They crossed the street and passed by La Plata Avenue School, a standard two-story red-brick structure, now quiet except for the playground. Rudy watched the black macadam radiating in the sun as two squabbling boys, maybe fourth-graders, slugged away at a tetherball, its chain clanging against the steel pole. Jonny tossed his popsicle stick and wrapper on the ground, then stopped.

Slob. Even Si wouldn't do that.

"I bet Hank let them have the tether-ball overnight. The ol' Negro never did that for me." He paused. "You liked this place, didn't you?"

God. Rudy had kept walking.

Jonny caught up. "Not me. Remember when you were Slater's little math genius?"

"That was arithmetic."

His tailbone aching, Rudy didn't respond to most of Jonny's jabber over the next few blocks. They came to a long stretch of upscale residences. Most were closed up, their air-conditioners whirring against the eighty-degree day. Unlike the cookie-cutter suburbs, these homes were built during the previous decades in a variety of architectural styles, most with extra lots. The diversity of La Plata's best homes contrasted with the conformity of their landscaping. Most yards boasted putting-green perfect lawns, manicured oleander hedges, avocado or citrus trees, and sometimes an exotic territorial like a century plant, jacaranda, or an endangered yucca—illegal to transplant but common in yards of expensive homes.

The boys approached the meticulous, vast front yard of the Wilsons' old but completely renovated two-story house. Its roof was Spanish tile, and the exterior had been remodeled with colorful designs formed by ceramic tiles embedded in white cement. A new Lincoln and an early '70s Chevy station wagon occupied two spots in their four-car garage.

Jonny looked askance at his house. "Our jap gardener's here. He's supposed to be finished by now—he looks in our windows."

"Bullshit, he's Matt's dad." Back in sixth grade, Matt Jojima was the fifth boy in their group before his family moved to Glendale.

"So? My mom says we're getting too many japs and spics. She doesn't want me around them anymore."

Big surprise.

They stopped at an ornate black-iron fence, where the gardener had just finished some delicate trimming nearby that always reminded Rudy of some creepy topiary in a favorite science-fiction movie. "So, you're just going to dump Artie?"

"No, I'll see him enough to get my Spanish homework."

Prick. "And what about Jews?"

Jonny put three middle fingers of one hand on the bridge of his nose, stroking downward, a common pejorative gesture at Truman for Jews. "Mom doesn't like Jews either, but she says Noah will probably be rich someday."

He'll be glad to hear it. Rudy glanced at the gardener, who was carrying yard tools over to his '50s Ford pick-up. "So, Jonny, do I still merit the honor of your acquaintance?"

"Why do you talk like that sometimes?"

To piss you off. "Like what?"

"You know what I mean. Anyway—yeah, we're still friends. Mom says that me and you are the only Christians."

She's an idiot. "Artie's a Christian."

"No, he's Catholic." Jonny pointed across the street at a two-story American colonial. "Listen, I'm friends with Walt now."

Yeah, now that you can drive. Jonny had recently passed his driving test and drove one-way to school every day with his mother.

"Rudy, why don't you come to *Saturday Night Fever* with me, Walt, Trish, and her two friends on Saturday? Mom's letting me drive the wagon on my own, and she'll pay your way."

Like hell she will.

Lugging a wound-up hose past the fence, the gardener bowed very slightly to Jonny.

Attempting to greet the man before he made another bow, Rudy said, "Afternoon, Mister Jojima." The gardener still bowed timidly before heading for his truck.

Oblivious to the gardener's obsequious gestures, Jonny looked at Rudy. "Paula is Trish's best friend; she's short, so I'll take her. Walt doesn't know who the other one is—you get her."

Man, think about this. No, he screwed up everything. "This sucks, Jonny. Remember we were all going to see *Star Wars* again, then poker and the Series? You should've told us."

"I don't care about any of that. I think Noah's right; you're just scared of girls."

I could beat the crap out of the little twerp. Who couldn't? Big man, Rudy.

"Okay, don't answer me," Jonny whined. "Fine, I'll get somebody else for the other girl."

"Yeah, you do that." Rudy walked off, his forehead pulsing again. He left the Wilsons' wide driveway, absentmindedly chewing the same fingernail as he continued up La Plata Avenue.

He was startled from his reflections by a garbage truck that rumbled by, coughing black smoke. *Man, what a day. At least it should be pretty laid-back at home tonight.* Rudy walked the last blocks to his street corner, looked toward his yard, then groaned loud enough to make a neighbor's dog bark. His Uncle Si's beige, rusted Studebaker, the old model that resembles a single-prop airplane without wings, was parked in front of the Lanier's house. *Dammit, Si was here last weekend. How do I get out of the house tonight?*

CHAPTER 3
Simon/1946

Mildred Krenshaw had always been proud of Simon, as she called him, especially when Si became the first of her three sons who "took to school." A bright, introverted boy, Si liked to explore his yard, the nearby park, and play games with his best friend and his sisters. Since Si originally started kindergarten a year late and was now doing so well, Mildred agreed to have him skip the second half of fourth grade. In 1946, students in Los Angeles public schools first enrolled in February or September, eventually graduating from high school in a summer or winter class. As a result, Si would be moving on to fifth grade in September, but Mildred was baffled by Simon's apparent confusion about the news that Miss Hartland, his previous first-grade teacher, was transferring to a fifth-grade vacancy and would be his new teacher.

Ten days after classes began at Parkview Place School, Mildred received a note from Miss Hartland saying that Si was indifferent to much of his work, except for reading. The teacher wrote that Si would use all of his free time reading the same library books on insects, the solar system, and the World Wars. Mildred knew that her boy's war interests revolved around his brother in the army and Simon's long-time fascination with military weapons, vehicles, and aircraft. He steadfastly remained on watch for the silhouettes of Japanese Zeros.

The teacher reported that she had tried to have Si tutor his friend, Greg, but it didn't pan out when Si had unexpected difficulty retaining new information and couldn't help Greg with comprehension. Mildred hoped her son just had early growing pangs; she was more concerned that he had gained weight that summer and was pocked with scores of scabs from insect bites.

At eleven-thirty on a Thursday morning, Mildred left her house for a parent-teacher visit. She descended the partially broken stairs of their one-story log home, one of the oldest houses in north Los Angeles, built in a strawberry field before the turn of the century with timber from the Sierra Nevada. Mildred's large family used every square foot of the long, narrow two-story house, but the anachronistic building struggled against disrepair on her sparse income and the skimpy funds from her estranged husband. In order to be with her children as much as possible, she worked on a production line—five-hour shifts, nine p.m. to two a.m., six nights a week at a nearby ceramics factory that had gradually converted back from assembling military parts.

Mildred walked through her mostly harvested victory garden that took up half of the front yard, fenced in by weathered grey pickets. She sighed. Next to the garden, a gnarly orange tree shaded their geriatric brown mutt, dozing near some fallen fruit and a few scrawny hens. Carrying a large hemp bag, Mildred pushed their wobbly wooden gate and left.

About forty, spare, and five-foot-six, she wore a long, seamlessly mended, pastel-blue cotton house dress that looked to be passed down from a heavier woman. Her deep, dark eye sockets were shaded from the sun by a well-worn flowery sunbonnet that protected her pale, gaunt face. Mildred's lustrous sorrel-brown hair, her most attractive physical feature, was held with a clip to fall down her narrow back.

She inhaled and looked up as she walked, pleased with the fresh air and flax-blue skies. She was grateful for the atypical weather, a result of a rare Pacific storm the previous day that had scrubbed out the smoke and sticky heat from the Los Angeles basin.

Mildred scrutinized the first houses on Halifax Street. She walked by an abandoned frame house, but she smiled at the next small place. It was classically Southern Californian with a trimmed lawn and semi-tropical greenery around a white stucco home with a russet-clay tile roof. Mildred then approached the defunct Griffith School, which she had always presumed was named for nearby Griffith Park.

Mildred stopped to stare at the lifeless, dilapidated building; she shuddered as if echoes of bustling and shouting children lingered from the forsaken classrooms and playground. She recalled bitterly when the school was boarded up in 1942 after nearly all of its Japanese-American students, many of them friends of Mildred's children, were rounded up with their parents and detained at a Civilian Conservation Corps camp in Griffith Park before their transfer to U.S. Army detention camps in Montana and North Dakota. The arrested families included about a third of the school's students, so Griffith School no longer had a viable population and was shuttered. The principal of Parkview Place School was pleased to enroll the remaining Griffith children into his student population, which had also declined during the war.

Shaking off the "willies" from her kids' former school, Mildred passed more houses, some of them well-kept the closer she came to the bus stop on Los Feliz Boulevard. She waited for one of the city buses that were gradually replacing the electric streetcars. Mildred got on a few minutes later and dropped a nickel into a machine. She listened to it rattle rhythmically, as if it were grinding the coins. After eight blocks, Mildred got off and walked up Parkview Place.

She put the bonnet in her bag and entered the venerable red-brick one-story school. The bell rang for lunch as Mildred entered the upper-grade hallway and watched the students crowd out of the classroom doors onto the lacquered wood floor, dusty after a half-day of dirty shoes and drifting chalk powder. Smiling at a teacher on hall duty, Mildred thought the kids were mostly well-behaved, some of them peeking into their lunch sacks; a few others pushed ahead to burst out of the back double doors.

Mildred watched the commotion subside, then a few teachers surfaced, including Miss Hartland. Now in her thirties, she was slim and about five-eight in a modest yellow summer dress, her tawny hair pinned back into a modern bun.

"Mrs. Krenshaw, wonderful to see you again."

"Afternoon, Miss Hartlan'. I picked a right busy time."

"Not at all, I switched duties today."

"'Preciate it." Mildred took her hand for a few moments as if they were long-time close friends. She peeked over the teacher's shoulder. "An' Simon?"

"Inside, finishing his lunch." They walked ahead. "It's so nice the heat has backed off."

"Yes'm, but accordin' to my cousin's almanac, it's not over." She paused. "We have a lemon tree; I'll send along a bagful with Simon."

"Fresh off the tree? Wonderful. Thank you."

They entered the classroom, and Mildred noticed how the orderliness of the room added to the feeling that the school hadn't changed much since opening in 1909. Five very tall windows with glass transoms looked out on the middle-class homes across the street. Opaque dark stain dominated the room's walls, shelves, cloakroom, and five rows of student desks bolted to the floor. High on the front wall, several feet from the flag, a solitary picture was hung above grammar, penmanship, and arithmetic charts, where Abraham Lincoln looked down on the desks with an uneasy smile.

Mildred saw Simon at a nearby desk, his lunch pail to one side. As he dutifully finished a carrot stick, Simon slouched over an open book with a B-29 bomber on the cover.

He looked up. "Hi, M-mom," he stuttered, then went right back to his book.

"Si, um, Simon, your mother and I are going to chat for a few moments. If you have finished eating, please put away your things, then you can go down to your duty a bit early."

"Yes'm."

Mildred watched Simon brace himself on the desk to get up. Almost five-seven, thick rolls bulged his white tee shirt, which had a patch on the front the size of a saucer, embroidered in red, white, and blue, a white star at its center. Mildred noticed Simon's chubby face, once tan in the summer, was now pallid in contrast to his dun eyes and mussy dark-brown hair. His locks didn't hide his oblong cranium, already in the high range of normal for an adult.

Si took his things to the cloakroom and left without a word.

"Mrs. Krenshaw, I didn't think you'd want to be talking about Si in front of him."

"Thank you, ma'am, but I don't think he cares. Is he eatin' lunch in here every day?"

"Yes, I decided to offer him a different duty, which he seems to like. He goes down to the kindergarten to help the teacher when they start in the afternoon." Miss Hartland presented a hand toward a chair near her desk, which had a folder, notepad, and pencil on top.

Mildred sat down. "Can you tell me y'r thinkin' on that?"

"Of course." She sat at her desk. "He was sitting around at noon with his books; I wanted him to be more active and involved. The children in kindergarten love it when he reads to them. I watched him there one day, and I believe he smiled."

Mildred covered her doubt with her own smile. "What about bein' with kids his age?"

"Yes, that's important. He's with them here and at recess." She picked up a pencil. "May I take a few notes?"

Mildred nodded. "How else is Simon comin' along?"

"Well, Si, um, Simon—"

"Excuse, Miss Hartlan', don't fret about callin' him Simon. I give up on other folks usin' his Christian name. I mean *gave* up—the twins'r helpin' me on my past-time words."

"Good for you, Mrs. Krenshaw," she said, sighing. "I know he doesn't leave home in a mess, but Simon arrives at school sometimes with shirttails out, shoes untied, even dirt or food on his face and clothes."

Mildred nodded and sighed. "Yes, I can't figure why he does that now."

"Neither can I. I'm afraid he is teased about his appearance; the insect bites made it worse. I'm glad they are healing." She paused. "Mrs. Krenshaw, I do put a stop to the teasing when I can, but I'm not always near him."

"'Preciate that, but Simon don't seem to care much about the teasin' neither."

"Yes." The teacher paused. "Since it has been so long since I worked with Simon, Mrs. Krenshaw, would you mind updating me about the rest of your family?"

"The whole lot of 'em?" she said as if she had fifteen children.

"Please."

"Well, it's seven kids now, includin' Simon. My oldest, Daniel, joined the army in '43—that boy knows right from wrong." She felt her enthusiasm wane. "Then there's Nicholas, supposed to graduate winter class—might take 'til June. He's home now with two broke bones from football. Next is Marguerite; she's doin' fine in ninth grade—an' helps me with the girls 'n all. I lost a baby after her." She bowed her head slightly. "So, there's a stretch before Simon." She smiled. "He's so good to his little sisters—especially the twins, Camilla and Catherine, in third grade. He's been good to Candace too; she's my baby in first grade."

"I wish I had the twins in first grade; maybe I'll have them in here," she said, smiling. "I've noticed that the twins and Simon don't avoid each other like some siblings do."

"On account a' them bein' together so much—all three of 'em brighter'n a new dime. Until now anyway." She frowned. "Well, that's the lot."

"And Mister Krenshaw?"

"Re-enlisted after V-E Day. He could a' been stationed here in the desert, but he said his best chance was workin' on planes in Seattle. Right off, he got discharged. He's still livin' up there, fixin' tires 'n such."

"I see. It sounds like Simon gets along well with his sisters—his brothers too?"

"Simon keeps Daniel's letters—reads 'em over 'n over. All them years between 'em, but they always been close," she said with a smile. "I'm thankful Daniel come home with nary a scratch after fightin' on them islands. One year left, thank the Lord. Daniel's wife, Sharon, stays with us—an' she's good to Simon too." Mildred's face beamed. "An' my first granbaby's due at Christmas."

"Congratulations, Mrs. Krenshaw!" She jotted a note while the light moment lingered.

"And your other son, how does he get along with Simon?"

"Simon bein' such a peaceful child, Nicholas'd tease 'im real bad until Daniel give Nicholas, um, gave him whatfor."

"Thank you for telling me about everyone, Mrs. Krenshaw; it helps me with Simon. May I ask one more question about the family?"

"Yes'm."

"Thank you. How do you think Simon would react if his father visited?"

"Imagine he'd go play with the twins. Before, he'd hide." Mildred bent her neck and torso forward a little. "When Simon got bigger, Sam'd say he was a misfit for not bein' like his brothers, an' a sissy for playin' with his sisters. Daniel's the closest Simon's had to a real father."

"If this is too personal, I can—"

"No, ma'am. When the boys was growin' up, Sam'd be okay to 'em all week, but not to Marguerite. Weekends, he'd be drinkin' an' mean, an' I'd try to get him outta' the house." She paused, her eyes still on the floor. "Sam'd hit us, then I got me Simon's baseball bat. Daniel finally run him off for good." Her eyes moist, Mildred straightened herself, shook her head, then her eyes met the teacher's. "Sam become a lush in the war—servicin' airplanes in England."

The teacher was silent for a few moments. "I'm sorry if I upset you with my questions."

"Jus' the truth. I hear tell it's good to get troubles out to somebody you trust. Two gals I know had worse beatin's, but they can't even talk about it." She dried her eyes. "It took a long time to figure Sam for a coward—now I always got my ol' club ready."

"I don't blame you, but let's hope it doesn't come to that again. Mrs. Krenshaw, I believe you're raising a fine family."

"We got problems like most, but we're gittin' on, thank the Lord." She sighed. "Money's always a problem, but I worry Simon'll get worse and make it harder on his self and the girls."

"And on you, Mrs. Krenshaw."

"I'll be fine. I believe my kids'll have me around until they all grow up—I seen a lot who don't even have that. What I aim for most now is for Simon an' my girls not to have a hard life."

"An admirable goal." The teacher paused. "I want to mention something that I think is remarkable about Simon." She took a tiny toy soldier from her purse. "This is a gift from him. It's very sweet that he is so generous. Back in first grade, I thought it was remarkable that he never seemed to expect anything in return from anybody."

"Yes'm, somethin' that hasn't changed." Mildred nodded. "Some folks don't even notice, 'specially the part about him not expectin' nothin' back. Started as a toddler—sharin' things'd make him happy. Difference is, now it's more like, um, a habit."

"It doesn't seem like it to me." The teacher put down the toy soldier in a standing posture, eternally plunging its bayonet at some foe. "Can you tell me how long since you first noticed that Simon had changed at home?"

"Well, he come back—um, came back—in August with the doldrums. You think maybe he's just comin' early to the change?"

"Oh." She glanced at the folder. "I don't believe so—not quite yet. You said Simon came back from somewhere. What did you mean?"

"Simon an' the twins always go first a' August to my brother-in-law's farm up in Kern County before comin' back for school. They take to the open space an' fresh air—can't blame 'em," she sighed.

"The girls don't get along with my sister, Melody, so good, 'specially Catherine, but their Uncle Ted dotes on all my kids."

"Sounds like they still have a wonderful time up there." She jotted again. "How did Si, um, Simon show the doldrums you mentioned?"

Mildred exhaled noticeably. "Simon was always a little bashful away from home, but it's worse now. I think you, me, um, an' the twins can see part a' my boy's missin'." She sniffled slightly. "Sharon knows it too, an' so will Daniel. Most others don't see it—but they's not obliged, just busy with their own life."

"I think I understand." She paused. "Please tell me more about Simon's changes."

"Yes'm," her face dour. "When the kids'r playin', he's not much a part of it anymore. He gets dirty like most boys, but now I gotta' get after him about all his personals—washin' up, takin' baths, sloppin' his food; he'll use the same shirt a week if I let him. An' Simon…" She bowed her head slightly again. "…sometimes he don't, uh, clean his self good—back there—I could tell from his underdrawers." She twisted a handkerchief she had taken from her bag.

Mildred looked up. "He's doin' a little better now, but I can't get him to stop pickin' his nose around people—don't look like he even knows he's doin' it. When I ask him if somethin's wrong or somethin' happened, he'll just say, *No, ma'am*, an' go on with what he's doin'."

During the explicit anecdotes, the teacher took notes and waited for Mildred to continue. "Simon always had a tummy, but it's turned to a big roll." She pursed her lips. "He eats more'n ever, more'n we can even afford. Sharon an' Daniel help some with the food, but they gotta' save every nickel they can."

"Of course."

"We try to make ends meet with what little Sam sends, my night job, an' the girls helpin' with piece work I take in. Even Simon'd collect bottles to help out, but now he started spendin' it on candy. Ain't sneaky about it—he just don't fathom how it matters. So now I tell him to keep three pennies for a sweet at the dime store, an' the twins remind him."

"What happens when you talk to him about how he eats and takes care of himself?"

"He just says, *Yes'm*, then he'll try to do things right—never contrary. After a few hours, it's like I never said a word, but he don't mean nothin' by it."

The teacher nodded. "Did you know that Greg is his only good friend at school?"

"Yes, they been friends for years—it's good they're in the same class now."

Mildred knew only too well that Greg was called *lamebrain* by some boys because he was a "slow kid." They harassed Greg over his given name, Gregor, dubbing him *Igor the Kraut*. Greg's father, the son of Austrian immigrants, was a wealthy banker, which didn't work in Greg's favor since prejudice was rife toward families associated with the Axis countries. Mildred puzzled over how Jews were often scorned as well, irrespective of Hitler's slaughter.

"Simon always took to helpin' Greg with homework 'n such, but not now. The Greisens is kind to my boy, an' we like havin' Greg over. They send me mendin' too—helps me save up so my kids can go to the matinee every month." Mildred sighed again. "Mostly it's Sharon takes 'em to the movies; she tol' me the twins wait to see where Simon sits when Greg don't come. The girls go an' sit with him, or he'd just be alone the whole time. Bless their hearts."

"Yes." Miss Hartland nodded again while finishing another note.

"My heavens, I never," Mildred *tsked*. "I'm just goin' on an' on like a ol' hen."

"I don't think so, Mrs. Krenshaw. I wish all parents cared as much about their children."

Mildred was silent for a moment. "That's real nice a' you to say, Miss Hartlan'."

"It's true, Mrs. Krenshaw." She checked her notes. "And Simon's stutter?"

"That's another mystery to me." Mildred rubbed her temple. "Simon was five when he got real sick an' the stutter come on. Doc Grant said it was likely to go away, an' it did, then never come back 'til now, but it's not near so bad like before. There's times he don't stutter at all, like singin' out loud. There's some reason for that?"

"I don't know. He also doesn't stutter when he reads to me or the children." She paused. "One activity he did participate in was the paper drive. He and Greg went all out."

"Yes, they was in all the drives durin' the war. He an' Greg'd hunt down metal scraps, cans, grease, an' what all. Simon even give up his toy soldiers, but Daniel sent 'im new ones. The drives fit right in with Simon's interest in the war, especially him wantin' to help Daniel."

"And who's to say he didn't? Good for Simon and Greg."

"Yes'm, but the war's over."

"Yes," with a solemn nod. "What else has or hasn't changed with Simon?"

"I recollect Simon readin' comics an' whatever took his fancy when he was five. Now it's mostly two army rule books Daniel give 'im, an' I keep 'n eye out for used kids' books for Christmas an' his birthday. His library books is the same ones he was readin' before."

"Yes, I know the ones."

"He'd do the crossword for kids I'd cut out from papers on the bus, but they was too easy, so I'd look for harder ones at the Goodwill. Now I'm cuttin' out easy puzzles again. He knows some words from his studyin' before, but like you say, he don't seem to learn new words." She paused. "Miss Hartlan', somethin' else good that didn't change—Simon's harmonica."

"Oh, yes! The kindergarten teacher says her children love his music. When did he learn?"

"You know Mrs. Amaral, his third-grade teacher?"

"Wonderful teacher; she just retired."

"Yes'm—shame my girls don't get to have her. She'd teach music with the autoharp an' let the kids have a try. She showed Simon the buttons 'n all, an' he took right to playin' songs. Daniel came home one day from the pawnshop with a mouth organ, an' Simon took to that quick too. Won't play for nobody but his self an' the family—an' now the kinders, I guess."

"What sort of music does he play?"

"Army an' cowboy songs, an' some little kids' songs he learned for Candace."

"Does he still learn new songs?"

"No, just the same ones, but he still plays 'em good."

"I'm sure he does," with a smile. "So, Mrs. Krenshaw, Simon was skipped partly because he started kindergarten so late. Do you mind telling me what caused that to happen?"

"Don't mind." Mildred looked up at a hanging light as if beseeching some entity to help her explain. "He started school on time, but before Thanksgivin' he come down with the scarlet fever an' strep—worse fevers I ever seen a body live through—rash, the strawberry tongue an' all. Doc Grant, Simon, an' us give it a fight, an' he made it, thank the Lord." She paused. "Then come the peelin' all over, includin' his tongue. All that an' the quarantine, he started kinder again the next February." Mildred saw Miss Hartland poke a page in the folder with her pencil.

"None of that is even in his records, Mrs. Krenshaw, except enrollment dates."

Surprised by the teacher's mild indignation, Mildred searched for a way to respond. "Um, I believe Doc Grant mailed a report to the school."

"Yes, I'm sure he did." She sighed. "How long since Simon has had a physical?"

"A while. I pay Doc Grant three dollars a month on what we owe plus a dollar in fresh produce when we have it. Bless him." She paused. "If it comes to Simon needin' to go to the doctor, we'll manage somehow."

"I think it might also be a good idea to ask the twins if anything unusual happened to Simon at the farm in the summer."

"Yes'm, I shoulda' tried that before. Maybe today." Mildred got to her feet. "I can tell, Miss Hartlan', you know he's a good boy, no matter him bein' different. Even before all this, some'd call him peculiar. I don't cotton to that at all."

"I don't blame you." She put the folder and notepad down.

Mildred tried to keep tears from welling in her eyes. "Maybe he don't show it, but I believe Simon cares for you like family, Miss Hartland."

"Oh, my." Her cheeks flushed a bit. "Well, that's very nice of you to say." The teacher placed her hand lightly on Mildred's shoulder. "I don't know if this helps, but Simon doesn't seem nearly as upset by all of this as we are."

Tears raced down Mildred's cheeks. "The way he is now—you think it's for good?"

"Sorry, but I have no idea, but I think your doctor is a good place to start."

"Yes'm, he's a good man, an' maybe he'll have ideas for what I can do for my boy."

"What *we* can do, Mrs. Krenshaw." She gently squeezed her arm.

After she visited Miss Hartland, Mildred wanted to talk to the twins as soon as they got back from school. Mildred returned home and took her knitting out to the ragged stuffed chair on their long porch. When the children arrived, Mildred, her face atypically stern, stood and raised a hand to hold back the twins. She waited for Simon and Candace to go into change while Greg, holding his pouch of marbles, walked over to play on the smooth dirt under the orange tree.

As she did with all of her children, Mildred called the twins by their actual names, Camilla and Catherine; to most everyone else they were Cami and Katie—nicknames coined by Margie when they were babies. The twins had started this day in clean jeans and t-shirts, but dust and dried sweat from recess and the walk home had soiled their clothes and faces.

A tad small for their age, both of the raven-haired girls had lean faces with dark eyes and small mouths. Cami's chin jutted out, Katie's didn't, and she had a short, impish nose while Cami's was longer and a notch crooked. With her symmetrical features, Katie could almost pass for cute while Cami was plainer. Mildred literally trimmed their thick hair around a colander, leaving them with a Prince Valiant look—very practical for the rambunctious twosome.

While the twins centered their lives around their imaginations, silliness, and unbridled curiosity, Mildred knew that Cami had an inchoate sensitivity for the plights of others, which Katie sometimes emulated in order to go along. Mildred was proud of their good marks in school, regardless of a few minor run-ins with the rules, mostly instigated by Katie.

The more the twins achieved, the less Mildred worried about them growing up to be pretty enough to find a husband. Now that the war had helped to stimulate more careers for women, Mildred hoped the twins would someday attend the public college near Hollywood.

Standing by her sister in front of the long, splintered wooden bench on the porch, Katie groaned. "Aw, Mom, can't we just—"

"...change, then go out and play?" Cami had completed the second half of their question, emulating Huey, Dewey, and Louie in the funnies. The girls had outgrown an imaginary, fat triplet sister, whom Katie sometimes blamed for their mischief. Occasionally, the twins still called themselves *Katie, Cami, and big ol' Fanny*.

Mildred returned to the chair and put the half-crocheted baby blanket on her lap. "No whinin', girls. For chores today, you'll pick twenty lemons each, then spell Marguerite with Nicholas 'til I come up, then you sweep under the big table from breakfast. After that, out to play. Now, you're to sit an' listen to me."

"Yes'm," with low groans. The girls plopped onto the bench.

"Lot a' homework today, Catherine?"

"No, we already did it."

"Too easy," Cami added.

"Good." Mildred broke her stern tone with just a slit of a smile. "I was wonderin' why you two never told me much about your time at Uncle Ted's farm."

Katie raised her brows. "Oh, that; we had, um—"

"…a swell time," the sentence divided between them again.

"That's somethin' I already know. Do somethin' new this year?"

"Yeah, Uncle Ted put up—"

"…a tire swing at the pond." This time, it was Katie who finished the sentence.

"Nice a' him. Your brother try it out?"

"Yes," from both girls, then Cami said, "Si was out there with us swimming—"

"…and chasing bugs until—" Katie covered her mouth.

"Until what, Catherine?"

She furtively yanked an earlobe. "Until dark."

"Girls, did somethin' different happen to Simon up at the farm?"

"Different?" Cami pulled an ear as if her mother wasn't aware of their signals.

"What're you hidin', girls?" Mildred closed her eyes, then opened them—much longer than a blink. "You girls know somethin's not right with Simon."

"But he's still smart," both of them said eagerly.

Mildred drew in a long breath and released it. "Only with some things."

"Well, he was, um—" Cami peeked at her sister.

"…sick up there."

"How sick, Catherine?"

"Aunt Melody made him stay in bed for—" The twins faced each other; Cami nodded, then Katie looked down, her lips trembling a little. "Mom, we have something to tell you."

"Catherine?"

She faced her mother. "I'm going to tell you the first part," Katie said, "then Cami the rest—she saw more of that part than I did."

"Alright, go on, but no cuttin' in now, either a' you."

"Yes'm," simultaneously, their heads down.

Katie looked up, her legs wobbling. "When we got home, we knew Si was acting funny. But not all that much, so we didn't see why we should get in trouble."

"Go on, Catherine."

She groaned and began to wring her hands. "It was about a week after we got to the farm when all of us went out past the cornfield to play under some oak trees, making up stories and stuff. Eric and Edith got bored and went back to the house. After a while, we were going to leave too, but I saw a wasp fly right into a hole in the ground. Si said they were yellowjackets and to stay away, but *he's* the one who always tells us bees won't hurt you, so we kidded him about it."

Cami distended her lower lip. "But he's never made fun of us for being afraid."

"Yes, Camilla, but it's still her turn. Go on ahead, Catherine."

Katie drew in a long breath. "Cami's right, he never has. So, we ran over to the hole and started yelling and dancing around it, pretending to be Indians."

"And then you dared Simon to do it?" Mildred's voice elevated a little.

"I double-dared him," Katie said, her head down again.

"Oh, girls."

"We're sorry Mom." Their lips quivered.

"Go on, Catherine."

"Yes'm." Tears welled up in her eyes. "Si came over and pushed us away from the hole, but that made us mad; we didn't know he was trying to help us. So, we started back to the house, then turned around and saw wasps all over him, stinging again and again, not flying off. He yelled at us to keep going, but we stopped and watched him try to run away with his shirt over his head, getting stung a lot more." Katie glanced at Cami, who was now sobbing quietly.

Katie continued. "Before he got very far, they finally started to fly away. We went to him; they were almost gone, but we got a couple stings. Si had bites all over, especially his face; it turned all red." She sniffled. "He could walk okay, so we took him back to the farm. From here on, Cami saw more than I did."

"How come, Catherine?" Mildred got up and sat on the bench with them.

"You know Aunt Melody doesn't like me." Katie's face contorted. "She says I get all the kids in trouble. Her little angel, Edith, starts most of it."

"Katie's right," Cami said softly. "When Aunt Melody saw Si, she just blamed Katie and sent her to bed the same time as Si." Her tone had become more adamant.

For Mildred, Melody's treatment of Katie echoed her sister's betrayals from long ago. She patted Katie on the arm. "You couldn't a' known them bees'd do that, so don't be frettin' about y'r aunt. Okay, Camilla, what about back at the house?"

Her face dour, Cami couldn't face her mother. "Si had a fever that wouldn't stop; the worst part was his face—it was red hot. I thought it would get all puffy like a kid at school who got stung, but it was just a little bit swollen. Aunt Melody put a wet washrag on his forehead, then tried some doughy stuff on the stings, then onions, potion, and something else real smelly. None of it helped, but she said Si was better.

"But he wasn't. Si was moaning and started to get the hives and a worse fever, so Uncle Ted told Aunt Melody to put away her remedies. He wrapped Si in wet towels from the belly to his head, then took him to the hospital overnight. Si came back red and sore with lotion all over, especially his face and neck, ears and, um, armpits. The doctor told Uncle Ted it was the worst stinging he ever saw. He said Si was lucky not to be allergic or to get stung in the mouth. But he told Uncle Ted that Si would be okay in a couple weeks."

"Praise the Lord for that."

"Yes'm," the girls said simultaneously again. Cami sat back on the bench.

"Is that all, Camilla?"

"Not yet." She turned to her mother. "Aunt Melody was complaining and angry all the time. She mostly ignored Si in the daytime, so we tried to get him what he needed. Uncle Ted took over at night, but Aunt Melody, she, um…" Cami paused. "She just got drunk at night. We didn't know if you knew about her drinking."

Mildred chuckled mirthlessly. "I been tryin' to keep that from *you*. She's been a drinker for years, but this sounds worse. We'll talk on that later. Keep goin', Camilla."

"After a week or so, Uncle Ted said Si couldn't travel yet. Then they argued about what to do with us. Aunt Melody wanted us to leave. Uncle Ted told her we still had time left. Aunt Melody was getting all mad at him and Katie. Then we heard Uncle Ted say again that—"

"…Si was getting better," Katie said. The twins had reverted to finishing each other's sentences. "He didn't want you to get worried about Si. We thought Uncle Ted was right—"

"…so why should we get you all upset?"

"M-hm. The right thing was to tell me this when you got home." She sighed deeply. "I'm not mad, but you two think a minute 'bout who got hurt by all that, then tell me, one at a time."

The girls looked at each other. After several seconds, Katie somberly peeked up at her mother. "Um, I think it hurt you most. You taught us it's wrong not to tell the truth."

"Yes, but I'll get over it an' forgive you girls." She turned to Cami. "What's your thinkin' on this, Camilla?"

She moaned, her lower lip blubbering; she released a long exhale. "Katie's right about you, Mom, but we also hurt Si because we didn't tell you right away; you didn't have a chance to do something. We tried to apologize to him, but he didn't get it at all."

Mildred embraced her sobbing daughters with both arms. They let go after several more seconds. "Girls, it's the two a' you who got hurt the most—keepin' this bottled up." Mildred wiped her eyes with a forearm. "God knows you love your brother an' never'd hurt him on purpose. I don't know who can help Simon, but I aim to find out. An' don't be holdin' onto no guilt over this. But like they say, you gotta' learn from mistakes. We all make 'em."

Cami finished drying her face with a sleeve. "Mom, what do we say to Si?"

"He don't blame you girls. Just treat Simon good like you always do."

"Mom," Katie said, still sniffling. "I'm not very good to Si, just Cami is."

"What're you sayin', Catherine?"

Her lower lip protruded. "When Si is really sloppy or dirty—I'm, um, ashamed if someone's around who's not family. I'm sorry."

"Truth'll hurt sometimes, Catherine." She faced Cami. "Camilla?"

"I can't help it sometimes either."

"It bothers me more," Katie mumbled.

"Girls, I'm afraid it'll be even harder when you come to be teeners. Simon's way a' doin' things now bothers me too, but he's ours, an' we gotta' stand by him best we can."

"Yes'm."

"Anything else you remember, girls?"

The twins stood and crossed their hearts. "That's the truth, the whole truth, and nothing but the truth—so help us God," both of them said in earnest.

"Mom, can we change now—"

"…and go play with Greg?"

"You two know what you're supposed to do first." Mildred got up as the twins started for the door. "Wait, girls. You're gonna' be playin' only with Greg?"

They stopped. "Si will be there—"

"…but he'll probably just read or watch."

CHAPTER 4
Rudy and Si

The expanding Black and White populations in Los Angeles during and after World War II came chiefly from the South or Midwest, and most immigrants arrived from Latin America, Asia, and the Middle East. Many newcomers moved into lower middle-class or impoverished neighborhoods, and the expanding population led to increased pollution—but most Los Angeles boosters saw nothing but blue skies overhead. Some of the populace knew that the grey, astringent air was not a passing problem, prompting a small but prophetic protest by some citizens of Azusa and Pasadena. To others, inured or brainwashed, every day was "another beautiful day in L.A." Many who resided in the city before World War II chuckled at postcards portraying L.A. with images of lush palms, green hills, and the HOLLYWOODLAND sign under azure skies. In fact, some of the palms were desiccated, the hills more grey than green, and the enormous advertisement that once promoted a housing development was missing its *H*, fallen due to a drunk caretaker or a gust from the Santa Ana winds. Either way, the sign became OLLYWOODLAND, and a Los Angeles wag wrote that the damaged advertisement was an homage to Oliver Hardy.

In the three decades since World War II, much of the growing middle class in Los Angeles was preoccupied with two strong but contrasting impulses. Many strove for more acquisition, especially gee-whiz technology, luxury homes and cars, plus the latest styles, goods, and services. Simultaneously, there was steadfast pining for the vanishing days of Mom at home, Dad at work, the kids in school with their own kind, and pious church services on Sunday.

Rudy had stayed on the corner, glaring at his uncle's ramshackle car. *Okay, think. How can you pull this off? Artie? No—too far, too late. Reed's busy. Noah? No way.* He left the corner, his rear end pulsing, and his head pounding up front again.

Relegating an escape from Si to the back of his mind, Rudy made his way down the middle of the idle block, ignoring its bisecting tar line, which he had pretended to tightrope as recently as ninth grade. If you could apply the word *mongrels* to homes, Ontario Place would be the street. It included two Pre-World War II cinder-block duplexes, several modest stick-built bungalows, an incongruous two-story A-frame, one pastel-yellow stucco, and the Lanier house—the largest on the block, much of it not visible from the street.

The one-level, light-blue home that Larry Lanier rebuilt bore little resemblance to the small frame house on four front-to-back city lots that his widowed father had left to him two years after Larry Junior graduated from high school. Larry Senior had started Larry's Plumbing well before the Great Depression as a word-of-mouth operation, and the business survived the '30s with discounted service and loyal customers.

Larry Junior's work on the property began before his marriage to Katie Krenshaw, whom he met after she won a parks department swimming race where he was the lifeguard. The wedding took place following her high school graduation in the winter class of 1955, two years after Larry took over the plumbing business upon Larry Senior's death.

Since Larry and Katie were going to be parents much sooner than they anticipated, he accelerated the expansion of the home and business. He and two newly hired plumbers tripled the size of Senior's old shop, then Larry soon began renovations to the house. Eventually, he would add a pod of three bedrooms and two baths, then a den and rumpus room—more than enough growing space for their daughter, Charlotte, born four months after the wedding, and the two or three additional children they expected to have.

Nearly seven years after Charlotte's birth, when they had about given up, their second and last child was born. Katie had kept it to herself that she thought Charlotte, a second-grader at the time, was turning out to be an innately stubborn and difficult child. Since Katie had expected and planned for another girl, she asked Larry to choose their son's name. He liked *Rudy*, and his mother-in-law, Gramma Mildred, suggested *Rudolph* for the birth certificate.

Months after Rudy's birth, Katie half-jokingly referred to him as "Gramma's boy." Over the years, if anyone intimated that Mildred spoiled Rudy, she'd take his side. That pleased him, but he was mortified when she called him Rudolph away from home, especially at Christmas.

After passing by Si's Studebaker, Rudy walked onto their front yard of mowed crabgrass. He made his daily check of their tall avocado tree, hoping against hope that it had borne its first fruit in years. To the right of the Laniers' one-level home, Rudy's close friend, Reed McCool, lived with Helen, his grandmother and guardian, in the left apartment of a small duplex.

Rudy liked to recall Reed's initial claim to fame at Truman—a stunt he pulled back in their first month of tenth grade. A coach and physical education teacher named Otis was generally despised by the boys, except for the elite athletes whom he favored. His stale practical joke was to tell a new student to go out for a long pass, then the coach would fake a throw until the boy was exhausted at the end of the playing field, and Otis would just stroll away with the ball, a sinister grin on his face.

After Reed witnessed this, he told Rudy about his plan-in-waiting. The following week, the stars aligned—Reed called it a good omen—on a day when there was a new student in their *IJKLMN* homeroom. His last name was Martinez, which was perfect since Otis especially liked to harass Mexican kids and wouldn't hesitate to perform his old ruse.

Rudy tagged along as Reed prepared to put his plan into action for later in the day. First, they explained the prank to Martinez, who was fine with it as long as he wouldn't get in trouble. Before P.E., Rudy went with Reed as he retrieved a navy-blue stocking cap he had left in his locker. He pulled it down to his brow for roll call, squatting behind Rudy and the squad of boys.

"Okay, shut it," Otis snapped at them, a football under one arm. Adept at wasting most of the first ten minutes of class, Otis droned through the names in alphabetical order. After a few minutes, he smirked and called out, "Martinez—"

Before Otis could say the first name, Reed shouted, "Here, sir," from behind the class.

"Okay, Martinez, let's see what you can do." Reed took off. "Go out for a pass—a long one." Otis turned away from the boys; Reed was already in range for a pass. "Look at the new boy go!" Otis cocked his arm. "That's right, go, boy!" he blared and hooted at the same time.

Rudy and the boys watched Reed run on, extending his hands as if to catch the pass. In no time at all, he easily scaled the chain-link fence and began to sprint down the street, raising his arms in victory while most of the class cheered, then laughed at Otis. That earned Reed a suspension and a nickname coined by Noah in his poor Spanish—*Mucholoco.*

Rudy checked Helen and Reed's place; he saw the front door was closed behind the screen. *He's probably still painting.* He walked up their extra-wide driveway past Katie's new blue Beetle, Larry's wide '68 T-Bird, and his decrepit Chevy pick-up filled with pipes and trash.

Rudy continued on to the shop, where Larry's van was backed up to one of three double doors. To the right, the rear lots were taken up by a walnut tree as old as the original house, a spacious yard much tidier than the one out front, a cinder-block building, and a patio next to a swimming pool, the only one on the street. Near an alley at the back of the yard, Larry's carpentry and plumbing cast-offs begat great heaps of just-in-case scraps—a source of scorn to an unctuous pair of Ontario Place gossips.

Larry built the mid-size kidney-shaped pool where Katie would take her 6:30 a.m. lap swim almost every day. Charlotte and her friends practically grew up in the pool until they became obsessed with their tans. When Rudy's friends came over, he joined in the frolic only when they came to his end of the pool, where his feet could touch the bottom.

His father's arc welder now crackling in the shop, Rudy walked toward the gate to see his dog, a true mutt—Labrador mixed with the proverbial god-knows-what. The black dog was medium-large, had droopy ears, a white patch on the chest, and his legs were too short for his sturdy trunk. When the dog was a puppy, Larry hoped its Labrador genes indicated a good hunter, but the dog turned out to be too slow, free-willed as a cat, and gun-shy—traits that didn't bother Rudy, who found himself with his first pet. He named the dog Stew—as in *concoction*.

Rudy was one of few incentives for Stew to leave his favorite tree-shaded spot inside the sturdy fence that surrounded the two back lots. Larry had installed it for security and because of Stew's one vice, digging up the neighbors' flowers. Although Stew had the run of the spacious yard, he had slowed with age and increasingly scratched the den's glass door to go in.

After putting down his books, Rudy opened the gate, where Stew was waiting quietly. In return for an ear scratch and a "good boy," Stew slobbered Rudy's fingers. He ran the hose to top off the water bowl; the dog lapped up a long, noisy, and seemingly appreciative drink.

"Here ya' go, boy." Like most days, Rudy used an old tennis ball to play fetch with Stew until the dog soon started to pant excessively. Rudy left the slimy ball in Stew's play box, then rinsed his hands from the hose. Stew followed his master to the patio near the drained swimming pool, where Rudy sat hesitantly in one of Larry's lacquered Adirondack chairs. *Damn, that hurts.* He switched to the patio couch. *The bastard really nailed me.* His headache forgotten, he yawned and lay sideways. *You're stalling, it's time for Si.* He patted Stew. *C'mon, get it over with.*

In greasy overalls, Larry came out of the shop to the back of the van. Rudy's father was about five-eleven, but not much overweight—a stout center on his high school football team. The main physical similarity between father and son was their coloring—Larry also had fair skin, brown eyes, a full head of dark-blond hair, and the same bushy brows. His prominent cheekbones contrasted with Rudy's, and Larry's muscular neck had lost tone over the years, but he remained ruggedly handsome.

Larry looked over and spotted his son. "Hey, Rudy," he called, softly as always.

"Hi, Dad. When did Si show up?"

"Not sure. He came back to say hi this afternoon."

Yeah—hi, Si and goodbye. I should be so lucky. "Why is he here today?"

"I didn't ask." He turned back to the van with a wooden figure in his hands.

Man, he started carving again.

Not long after Larry's Plumbing began to flourish, Larry had been drafted to serve in Vietnam. When five-year-old Rudy began to understand some implications of this news, he began to cling to his father. One night, he found Larry preoccupied in the shop. After he showed Rudy his animal carvings, Larry asked him to keep it to himself, but Katie eventually found out.

After Corporal Lanier returned from his four-year stint with the Army Rangers, decorated and physically unharmed, he preferred his own inscrutable thoughts over conversation with most anyone. His Sunday refuge became fishing alone at a public-access lake near the Tehachapi Mountains, north of Los Angeles County.

In those days, Katie sometimes coaxed Larry and Rudy to take in a ballgame or a movie. Rudy liked the outings, although he and his father had little to say to each other. Katie also encouraged Larry to give his son a chance to learn carpentry or fishing, but Rudy preferred a book or a rook over pounding a hammer or gutting a fish.

"Tell her I'll be out here a while," Larry said, his voice barely audible.

Rudy started to go in. "Okay." *He won't make it, and Charlotte has a date. Good—no sit-down dinner with Si. I'm still probably stuck with him.*

He walked toward the side door, the family's usual entrance and exit. Rudy climbed the three steps, opened the screen door to the kitchen, the only relatively large room in the original house. Much of it was taken up by Larry's custom oak table, which sat eight and was the center of household activity. He had also added a nearby utility room ample enough for large appliances and a wide wardrobe where Rudy kept his best clothes. *Si must be in the living room—probably reading Louis Lamour or just sitting there.*

Rudy assumed his mother was at her desk—off-limits when she was working on the plumbing accounts. Katie's usual hours weren't over until around five, so Rudy lingered in the kitchen. A mild headache reminded him to take off his hat and check his injury. He applied a cold washrag above his ear; only a few crusts of dried blood showed up on the cloth, but he did find a lump. *Shit, keep the hat on or Mom will freak. Why is the headache nowhere near where I hit the sidewalk? You'll live, lie down for a minute.*

Rudy walked the short hallway from the kitchen to his bedroom, where he changed from his dirty clothes and sat almost delicately on his single bed. His windowless interior room was once the utility area and a half-bath. Larry had partitioned off the toilet, shower, and sink, which allowed the remaining space to become a small bedroom with no closet. Rudy could have taken one of the newer rooms, but he liked the solitude here, away from his sister. If the kitchen was busy, he often used earphones to listen to Credence Clearwater, Tom Petty, or an Angels game.

Hm, the hubcap. He stood, then took a couple of steps to the bookcase for his notebook of observations, which he had named, *Nobody Saw.* Sitting gradually on the bed again, he started to write about the shiny hubcap he watched rolling in the street before it was mashed by a truck. He contrasted the functioning object with its sudden destruction.

Rudy looked at the clock; he'd been writing for ten minutes. *You're stalling again.* Sighing, he put the notebook away, then walked to his compact bathroom. He climbed onto the chair, lowered his pants and shorts, turned around, and looked in the mirror. Together, the two bruises on his right butt cheek had left overlapping marks the size and color of a crimson maple leaf. On closer inspection, he saw four round, smaller, and darker contusions within the bruises. He touched one and immediately withdrew his finger from the stinging pain. *The goddam ball-bearings.* He removed his t-shirt to check where Harry shoved him in the chest. He found one bruise, not half as dark or painful.

A dull ache thudded in his forehead. He touched the back of his crown, cleaned the dry abrasion, and decided his hair was just long enough to conceal the lump. He did his business, got dressed, then walked into the kitchen and stopped to answer the phone. He stayed on his feet, thinking he could smell Si's rank presence. *Good god.* "Hello."

"Rudy?"

Noah. "Yeah." *What do you want?*

"What happened with Harry?"

"We re-broke his arm."

"Yeah, right." He paused. "Hey, what about the World History report due next week?"

Ah, that's what he wants. "No school Monday. You have plenty of time."

"If I don't have it done by tomorrow night, then I can't go anywhere on Saturday."

Tough shit.

"My dad grounded me until I do it all myself—probably something he got from the Old Testament. Could we work on it before school tomorrow? You said you would help."

Don't be a shit, Rudy. "Alright, I can get you started tomorrow at the bench."

"Great. Then, the library after school?"

"Si showed up. Mom will have me doing something with him."

"Well, I think Fineman can help me after you get me going. Ya' know, the last time I saw your uncle, he kind of reminded me of you—mostly his shape and—"

"Not funny."

"Okay, okay. So, I guess you want out of there tonight. Where will you go?"

Maybe Reed's taking a break. "I'll probably call Reed."

"That should be loads of fun. Mucholoco's still in school?"

Technically, you prick. "He is. Why don't you say that to his face?"

"Hell, I don't have any reason to talk to him; Jonny calls him psycho."

Screw Jonny. "Jonny ruined Saturday; he's going with Walt to that disco movie."

"Correction, he's going with Walt *and* some girls. He called me. I'm going with them if I get my report done. Dad still thinks I want to go to a movie with you guys."

So did I. "Whatever happened to not dating girls who aren't Jewish?"

"Walt said Trudy wanted it to be a blind date; it's possible she could be Jewish."

Sure.

"But I could go for any cute little *goy* who shows up," Noah said with a snicker. "Jonny told me you got mad. You passed up an easy in with a girl, man. Why are you so pissed at him?"

Want to hear what he said about you and Artie? "Because he screwed up our deal without even telling us."

"*Ffff,* I have a two-word answer for that—girls." Noah laughed. "Rudy, he's driving now, for god's sake. It's a good deal for us until somebody else gets a license. Why don't you at least call him and smooth it over?"

Not if I can help it. "I'm not calling him—see you tomorrow."

"Yeah. Jesus, you're so damn serious."

Rudy hung up. *He can do his own friggin' report.* His entire head seemed to tighten. Rudy opened one of the unstained oak cabinet doors that Larry had been renovating and found the aspirin bottle empty. *None in my bathroom either. Crap, it's not that bad.*

Books in hand, he passed the hallway that led to the two original bedrooms; one of them was Larry and Katie's. Rudy entered the dining room, one of only two rooms from the old house that Larry had not completely renovated. Grandmother Lanier's cherrywood table and six chairs stood before a walnut buffet and cabinet that displayed antique dishes now used only on Thanksgiving and Christmas. Rudy left his books on the table, his usual homework spot.

He started into the oblong but compact living room, which Larry had left as it was to honor his sister's wish to hold onto some of their mother's belongings. Folksy décor, knickknacks, and early-American furniture took up most of what had become more like a parlor, although the front door was used infrequently.

Si was sitting at the far end of a well-preserved ruffled sofa. Facing the picture window to his left, he slouched over the armrest, his elbow touching the oak end table, the side of his head leaning on his open left hand. Rudy expected to find his uncle the same as always. His polo shirt would be too small, accentuating his "spare tire," one of two physical features common to Rudy and Si. The other was their outsized skulls—Si's was bald and shiny except for grey hair in back, buzzed as short as his dark beard shadow.

The rest of Si's clothing would be the usual navy slacks, brown belt, white socks, scuffed black loafers—and his one extravagance, a silver-banded Bulova that he rarely checked. As Rudy approached him on the shag carpet, Si appeared to be daydreaming and didn't notice he wasn't alone. One of his index fingers picked at a penny-sized scab on his neck.

Gross. What's he thinking when he's spaced out like this? Rudy noticed two gift-wrapped boxes, one pink and one blue, on an end table. *Oh boy, let's see, a cowboy shirt?* He came closer to Si, whose appearance was just as Rudy had anticipated, except his last shave had left angry red blotches of psoriasis, already spiked with short black whiskers.

God, that could be me in ten years. Rudy saw dandruff flakes on the shoulders of Si's brown shirt; white strands of hair curled out of his ears. *You could braid the damn things. What if Libby saw him? Uh, he's my dad's army friend; he has shell shock. Terrible.*

"Hi, Si." Rudy tentatively offered his hand.

Si stopped daydreaming and turned from the window. "Oh. Hi, Rudy." Si didn't quite look him in the eye. He slowly reached up.

Grin and bear it. He took Si's hand, noticing black crescents of dirt under his long fingernails. Although Rudy knew his own nails were clean and trimmed, he checked them anyway. They were fine, except for one gnawed, raw pinkie. *Crap—when did I do that?*

"When did you get here, Si?" *And why on a Thursday night?*

"I took an early shift—got here, um, maybe at three?" he said in his low, croaky voice.

"You see my mom?"

"Yes, she's working."

Si turned back to the window, and Rudy noticed an old issue of *True West* next to him. He had seen Si's stacks of adventure periodicals in his efficiency apartment in a small town in Orange County. After two years in Korea, Si was honorably discharged by the Army and took a custodial job at a shipping company. At first, he took the bus to L.A. to visit Mildred, Katie, and Cami. A few years later, Si bought a car and started visiting at least every other weekend.

Rudy saw Si's dog-eared pocket dictionary and a crisp new crossword magazine next to him: FUNCROSS—1978 JANUARY-MARCH EDITION—ADULT EASY. Among red and pink hearts, it implored: SHARPEN UP FOR THE BIRDS AND BEES!

Stupid. "Si, are those puzzles as easy as it says on the cover?"

"No. A lot of the clues and words are new to me. I can look up some of them."

"That's still pretty good." *Phony, Rudy.* "Would you like to watch the tube?"

"Yes." Si pointed to the gifts. "The square one's for you," matter-of-factly.

He wants it opened. Rudy picked up the present, wrapped in dark-blue paper printed with rocket ships and planets. *AOK, Houston.* Rudy removed the paper. The box inside had circular openings on all sides, revealing a red, seven-inch-diameter playground ball inside.

Hot dog. "Thanks, Si."

"Welcome. Your own ball to play curbs."

Whatever that is. "Right." Rudy turned to a *ticking* noise behind. A large wasp repeatedly collided with the picture window as if to fly through it. "Damn."

"*Vespid—genus Polistes.*"

Great. "I'm getting the flyswatter."

"It's a paper wasp; he just wants out—won't sting."

Sure. Already in the dining room, he entered the kitchen and found the flyswatter. His butt stiff, Rudy limped to the parlor; Si was on the sofa. *Get the damn thing.* "Si, where is it?"

"I let him out."

"How?"

"The front door."

What? Forget it. "Okay—TV."

"Rudy, Doc Grant told me you write stories."

Why would he say that to Si? "Yeah, I try."

"Do you have one I might like?"

What? He means it. "Um, one of the stories is about a nearly extinct animal."

"Can I read that one?"

"Okay, I'll get it for you later."

"Promise?"

Brother. "Sure, Si. Ready for some TV?"

About the same height as Rudy, Si boosted himself to his feet by putting both hands on one armrest to stand up.

*God, **I am** getting as fat as he is. Well, you blew off the diets, lard-ass.* A waft of Si's ripe body odor reached Rudy. *Oh, man—worse than ever.*

Leaving the parlor, Rudy held his breath and moved ahead of Si, who, like Rudy, was limping slightly. They went by the hall that led to the newer bedrooms, including his sister's and one appointed attractively for guests. Rudy had refused the third room. It remained mostly empty except for a chest of drawers and a fold-out bed, where Si slept on his frequent visits.

Rudy and Si stepped under a red-brick arch down one stair to the add-on den, about a twenty-square-foot room with a tongue-and-groove lacquered pinewood floor. They walked by a bathroom door with a corny outhouse plaque, then Larry's varnished pine wet bar, which included an old fridge long-ago painted royal blue and mustard yellow. The walls and ceiling continued the pine motif to the den's far door to the backyard.

The center of the den was taken up by furniture arranged toward a focal point—a new twenty-three-inch color TV that Katie bought impulsively, then rarely watched. A brown leather sofa, two matching recliners, and two stuffed armchairs formed a great *U* around the Zenith. Larry's pine handiwork also included six chairs that circled a hexagonal card table complete with drink holders and a green felt surface. Four TV trays, once darkly stained but now fading, hung on a wall rack; the outside tray showed a beginning-to-peel L.A. Rams sticker.

For fresh air, Larry had built the den with eight louvered windows, each with a thick dark curtain to keep glare off of the football games. A sun-bleached poster, taped crookedly to a wall, showed a smirking L.A. Rams lineman posing to make a tackle, the washed-out colors of his uniform lighter than the gold and blue refrigerator.

Si sat in his usual spot at one end of the sofa while Rudy leaned over to the card table to pick up the silver *SPACE COMMAND* remote control. Rudy turned on the TV, then sat on the arm of a stuffed chair. "Si, want to see how the remote works?"

"Okay. Rudy, is Charlotte going to be here tonight and get her present?"

"I don't know." *And don't care.*

Charlotte mostly ignored Si, but she made a show of being nice to him around their Grandmother Mildred. Rudy had seen Char's friends ask Si condescending or "naughty" questions when Charlotte was out of the room, then giggle at his answers.

Rudy went over to the sofa to show Si the device, shaped like a pack of extra-long cigarettes. He pointed to one of the buttons. "This turns it on, and this controls the sound; you can even mute it." *See if he gets that.*

"Why do you mute it?"

Of course he gets it. "Then you don't have to listen to commercials."

"Oh. I like commercials."

"Then leave the sound on." Rudy turned on the set. "These buttons control the channels."

"Shouldn't I ask Katie first?"

Rudy rolled his eyes, confident that Si didn't notice his body language. "No, you don't have to. You can turn it on whenever you want." He handed Si the remote.

"Okay." Si put the device down on the sofa right away.

Nice try. He'll still ask for permission. The TV set had warmed up to show a kitchen scene in an old Jackie Gleason re-run. "Si, you okay with this?"

"Yes. Any westerns or army or space shows?"

"Later tonight, probably." Rudy stood.

"This one, then." Si attentively watched Ralph's neighbor, Norton.

Okay, he's fine. Rudy went out the sliding glass door at the end of the den, then down two steps to the backyard pavers that led to the rumpus room. Still about fifteen minutes until his mother would be finished, he wandered over to Stew and took the slobbered tennis ball out of the box. The dog growled at a car in the driveway, its motor dieseling to a stop. Larry had bought the '70 Chevy Malibu for Charlotte's twenty-first birthday nearly two years before.

"It's okay, boy, it's just the wicked witch." He dropped the tennis ball back into the box. "Sit, Stew, maybe she won't see us."

CHAPTER 5
Five Sheets to the Wind

World War II had kick-started Southern California's economy with the production of ships, airplanes, vehicle components, and oil—creating the perfect Petri dish for the seemingly limitless post-war construction of homes, office buildings, factories, supermarkets, department stores, and infrastructure. The mass production of penicillin improved life expectancy, and the unsurprisingly high post-war birthrate along with a wave of newcomers added even more stimulus to the economy, but not even a fourth of the city's Japanese-American citizens returned from the detention camps or the war.

The entertainment industry hardly skipped a beat during the war, dazzling the U.S. and the world with celebrities—some with stand-alone names like Sinatra, Satchmo, Bogart, and Hepburn. Rejected in 1943 and resurrected in 1946, a sentimental and quirky movie, *It's a Wonderful Life*, became an icon of Americana along with its leading man, James Stewart.

After the United States prosecuted the war to its apocalyptic conclusion in Japan, the once-sleepy city of Los Angeles began to develop a conceit similar to New York's. While the "Big Apple" kept reaching for the sky, the leaders of sprawling Los Angeles began to consider their city the western hub of North America, increasingly confident that Americans—in one way or another—would have to go through L.A. to get what they wanted. In the '40s and '50s, the World War II generation spawned a sub-culture that would challenge the status quo in the '60s. Los Angeles and New York naturally emerged at the forefront of that societal transformation.

The Dodgers left Brooklyn for L.A., where the city accommodated them by removing a long-established Mexican-American agricultural enclave for a new stadium. Jazz and blues hung on, but the big-band era stood aside for Elvis, Aretha, the Beatles, and Springsteen. On both coasts, television overwhelmed the movies until the two industries began to meld.

The Watts Towers, finished by an Italian immigrant in 1954, survived later revolts that ended with loss of life and hope. JFK, MLK, and RFK often visited the City of the Angels before all were lost to an implausible triad of vile assassinations, the final one in a Los Angeles hotel.

By the '70s, the county's population exceeded seven million, and one of the world's largest electric rail systems had succumbed to an unrivaled network of freeways. The Sylmar earthquake killed sixty-four and wasn't even "the big one." Luxury homes went up amidst sage, scrub, and dry grass, then some of those neighborhoods went down in flames or mudslides. The iconic HOLLYWOOD sign had been repaired, but on many days it could hardly be seen for the dingy, sallow air.

Partially hidden, Rudy watched Charlotte take her tennis gear out of the Chevy and walk past the small porch to its back stairs, not far from the yard. She was about to step up to the side door when she spotted Rudy and Stew in the pen.

About the time Rudy was born, his Aunt Candy had been brainwashing Charlotte to love dolls, princesses, and the cutest outfits for school. Years later, Rudy and his parents were surprised when the previously sports-phobic Charlotte rejected the Truman High School dance team for junior varsity tennis.

Encouraged by her inchoate athleticism, Charlotte determinedly took lessons both summers before her senior year, when she starred for varsity and placed third in the city in singles. She boasted that one of L.A.'s private colleges had practically offered her a scholarship. Her mediocre academic history and test scores put a stop to that, and she compensated by convincing herself that she hated school and tennis.

Living at home, Charlotte worked in retail and enrolled at L.A. Valley College for something to do. Now she was a third-year sophomore taking advanced tennis lessons again, eligible to transfer in December to any four-year college that would accept her.

Charlotte had Katie's dark hair and eyes, and her father's sinewy face and neck. Her angular features were countered by her button nose and make-up cleverly applied to her tan face. About five-seven and lean, her tennis shorts showed off firm calves and thighs, and she wore a stiff bra under a tight t-shirt, exaggerating her small breasts.

Now Charlotte turned to Rudy and removed her sun visor. Before leaving the car, she had released her ponytail; freeing her black hair to fall unkempt almost to her shoulders.

"So, you really did start playing again?" Rudy looked down to pet the dog.

"What was your first clue, Gramma's boy? So, that's all you're up to, petting that ugly dog?" Stew growled. "Control that bitch."

Shit, here we go. Rudy kept petting. "*He* is not a bitch, and *he* only growls at you."

"Still a bitch. So, Si's here again, a good excuse for you to be a dickhead."

"He asked about you. He thinks you care about him. What a joke."

"You're so full of crap. You think he doesn't know you can't stand to be around him?"

That's right, he doesn't know. "At least I don't pretend to like him."

"More bullsh—" She stopped to listen to some loud traffic noise. "That's Wayne's heap—see what you did? Get your fat ass out front and tell him I'll be there in ten minutes." Charlotte took the last step up to the door.

"Do it yourself."

She stopped, turning to him again. "C'mon, Rood, there's a buck in it for you."

Not this time. "Three."

"Damn thief. Okay, ask Wayne for it. Go!" She hurried inside.

I'll never see that money. Wait. After all, it is Wayne. Maybe a little extortion.

Two years younger than Charlotte, Wayne was her steadiest boyfriend ever—going on two months. Rudy thought she was getting desperate, and that Wayne was probably boasting about dating an older girl.

Limping again from his sore posterior, Rudy ambled deliberately down the driveway to the street, where Wayne had just parked his '55 Pontiac Starchief convertible. "Way more cool than any '57 Chevy," according to Wayne. Advertised as sleek and elegant in its day, to Rudy it was just another crappy old GM car.

Wayne had purchased the Pontiac with a plan to "cherry it up" so he could cruise Sunset Boulevard with the top down as if he were a surfer. Rudy smirked at the car's unchanged condition: its dented and rusted two-tone red-and-white body, a perpetually one-quarter-open and ripped convertible cover, a shattered spotlight, bald tires, and a pocked, opaque front window.

His radio blaring rock oldies, Wayne used his forefingers to drum on the steering wheel. When he saw Rudy, Wayne revved the engine, smiling at the roar from his custom muffler and dual exhaust, the only significant alterations he had made to the car.

I'm so impressed. "You want Shar's message or not?" Rudy hollered, but Wayne didn't let off the accelerator. *Screw him.* Rudy turned to go.

Wayne killed the engine. "Hang on, Rood," in a whiny, patronizing tone, "I was jokin'."

Rudy turned and looked at him across the seats. As usual, Wayne wore a gaudy Hawaiian shirt to distract from his gawky neck, allergy-red nose, and greasy tan hair. One feature, cornflower-blue eyes, salvaged him from complete homeliness.

"Shar needs ten minutes; she said you owe me five bucks for my trouble."

"What trouble? Hell, she won't be out here for half an hour. C'mere."

Rudy took a step forward; "Return to Sender" blasted from Wayne's radio. "Turn that crap down if you've got something to say," Rudy shouted. Wayne adjusted the volume; his gamey cologne wafted into the street. *Ack.* "So, Wayne, what'll you do with this beauty when it rains?"

"You don't know crap about the time and bread it takes to fix up a classic. Watch this." He turned on his lights and pointed to the hood ornament. "Ain't that bitchin?"

Bitchin? Good god. "What are you talking about?"

"The chief lights up—I fixed it. You can see it good when it's dark."

"If that don't beat all, Goober," in a passable Gomer Pyle accent.

"Where's *your* goddam wheels?"

"I'm looking for a real classic, maybe a '61 Corvair."

"Shit, that ain't a classic."

"A classic piece of crap, just like this."

"What's your problem?"

"Wayne, anyone ever tell you the '50s are gone and so is Elvis?"

"I suppose you like coon music," he said, spittle on his lip.

"I suppose you don't know that Elvis liked Black gospel and jazz."

"That's BS," inertly, then he grinned. "Hey, don't let's argue. I want to ask you somethin' about sweet Charlotte."

Sweet, my ass. "I still don't know anything you'd want to hear."

"C'mon, you never told me what she really likes—you know," with a theatrical wink.

Same ol' shit. "You mean something that would make her *really* appreciative?"

"Yeah, that's it." Wayne slid eagerly across the seat.

"It'll cost you the five bucks you already owe me."

"I need that for popcorn."

"She'll buy it."

Wayne sat up, dug out his wallet, and handed over the five. "Alright, let's hear it."

Dumb shit. "Okay, what she *really* likes is…" He paused for effect. "…coconut pudding."

Rudy walked off, but it took Wayne seconds to respond. "What? Gimme that five back."

Ten feet or so up the driveway, Rudy scowled back. "Come and get it." *What if he does?*

"Friggin' fat little fucker," Wayne blared but stayed put.

"Ah, alliteration. Good going, Goober," Rudy called back, then he heard Wayne grumble and turn up The Everly Brothers.

Rudy went to his room to get the story that Si had asked for. He walked through the house and down to the den. His uncle was still ensconced on the sofa, but he had let in the dog. Si stared at Jackie Gleason's signature stage exit: *And away we go!*

"Si, how was the show?"

"Good," he said, staring at a toothpaste commercial.

"Here's that story you wanted to read." Rudy handed it to him, then patted Stew, dozing on the dog bed in the corner—his other inside spot along with the blanket in the kitchen.

"It's typed—good." He checked the TV. "They said another Jackie Gleason is next."

"Okay, I'm going out to see my mom." Rudy took his time to cross the den. He slid open the glass door, went out, then traversed the pavers over to the rumpus-room door. He opened it and saw his mother working in her office in the far-right corner while John Denver crooned and warbled from her cassette player.

Constructed with double walls of cinder block, including hundreds that Larry had scavenged, the rumpus room originally resembled a vacant church basement. Now, besides Katie's small office, the room had a half-bathroom, a storage room, regulation pool and ping-pong tables, and a 12 X 15 tile dance floor set an inch above the concrete.

Over the years, the Laniers, Krenshaws, and friends decorated the drab grey walls for parties, dances, receptions, and rites of passage—even a *quinceñera* for the daughter of one of Larry's plumbers. However, the rumpus in the rumpus room had diminished to a rare party or Rudy hanging out with friends to shoot pool and play ping-pong. Even the annual Thanksgiving gathering there with family and friends was now in question. With fewer activities each year, the cavernous room became impractical and inconvenient; they had tentatively planned to celebrate the upcoming holidays in the den.

Katie's office had a rarely-used swamp cooler in its only window, but the rest of the hall was windowless like a fruit warehouse and stayed surprisingly comfortable until the late-summer heat found ways to creep in. Rudy walked by the dance floor toward Katie's small corner office with glass panes for walls on two sides, one with a doorway but no door.

She was preoccupied with her electric typewriter, so Rudy turned back to enter the nearby half-bathroom. He checked his head again in the mirror, then went back to her office and stood several feet behind her. John Denver exulted—*I've seen it rainin' fire in the sky...*

He heard the furious clicking of her typewriter. *Man, she's flying* He knew her fingers were a blur as if they weren't touching the keys. On a coaster by the typewriter, Rudy saw a small glass that contained ice melt and cubes from what had been a short highball. Like a "dame" in a '40s movie, half of a cigarette dangled from the side of her mouth. Next to her roll-top desk, she had piled some work on a file cabinet beneath a wrinkled poster on the wall of a female Olympic swimmer.

Rudy cleared his throat intentionally before speaking over the music. "Mom?"

"Yes, I heard you come in." She shut off the IBM; it rattled for a few seconds to a stop. Katie turned to him, her brows slanted. She was wearing one of her grey sweatsuits that she often kept on all day from October to March. "Five more minutes?" she nearly shouted over the music.

"Okay with me." His aching gluteus prompted Rudy not to sit on her torn, semi-retired, visitor's swivel chair.

"Pshaw," puckishly, "jus' foolin' y'all—like yr' gramma says." She hiccupped. "Had enough of this crappy account anyway—just need to tidy up." She began to shuffle some papers.

Time had treated Katie well until recent years when she began drinking more and took up her old smoking habit. At about five-five, she still wore a neat black pageboy, indifferent to the grey around the edges. Age and tension lines had taken their toll on her symmetrical face, but she was only a few pounds heavier than "little Katie" who married Larry Lanier.

Rudy glared at her glass. *Only one sheet—works for me.* When Rudy was in junior high, he made up a five-level scale for her inebriation. He decided that the old bromide, *three sheets to the wind,* didn't apply. The two levels after sobriety ran from happy to giddy, then levels four and five went from raucously silly to loss of control, the worst stage of all. Cold-sober, she was sullen, and Rudy avoided her, then he tried not to be too enabling when her once-spirited personality surfaced after a couple highballs. Level five would drive him outside or to his room.

In the years between the births of her two children, Katie enrolled in night classes to study accounting. She soon became the bookkeeper for Larry's Plumbing and did the same for her church, pro bono, and also volunteered for school activities. She stayed in touch with her siblings, especially Si, Danny, and Cami, who had a master's degree and was now a relief official in Ethiopia. Over the years, Katie's work for the business expanded while involvement in the church and schools decreased; even her daily swimming fell off to only once or twice a week.

Katie reached up, knocked over a photo frame, tittered at the harmless accident, then turned off the music, sat in her chair, and regarded her son lackadaisically. "I have a couple things to talk to you about," she stammered slightly. "You have somethin' to tell me?"

"Yeah, Dad said he won't be in until later."

"Another toilet that can't wait."

Rudy thought her words sounded both resigned and sarcastic. While she fiddled with an errant paper, Rudy was fixated on the smoke and dust motes floating in the light from her window. *What are those specks made of? How do they*—

Katie broke the silence. "Why don't you sit down, Rudy?"

No. "I'm okay." He folded his arms and leaned on the doorless frame.

"Rudy, know what I heard? Electric typewriters are done for. They're coming out with personal computers. You type whatever, then use a disc to store or bring back information, even a hundred pages. Sounds too good to be true—probably is."

"Sounds like it would help you." *So, what's my assignment with Si?*

Katie mashed the cigarette butt in a green ashtray that Rudy had kilned in third grade. She rolled back two or three feet from her desk. "Alright, what's on your mind?" Her voice was slightly more abrupt.

Yeah, probably just the one drink. "Um, there's no aspirin in the kitchen."

"Check the grocery bag on the sink. Are you still having headaches?"

"What are you talking about?"

"Why do you think we were out of aspirin? You've been taking a lot."

"No, just once in a while."

"Probably your hormones." She scooted forward, rummaged around in a drawer, then reached across to hand him a tiny yellow aspirin tin. "Just keep it."

"Thanks." He looked at the tin, then at her. *C'mon, get to Si.* "Mom, Si mentioned something about playing *curbs*. Do you know what he means?"

"When did he say that?"

"A little while ago. He gave me a playground ball."

"Good ol' Si." She stared at her glass. "Curbs was a game we played in El Rancho."

"What should I do with the ball?"

"Don't ask *me*."

"I'll give it to the school." He turned away, took one aspirin dry, and put the tin in his jeans. "Mom, why is Si here two weeks in a row?"

"He's here for Gramma and Grampa's anniversary party on Sunday."

"Right, I forgot, but I didn't know he was coming."

"For his mother's party? You know he won't be in your way."

Especially after I leave. "Why is he here early?"

"He took a vacation day tomorrow to help with the party."

Help? Give me a break. "Is he staying at Gramma's one of the nights?"

"Here, all three nights."

"Would've been nice to know that."

"Why, so you could be somewhere else?"

"That's not what I meant." *Liar.* "Well, maybe he could take a bath before Sunday. The parlor smells like a locker room." He looked up at her window.

"Now you're whining. Is that all; anything else on your list?" she asked in a snide tone.

He was watching the dust motes again. *Some are floating up. How? Write it.*

"Am I boring you, Rudy? Come on, drag out one of the oldies— like you can't stand to watch him eat." She shrugged. "I don't know why you even watch."

Okay. "It's so gross that I can't help but look, like a car wreck."

"Jesus wept." Katie had picked up that phrase after she started calling herself, *a Christmas Christian.* The door opened at the far end of the long room. "It's your sister."

He turned to see Charlotte a few feet inside the door. *Damn, she should be gone by now.*

Katie's eyes drooped. "Rudy, I'm dragging your father to a wedding party tomorrow night. I'd like you to be here with Si."

Crap, there it is. "Why?"

"Because nobody else will be here."

So? No, not this old argument—just do it. "Okay."

"Good. And you'll have to take the bus or walk home with your friends."

Friend—Artie. On alternate Fridays, Katie or Larry picked Rudy up after school to go to a clinic for a weight-loss injection. "Good, that shot hasn't been helping anyway." He pinched the thick fold of adipose near his waist; he saw Charlotte getting closer.

"You didn't stay with the diet; we'll talk about it after I see what

Shar wants."

"Diet?" Charlotte said, now in a blouse and skirt. "You mean Rudy's get-fatter diet?"

"And you're on a fathead diet," he responded in a flat tone, "a very unsuccessful one."

"Alright, don't start, you two," Katie said offhandedly, then she snickered, pointing to the unopened pink gift in Charlotte's hand. "Another Barbie from Si?"

"It isn't funny anymore—ten years since I played with the damn things." She moved over to sit on the visitor's chair, away from Rudy.

Katie grinned. "Shar, Si likes to watch you open his gifts."

"I thanked him. I'll just keep saving them in case I have a daughter someday." She noticed Rudy's smug grin. "Don't say anything, snot." Charlotte pointed at Katie's finished drink. "I need one of those more than you do."

"Bottle's empty. No damn lectures."

"Jesus." Charlotte glanced at Rudy. "Mom, you gotta' do something about the snot. He tricked Wayne out of five dollars."

Rudy scoffed. "Yeah, I really shouldn't take advantage of somebody that stupid. You told me to get the money from him."

"Not five bucks. You also pissed him off—made fun of his car and music."

"And *he* said that I probably like *coon* music."

Katie made a dull sigh. "No more of that talk."

Rudy turned to his mother. "I was quoting Goober out there."

"So?" Charlotte challenged. "Then you tried to pick a fight with him."

"What?" Katie blurted out a laugh. "Rudy picked a fight? Jesus, Charlotte, how can I believe anything you say after that?"

Charlotte sneered. "You don't believe anything I say anyway."

"Rudy," Katie said, chuckling, "did you really do that?"

"He wanted the five back, so I just said to come and get it."

Katie was still smiling. "You were bluffing, right?"

Maybe. "I guess so. Wayne is such a—never mind."

Charlotte's eyes darted to Rudy. "He's gone, fat-ass—we broke up."

Rudy thought she sounded more factual than angry. He shook his head. "No loss."

"Enough, Rudy," Katie said flatly, then faced Charlotte. "You broke up over *that?*"

"Wayne wanted me to pay him back." She spun in her chair. "I called him a Jew; we both got pissed. If not for Rudy, this shit wouldn't have happened."

Still leaning on the doorframe, Rudy looked at Katie. "She didn't even like the dimwit. She should thank me."

"For messing in my business?" Charlotte fumed. "Look, I'm outta' here in December." She faced her mother. "My grades are up, I'll get a part-time job, share rent with Amy, and apply for tennis scholarships for next fall."

Katie groaned. "Won't you be too old for college tennis?"

"No, I won't, and *that's* what I'm doing."

Rudy mimed a prayer with his hands. "Make it so."

"Quiet, Rudy." Katie's tone was still lax.

Charlotte got up and took a step toward Katie's desk. "Is that the best you can do, Mom?" She turned and started toward the den, calling back. "I'm not eating with Rudy; Si would be better. I'm going to Amy's."

Katie waited until Charlotte went out the door. "Well, at least she might finally finish junior college." She hunched her shoulders. "You two are still so awful to each other."

"Actually, what you just saw isn't common anymore—we're good at avoiding each other." He paused. "You were going to tell me about the shots."

Katie looked up from staring at the ice cubes. "Rudy, you and Shar could end up like half my brothers and sisters—barely speaking to each other."

"I should be so lucky. Mom, what's the deal with the shots?"

Katie burped without opening her mouth, holding her glass as if for comfort. "Alright, your grampa said the drug was a scam, not meant for weight loss, but he's sure it didn't harm you. I should've gone to grampa first instead of listening to June."

Yeah, dump that old windbag. "You were just trying to help."

"He said no more shots; maybe a new diet."

Try, try again. "Okay."

"You're not all that fat anyway." Katie paused, then grinned slightly. "For Friday, we'll give that new pizza delivery place up on San Fernando Road a try. I'll set it up—"

Pizza with Si? "Mom, tomato sauce always gives me heartburn."

"Everything gives you heartburn. Fine—easier for me. I'll leave sandwich makings."

I'm not cleaning up Si's mess. He massaged his forehead with a thumb and forefinger.

"Is your head aching right now?"

"A little."

"Take another aspirin." She sighed. "Besides the gift, did you talk to Si?"

"Yeah, he asked to read one of my stories. I got it for him."

"Really," she stated. "Is he watching TV now?"

He nodded. "I showed him how to use the new remote control."

"See, you're only mean to him in your head. Something we have in common."

She says that now after all these years?

"I didn't mean that." Her phone rang. "I'll keep it short." She answered the call, then was silent for several seconds. "Marcie, it's almost six; I need to start dinner." She kept listening.

Rudy bit the remnants of the nail on his pinkie and heard Katie say *yes* or *no* three or four times. He watched the dust motes until she finally finished.

"She just wouldn't stop. How was your daydream?"

"Just thinking."

"Stop chewing your nails. Where were we? Um, Si, I think." She paused. "I thought you understood that Mom, Danny, Margie, and Cami want Si to visit whenever he needs to; they don't want him to ever feel like he isn't welcome."

Right, we wouldn't want that. "Why didn't you include yourself on the list?"

"I'm not as adamant. Si is attached to us, no matter what we think of him. Within limits, I'm sort of Cami's stand-in. She expects to move back to L.A. next year, then Si won't be here as much. For now, maybe you can do us all a favor and just survive for a few days."

Like I have any choice. "I'll be fine."

She got up from her chair. "Rudy, I think we cleared up some things."

No, we didn't. "I guess."

Katie stood, stepped forward, and pecked him on the cheek, her pungent breath right in his face. "Okay, it's Si's favorite tonight—

beef stroganoff."

His nose contorted. *He'd eat gruel if she cooked it. She's right, I'd never say that to him.*

They walked to the doorway. "Hamburger and raw vegetables for you, Rudy. Since your father isn't coming in, I assume you'd rather not eat your burger with Si and me."

Right, neither of you. "I'll cook it later. Can I make a call on your phone?"

She faced him while she was leaving. "Hopefully," she teased, "to call some cute—"

"Okay, Mom." A sharper headache struck Rudy as she left. He touched the aspirin tin in his jeans, then walked to the half-bathroom. Although the headaches started months before, Rudy didn't think about them much since aspirin always helped. More recently, the trade-off was a strange malaise, an overall fatigue. Hoping to avoid that, Rudy took only half an aspirin, leaving two and a half in the tin. Back in the office, he remained standing as he dialed Reed's number.

CHAPTER 6
Mildred and Seth

Two days after talking with the twins and Simon's teacher, and as soon as her four youngest were in bed, Mildred left Sharon in charge and made a long-distance call to her sister, Melody, from a neighbor's telephone. The lady took fifty cents on top of any charges—an outrageous sum to the several families nearby who still didn't have a phone. Although it was more than a year since V-J Day, many considered the woman to be a war profiteer. Mildred reluctantly used the lady's telephone only for something urgent.

She called the Kern County number. "Lo," Melody answered abruptly. Ten years before the war, she and Ted sold their farm in Missouri at half-price and moved to California.

"Melody, how're things up there?"

"Milly. Nothin' difrint. Kind a' late t' be callin'."

Melody's voice was so sluggish that Mildred knew she had been drinking. She told herself to try not to rile her sister. "I need to ask you an' Ted somethin'."

"He ain't here. Hope it ain't money. Savin' t' go see Ma," Melody slurred.

"I know that. God in heaven, Melody, soused in front a' y'r kids?"

She didn't answer right away. "They's in bed. What's it to ya'?"

"Nothin'." Mildred thought Melody became a little more alert, regardless of her rancor.

"How much ya' want, Milly?"

"No money—you know I paid back every red cent durin' the war."

"Then what do you want?"

"Concernin' Simon."

"Boy's more touched ev'ry day—an' I ain't sure I'll let that Katie up here again."

"Don't be talkin' down my kids, Melody," some ire in her tone. "Tell me about Simon bein' sick this summer."

"Weren't our fault—boy playin' aroun' with a hive."

"Yes, but what'd you do for his stings?"

"What Momma always done—poultice n' all."

"Ya' make it sound like nothin'. He come home with maybe a hundred scabs."

"Was you here or me?" When Mildred didn't answer, Melody went on. "Ted tol' me the boy wasn't breathin' right, so he took 'im in—waste a' money."

"Then what?"

"They tol' Ted they was so many stings it was like poison..." Melody rambled through her version of Si's recovery, some of it at odds with what the twins had said. "...an' y'r listenin' to that know-it-all, Katie. I was tryin' to get shed of all of 'em, but Ted spoils—"

"What about callin' Cousin Marshall in Burbank? He'd a' got us a message."

"Some kind a' thanks." Another long pause. "Keepin' 'm here was Ted's doin'. He tol' me don't tell you 'bout the doctor bill, but y'r not even askin' 'bout that."

Mildred restrained her anger again. "Send me how much; I'll pay it."

"Take ya' two years."

"Won't argue no more, Melody. What'd ya' mean 'bout Simon bein' touched?"

"*Ffff*, he'd hardly talk, eatin' like a pig n' all. Ted got ornery, sayin' the boy's jus' two weeks outta' the sick bed."

"It's all comin' to me now."

"What's 'at mean?"

"Nothin'. Give Ted my thanks for the care he give Simon."

"Some kind a' nerve sayin' that, Milly."

"Bye, Melody." Seething about the conversation, Mildred left the neighbor's place and started home mired in self-recrimination for not knowing that Melody's drinking was worse. "Lord. Never they goin' to visit her again by themself," she promised aloud.

Before she got home, she decided to take Simon to Dr. Grant as soon as she could. Mildred sent a note on Monday to let Miss Hartland know why Simon would miss class on Tuesday morning.

Two days later, wrapped in her light-brown terry-cloth bathrobe, stiff from years of laundering, Mildred sipped her coffee just after dawn, gazing from the kitchen table past their old fig tree. She listened to the stillness until it was broken by the uneven, constant chatter of a mockingbird on a power line. "Good mornin' to you, Gabby." She allowed herself to relax longer than usual since Sharon would be getting the girls ready for school after Mildred and Simon left for the doctor's office.

Dr. Grant took patients on a first-come basis up to ten o'clock, so Mildred had planned to leave early. She was tempted to take Sam's old Dodge that Nick had brought back to life, but Mildred didn't want to use even a dime's worth of gasoline.

Mildred woke Simon, then returned to her bedroom to brush and gather her lush hair and clip it behind. Frowning at a tinge of sallowness in her face, she then noticed the slight protrusion of her cheek bones. She applied a few touches of make-up and dull lipstick, then donned her "presentable" outfit—a lemon-yellow cotton dress. Mildred frowned at her once-noticeable womanly shape in the mirror. Her dress disguised the only significant fat on her body—a small paunch of loose flesh and her beginning-to-droop breasts.

She went to the kitchen and packed some items in her large hemp bag. Mildred called Simon, then she made a peanut-butter toast sandwich for him. He entered in his good pair of jeans, a faded-green poplin jacket, and his t-shirt with the *Captain America* patch.

Mildred gave him the toast, and they left for the doctor's—about a mile away. To walk there on Los Feliz Boulevard, they had to cross the bridge over the Los Angeles River—a weak stream dissecting a massive concrete aqueduct. Very rarely, run-off from a downpour would surge from the hills to flood the channel into a raging torrent.

They continued across the bridge and Mildred looked up at the greyish-green chaparral foothills of Griffith Park, part of the low range often called the Hollywood Hills that separated the L.A. basin from the San Fernando Valley. She watched Simon finish his sandwich.

"In your check-up, Simon, Doc Grant will likely be askin' about this summer when you was at Uncle Ted's farm. Promise to think hard an' tell all you recollect?"

"Yes'm." He gouged peanut butter from his gums, then sucked it off his finger.

Mildred brushed off his crumbs, then they came to Riverside Drive and the Mulholland Fountain, a taken-for-granted monument to most locals, although tourists were awed to hear that the big studios filmed it as a stand-in for European fountains. Mildred and Simon walked on to an area on Riverside checkered with vacant lots and a few rundown houses. They approached the doctor's well-preserved, two-story, cobalt-blue frame house—as incongruous on this street as the renovated black and dark-green Model-A Ford parked in the driveway in front of his long garage.

As they came closer, Mildred checked the familiar garden that ran along the sunniest side of the doctor's house. She admired his semi-tropical blossoms that had endured the shorter, cooler nights—a respite of color on the dingy street. "Doc Grant's a special man, Simon, helpin' folks with his way of doctorin'—an' a man growin' a flower garden an' bein' proud of it."

"Yes'm." They climbed four stairs and passed beneath the familiar brown shingle that displayed SETH GRANT M.D. in white letters. Mildred and Simon took the steps up to the door to his front porch, a house number above, and a custom sign at adult eye level:

OPEN 8-1. Appointments 10-1 (House Calls after 2)
OLYmpia-6465. CLOSED SUNDAY and P.M. SAT.
PLEASE LEAVE MESSAGE ON PORCH.

She released his hand and opened the door to an enclosed, long veranda with a lacquered bench as you might see in a train station. It ran the length of the porch below four standard windows facing the intermittent traffic on Riverside Drive. As always, three yellow pencils, a blank 5X7 note pad, and small envelopes were set out on a white table opposite the bench.

Mildred didn't bother with the handle to what was once the front door of the house, its top half made of glass, a drawn blind inside. "We're earlier'n I expected, Simon, but that puts us first in line." They took the first two spots on the smooth bench.

A sixtyish woman in heavy makeup and a prim long dress entered, ignored Mildred's friendly nod, then she sat passively a few spaces away from them. Si started to unroll his comic but stopped to insert a pinkie deep into his ear canal and wipe the finger on his pants. Mildred saw the woman's painted clownish eyes turn away from Si's pant leg, then she looked down her nose at Mildred's hemp bag. Si opened the comic, and the lady scooted another foot away.

The slats of the venetian blind inside opened, then Dr. Grant stepped out. "Morning, everyone. I thought there might be some early birds out here. Hello, Mrs. Warner, and here's Mrs. Krenshaw and Simon, our young entomologist."

"Doctor Grant," the lady huffed from her seat.

Mildred stood respectfully with a half-smile, pleased that the doctor again used Simon's real name. "Good mornin', doctor." She nudged Simon's arm.

He got to his feet and reached out to shake the doctor's hand. "M-morning, s-sir."

"Sir? Why, it's always Doc Grant to you, son."

He didn't answer, and the woman sneered as Si sat and opened his comic again.

"Feeling a bit reserved today, Simon? That's okay, it is awfully early." The physician turned to Mrs. Warner to ask her a question.

Mildred reflected about how her four youngest children had known Dr. Grant all of their lives and had always been fond of the man who often emitted the jolliness of Santa, if not his appearance. Now a bachelor in his mid-forties, he had fringes of brown hair circling his shiny skull. His reddish tan had faded from summer, leaving his lean face rough and slightly pocked around a few premature wrinkles. Nearly six feet tall, Dr. Grant seemed as lithe and hearty as an athlete in his twenties. His tweed sport coat fell to his trim waist from incongruously square shoulders. His one accessory was a wristwatch, but his brown bow tie gave his otherwise drab appearance a jaunty touch.

"Well, Mrs. Krenshaw, you're first. Is Simon my patient today?"

"Yes, doctor, but I'll want to talk to you first," she said forthrightly, glancing at the other woman as Simon read his comic.

"Of course. Come in please, everyone." He held the door for Mrs. Warner, then the doctor followed Simon and Mildred inside.

She always thought the spacious waiting room seemed more like the living room it once was—with overstuffed chairs and a sofa beneath generic prints of farms and the shore. At the center of the room, a long coffee table had the customary stacks of *National Geographic*, *Look*, and *Life*. Simon sat in one of the soft chairs and opened his comic.

"My assistant is off today. Be right with you—sign in, please."

Mildred watched the doctor enter the door to the lavatories and two examination rooms; the top half of a third door was glass, where part of the kitchen and some stairs were visible from the waiting room.

The two women approached a large office desk; it had a phone, calendar, typewriter, file cabinet, and a few personal tchotchkes. Mildred signed and dated her entry in a notebook next to a small valet bell. At the top of the sheet it said, PLEASE RING BELL ONCE AFTER SIGNING, which she ignored since she had already spoken to the doctor.

While the other woman signed, Mildred sat, bag in hand, near the door that Dr. Grant had entered. She heard the lady huff, ring the bell, then sit as far from Si as she could. The doctor came back out with a steady smile; he had removed his coat, revealing a stethoscope and black suspenders over a short-sleeved white business shirt. The doctor gave some papers to Mrs. Warner, then held the door open for Mildred.

She eyed the familiar room. It had likely been a master bedroom until the trappings of a clinic took over: a padded examination table, sink, two tall medical cabinets, a magazine shelf, and three sturdy oak chairs near a blood-pressure apparatus secured to one of the white walls. A steel scale with iron weights stood in a nearby corner next to the obligatory eye chart.

The doctor's business area took up all of a far corner of the room. His desk was cluttered with papers, folders, and books. File cabinets and overflowing bookshelves covered one wall. Another had diplomas, a daguerreotype group portrait, and the room's one window, open to the warm breeze. A haggard Hollywood Stars baseball cap hung crookedly on an arm of a wooden hat rack.

Mildred and the doctor walked over to the chairs near the examination table. She took a seat, modestly folding her hands on her lap. Usually shy when speaking alone with Dr. Grant, she looked him in the eye this time as he sat halfway back in a chair a few feet away.

"Well, Mrs. Krenshaw, staying ahead of that big outfit of yours?"

"We're doin' okay, doctor."

"And Nicholas?"

"He's mendin' up fine. Thanks again for checkin' on him that night."

"You're welcome, Mrs. Krenshaw." He flipped open a notepad.

She creased her lips resolutely before opening her bag to take out a small pocketbook. "I have a payment plus two extra dollars, but I don't see us catchin' up for a while."

"I'm still enjoying some of your victory garden. We can catch up with that bill later."

"'Preciate it, but please take this." She leaned across from her chair, giving him three rumpled dollar bills and eight quarters, then returned the pocketbook to her bag.

She watched him put the money casually on a table tray, the stack of quarters leaning precariously. As part of being the Krenshaws' physician, Seth was, of course, also Mildred's doctor. He always examined her with professional distance, but after her separation, the doctor was uncomfortable with her exams, so he brought in his assistant when more personal protocols were necessary. Seth's approach seemed respectful to Mildred, but she didn't ask about it, nor did he explain.

"Mrs. Krenshaw, may I ask if Sam is keeping up with support for you and the children?"

"Not regular." Mildred leaned over to her bag. "Got something else here." She took out two canning jars and handed them over to him. "Orange-lemon marmalade from our two trees."

"And all of your hard work. Wonderful." He set the jars carefully on the floor. "Thank you, Mrs. Krenshaw. I was just about to buy store jam—so let's call this ample supply another dollar off of your bill."

She turned slightly downcast. "Afraid Simon'll be addin' to what we owe."

"Well, we'll see. It does appear that he gained weight, but I believe I can help him with that. Won't cost much if he's willing."

"Don't believe he cares 'bout it one way or the other."

"Well, overweight children are sometimes distraught and don't talk about it."

"*Distraught* is troubled?"

"Yes."

"If he's troubled, he hardly shows that neither," she said, turning slowly away.

"Mrs. Krenshaw, I can see that *you* seem to be upset."

"It's not about me, doctor. My boy's not right," she said, determined but polite.

The doctor left a long pause. "How is Simon not right, Mrs. Krenshaw?" His tone was soft, almost apologetic.

"Hard to explain." She breathed a full sigh. "It's how he acts, the way he'll do things, peculiar like." Mildred told herself not to speak so countryfied.

The doctor finished jotting a note. "Well, what about Simon's usual interests?"

"Not like before."

"What do you mean by *before*?"

"That's why we come, um, came, today," she answered, starting to choke up a little. "Don't think there's time to tell it all." Her lips quivered; two tears raced down her cheek.

"My goodness, Mrs. Krenshaw." He stood, barely touched her shoulder, and handed her a small box of tissues. "Excuse me, I'll go out and see if Mrs. Warner is finished, then you can tell me what has been going on with Simon."

She sat up straighter, holding a tissue. "I'm sorry, doctor."

"No need. I'll be right back." He hurried to his desk, rummaged around, then went out to the waiting room and returned a minute or two later. "No one else there; we'll be fine for a while." He put Simon's thick file on the exam table.

Mildred noticed that Doc Grant sat one chair closer to her. She made a long sniffle, then a sigh. "Simon readin' his *Captain America*?"

"Yes, he looked up at me once, and I think he gave me a little smile." She groaned almost imperceptibly.

The doctor didn't respond right away. "I'm sorry, did I say something—"

"No, it's me needs to apologize." She closed her eyes, took a full breath, then looked at him again. "Guess I'm gittin' touchy 'bout all this."

"I know you wouldn't be upset if there wasn't good reason."

"Not so sure. I just can't figure what's ailin' Simon; why he acts so different."

"It sounds like that's where we should start."

Mildred explained recent examples of Si's altered behavior to the doctor, who listened intently, interrupting only for some clarifications.

Mildred finished with what she knew about the wasps attacking Si in the summer.

"Do you think the twins told you everything about what happened?"

"They maybe left somethin' out, but I believe 'em." Mildred's mind flashed to the frequent cuts, bumps, abrasions, and fevers the twins had presented to the doctor over eight years. "You know more'n anybody 'bout their mischief." She felt a brief rush of warmth in her cheeks.

"I suppose the twins can be a handful at times." He paused. "Please tell me about the first aid Simon received after the stings."

Mildred began to describe Melody's home-spun methods, but the telephone rang.

The doctor, grumbling a bit as he stood, dispatched with the call, then returned to Mildred and placed a plain cloth sack down by his chair. "The telephone's off now—sorry." He sat again. "So, you were about to tell me about the first aid."

Glum, Mildred nodded, then explained Melody's treatments, and what the hospital told Ted about Si's condition.

"They didn't say that he was in anaphylactic shock?"

"Doctor?"

"Sorry. An extreme allergic reaction."

"No, they said he had so many stings it was like poison." The bell rang once in the other room. "You're needin' to go, doctor. I can wait."

"Thanks, but after I handle it, I'll bring Simon in for his check-up."

Mildred sighed heavily. "Maybe he'll talk more to you, doctor. Thank you."

"Of course, Mrs. Krenshaw."

Mildred heard Dr. Grant lead someone into the other exam room. As if she were cold, she folded her arms, praying silently that the doctor could help Simon.

After fifteen minutes or so, he opened the door and came in with Si. "Do you mind if your mother stays with us, Simon?"

"No, s-sir."

Mildred had been staring toward the window. "Simon, finish your comic again?"

"Yes'm."

"Near time for the new *Captain America* to come out, right?" Simon's mien warmed very slightly, well short of an actual smile, but it was good enough for Mildred. She didn't think anyone sensed that very infrequent subtle change in Simon's visage, but the possibility that both Miss Hartland and Doctor Grant might have noticed gave Mildred a ray of hope. She gave Simon a full smile. "Doc Grant's ready to start your check-up an' ask some questions."

"Yes'm."

Dr. Grant cheerily patted the exam table, but after observing Si's inability to climb up, the doctor gave him a boost. The boy passed involuntary gas near the doctor's face, as in some cartoonish scatological gag.

"Okay, Simon. All set?" he asked as if the fart hadn't happened.

Mildred *tsked*. "Simon Peter, say excuse me."

"Hm? Excuse m-me," he said to his mother.

Seth stood near his patient. "Simon. I like your *Captain America* shirt."

"Mom m-made the patch."

"Oh? Your mother is sure good at making things."

Mildred shied away.

"Yes, s-sir. She m-makes the best cookies."

"I bet she does." He smile-glanced at her. "Simon, may I ask you a few things?"

"Yes, s-sir."

"Good. How do you think it's going for you this year in school?"

"I don't know as m-many answers."

"Answers aren't everything, Simon."

"Oh."

"Are some of the children bothering you?"

"A little, I guess."

"I'm sorry to hear that. Have they hurt you?"

"No. If they call m-me names, I walk away. They m-mostly don't bother me."

"Do you worry about them?"

"No."

"Well, that's good." He paused. "Simon, your mom said you visited your uncle's place last summer, and that's where you got all those bites. Were they mostly mosquitos?"

"M-mostly wasps, bees, and red ants. S-suborder *Apocrita*."

"I didn't know that classification, Simon. Do you know what kind of wasps stung you?"

"Western yellowjackets, *vespula pensylvanica*."

"I see. Some say paper wasps and yellowjackets are the same, but that isn't true, right?"

"Yellowjackets usually nest in the ground; they get m-madder than paper wasps."

"How many times do you think the yellowjackets stung you?"

"Lots. They don't lose their s-stingers."

"Right. What do you remember from when it was happening to you?"

"Um, chasing the twins away, covering up with m-my shirt. It hurt real bad."

"I bet it did. It was brave of you to distract the yellowjackets from your sisters."

"Oh."

"Do you remember getting hurt badly at the farm, besides the wasps?"

"No, s-sir."

"What do you remember from right after the wasps stung you?"

He didn't answer right away. "Um, I don't remember. M-maybe if I think."

"Okay, I'll ask again later. Well, Simon, let's begin your exam."

Mildred watched the whole process as Dr. Grant led Simon to the scale first, then checked his temperature and blood pressure. The doctor took a few notes, then asked Simon to remove his shirt. He made a quick inspection of the insect scabs, then searched for obvious health issues with Simon's head, heart, lungs, and reflexes. Mildred spoke only when the doctor occasionally asked her to corroborate some routine medical history. She noticed that Seth started the exam with a jovial bedside manner that became more business-like by the time he finished.

"Well done, Simon. I wish all my patients were so cooperative. I'll be right back."

Mildred smiled at her son as he put on his shirt. "You likely have time to read, Simon."

Dr. Grant had gone over to his desk, perused a book from a shelf, and jotted notes before he returned, beaming at Mildred and her son. "Simon, aren't you quite the war historian?"

"I know s-some things. Were you in the war?"

"The last one? No, I was in the first war—Europe in '17 and '18."

"World War I. Were you a captain?"

"No, just buck-Sergeant Grant," with a casual salute.

Si nodded as if to approve of the gesture. "Did you use your rifle, S-sergeant Grant?"

"Mostly bandages—I was a stretcher-bearer, then a medic." He paused. "Well, Simon, you seem to be in good health, except for your weight."

"I'm too fat."

"You are overweight, but you haven't had your adolescent growth spurt yet. Do you know what I mean by that?"

"You grow faster when you're a teenager."

"That's right, but it probably won't take care of your weight. I have some ideas that should help, but we'll talk about that another day. I have some more questions. Simon, do you happen to know any of your brothers' or sisters' birthdays?"

"Yes, S-sergeant." Si recited all but one. "I never learned Nick's, s-sir."

"That was very good, Simon." Dr. Grant had him listen to sets of numbers, then say them backward. Si had difficulty with a set of four numbers and couldn't do five.

"Thank you, Simon. Now we'll try to remember some words; most of them will be easy for a crossword guy like you. I'll say a word, and you just tell or explain what you think it means. If you don't know, just say so. Got it?" Si nodded back. The doctor started with three simple words; Si knew them right away. "The next word, Simon, is *mule.*"

"Cross between a horse and a donkey."

Mildred half-smiled at Si's quick response. The doctor continued with some words that were common but more obscure. Si hesitated but came up with plausible meanings for the first two. He didn't know the next two; Seth defined them, then asked Si to repeat them in two short sentences. "Good, you've got them. Now try to remember what those two words mean while we talk about something else for a minute. Okay, Simon, did you see my car outside this morning?"

"Yes, s-sir. M-model-A Ford Coupe. I know lots of old cars."

"That's impressive, Simon. Do you remember the colors of my Model A?"

"Black."

"Yes, that's the main one." The doctor waited. "Okay." He pointed to Si's comic. "Simon, can you tell me what Captain America is up to in your comic?"

"He's always after Red spies."

Seth waited again. "How does he try to catch them in *this* comic?"

"He fights them."

"So, when you read it next time, will it seem like a new story?"

"Some of it."

"Okay, back to the wasps. Did you remember anything from after they stung you?"

"My aunt put s-smelly s-stuff all over, and then a doctor."

"Did the doctor come to see you?"

"Um, I guess so, to put the medicine on."

"Then how were you doing?"

"Scratching a lot." Si's placid visage turned a shade anxious. "Katie was crying, but I couldn't play m-my harmonica for her."

"I see. And what did you do in the weeks before you came home?"

"I had m-my books and comics with me. Um, we played outside."

"What else do you remember, anything at all, about your vacation?"

He looked at his mother. "Uh, maybe Uncle Ted made ice cream like last year?"

"Good, Simon. I'm going to ask you again about a few words."

Mildred watched him answer the first three easily, but he didn't know the two he had just tried to learn. Mildred thought that the next word, *chrysalis*, would be difficult for most adults, but Si answered as if he had been asked his name. She decided that the doctor did it on purpose.

"Very good, Simon. All of this talk of insects reminds me of something. Do you remember what I told you last year about my flower garden?"

"You s-said Greg and I could come over and s-study insects."

"That's right—I might have some that are different from those in your mom's garden. Did you know that you can find insects and spiders in the snow?"

"In the s-snow?"

"Yes, sometimes. Have you ever been up to the snow?"

"No, s-sir."

"Well, I go hiking every year in the fall and search for wildflower seeds, animals, even insects. I usually drive up to Mt. Wilson; I heard they have a few inches of snow already. Would you like to go? We could make it a picnic."

"I can make sandwiches and cookies for you." Mildred's eagerness made her shy away again.

"Hear that, Simon?" He briefly put his hand on the boy's shoulder. "Is it a deal?"

"Yes, s-sir. Can m-my m-mom and the twins come?"

"Good idea—the more the merrier."

Mildred cleared her throat. "Simon, maybe we'd be putting the doctor out."

"Not at all, Mrs. Krenshaw."

Her face warmed again from his enthusiasm. "Um, seems I'll be bakin' a lot a' cookies."

"Fine, it's all settled then. Simon, I bet you know the date for Armistice Day."

"Yes, s-sir—eleven, eleven."

"Yes, next Monday, and school is closed." He faced Mildred. "Pick you up at nine a.m.?"

Mortified by another blush, she nodded in agreement.

"In your little Model-A?" Si asked quietly.

Mildred muted a gasp. "Simon Peter, my goodness."

"It's okay, Mrs. Krenshaw. Simon, I also have a larger car."

"Doctor, you sure 'bout this?" she asked.

"Yes, we'll have a lot of fun." The doctor told Si he could get down; he slid haltingly off the table. Seth picked up the cloth sack from the floor. "Reach in for a prize, Simon."

"Okay." Si took out the first thing he touched, a five-inch narrow cylinder of woven red and green bamboo. "Chinese finger trap. Thanks. I have s-something for you."

"You do?" The doctor and Mildred watched Si dig into his jeans.

"Here." Si held out a grey oval stone smeared slightly with peanut butter.

Dr. Grant accepted the gift, rubbing it. "Why, it's unusually smooth. Look at that shape, plus a white streak too. Thank you very much, Simon."

"Welcome." Si sat in the extra chair. "You could put it in your garden."

"Actually, I have a special place for it in my rock collection. Simon, while your mother and I talk about your check-up, do you want to stay in here?"

"Can I wait out there?" The doctor nodded; Si got up and left with his toy and comic.

File folder and papers in hand, Seth scooted the chair closer to Mildred. "Okay, Mrs. Krenshaw, before I start, do you have questions?"

"Yes, doctor."

"Please go ahead."

"Was you expectin' Simon *not* to listen to us if he stayed in here?"

"Yes, that's right."

"An' you expected he'd pick goin' out there?"

"I wasn't so sure on that."

"So, you was learnin' more about 'im even then."

"Yes, I was trying to. Very perceptive, Mrs. Krenshaw. Another question?"

She demurely looked down at her hands. "You expected Simon to know that last word?"

He smiled. "Yes, I'll get to that in a moment. I have one question for you. I believe you said his uncle took him to the hospital?"

"Yes, but he didn't remember it."

The doctor nodded, then began his report, earnest but not grave. "…and other than his weight, Simon seems to be healthy." He paused. "As you know, he has difficulty remembering or retaining recent experiences, which is very concerning. However, it is remarkable what he remembers from before this happened." He paused. "Simon also doesn't seem to be very aware of how he has changed, even the mild stutter, which should likely go away again."

"I guess that's a piece a' good news."

"Yes, but my guess—and it is only a guess—is that his symptoms might indicate some sort of brain disorder or damage." Briefly downcast, the doctor continued. "I'm sorry, Mrs. Krenshaw, all of this must be very hard for you." He sighed. "As for the causes of Simon's condition, all I have so far is my opinion. I believe that his symptoms might have resulted from his horrible bout with scarlet fever, his other high fevers over the years, and, of course, the recent high fever after the mass envenomation." He paused. "Sorry—that means hundreds of stings."

She furled her brow, took a tissue, dabbed her eyes, then sighed deeply. "What can they do about it, doctor?"

"I'm afraid nobody knows how all of this fits together. We are just beginning to scratch the surface on figuring out the brain and the nervous system. For now, I'll do some research, make some contacts, and I think I need to consult with a brain specialist."

She dabbed her eyes. "That's real expensive, right, doctor? I believe in payin' my way."

"I know you do, Mrs. Krenshaw, but please hear me out. This would be a consultation with Doctor Norman at USC. He is a brain expert and will gladly consult with me about Simon and share the latest research—no cost."

"He must be fair to regular folk—like you, doctor." Embarrassed again, she turned away.

"Um, thank you," he said awkwardly. "Whatever we find out, Mrs. Krenshaw, Simon is still a wonderful boy."

She raised her head. "Yes, but if he don't get better, what'll Simon do when he's grown?"

"It's hard, but try not to worry too much about it for now."

"Yes, doctor." She slumped again but didn't cry. Mildred looked up. "Doctor, you already done somethin' for Simon, even if he don't show it much. Even before all this, most folks'd treat Simon like he wasn't there, 'specially since he keeps to his self." She shut her eyes for a moment, then made eye contact with him. "He recollects you always treat him good. In Simon's way, I believe he still cares for you more than most other folk."

He smiled, then Mildred got right up to the sink and splashed a little water on her face.

Seth turned to her as he started for his desk. "Mrs. Krenshaw, with your permission, perhaps I can catch Doctor Norman right now, or leave a message to ask for a conference."

"Yes, doctor." While he made the call, Mildred settled into her chair, sniffling quietly. Several minutes later, Seth returned. Mildred thought he was trying to appear encouraging.

"Mrs. Krenshaw, Doctor Norman agreed to consult with me on Thursday afternoon. Then, if it's okay, I'll drop by that night around eight with the information."

She dabbed her face again. "That suits me fine, doctor. Thank you."

CHAPTER 7
Reed's Wheels

To most students at Truman High School, the only thing "cool" about Reed McCool was his last name. His main advocate there was a counselor, Mr. Collison, who considered Reed to be one of the most talented students at Truman. Nevertheless, Reed was held back in tenth grade due to unexcused absences, poor grades, and suspensions for his antics.

Reed had tried to drop out of school after that, but various authorities made him return. Finally, an agreement was made with Helen, social services, and Mr. Collison. Reed would study for his GED in the fall until he passed it or turned eighteen in November. He also had to continue behavioral therapy, a stipulation of a prior court order. When Reed began to show up at school again, only Rudy, Artie, and a few of the school's marginal drop-outs spoke to him intentionally.

Reed was studying half-day in Mr. Collison's office and was showing up three or four times a week—good attendance for him. Monday and Wednesday nights, his grandmother Helen tutored Reed for his GED, just as she did before with his regular homework. Rudy often went to Helen's those same nights for math tutoring, and if Reed didn't show up, she would still help Rudy with his math, then share some literature, art, or music with him.

Reed answered Rudy's call after a few rings. "Carradine residence."

"What's that supposed to mean?"

"Rudy, my man, you never heard of John Carradine?"

"Some old actor. So?"

"He's a *great* actor. Gram says we're distant cousins. Told you I had acting genes."

When Reed was eleven, his mother signed him up for *Broadway or Bust,* a modern dance academy for kids. Reed excelled for three years until he reached the age limit for boys. Then, in junior high, they put on plays twice a year, and Reed always had central roles—his main incentives to attend school. He had also been in the ensemble for years at a local community theater, which included some short speaking parts before he could no longer pass for a child.

At the beginning of tenth grade, Reed won the male lead in *Oklahoma!* but had sharp differences with the drama teacher. An art teacher who was supervising set design suggested that Reed be the student art director. He took up the challenge, creating three moderately surreal sets of the Oklahoma plains, a farmhouse, and a barn—which turned out to overshadow the play's lackluster performances. Reed's Art and French classes were the only ones he passed, both taught by the woman who had maneuvered him into set design.

"Did I catch you on a break, Reed?" *And what are you doing tonight?*

"I hit a dead-end with that painting for now, so I'm finishing my *Playboy* interview. When they call, I'll have it ready and waiting. I used questions like the ones they always have."

Okay, ask the obvious. "Why would they want to do an interview?"

"Don't worry, eventually they will. That's not all—Disney's auditioning guys my age for some cheesy animal movie—I think I'm a shoo-in for the part."

"Are you saying that you have an audition?"

"No, but I will." He paused. "I was about to call you. What are you up to?"

"Just homework, you?"

"No more homework for me."

"How come?" *Kicked out again.*

"Tell you later. I saw Si's car—that's a good omen."

Another omen—Jesus.

"Rudy, I was about to call you; I know you want out of there."

Yes! "Yeah, tonight especially; I have to babysit him tomorrow night."

"Easy on him, Rudy." Reed paused. "Hang on a second." He spoke interrogatively away from the muffled phone. "We haven't eaten yet; Gram's asking you over for dinner."

God, one of her vegetarian delights. "It's last minute—isn't it too much trouble for her?"

"No way. Gram always wants to expose me to your positive influence," he said with a chuckle. "Don't worry, it's tomato soup; even *you* will eat that."

"Yeah, funny. I was cooking for myself tonight, so it should be okay."

"Good. Rudy, I'll get us outta' here for as long as you want. One thing, bring a flannel shirt. Oh, and fill your old canteen. I'll explain later."

Another Reed mystery. "Be there in a few minutes."

Rudy was once told by Katie that Helen Crowley was the "neighborhood intellectual," and a few people on the block thought she put on airs about it. A retired city librarian and a long-time student of psychology, Helen held a weekly meeting on aging issues for elderly women. Larry had always been casually acquainted with her, but after his marriage to Katie, Helen became closer friends with some of the Laniers and Krenshaws.

Rudy rang the kitchen phone and let Katie know he was eating at Helen's. He hurried to the rumpus room closet, found the canteen, and borrowed a green flannel shirt from his father's gear. He filled the canteen, then went out to the backyard. *Man, dusk already.* He jogged over to his shortcut—dim in the day, black at night—between one side of the Lanier's house and a six-foot oleander hedge on the duplex property.

Half-convinced that the path didn't spook him anymore, Rudy race-walked ahead, then he stopped to listen to some rustling in the oleander. *What was that?* He ran the rest of the way, then around the hedge, where he caught his breath. *Jesus, Rudy—it was nothing.* His rear end painful from running, Rudy crossed the small lawn, climbed two stairs to the porch, then passed a curtained window to Helen's door.

Hearing Helen's weak footfalls on the wood floor, Rudy knocked softly, then put the canteen down off to the side. The door opened, and Helen, frail but steady, stood there with her sturdy driftwood cane. Decked out for autumn regardless of the warm day, she wore a goldenrod cotton skirt with a crocheted brown wrap. In her mid-eighties, she kept her long white hair up in back with a barrette. Behind her bifocals, time had wizened her face so much that her features were nearly lost, but Rudy was always struck by the intensity of her hazel eyes.

"Well, my student of modern literature." She couldn't quite form the full smile that Rudy knew she intended. "Come in, Rudy; haven't seen you in a while. You look a bit, um, winded."

"I'm fine, Helen." He inhaled pungent molecules of soup wafting in from the kitchen. *That's tomato?* "Um, thanks for inviting me."

"We're always pleased to have you here—and we have a little celebration."

Celebration? "Thank you, Helen."

She saw the flannel shirt tied to his waist. "Then who knows what you two are up to?"

Yeah, who knows? She left her cane just inside the door; he followed her slow pace into the living room. "So, how does my favorite Dodger fan think it's going in the World Series?"

"Tied, the newspaper says." She glanced at his Angels cap. "I'm not much of a fan, but I am furious that Vin Scully is not on the radio, not even on Melba's television. Every old widow in this city is infatuated with that man's voice and sense of humor. One of his commercials interested me in sausages, and I don't eat sausages."

"So, it's the damn Yankees *and* the damn networks."

"Precisely." She left him and puttered into the kitchen to attend to the soup.

Helen's living room was about the size of a master bedroom in a small house. The furniture included a settee, coffee table, one padded armchair, a rocker, and a writing desk—all of them partly or completely made of wood, but of no consistent type or grain. A darkly-stained grandfather clock stood in one corner, marking each second with a hollow noise that always sounded, to Rudy's amusement, like *klok.*

Helen's grey tabby, Agatha, napped on the rocker; Rudy petted her and scanned Helen's nearby books—mostly hardbacks shelved from floor to ceiling. The front window had a tall, full bookcase to the left and a long table on the right for her classical records and an old Philco radio. That table was also home to *Peter Rabbit, Aesop's Fables, The Jungle Book,* and other fantastical children's literature. His taste for her books had progressed over the years from *Doctor Doolittle* to *Pogo* to Rudy's first novels, *The Pearl,* and *The Old Man and the Sea.* Helen also loved the old classics, but she once told Rudy she had hopes that contemporary literature could hold the ramparts for young people against television and the incipient computer age.

Hers was the only house Rudy had ever been in that didn't have a TV, but Helen's décor, gathered mostly from her travels, fascinated him. The items were mostly from Africa or Latin America, including small tools, carvings, baskets, and idols crowded around bookends. Above some of the bookcases, Helen displayed a few of her own charcoal drawings, capably rendered, including dark cityscapes and wan portraits of needy children. They were set off by two watercolors of peasants—a dark, tall, white-robed man driving lean cattle past an umbrella thorn tree in an African savanna; the other was an indigenous woman with coal-black hair and a colorful poncho, grinding corn into *masa* at a mud hearth.

Reed had inherited a knack for art from Helen, but he kept all of his work in his studio, which was also his bedroom. He admired surrealism, and Helen believed his work uniquely echoed Picasso; Reed boasted that it would all come out in a spectacular debut. Rudy didn't "get" his art, but it was clear to him that Reed's intricate shapes, designs, and use of color showed talent.

Although Rudy was nearly two years younger than Reed, they came to rely on each other as children to share their struggles. Reed, an only child, occasionally related troubling accounts of his father, who physically abused Reed and his mother. When he was thirteen, Reed executed a cunning ruse that sent Will McCool to jail for child abuse. His mother was hospitalized at the time, so Reed moved in with Helen, and guardianship was soon granted by the court. Reed was allowed to visit his mother every month at the mental hospital, depending on her condition.

Helen returned. "So, how have you been, Rudy?" She stood near the coffee table, stacked neatly with issues of *The New Yorker*, *Atlantic Monthly*, and *National Geographic*.

"Fine, thank you." He peeked over her shoulder to see if Reed might be coming in from either the kitchen or the short hallway.

"Reed will be a minute—he's finding a stopping place on something he's writing. I told him I heard you coming." She sat on the rocker, and Rudy eased his tender posterior carefully into the armchair. "Rudy, do you like tomato soup with cheese dumplings?"

God, no. "Helen, excuse me for asking, does it happen to be white cheese?"

"Sharp yellow, but I have an alternative I think you'll like."

"Thanks." *For putting up with me.*

"Of course. How are you doing with your Algebra, Rudy?"

"I'm mostly lost. They still explain things with little sayings like, 'Whatever you do to one side, you do to the other.' If I ask them to clarify, the teacher and the math dorks laugh. Thank god it's my last math class—I'll probably get a *D.*"

"I see. Are any of those, um, *math dorks* in your advanced English class?"

"Yes, two of them get their only *B*'s there because they don't participate in discussions."

"And does anybody mock them?"

Yes. "Yeah, I get your point."

"Rudy, there are rare geniuses who see the world from a scientific, artistic, and humane point of view. Perhaps they are the ones who can save our planet from ourselves. You and Reed see the world from an artist's perspective, which is vital for any culture to survive."

What? "How could that be? I don't have any skills or talents like Reed's."

"Not the same ones. Reed writes when it suits him, but you are a writer."

"Thanks." *But I don't think so.* Rudy stood and noticed that her eighteen-inch-tall, hand-carved elephant, its natural wood dark brown, had recently been re-positioned on its shelf. Rudy eyed it carefully, discovering a baby elephant carved into its mother's haunch.

"That's amazing, Helen. I didn't see the little one before."

"Yes, it's quite subtle." Helen waited for Rudy to face her. "So, Reed said that Si's here."

"Yeah, supposedly to help with the party." He poorly disguised a low groan.

"So, his visits still upset you."

More than ever. "A little." He checked the kitchen for Reed.

"I see." She paused. "Did you bring one of your stories to leave with me?"

"I haven't finished one for a while." Rudy paused. "I know—I need to write every day. I do on most days—usually about everyday things I notice."

"That's the ticket, Rudy. We'll definitely talk more about that next time. She scanned a nearby shelf. "Rudy, is this a good time to start you on another book?"

As long as it isn't 'War and Peace'. "Okay."

She stood and reached for a thin hardback. Helen handed it over; the original cover was protected by brown paper. Rudy was always grateful for the loan, but he might not pick up the book for days. Even if it took a month to read, he usually liked the story and also the discussion with Helen. Nobody at school, except Reed and Artie, knew that Rudy sometimes studied with an old lady and read her books. Knowing that some guys would be merciless about Rudy's time with Helen, Reed and Artie just considered it nobody's business.

Helen sat again. "A first edition, so it's double-covered—please handle with care."

Rudy put it on his lap. "It won't leave my house. Thanks, I'll start when I can."

"Good, it's another Steinbeck novella, but it's not at all like *The Pearl.* Those two books lead you nicely into one of Steinbeck's longer works. Some people find this story too morose, but there's so much more to it than that. I'm anxious to talk to you about it."

Morose? Like morbid? Look it up.

Reed entered the kitchen from its other end. "Soup on?" he called to Helen, then went to the stove to sample the aroma. Reed strutted into the living room; Rudy was curious about the ironed white business shirt he wore with ragged jeans and worn-out sneakers. Like Rudy, Reed was about five-ten but inaccurately described sometimes as "all skin and bones." His sinewy legs had made him the fastest runner in school since junior high, but Reed rejected the track team or any official competition. He could also hit most any target with a rock—a star pitcher in Little League the one year he played. Reed's wavy hair was a lighter brown than Rudy's; longer but not unkempt. A few girls at school had taken notice of Reed's even facial features, azure eyes, and rangy physique, but they mostly avoided him.

"Hey, Rudy, what's up? Another novel? Gram's going to make you into an English teacher." Reed put down the flannel shirt that had been on his shoulder, then moved around the room peripatetically searching Helen's books until he stopped to inspect one shelf.

"Dinner's not quite ready." She watched him, tenting her hands as she often did when she was thinking. Helen hobbled over to Reed. "What are you searching for?"

"Anything on the concept of being superstitious but not religious."

"I see. I'm sure there's something, but not off the top of my head."

"Maybe we'll go to the library when there's time."

"Yes, of course." She paused. "I'll check the dumplings. We can go on in."

They entered a kitchen so small that Helen's "ice box," as she called it, was relegated to the back porch. The rest was compartmentalized by function. The sink and counter took up one nook, the stove another, then a square oak table with pillowed bench seats filled the tight space where they took their meals. The white-tile linoleum floor, pastel-green walls, and the sink area were neat and clean, but not obsessively. A few dirty dishes were piled on the counter, a dish towel had fallen to the floor, and drops of salmon-colored soup dotted the white stove.

Reed put his shirt over the back of a chair, and Rudy tried to sit normally, regardless of his sore rear end. The table was set with blue cloth napkins, utensils, coffee cups, a carton of milk, homemade cookies on a plate, and a glass tray with raw vegetables. Rudy took off his baseball cap and set it on the floor.

"Thank you, Mister Manners," Reed said with a grin.

Rudy scoffed slightly, then faced the back of the table and Helen's old-fashioned cast-iron toaster in its usual place. Pyramid shaped, you put a slice of bread on each side of its naked coils, then after the first sides were toasted, you flipped the bread until the backs were also seared with images of the coils. To Rudy, the utility and durability of the familiar appliance seemed to be emblematic of Helen.

"Is milk okay, Rudy?" Helen asked from the stove. "Or I have juice and coffee."

Ugh, or cough syrup. "Milk's fine, thanks." Rudy and Reed chomped on carrot and celery sticks before Helen served large bowls of tomato soup—three dumplings for Reed, two for her, and one for Rudy; she also brought him a glass.

Geez, a drowning lump of cheesy flour—at least try the soup. He poured some milk, then picked up the spoon and took a couple of sips of the broth. *Watery, but it's okay.* He took another sip and saw Reed cut a hunk of dumpling, cheese oozing out like yellow lava. *Gross.*

"Something wrong, Rudy?" Helen's bifocals fell gently from her nose, caught by a thin silver necklace attached to them.

"No, um, the soup's fine."

She made another partial smile. "There's no cheese in your dumpling, Rudy."

"Oh." *Okay, try it.* He cut out a small piece from the dumpling and put the dry part in his mouth. *Hm, like a plain donut.* After that, he thought himself bold for tasting the bottom part, soaked in soup, then he finished the dumpling.

"There's another plain one, Rudy," she told him. "Would you care for it?"

"Yes, please," he answered sheepishly, but gratified to be eating something new. She took his bowl to the stove, then returned it to him.

"Rudy, eat up; I'm finished." Reed stood, carried his bowl and coffee cup to the sink, and rinsed them.

"Now you hold on, young man." Helen playfully shook an index finger at Reed. "We have our little celebration."

Reed turned from the sink. "C'mon, Gram, it's no big deal."

"Rudy, Reed passed the GED test, eighty-five or more in each subject, except math."

"What? You've only been studying for a few weeks."

"Collison said I was ready, so I took it. They all thought I'd be there until my birthday, except Gram and Collison. I don't know how he can stand that place. Anyway, I had to guess on some of the algebra and geometry—still made it."

"I wouldn't pass that part, for sure. That's great, Reed." Rudy ate more of the dumpling.

"Yeah, so much for high school—bigger fish to fry."

"Okay, Mister Carradine," Helen teased, then stood up to retrieve a black and yellow envelope from a kitchen shelf. "I have something for you." She handed it to him.

"Alright, looks like a good ol' Western Union money order. Still don't trust banks, Gram?" He opened the envelope, peeked at the amount, his eyes cartoonishly wide open.

"My god, why so much?"

"That should help your projects; maybe you can even take up modern dance again. I wanted you to have it when it would be the most helpful."

"Thanks, Gram." Reed embraced her lightly.

Man, there's a first.

"My goodness." Helen had a trace of a blush on her cheeks after they let go of each other. "Well, it's time for the young people to go out for a good time. Be sure and take some cookies—oatmeal-walnut—raisin sweetener."

Reed stared at the envelope, put it in his shirt pocket, then took two of the large cookies from the plate. "Thanks again, Gram. Rudy, I'll be on the front porch."

Rudy finished his soup, took the bowl to the sink, then turned to Helen, who was taking a bottle of sherry and a delicate wineglass from a shelf.

"Thank you, Helen, I really liked that." *Shouldn't have eaten both dumplings.*

"You're welcome. Next time we'll do it with jack cheese."

He smiled, picked up his hat, and put it on quickly, scraping the small lump. *Ouch, damn it.* Rudy thought about passing up the cookies, but he took two. *Give them to Reed—sure you will.* "These look great, Helen; I'll eat them later." He picked up the book and his shirt, then buttoned the cookies into a pocket. "Thanks for the book, Helen; I'll take good care of it."

"I know you will."

"Well, um, Reed's waiting." *Probably smoking.*

"Have fun, but don't take off too far. It's almost eight."

Too far? He thanked her again and left.

Outside, Reed was under the porch light, sitting on the steps and blowing cigarette smoke up at the light. Rudy came closer, an acrid cloud pierced his nostrils and made him hack out a cough. He stayed on his feet. "Reed, does Helen know you smoke?"

"Sure, she's an ex-smoker. Gram just tells me to smoke outside and keep it to four a day. Anyway, a lot of the ladies like a man who smokes. You know, suave and debonair." Reed stood, flourishing his left arm as if it held a cape. He laughed at himself and tossed the cigarette, grinding it into the walkway with the toe of a sneaker.

"And what do the *ladies* think of your crappy jeans and tennis shoes?"

Reed smirked. "C'mon, Rudy, you've seen me in fine threads when I need them."

"Rented, right?"

"For now." He took the Western Union envelope out of his shirt pocket.

"You're going to blow that on clothes?"

"Rudy, she gave me eight thousand bucks."

What? "My god."

"Yeah, I'm re-thinking some of my plans." He put the envelope in his chest pocket. "It's a good omen for sure. It changes everything," with a confident nod.

"You still want me around tonight?"

"Why wouldn't I? I promised I'd get you out of the house. Besides, I can think while we're out." Jangling some keys, Reed beamed, then pointed to a vehicle parked at the curb.

There was just enough light for Rudy to make out its strange shape. The car was on a rake, the back higher, and the frame declined to the front fender. "That's yours? Is it what I think it is?" Rudy was squinting.

"A '61 Citroen—very stylish French automobile," raising one eyebrow pompously.

"Oh sure, stylish. Remember the old Citroen joke?"

"Yeah, *shit-trown* all over it—so stupid, just because it isn't like a square American car. The Citroen is aero-dynamic—won all these awards for innovation. My old man bluffs that he'll sell it, but it's been parked and covered for years behind a fence in back of his place— doesn't even have 60,000 miles on it."

He's all in on this. "Wait a minute, won't your dad see it's gone?"

"Screw him. It'll be a month before he notices." Reed opened his wallet and flashed a small card at Rudy.

Hold on. "What's that, your license? I thought—"

"I only have the permit. The license is fake, but I'll have the real one on my birthday. I told Gram that the court let me take the driving test and that I registered the car. I didn't like lying to her, but Mom did sign all the papers over to me—it'll all be legal in three weeks."

"You lied to Helen again?"

"Like I said, I don't like doing it. Shit, Rudy, I can't do what I need to do without wheels. She'll understand."

"I know your plans are important, but—"

"Listen, I'll apologize to Gram and get it all square. I'll tell you later tonight what I'm thinking about."

"Why don't you just wait three weeks?"

"I need to drive the car a few times to take care of some minor repairs."

"What if you get stopped?"

"Ha! I follow all the damn traffic laws and play the role of Mister Respectable," he said, high-toned and theatrical. "Ergo my corny shirt, clip-on tie, and parted locks," pointing to his hair. "Today's only the second time I drove the Citroen, but I've been driving for a couple weeks—no problems with the cops."

"Driving what?"

"This is L.A., right? Some guys at midnight-auto loan cars—ten bucks an hour."

"What's midnight-auto?"

"You don't want to know. The other night, they got me a sticker for the Citroen's license plate and helped me move it and get it running—just needed a battery and some re-treads—still needs a few small parts. "For now, let's give this baby a spin—see if she's up to it."

"Really? You want to take it out tonight?"

"It's way after rush hour, and I know how and where to stay away from traffic."

"Reed, you've never asked me to do something like this."

"Like what, go for a ride with a juvenile delinquent? Look, even if I got in trouble, which I won't, the worst you would get is a slap on the wrist."

"I don't know." He took another glimpse of the Citroen. *Damn, what if—? Crap, chicken-shit, he'll do it anyway. Keep an eye on him.*

"What do you say, Rudy?"

C'mon. "Okay." He picked up the canteen from the porch. "Alright, let's go."

"I suppose you have some place in mind?"

"Actually, two places. I'll have to check my coin."

Great. "You still have that old thing?"

"Of course. Some of my best decisions have been made by this coin."

How many of your worst? Rudy watched him remove the coin from his pocket and palm it. Without looking, he turned it over a few times in his hand, then slapped it onto his other arm.

"I suppose you still won't let me see the coin up close."

Reed laughed. "You know that would jinx it." He peeked under his palm. "Off we go."

CHAPTER 8
Spam

As Rudy squirmed to get his tender butt into the front seat, Reed was preoccupied with clipping his tie and fixing his hair with a small comb. He drove the Citroen across Glendale Boulevard and through the Parkview neighborhood to Los Feliz Boulevard, where he took a left in sparse traffic and crossed the bridges over the L.A. River and the Golden State Freeway.

Not completely convinced by Reed's story about the car, Rudy saw that the interior did seem to be in good shape, except for dust on every surface and the indistinct stench of something dead, maybe a mouse.

Rudy carefully dropped Helen's book on the flannel shirt between his feet. "Reed, are you going to tell me where your damn coin is sending us?"

"Sure, when we get there." Reed passed Griffith Park's main entrance and the fountain.

Rudy watched the oval streetlights flip by as if animated in a zoetrope, then he saw the Citroen's headlights reflect the wide picture windows of expensive homes on Vermont Avenue. His head pulsing, Rudy settled back even more, his mind almost blank, mesmerized by the regular intervals of the streetlights, a sensation he had experienced many times over the last several years while riding in his father's car. *Damn, don't let it come.* He fell into a daze. *So strong and dark—like when it's all over, and I was never here.* Instead of escaping his torpor, Rudy sought the lights, drawn to their terrible truth. *Nothing here—a void.*

"Man, Rudy, what's with you?"

What? His body jerking upright, the seatbelt tightened on one of the chest bruises from Harry's shove. *Damn.* "I guess I was dozing off." *Sure you were.*

"No way—you were high, man. Don't know how you did it. Can't be weed, did you bring a little something else? I'd like to check out where you were."

No, you wouldn't. "Crap, I wouldn't have anything like that."

"You never know, Rudy."

"Just forget it."

"Okay—forgotten." They passed the last homes, then a public golf course.

"Where are we going, the Greek Theater?" Rudy tried to joke.

"Funny. You'll see." A couple of blocks before the theater parking lot, he turned left on a dirt side-road, not much more than a cleared firebreak, dry underbrush on both sides. Reed drove on for another few minutes on the rough road, then around a curve. He entered a wide turnout, his headlights exposing a venerable, thick evergreen oak away from the road. He yanked off his clip-on tie. "You remember this place, Rudy?"

"Sure, the trailhead for the old Scout trail."

Reed drove around an outhouse and a hitching-rail up to the oak. "Okay, this is it."

"This is what?"

"Where we park." He shut off the motor, then the headlights; they squinted through the windshield into the dark.

What the hell? "You want to hike that trail at night?"

"When we were kids, we built a fort around here. Remember?"

"Not at night we didn't."

"It's safer here than walking home from school. Here's your chance to take on the dark."

He's just trying to help. "Alright, should I bring the canteen?"

"Let's leave it. If we hydrate now, we'll be fine." He picked up some work gloves from the floor, handing a pair to Rudy. "You'll need these. One thing I screwed up—should've had you bring your own flashlight, but we'll be okay." He held up his plastic light. "New batteries."

They drank water until they were satiated. Reed took off the semi-formal shirt, then buttoned his red and black flannel over his t-shirt. They got out, the gloves in their back pockets.

"Why the shirt now?" Rudy asked, then waited a moment. "It isn't cold."

"You'll see in a while. Swami predicts you'll put yours on too."

Rudy tied his shirt around his waist, then Reed led him with the light past the oak and back onto the dirt road.

"Reed, aren't we going on the Scout trail?"

"No, we stay on the road for a while."

"I won't even bother to ask again what we're doing."

"Good." They soon came to a dilapidated Dodge Dart parked by a NO PARKING sign fastened to a rusted metal gate that crossed the road. "Didn't expect anyone up here tonight."

"I didn't expect *us* up here tonight."

"Like Gram says—patience, Prudence."

Rudy looked at the Dart. "What are they doing up here?"

"My guess would be making out." They walked on, skirting the Dart and the gate.

"Reed, is this a good time to tell me about your plans for the car and the money."

"Not yet. I'll get to it later."

With occasional small talk, they continued on the slight incline for about fifteen minutes before the road narrowed into a wide trail. Right behind them, a creature of some kind broke off into the dark. Reed immediately checked with his light.

Damn, it was pretty big. They started off again, now on hard, rocky ground. "You see what it was?"

"No. Take your pick: rabbit, 'possum, skunk, feral cat—"

"Reed, I read that a mountain lion was spotted up here once."

"More than once—right here, smack in the middle of L.A. It hasn't caused any trouble that I know of."

Jesus. "Did it escape from the zoo?"

"No, this is the end of the Santa Monica Mountains, just wild enough for a puma or two."

Two? Rudy slowed down and discreetly took out and opened the aspirin tin. He took one dry. *Damn, only one and a half left—should've filled it.*

"So you *were* holding out on me. What is it, Rudy?"

"Aspirin. Want one?"

"Funny. You've got a headache?"

"It's not bad."

The trail became firm dirt again. After another ten minutes or so, Reed stopped at a sprawling elderberry the size of an aged apple tree, many of its leaves fallen for the cooler months. "Okay, this bush is my first marker. Now we go up."

"For the real fun and games." His butt felt like it had been kicked again.

"C'mon, Rudy." Reed led him up an embankment to some chin-high undergrowth in back of the elderberry. "Okay, look up there." He pointed to a distant tree—its faint black outline etched by light from the city. "That oak up there is my next marker." He pointed his light toward the tree, then moved his arm like a clock's second hand to the right, then held it there. "About ninety degrees. We angle up that way, more or less."

More or less? At least he didn't consult the coin. "We go right into that wall of brush?"

"Not as bad as it looks—there are some gaps. Eventually we'll hit a trail, and on the way, we'll see that oak up there again. The quieter we are," in a low, guttural tone, "better the chance to see a critter or two."

"As long as the critter is no larger than a 'possum," Rudy answered, as quietly as Reed.

"C'mon." They put on their gloves and walked off into dry scrub, some of it over their heads. Although Rudy tried to help, Reed handled the brunt of the bushwhacking, shoving aside pliable branches, dry sticks, and dead limbs. Much of the chaparral was so dense that they had to go around.

They went on for at least fifteen minutes until Rudy stopped to remove a hefty dead limb that Reed had easily jumped. Rudy muffled his voice. "Man, I'm glad you brought these gloves."

Reed stopped. "Yeah, a basic necessity. Speaking of which, I need to do my duty like a good boy scout. Be right back." Reed's light disappeared into the brambles.

Shit! Pitch dark in here. Easy, he'll just be a minute. Give your ass a break. As Rudy's eyes adjusted, a gibbous moon shined brightly enough through the haze to cast ethereal silhouettes of branches onto his feet. One bush was so stout that he rested against it. Although he couldn't see the lights, the hum of the city seemed louder. He shuddered, then checked the spot where he thought Reed took off. *What's taking him? He wouldn't just split as a joke.* Rudy caught a glimpse of a small dark form fluttering by. *Damn, a bat?* Then he jumped a little when a stick cracked nearby. *That better be him.* He turned to see a light jittering through the thicket.

Rudy left the sturdy bush and tried to hide his relief. "Damn, what took so long?"

"Take it easy," Reed said, barely audible. "I had to find some leaves after I took a dump."

"Gross," he murmured, "I thought you were just taking a leak."

"Could've done that right here. What would you do, crap your pants?"

Never. "I think a bat swooped by me."

"There's a lot of 'em around here. They won't bother you on purpose."

How reassuring. Starting off again, the non-trail was now on a noticeable incline. *Keep up and don't fall on your ass.* Rudy shoved a branch out of the way, but it seemed to reach back and snag his t-shirt. "Shit." He hoped he sounded more startled than scared.

Reed turned to him. "The ghost of Griffith Park?"

He freed his shirt. "Hilarious."

"Rudy, I'm *not* trying to scare you."

"Fine. It's time for the other shirt. You were right, Swami." Rudy untied the flannel from his waist and put it on. "Now where?"

"Still a while until we meet the trail. Feel the breeze? That's good."

"Why?" *Patience, Prudence.* "Never mind." *Get closer to him—maybe see what's ahead.* Rudy moved up so they were side by side. They made their way together around drab sage of all sizes, coyote brush, wild blackberry briar, manzanita, and an occasional oak or sycamore.

"Stop a sec, Rudy." He aimed his light toward a relatively open rocky area surrounded by vegetation taller than Reed. "There are places to sit here if you need a break."

His gluteus throbbed. "I'm okay. I don't need to sit." *Anywhere out here.*

"Alright, we can see that oak again now." Reed led him to a small opening in the copse and pointed up at the tree's outline. "It's a marker again in case you do this some other time."

Maybe in broad daylight. That tree doesn't seem much closer. "How is it a marker now?"

"It shows the way to the path, we start off about thirty degrees to the right of the oak."

Desiccated twigs and leaves crunching under each step, Reed and Rudy took that direction, but the marker was soon out of sight. Nearly silent, they bushwhacked through more thick growth on a steeper incline for about a half hour. Reed stopped.

Good—catch your breath. He inhaled and exhaled noticeably. "Why did we stop here?"

"This is it."

"This is what?"

"The trail." Reed shined his light uphill along a worn path no more than two feet wide. "I guess you'd call it a deer path," he said under his breath, aiming the light straight down to some tiny tracks. "The smaller animals use it like a freeway to get around. We follow it up to the tree."

Rudy saw that the oak was visible again and now seemed closer. They started up the narrower and steeper trail, Rudy behind again. The underbrush was almost as dense as before, but it was mostly off to the sides, branches poking them intermittently.

"Some freeway, Reed."

They continued on up for several minutes, the darkness intensifying with taller and thicker vegetation looming over the path. Reed paused occasionally to investigate something with his light. *He's letting me catch my breath—fine with me.*

Reed soon came to a stop, shining his light to both sides; Rudy was surprised to see the vegetation was shorter, not even knee-high. They took a few more steps into a wider and more level break in the path. Then, without warning, Reed shut off the flashlight, leaving only negligible light from the moon.

Damn! Rudy stopped, literally in his tracks. "Funny, turn it back on." He could just make out that Reed was facing him.

"Rudy, I'm still not trying to scare you," his voice low. Reed kept the light off.

"I just wasn't expecting it." An ache in his forehead started again.

"Okay, I should've warned you. But now the light stays off and no talking at all."

"What?"

"Just trust me," in a hoarse whisper. "What we're going to do is turn around and look back—then listen. No talking."

What the hell? Rudy turned around. Beyond the wide spot, the breeze had cleared out most of the haze, and they had gained more altitude than Rudy expected. He had seen the lights of Los Angeles before, of course, but not like this. *Why are they brighter; so many more of them?* Even a scattering of the more lucid stars and planets had appeared above. Rudy heard a cacophony of faraway motors, horns, sirens, helicopters, airplanes, and the rumble-clatter of a distant freight train. Those noises melded into a steady din until some closer sounds, as if waiting for a chance, reached Rudy's ears one by one: a cautious chirr of crickets, a locust's steady buzz, shrill caws of a raven, the muffled bass of rock music, and the echo of a faint shout.

Reed nudged his arm. "Not bad, huh?"

Rudy kept listening and taking in the vista for a few more moments. "I never imagined." He left a long pause, vaguely cognizant that his headache had subsided. "Really something," he said softly, as if he might be bothering someone.

"Like that trip you were on in the car?" he asked, as quietly as Rudy.

"Not at all, this is relaxing."

"It's even better when you breathe all the way in."

"What?"

"Gram says that's part of what some Buddhist monk calls *mindfulness.* He's Vietnamese, I think. Gram can tell you all about him."

"She probably has a book he wrote."

"Yeah, all of them. I'm not much into it, but Gram showed me how to slow things down when I'm doing too much at once." Facing the city again, Reed took some deep breaths. "Rudy, there's a place right around here with an even better view."

"The observatory?"

"Nah, too close to the city and too many people." He turned on his flashlight and aimed up at the oak—squat-shaped but almost thirty feet tall.

What? "No way I'm climbing up there."

"See all those low limbs? It isn't a hard climb—some other time."

Fat chance.

"The beach is also good for doing this, if you pick your spot." He turned off the light again. "Night is best—lasting, unique, unpredictable, and with a sunrise—less popular but more worthy and hushed than sunset."

Pretty heavy. "You ever paint anything like this?"

"No, but my work is influenced."

They were silent again, watching the city for a couple more minutes before Rudy spoke faintly. "Do you usually do this sort of thing alone?"

"Yeah. Most people would say it's nuts, but I knew you'd get it."

Really? "Um, is it too late to drive out to the beach?"

"No, my coin sent us *here*. Not enough gas to get to the beach and back anyway, and all I have is eight thousand bucks hidden in the car." Reed snickered.

"I have my gramma's emergency twenty."

"Nah, we'll do it some other night. I have something else up here to show you anyway."

What? "I thought this was it."

"You're doing great, Rudy. C'mon."

Reed turned on the light, and they started off on a better trail, more level, not so narrow, and the vegetation not as close. A few minutes later, Reed turned to him. "My idiot therapist says I'm so self-centered that sometimes I isolate myself from people. That's the only thing he ever got right—I'm interested in people who *really* see what's right there in front of them."

"I think I get you."

"That's because you notice almost everything—not just living things; you notice shapes, sounds, or changes in inanimate things like dirt or cobwebs—"

"Or hubcaps."

"What?"

Rudy explained the flattened hubcap. "I write that stuff down."

"Of course you do!" he said, enthused but not loud. "If I wasn't into what I do, I'd be painting poodles playing poker." His upbeat tone turned more solemn. "What I'm getting to is this—I know three people who see what I can—Gram, a girl I know, and you."

Ah. "That's why you expected me to, um, *get* looking down at the city."

"Yes, but it means you're curious and aware, not crazy. A book I read said craziness is often like beauty—in the eye of the beholder."

"That's a relief. Are you dating this girl?"

"Actually, she's no girl. It's not like that, but I do love her. I met Diana in group therapy months ago. She's a sculptor; her work is brilliant. Diana notices everything, but she only talks to me and her girlfriend about it. Anyway, sometimes I do tune into the anxiety of others—with you three anyway." He paused, downcast. Some birds had apparently heard them and fluttered in the underbrush. "I see more grief in Diana than I could ever imagine."

Man. "That's rough. I'd like to meet her sometime."

"Yes, I want you to. She's mostly isolated and travels when she can—alone." Reed turned silent as they removed a huge dead bush, then went on. Two or three minutes later, he cleared his throat and turned to Rudy. "As for Gram, she grew up optimistic, expecting the world to redeem itself for its, um, 'atrocities and proud ignorance,' as she says. After she retired, Gram was into big causes until the King and Kennedy assassinations in '68. Hardly anyone knows how deeply discouraged she was; still is, in a way. But she's okay with her life—her books, art, and music—and Agatha, my mother, and me, I guess. Am I bumming you out?" he asked over his shoulder.

"No, Helen's a good friend, one of a few adults who doesn't talk down to me. Is she okay with you telling me all that?"

"I'll let her know, but I know she's fine with it, especially since it's you."

Okay, my turn. "Alright, so what's *my* big anxiety?"

Reed exhaled through his lips like a horse chuffling. "You already know it's fear—but one of your fears is more complicated than the others. It relates to Si."

What the hell? "I don't get you, but let's drop it for now."

"Fine." Reed's light sliced into the darkness ahead. They continued on the good path for several more minutes in silence. Reed stopped, leaned down, and tied his shoes. Then he cast the light on Rudy, who was brushing sticks off his shoulders.

Shit! He yanked off the flannel, then his t-shirt, flapping the two shirts as you would dusty rugs. Then he shivered, jiggling his boy-breasts.

"Rudy, what was it?"

Damn it. Discomfited by his exposure, he put the shirts right back on. "Nothing."

"Bull, you had the heebies, man."

"Okay, I think it was a damn spider on my neck. Let's just go."

Reed started off, his light flashing into the briar on both sides. "You'd practically have to sit on a spider to get bit out here."

"And I suppose that goes for bees during the day."

"Sure, if you don't mess with them."

"Yeah, that's what Si would say."

"I've seen him watching bugs. What's that all about?" Reed came to a thick dead tree limb that had fallen across the trail; they pushed it off to the side, then trudged ahead. "Rudy?"

"Okay, Mom said Si studied insects as a kid—still likes them; knows some scientific names."

"I didn't know that, but I've wondered about some of his words that just pop up in Scrabble. He'll spell something like *pupa* or, um, *formic*."

"He remembers most everything from before fifth grade, but not much after that." Rudy momentarily lost his footing in a shallow hole. He remained upright, but he winced from another sharp pain in his rear. *Klutz.* Reed had turned the light on him. "I'm all right," Rudy said gruffly.

"Okay, let's go." They continued hiking and stopped only to move or break off an occasional limb or branch.

"Rudy, you told me when we were kids that Si was in Korea and won a Purple Heart, but you never mentioned it much after that."

"All right," he said, his tone resigned. "So, Si knows all about the wars, especially World War II—knows more about that than Korea. Si knew everything about the M-1 rifle years before he touched one, then he bought his own rifle when he got back from Korea. He keeps the damn thing without ammo at his place—keeps it cleaner than himself." He chuckled.

"I don't think he can help that." Reed bent a limb out of the way. *A real knee-slapper, Rudy.* "Yeah." They hiked on.

"He was still in the Guard when he was called up for the Watts riots. Thank god somebody was smart enough to assign him to KP."

"Does anybody know why he's the way he is?"

Rudy stopped and turned to see the city again, but most of the lights were not visible. He explained how Si saved the twins from the yellowjackets. "He hasn't been the same since, but after all this time, they still don't know for sure if the stings were the cause."

"Hm, checkers and chess."

"What?"

"Si beats me in checkers, but he can't even learn chess. I guess that makes sense now. So, how could they have drafted him?"

"They didn't; he joined when he was eighteen. Si barely passed the tests—my dad said they probably bent the rules."

"Man, I didn't know most of this. Why didn't you tell me?"

"I didn't think you'd be so interested."

The trail leveled off even more. "Look, Rudy, I could interview

Si, write his story; sell it for a movie," he said enthusiastically, then hiked on.

After a few minutes, Reed stopped, turned around, and waited for Rudy, who had been struggling to keep up with a faster pace. "Want to help me, Rudy? You write even better than I do. We'd all be famous—no shit."

He won't drop it. Rudy exhaled deeply. "And what would the story be?"

"No sweat. 'Simple man foils commies in Korea.' It would be like a memoir made into a script—names changed, except for Si's." They started off again; the trail was a few inches wider.

"Reed, it wouldn't work. All he could tell you about is army equipment and regulations; he knew most of that as a kid from Danny's manuals. One thing he will tell you is that he had to eat too much Spam in Korea."

"What?"

"Gramma told me he hated it as a kid—one thing we have in common." His tone was bleak. "That's the *only* thing he hates, as far as I know."

"That would be pretty funny in the script."

"You don't get it," Rudy bristled, "he can't tell you about the fighting or the other soldiers, or even much about his sergeant. That guy brought Si's medal and talked to my gramma. He told her the soldiers gave Si a lot of crap at first, but they eventually started to ask him to play his harmonica."

"So he learned that when he was a kid too." Reed tossed away a long branch, then they went on. "That's more good material. I bet Si would tell me a lot of things like that."

"Man, you're nothing if not persistent. What I just told you was from the sergeant, not Si. He just did what the guy told him. Si was a good shot, so the sergeant kept him under his wing, telling him when and where to shoot. He won the Purple Heart because a bullet nicked a leg bone. Si doesn't remember any details—just says he got hurt."

"That's why he limps a little?"

"Yes, and that's all we know about his combat. Doesn't a script sound like using him?" he asked, raising his voice a little.

"Any profits would be his." Reed was silent for a minute or two as they walked. "Okay, you're right. I thought a script might help me open some doors. I'd still like to talk to him."

Relax, he'll be back to his own plans in no time. "Fine, just check with my gramma first. Let's change the subject." They breasted an easy hill on to flat ground.

"This is sort of a summit—it's gradually downhill from here." They descended into some tall shrubs and an occasional tree.

Rudy looked at the thickets around them. "You said there would be a view up here."

Reed turned back. "Never said that—I told you there was something else to see. You're going to like it."

More damn mystery. They went on for a minute or so. Reed slowed, aiming his light up into a tall ash. The darkness closed in on Rudy again. *Damn, let's go.* He took a step toward Reed, cracking a branch.

"There was an owl there," Reed said; they went on. "I want to ask you something."

"All right." *If it's not about Si.*

"In the car, you had your hat off when you were, um, kind of out of it. I saw that wound on your head, and now you're walking funny like your back hurts. What happened?"

Rudy sighed. "Harry kicked my ass—literally." As they walked on, Rudy gave him a sketchy account of the incidents up to where they started fighting at Sikes's place.

"Jesus, maybe we should go back home so you can take it easy."

"I'm okay, mainly a sore ass." Rudy finished the story as they hiked on.

Reed stopped and turned to him again, the beam at their feet. "So it was Artie who remembered what I told both of you about bullies?"

"Yeah, he's your protégé for sure."

"My man, Artie." Reed smiled and shook his head as they went on. "Artie's right, Harry is mayhem waiting to happen. Rudy, I never look for a fight; I can get away from most guys or avoid them in the first place. Artie hasn't agreed with me on that, but from what you said, it sounds like he's changing his tune a little. The main thing to remember is that fear is natural, but you can't let it stop you from thinking, which is your main advantage against bullies, who are usually stupid. The hard part is defending yourself if nothing works."

"Yeah, Artie's going to teach me some basics in boxing."

"He said he'd help me with that, but I never found time. I hardly ever see him anymore; maybe I'll give him a call."

"Good." Rudy paused. "How did you come up with your strategies for bullies?"

"I've been around violence all my life. You either learn to deal with it or end up in and out of jail your whole life like my ol' man."

Jesus. "Makes sense to me." His gut was roiling.

Not saying much, Rudy and Reed resumed walking until they heard some repetitive, hollow cooing. "Owl again?" Rudy whispered as they stopped again.

"Mourning doves. Is that your stomach?"

Hurts like hell. "Yeah." *Not to mention a damn headache.* "I'll just eat one of Helen's cookies." *Sounds terrible.*

"Rudy, are you pissed at me for butting into your business?"

"No, let's just see what you've got hidden up here."

"You don't seem so spooked by the dark anymore."

"Yeah, maybe this is a first step, but no way I'd come up here by myself at night."

"At least you admit it."

Not to anyone else.

"Okay, the show must go on." Reed's tone was more upbeat. They continued on level ground until they came to a small clearing. Reed beaconed the light all around, revealing worn paths from different directions. They fed into a much wider trail, perhaps an old firebreak.

"Reed, do you know where those other trails come from?"

"All over. You'll soon find out why."

Man, what could be up here? They started on the firebreak, which soon became a steep, steady downgrade of dirt, rocks, and sparse low scrub with thicker growth off to the sides. Reed began to descend in a semi-gallop, as if skipping stairs. Rudy's backside protesting, he followed at less than half his friend's pace, but Reed slowed down on and off for him. After about fifteen minutes, Rudy caught up where the firebreak abruptly ended. Still on a steep decline, Reed cast the light off into the tall sage around them, then he aimed it down by their feet, revealing faint paths off to the left and right.

"You choose which way. They both work out about the same."

For what? "To the right, I guess."

"A fine selection, *monsieur.*" They started off in five-foot undergrowth and a few trees, but the narrow but trodden path was visible below. The main difficulty was traversing the slanted hillside, each of them with his left foot below to maintain balance.

Rudy eyed the moderate drop-off from the path. "What if we fall that way?"

"There's plenty of limbs to stop you."

Comforting. "How far now?"

"Minute or two." The path led them through taller thickets where Rudy saw broken branches above in Reed's light. They soon entered a blanket-sized open space, the terrain still slanted downward. Rudy could see well enough to make out a patch that had been trampled over time, just a few dead trunks of bushes sticking out.

Reed shut off the light. "Okay, Rudy, sit on the dirt, then look downhill."

Again? He found a surprisingly soft and sandy spot while Reed settled a few feet away. Rudy spread out his flannel and sat down, his feet ahead and below. *Damn, that feels good.* The branches had been partially thinned; he zeroed in on breaks in the foliage, moved closer, and saw an amphitheater below. Rudy did a double-take. "Man, the Greek Theater."

"Yeah, you guessed it back in the car."

Weak security lights and the scant moonshine made it dusky over the classic U-shaped venue. Long structures left and right of the stage resembled oversized boxcars with renditions of Greek columns out front. A building at the back of the *U* could pass for an antebellum mansion, its façade serviceable as a stage backdrop. Center stage faced hundreds of rows of seating and, above, a live audience of two.

"Reed, you could watch the shows from here."

"Yeah, that's the general idea. It's called *cheapskate hill*; people sometimes haul up lawn chairs and picnics. Some performers, like Harry Belafonte, are cool about it and call up to you."

"Man." Rudy noticed two beer cans and a paper bag nearby. "What about the cops?"

"They won't hike up here if nobody's causing trouble. It's been going on for years; I hope some pencil-pusher doesn't put a stop to it. If they use sets on that stage, I'll design one."

"What? That's one of your goals now?"

"Sure, why not? Set design fits one way or another with what I do—a back-up plan. Gram also got me thinking about dance again—crucial for a lot of acting roles. I could take a refresher class in dance, a course in set design, and maybe even voice, then start pulling it all together here or in Vegas. Then it's off to New York. Thanks to Gram and Mom, I can start preparing—the omens are all good. Sound any crazier than my other plans?"

"Actually, it sounds more realistic—get more training and experience first."

Reed stared at the theater for a few seconds. "It does sound pretty conventional."

That's not what I meant. God, now what's he thinking?

CHAPTER 9
Armistice Day

On Thursday evening, Mildred watched the Model A pull up in front of the house just before eight. She prayed for good news as she went to get Simon.

Seth got out of the car carrying a file folder, then approached the stairs as Mildred and Si came out. He smiled at Simon before turning to her. "Nice for a November evening, Mildr—um, Mrs. Krenshaw."

"Yes, doctor, good evenin'. Would you care to come in?"

"Thank you, but let's make it the three of us. The bench will be fine."

"Yes, excuse me a minute."

She went in and told Margie they would be on the porch, then asked her to keep the girls in. Her daughter grinned, then Mildred *tsked*. "Marguerite, enough a' that; this is important."

Mildred grabbed her light sweater and Si's poplin jacket, then returned to the porch, where Seth and Si were talking. "…Simon, all set for our picnic to the mountains on Monday?"

"Um, Armistice Day. Yes, s-sir."

"Snow or not, at least we'll identify some trees, maybe more." He reached into his folder and handed Si a new comic. "Simon, find out how Captain America is doing with those spies."

"Yes, s-sir." Simon accepted the gift, his eyes opening just a crease wider.

Mildred pointed to the comic. "Simon Peter?"

"Yes?" His eyes were still trained on the cover. "Oh. Thank you, Doc Grant."

"You bet, Simon."

"Mom, can I read my comic now?"

Mildred smiled. "Yes, Simon, maybe over at the other light." She gave him his jacket, and they watched him walk down to the other end of the long bench. "Thank you, doctor."

"My pleasure. It's not often you get to buy a present you know is really wanted." He put down his folder on the bench, then waited for Mildred to sit a few feet away before he sat.

"Doctor, please don't take it personal if he don't seem excited about the trip."

"Of course not. Perhaps we don't really know if he's excited or not."

"Yes, food for thought, like my ma says. Oh, my manners. Would you care for a drink?"

"No thank you, Mrs. Krenshaw." Seth cleared his throat, then checked some notes in his file. "Well, we'd better get going on this."

"Yes, doctor."

He sighed. "Unfortunately, Doctor Norman agrees with my conclusions—and my lack of conclusions…" He repeated much of what she already knew. "He said most research is focused now on severe brain injury, especially from the war." He exhaled noticeably again. "Doctor Norman brought up another point. He said that some of Si's symptoms are not unheard of and are being investigated by a few researchers in children's psychology and medicine, but they have barely started. We have no idea how many years until they have some answers."

"Any chance at all he could jus' get better on his own?"

"Doctor Norman agreed that the stuttering will likely go away. It's not impossible that Simon could improve some—we just don't know, but he also said it was unlikely that Simon will get worse, unless he has extreme fever again. Doctor Norman would agree to an appointment for Simon, but he suggested we wait to see if there is any change. I agree with his recommendation."

"Doctor, I'll be trustin' you to tell me if he needs to go to the other doctor."

"Thank you, Mrs. Krenshaw. Meanwhile, I'll see Simon regularly for brief observations—unless he has another illness, of course. I'm sorry; I wish I had better news."

Her eyes teared up as she stared at her son at the end of the bench. "Is there some way *I* can help him?"

"Yes, you can continue to provide an active and stimulating environment."

She closed her eyes as if in prayer, then opened them, her face resolute. "An' I can jus' love my boy no matter what."

"Yes, that's most important of all."

On Armistice Day, the morning began in the upper forties, unusually cool for Los Angeles, even in November. Mildred heard Cami and Katie romping excitedly on the porch, and she wondered if Simon had joined them. Brushing her hair, Mildred peeked out of Margie's window and saw the twins throwing their outgrown sweaters at each other while Si read his comic in his jacket and favorite t-shirt. The three of them were also prepared for the snow in forest-green mittens and stocking caps.

"You girls behave now," Mildred called from the window. "I'll be right out." She saw a long, black car with wire wheels and whitewall tires roll up in front, stopping at the curb outside the fence. Mildred heard her children react.

Katie gasped, holding Cami's arm. "It's one of those long cars—"

"...for dead people!"

Si put down his comic. "A '41 Packard Clipper. Ike had one in the war."

"Smarty-farty, we saw some army cars—"

"...they're green with a star on the side."

Mildred watched the doctor get out and start for the gate. He had dressed for the picnic in khaki work pants, a heavy dark-blue cardigan, and brown boots. She came to the front door in time to see Katie and Cami gallop down the steps.

"Doc Grant, Doc Grant!" they shouted, latching onto one of his hands.

Smiling, Mildred stayed back from the screen door to watch for a moment.

"Good morning, girls; that's quite a welcome." They started up the rock path. "You know what? It's been cool enough that I think there might actually be some snow left up there."

"Yay!"

"Okay then, I see Simon; we just need your mother."

"Doc Grant, Mom's not quite ready—"

"…she's gussying for you."

Cami shook her head. "Is not, she's just finding something of Margie's to wear."

The doctor chuckled. "I thought you two were always thinking the same thing."

"Not always," they both said, releasing their hands from his.

Mildred was smiling at their conversation, then Margie and Candy walked by her onto the porch. "Thank you, girls," she told them. They placed a picnic basket and a cardboard box next to Si on the bench; the twins ran back up to check out the food. Margie and Candy waved to the doctor; he waved back before they went in. Seth called over to Si and the twins, asking them to put the picnic things out behind the car's trunk; he told them they could get comfortable in the back seat. Katie and Cami giggled on their way out to the shiny automobile; Si followed.

Exhaling fully, Mildred came out onto the porch carrying her hemp purse. With Daniel's red mackinaw draped over one arm, she descended the stairs. Margie had outfitted her mother in used but respectable loose black slacks, a white blouse, and one of Sharon's modern bras. Her auburn hair was not pinned up and fell over her shoulders. She was surprised how loosely her daughter's clothes fit.

Mildred caught Seth admiring her, then blushed. "Good morning, doctor," saying *morning* instead of *mornin'*. Mildred offered her unsteady hand.

"Yes, another fine day." He gently held her slim, cold digits for a moment. "You look wonderful, Mildred. It's *Seth* today—this is, after all, an outing." They started down the path.

Mildred's cheeks were warm again. "Not sure I can remember that, doctor."

"Well, you already forgot," he chuckled amiably.

"Guess I did, um, Seth."

"Now that wasn't so bad." He pointed to the house. "Mildred, I have plenty of room in the Packard for Marguerite and Candace to join us."

"Thank you, Seth, them—um, those two are already preparin' for Thanksgivin'."

"Never too early." He opened the gate for her.

She nodded her thanks. "Not for the pair a' them."

"Will Daniel be here for Thanksgiving?"

"No, maybe Christmas." She faced the Packard. "I didn't expect such a fancy car."

"It was my dad's before he passed a few years ago."

"Oh, I'm sorry." They approached the car, the twins watching them, bug-eyed, from the back seat. Seth held the passenger-side front door open for her—the girls stifled more giggles.

"Thank you, Seth." She was thinking, *First time for everythin'*. She easily maneuvered herself into the passenger side of the front seat as the door closed behind with the neat click of a perfect fit. While Seth walked briskly around front, Mildred inspected the interior. Its broadcloth headliner seemed new—same for the woodgrain panels and moldings. The dashboard had an array of gauges and knobs with spotless ivory-colored faces encircled by silver borders.

Mildred checked the kids; Si had already settled in the middle of the back seat as the twins experimented with the window cranks, ashtrays, and footrests. "Land sakes, girls, not so rambunctious. You'll break something."

Seth opened the driver's door. "Almost forgot the provisions behind the car; that would have made for a fine picnic."

Mildred smiled modestly and drew a forefinger across the dashboard. "Wish my house was this clean." Her face was warm again.

"I try to take care of it like my dad did. It's like a hobby now, along with the Model A." He pumped the gas pedal, turned the key, pushed one of the buttons, and the motor started. Seth put the transmission in first gear, then turned back to the kids. "Everybody ready for a picnic and maybe some snow?"

"Yay!" from the twins.

"How about you Simon, are you ready?" Si nodded. "Good. Okay, girls, you need to sit down now. It's dangerous to be up when we're moving."

They sat grudgingly, Si between them. Mildred took a glimpse of Seth before turning to the twins. "You two mind what Doc Grant says."

Seth checked for traffic and started away from the curb. "Where did you kids get those fancy mittens and stocking caps?"

"Mom knitted them—"

"…in just a few days!"

"She did? And the three of you even match."

"Not much choice in that," Mildred interjected. "Just some ol' Christmas yarn."

Seth looked in his rear-view mirror at the kids. "Most of this excursion is new to you, so it should be interesting just to watch where we go. We can also have a little music."

"In the car?" from Katie.

"Yes, right here." He reached forward, turned on the radio, and tuned into one of Sousa's peppy military anthems.

Mildred smiled back at her children, the girls tramping to the beat from their seats while Si tapped his toe on a footrest.

On the way to Glendale, Seth checked on the kids and saw Si trying to say something. The girls moaned when Seth turned down the music. "Simon?"

"*Field Artillery S-song*, World War I. Happy Armistice Day, Doc Grant."

The girls looked at each other. "Happy Armistice Day, Doc Grant."

Mildred turned back to smile at her children, especially Simon.

Seth chuckled. "Well, thank you very much." He turned up the music—the beginning of *Taps*. Si held up his harmonica, and Seth lowered the volume again. "Si?"

"I can play *Taps*." They listened to Si's slow, emotive version up to the last long note.

"…God is nigh," Seth said, glancing at Simon. "Wonderful. Thank you, Simon."

"Welcome."

His eyes glistening, Seth faced Mildred. "Sorry." He paused. "So, so many boys."

She touched his arm, nodding; he summoned a smile. "Okay, kids, off to the snow!"

"Yay!" from the twins again.

Seth turned the radio up, then tuned to a station that was playing the new singing sensation, Frank Sinatra. The girls convinced Si to play rock-paper-scissors until the car left Glendale, where they came to a long block of large new homes. Si opened his comic while the twins gawked at the neighborhood.

"Are these people—"

"…millionaires?"

Seth chortled. "No, girls, but they are well off, as far as money goes."

"Are there doctors who live here?" Katie asked.

"Oh, I wouldn't be surprised."

"Why don't you live here—"

"…in a place like *that?*" Katie pointed.

"Not my cup of tea, girls." The car approached a sign ahead: LA CANADA.

Mildred turned back to the twins. "Girls, please, not such private questions."

"Yes, ma'am," Cami said. "Doc Grant, why does that sign say Canada?"

"This town is called *La Cañada*. It's Spanish—something to do with canyons."

Katie groaned. "How long until the snow?"

"A little while still." Seth turned left to continue on Highway 2, then he came to dry chaparral on both sides of the road. The radio broadcast had become mostly static; he turned it off. The Packard approached a sign: ANGELES NATIONAL FOREST.

"Forest? It looks like Griffith Park," Katie groused.

"Right you are, but not for long. See all the trees and snow up there?" Seth pointed toward Mt. Wilson.

"That's so far away," the girls said, nearly in unison.

"Yes, but we're gaining altitude; the snow starts long before that. You girls have never been up to the snow?" he asked as if he didn't know their answer. "Never played in it? Never built a snowman?" His inflection rose with each question. "Never had a snowball fight? Never made a snow angel?"

"No, no, no, and no!"

"Si, you can make snow angels with us—"

"…we saw how to do it in a movie."

"Okay."

"Attaboy, Simon." As Seth drove on, the flora by the curvy road transitioned into oak woodlands, then they soon came to the first evergreens. "Si, do you know what that tree is?"

Si stopped reading and caught sight of the tree. "Um, pine. I don't know its real name."

"It's *Pinus Ponderosa*; there are lots of them ahead, also some fir." He drove through slush on one side of the road. "Okay, eyes open, kids. You're going to see snow any time now."

"Yay!" Katie pressed her nose onto the left window, Cami onto the right.

A small white patch appeared next to the road on Cami's side. "Katie, there it is!"

"Can we stop now?" they both squealed.

"That's not even enough to play in, girls. Hang on, just trust me."

"Awww, it's plenty."

"Look up there." Seth pointed ahead to where you could see that the road had been cleared, forming a bank of about two feet of snow off to the side.

"See how deep it is! *Now* can we stop?" Katie asked.

Seth snickered. "That's wet and dirty. A few more curves."

"Seth," Mildred said quietly, "you're not teasin' are you?"

"Why Mildred, of course not," grinning. "Have you ever been up here before?"

"When Sam was in the CCC, but not in winter. That heater feels good."

He turned to the girls again. "Guess what, your mom's never been to the snow, either."

"Now can we stop—please, please," they answered. The girls rolled their windows part-way down and stuck out their hands. "It's freezing!" They rolled the windows up right away.

"Not quite, I'd say it's about thirty-five degrees. Everybody get your sweaters on." A sign by the road read, CHILAO FLATS *Angeles National Forest.* "Okay, here's the campground."

"Yay!"

He turned off the road into a driveway with about three inches of snow and the tracks of a car that had entered and left. Seth's heavy Packard easily negotiated the short road into the campground, where slightly deeper snow was undisturbed but melting. A forget-me-not blue sky peeked through the limbs of tall ponderosas while plops of wet snow fell intermittently below.

Seth stopped at a campsite; the girls bolted out the doors to an open spot in the trees and immediately started throwing snow and screeching at each other. Si had gotten out but was standing by the car. "C'mon, Si!" the girls shouted.

Mildred, now bundled in the mackinaw plus a scarf from her purse, turned to Seth. "Can we maybe jus' watch for a spell?"

"Sure, I'll leave the motor on for the heater."

Si slowly approached the girls, and they immediately threw snow at him; he scooped some up and threw it well short of Katie. The girls kept throwing snow at him and each other, but Si stopped playing until Cami and Katie convinced him to make a snow angel after they made several of their own, laughing at the shapes.

Seth turned to Mildred. "Are you going to be warm enough to venture out to a table?"

"Another minute? I'm not 'customed to this—sure not botherin' the twins."

He nodded earnestly. "The girls try so hard to involve him."

"Yes, they don't see it as a chore."

The kids started on a snowman, but the snow was too wet to roll into a base. They began to pile it up, and Si worked steadily this time until the twins were pleased with it. Si then watched his sisters work on the torso.

"Well, shall we see about the picnic table?" Seth asked Mildred.

She told herself to be a good sport. "Okay," forcing a smile.

Seth shut off the engine, buttoned up his sweater, and put on some thin black gloves. Mildred stuffed her bare hands into her pockets as they got out, then Seth found a pair of work gloves in back and came around the car to give them to her. "A bit dirty and large, but these should do in a pinch."

She put them on. "They work just fine." Mildred and Seth sloshed over in the melting snow to a table, occasionally checking the kids. "This is so beautiful, Seth. Thank you." Her voice carried a hint of a shiver.

"My pleasure, but I think you're still chilly. Shall we have our picnic in the car?"

"I'm not always such a wet blanket, but that sounds good."

"Wet blanket? That's a laugh—let's go." He put his arm around her as they started back. "Are you okay, Mildred?"

"Yes, just cold." She allowed him to move an inch or two closer.

"I planned it this way," he chuckled, "just to put my arm around a pretty lady."

"Oh my." Her face flushed again. "Now *that's* a laugh."

They came to the car, and Mildred shuddered, sucking air in through her teeth. Seth opened the passenger door. "Okay, Mildred, let's get that heat going." He shut the door and hurried around the front, got in, started the engine, and checked to be sure he had left the heater switch on. "Won't be long now."

Teeth chattering a little, she said, "Seth, am I bein' forward to ask for your arm again?"

"Of course not." They met in the middle of the seat; he extended his arm around her.

"Thank you, Seth." She was silent for several moments. "Yes, that's better already."

They watched the children. Si was back with the girls near the snowman, which sported a green stocking cap and a pinecone nose. Si had been granted the sacred duty of selecting the eyes; the girls cheered him on as he inserted two dissimilar stones above the pinecone.

"Three wonderful kids, Mildred."

"Thank you. They do take to you, always have."

He sighed. "Mildred, you must already know that I'm very fond of you."

Looking at the kids, she sighed, then turned to him. "And I'm very fond of you, Seth."

"Mildred." He cleared his throat. "I'm asking to be the best father I can to Simon and the girls, and also be the best husband I can to you."

"Seth," her eyes tearful, "we're jus' from simple farm folk, and—"

"And I care so much for all of you; I don't want you to ever have to struggle again."

CHAPTER 10
Andy and Barney

Reed turned to eye the amphitheater. "They built this place around 1930, then hardly used it for about fifteen years; the big building in back was used as a barracks during World War II."

"No kidding? Where did you find out about all that?" Rudy asked.

"Gram. She knows a lot of L.A. history."

"How often have you been up here for a show?"

"A few times—when they had talent I liked."

"Must be cool, no matter who it is."

"First time, yeah. I should've brought you here before. Now that I have wheels, we can come up to see someone we both like." He pointed ahead and down. "You been in the audience?"

"Once, with my mom when I was eleven. Someone gave her two tickets to John Denver, her favorite. Dad didn't want to go, so I did. It was a lot of fun."

"John Denver's pretty cornball, but I like his—" Reed stopped.

"His what?"

"Hang on," he mumbled, then listened.

"Why are you whispering again?" Rudy had also hushed his voice.

"I heard something scrambling out there." He listened again. "We probably scared off another animal."

Okay, show's over. "Reed, this is great, but—"

"Yeah, let's go."

They stood, then quietly started back, lurching across the grade, right feet below this time. Before the firebreak, Rudy's toe caught on a root. He lost his balance and slid several yards down into sticks and dry mulch. His rear end took the brunt of the impact before he latched onto a hefty branch, his butt pounding. "Shit." Holding on to what was actually a sapling, Rudy struggled to his feet.

Reed shined the light down on him. "Need help?" he said, just loud enough to be heard.

No, dammit. "I'll make it." It took him three or four minutes to clamber up close to Reed, who reached down to give him a hand. Rudy stood up in Reed's light and struck the sides of his jeans with his cap. A headache added to his pain. "Double-shit," he grumbled to himself.

"If you're okay, let's keep moving," Reed stated quietly.

"Yeah." *I knew it; he's worried about something.*

They worked through the bramble up to the edge of the firebreak, then Reed hurriedly brushed off a layer of dirt and twigs from Rudy's back and shoulders. "Alright, let's go."

Rudy saw a light flickering less than twenty feet away on the firebreak. "It's them," came from the direction of the jiggling beam.

A second voice shouted, "Shut up!" as Reed directed his light toward them.

The silhouette of the first one, about Rudy's size, showed him stumbling along with the flashlight, but the other guy had already passed him in a downhill gallop and was almost to Rudy and Reed. "Don't you move, fags," he shouted.

In Reed's light, Rudy could only make out that he was over six feet tall. *Reed didn't take off—hang tight. Damn, what do they want?* Standing slightly ahead of Reed, Rudy scrutinized the taller one as he approached. He was at least six-three, had a sturdy build, and wore hiking boots, a camouflage hat, and battle fatigues—a knife handle protruded from a sheath on his belt. His face was bootblacked; his eyes reflected Reed's light like tiny high-beam headlights. The shorter but stocky one stepped forward, a small pack on his back. Long hair circled his uncamouflaged full-moon face, and he wore a loose dark t-shirt, jeans, sneakers, and a scruffy L.A. Lakers cap. *They're older than us—jerk-offs still playing army, but that damn knife is real.*

Army guy put his small light in a pocket, snatched the flashlight from his cohort, and directed it at Reed from a few feet away. "Light off, faggot."

Reed's light stayed on. *He must be planning something.*

"Turn it off right now, goddammit!"

Rudy watched Reed switch off the light and place it on the ground. *What? The guy didn't say to put it down.* Rudy faced them. "We're not bothering you, and we only have pocket change. Why don't you take it and go?" *Some bluff.*

"Shut up, fat-ass." Army guy spat on the ground. "Aww, you two must wanna be alone. We saw you getting all comfy back at the theater."

"Andy, I don't like this," the shorter one said in a calming tone. "We should've left after we saw their car. We can still just go."

"You shut up too. I was right about their sissy car. We found us some naughty boys up here," cackling, straight-faced. Andy kept the light on Reed. "Get the ropes, Barney."

Andy and Barney? Ropes? What the hell?

While Barney removed his daypack and reached inside, Reed whispered to Rudy from just behind. "Rudy, more tough talk."

And piss this guy off? Just do it. His head aching, Rudy took a step forward. "So, you're out here looking for someone to hassle," he blustered. "Too chicken-shit to harass someone in town?" *Damn, don't overdo it.*

"*Hair-ass*, what the fuck is that?" Andy sniggered.

"Keep talking," Reed whispered, then he dashed straight into the dark copse.

"Shit." Andy took a couple of steps toward the briar, then stopped.

"You can't find him in there, Andy. Let's just forget this—"

"Hell, we got bait right here. If he don't come back soon," lowering his voice, "I got a way to get him. This fat-ass prob'ly can't run ten feet, just like you. Tie him up anyway."

"Andy, you said you weren't going to do any of that shit tonight."

"I don't know yet," clipping Barney in the back of the head; his cap fell off. "And keep your damn voice down." Barney had taken the glancing blow stoically, then Andy circled Rudy twice, mumbling to himself before he jerked his light toward some noise on the firebreak.

Reed better have a brilliant plan. Distract them. "You're making a big miscalculation. You can't—"

"*Miss-cal-kyoo-LAY-shun*—shit." Andy spat again, this time between Rudy's feet.

Go on. "He's not coming back; he's halfway to his car, and then he'll get the cops. Why don't you just take off before you regret it?"

"Regret what?" Andy put his foot behind Rudy's calf and pushed him; he landed on his bruised rear, writhing in pain. "Aw, you pansy, that was nothing." Blinding Rudy with the flashlight, Andy grabbed him by the collar, made him stand, then released him. "Barney, I bet this one has some easy money for me."

Yeah, hundreds, prick.

Barney put his cap on. "Andy, just take it and let's go."

Andy grumbled in Barney's direction. "Always bitching 'bout everything." He checked the firebreak again, then turned toward the thumping noise well behind them. Andy shut off the light, then waited, gripping Rudy's arm before a helicopter flew right above, hugging the hills on its way from the L.A. Basin to the San Fernando Valley. Mesmerized by the proximity of the aircraft, Andy craned his neck to watch. "Real chopper," he mumbled.

As the helicopter's running lights began to fade, Andy escaped his reverie and turned on his flashlight. "Sit down, fat boy." Rudy complied as Andy took a last glimpse of the distant helicopter before turning back to Barney. "Damn it, I said tie him up."

With several long pieces of nylon clothesline in hand, Barney picked up Reed's flashlight. "I wonder why he put this down?"

"Because he's stupid, so now it's yours—stupid."

Barney turned on the light, set it behind Rudy, then began to tie him up.

Why so loose? Keep talking. "My friend—"

"Shut up," Andy snarled. "Shit, he did take off." He checked the trail before turning back to see Rudy fooling with the knots. Towering over him, Andy cuffed Rudy on the head, but on the opposite side of the wound from earlier that day. Andy pushed him roughly over onto his side, then secured the ropes. "Barney, if he messes with the rope while I'm gone, put the light in his face. If he sits up, push him over—and *no* talking to him." He threatened Barney with a fist.

Barney cowered a little. "Alright, alright—where are *you* going?"

Andy lowered his arm. "The skinny fag don't know my shortcut down there. I'll get 'im," patting his sheath.

"Don't cut him, Andy."

"Shut up. I will if I want to." He grabbed more clothesline from Barney's pack, took out his penlight, and stuffed the flashlight into a back pocket. Andy skulked up onto the firebreak, grumbling. He aimed the light all around, then started to lope uphill, following the tiny beam.

Shit, Andy and Barney of Mayberry—Andy's brilliant idea. He'll kick my ass or cut me whether he gets money or not. Reed must have something going on. What's Barney's deal? Rudy's head started drumming again. *Get him talking.* "Barney, did you guys go to Truman?"

Barney sat down, then calmly aimed Reed's light up at the trail. While Barney was distracted, Rudy had rolled onto his back and managed to rock into a sit-up.

"Hollywood High. They kicked him out; I almost finished."

"You quit school for petty theft?"

"I wish that's all it was." Barney got up. "If he comes back and finds you sitting up, he'll beat us both." He gently pushed Rudy back onto his side and put the Angels cap next to him. "Sorry you got hit; I can't control him." Barney sat and turned the flashlight toward Rudy again.

He's not into this at all. "Not your fault, Barney." Rudy listened to the chaparral, but distant sirens dominated any nearby sounds. "Barney, have you and Andy been friends long?"

"He's my brother."

"Oh." *Good god.* "My name's Rudy. What's your real name?"

"You don't believe it's *Barney*?" He chuckled miserably. "I'm Earl."

"Do you do this all the time, Earl?"

Earl, ere Barney, scoffed. He got up to help Rudy back into a sitting position. "No, but Garret makes me go sometimes. Some nights, he drives all over—anyplace people park to make out. He flashes his knife; I hold the money. Sometimes, he makes a guy show himself to the girl, then laughs. I try to talk him out of some worse shit he does to queers; he says the cops don't listen to them. I don't think he really believes you two are queers, lucky for you."

He doesn't sound very sure.

"He'd beat me if he knew I told you all this." He sighed. "The more I disagree with him, the more he hurts me, so I try not to. "

Damn, has that creep messed with Earl? "Do you two live alone?"

"With our ol' man—he's a cokehead. It's more like he lives with us. When his government check runs out, Garret makes me go out to help him get money and drugs. The old man is big, and when he isn't wasted, Garret's scared of him."

"Why don't you let him get caught, or turn him in?"

"Before my dad got worse, I promised him I'd try to keep Garret out of jail. They charge me for whatever Garret does anyway. He's been in twice for a few days, and so have I."

"It sounds like you're trapped."

"I get by." Earl stood and shined his light on Rudy's wrists. "I'm going to untie you before Garret comes back and fools with you." Earl easily freed his wrists and ankles.

Now what? "I'll hide and wait for Reed. What about you?"

Earl stood. "You really think your friend will be back?"

"I know he will."

"Believe it when I see it, but maybe I'll—" He spotted a small light on the trail. "Damn, that's Garret." Earl paused, then whispered. "Drape the ropes and act like you're still tied up; fall on your side."

Garret, limping noticeably, came closer with the penlight. "Fuckin' Earl, I heard you say my name thirty feet back," he snarled. "Having a nice goddam chat?"

"Sorry." Earl kept the light on Garret.

"You're a sorry little shit alright." Garret touched a gash and some blood on his face.

Earl gawped at him. "What happened?"

Reed happened—ha!

"Sneaky chicken-shit threw rocks from the bushes." He dabbed the wound with a sleeve. "Got me here and my knee. I chased him with my knife, but he got away in the woods."

He's probably right around here.

"Then let's just go," Earl told his brother.

Garret slugged Earl hard in the arm. "Little prick!" He took out his hunting knife and the larger flashlight, then pointed the light at the thickets, his hand and the beam shaking. "Hey, faggot!" he shouted. "C'mon on out for this guy's fat ass before I tattoo it!" He dabbed his cut again, put the flashlight back in his pocket, and turned to Earl. "*You* watch for him, dammit."

Earl tentatively aimed Reed's light at the trail. "I checked this guy, Garret. He's broke."

"Yeah? I'll see for myself, an' at least I'll have me a little show. Untie him."

Earl hesitated. "No, I won't do it."

"What'd you say? You'll fucking do what I tell you." He took a few steps to Earl.

Earl cringed. "No."

"Stupid runt." Garret raised his arm to strike him again.

"Leave him alone!" Rudy screamed as loud as he could in case Reed was nearby.

"Yeah? I had it with you, queer-bait." Garret moved to Rudy and roughly yanked him up to a sitting position, his arms behind. Garret trained the light into Rudy's eyes again. "I'll have your money right now."

Stall. Rudy turned away from the light. "I can't get it without my hands."

"Untie him, Earl. Now, goddammit." Garret turned to the firebreak again. Earl went to Rudy and acted as if he had difficulty untying him.

"What's taking you?" Garret turned back to them. "Shit, I didn't say untie his ankles. Jus' get outta' my way." He shined the light on Rudy. "The wallet, fag."

Earl backed off a couple of feet as Rudy stood, sliding his hand into his back pocket. He turned the wallet inside out, dumping his learner's permit, three one-dollar bills, and other papers on the ground. He tossed the wallet to Garret. Rudy reached into his front pockets, held the aspirin tin, and pulled out both pocket liners—a few coins and his housekey fell below. "There, three bucks and change. Don't spend it all in one place."

"Wise-ass." Garret checked the wallet, then threw it into the dark. "Sit down and gimme your shoes."

Damn. He sat, yanked off his sneakers, and lobbed them in front of Garret's feet.

He picked one up. "Hm, looky here, I bet mommy made you this little secret pocket. Let's see, here's a twenty. You an' Earl lied, fat-ass." He checked the other shoe, then fired them at Rudy; they glanced off his arm and torso. Garret faced Earl. "Keep that light on him, dammit."

Earl complied, but he aimed Reed's flashlight a few feet away from Rudy, who furtively pulled on his sneakers by the heel notches.

Garret had been searching inside the small pack with his penlight. One arm behind, Garret returned to Rudy, who was in Earl's light again. "Easy, fat-ass, I ain't gonna' hurt you..." He acted like he was leaning down to pick up one of Rudy's coins, then, with a sock now on his hand, he threw a hard left hook to Rudy's cheek. "…much." He horse-laughed as Rudy buckled over.

The blood in Rudy's mouth tasted salty. He touched his right jaw. *Shit, even worse than Harry. Bastard knocked a tooth loose.* He sat up, pressure around his eyes; his nose was running. *Don't start bawling; he'd love it.* Rudy defiantly put his cap on his throbbing head.

Earl helped Rudy to his feet and turned to Garret. "You got your damn money and still hurt him. That's the kind of crap that will land you in jail for good."

Garret came closer to them. "Aww, you two faggots want me to stop?"

Shit, he'll nail me again. His jaw throbbing, Rudy recoiled, bracing himself, but Garret shoved Earl hard below the neck; he fell, his head thudding straight back on the ground.

Garret pointed at Earl. "Stay there, goddam sissy."

Rudy spat out a glob of blood. "Stay there? You knocked him out."

"Bullshit—he's moving." Garret took out his knife and pushed Rudy over. "Alright, let's see what you got. Pull 'em down," shining the light on Rudy's zipper.

Rudy couldn't stop a few tears. "I won't do it." He scooted himself back.

Garret, his knife reflecting the light, stepped closer to Rudy. "Poor baby."

Do something. Sniffling, Rudy desperately reached behind for a rock, anything to defend himself. He found a soft spot and scooped out a handful of dirt. Garret leaned down for him.

"No!" Rudy flung the sandy dirt directly into Garret's cut and bloody face; he howled in pain. Rudy got up, staggered over to the trail, and tried to run uphill. *He'll catch me—shit.* He stumbled but kept going. *What the hell? He should've caught me by now.* From far behind, he heard Garret squall in pain. Rudy turned; Garret's flashlight fell to the ground and went dark.

Reed got him again! Nearly winded, Rudy walked backward uphill until Garret's small light came on and started to move. *Go!* He turned and ran on, breathing hard, then he stopped again to check behind. Rudy's stalker shined his penlight into the bush, then a rock larger than a baseball hit him in front. In a rough image drawn by the weak moonlight, Garret groaned and held himself as if taking a pee.

That got the creep. Keep going. Rudy turned; the incline had left his lungs burning, but he didn't pause until he heard distant footsteps behind. *Shit, move.* He tried to hurry, but the approaching steps grew louder. *Go into the bush.* He turned to change direction.

"Easy, Rudy, it's me. He's way back there."

Rudy could barely see Reed. "Man, the damn cavalry." He exhaled through his lips.

"Except my horse sprained an ankle," pointing toward his foot. "I got back down there in time to see you get him in the face with the dirt—not bad, Rudy."

"I was scared shitless." He took another deep breath, his head hammering again.

"Yeah, but you *did* something about it. Did they hurt you before I got there?"

"The bastard sucker-punched me in the jaw and, um, he wanted me to pull my pants—"

"A goddam molester? Jesus." He checked the firebreak behind. "No sign of him yet, but he's a hulking son of a bitch. He'll be coming in a little while."

"I'm gassed, Reed."

"After he recovers from that rock in the balls, he might be able to move faster than we can. We'll have to go into the tulies." Reed glanced behind. "How's your jaw?"

Rudy held his cheek; it had begun to swell. He spat out blood, but not as much as before. "Hurts, but I'll be all right. The big guy is Garret; he was sure he'd catch you."

"Not even close. I missed him with the first rock, then I got him twice before the dumb sucker went back down to you. I was following him from the scrub when I twisted my ankle; you got him right when I caught up." He checked the trail again. "Where's the other guy?"

"Earl—they're brothers." Rudy briefly explained what happened. "...and Earl wasn't moving very much."

"He did that to his own brother?"

"He's a psychopath, like Harry."

Reed squinted at a wavering glimmer of light coming toward them. "Well, he hasn't had enough or he's trying to get out to his car. Probably both. We've got to whisper."

Rudy faced a wall of briar. "We're really going in there?" he asked, his voice subdued.

"Not very far. C'mon, pick up some rocks on the way."

Move it, Rudy. He gathered what felt like river stones as they left the firebreak.

"Now, quiet as you can; try to watch where each of your steps will land." Reed pointed off to thicker scrub. "We're going that direction about twenty more feet. He'll never see us," he said with a grin so wide that Rudy could see it easily.

Good god, he's enjoying this. Rudy plodded on until Reed stopped, and they piled up their ammunition.

"Good, Rudy. Okay, get down; we can see enough from here."

"I need to get on my knees. My butt needs a break."

"That's fine. When he comes, just be completely still."

"Let him go by?"

"I'd be okay with that if I was sure he'd keep going. I think another rock or two will keep him moving."

"What if he comes in after us with that knife?"

"He's beat up pretty bad and not quite stupid enough to take a rock point-blank. Okay, now we just wait." Reed's voice was muted, his eyes trained on the trail.

They held still for another couple of minutes. Now on his knees, Rudy was trembling a little. *Damn, we're dead if he's wrong.*

"There he is, Rudy."

Rudy saw Garret's burly frame bent forward, but he lugged himself along in the weak moonlight faster than seemed possible. He had one hand on his face, the penlight showing the way ahead. *He looks like shit—he wants out.* Rudy turned to tell Reed, who had picked up a rock about a quarter the size of a brick. *God, that could kill him.*

Reed checked Garret's pace, waited until he was nearly out of sight, then stood. Like a basketball hook shot, he flung the heavy rock over the undergrowth and a little downhill.

"Shit." Garret grumbled after the rock thudded somewhere behind him on the firebreak.

"That couldn't have hit him," Rudy said under his breath.

"No," Reed whispered back, "and he didn't sound very scared."

"Now what?"

"Find out if he left." Reed handed him an oval stone about the size of an egg. "Let's wait a minute." Rudy listened while Reed gauged the arc with his arm and hand. "About there—behind him, so he can't see where it comes from." Rudy flung the stone.

"Ha! Missed again, faggot. I'll get you someday."

"That was great," Rudy murmured with a grin.

Reed put an index finger to his lips. "He could be faking."

No, the creep wants out of here. They picked up rocks and waited for any noise or a glimmer of light. Rudy flinched at some rustling in the dry vegetation. *Shit!* He cocked his arm.

"Easy," Reed said under his breath. "He makes a lot more noise than that."

Rudy listened carefully again. *Damn, what about Earl?*

Reed tossed a small rock; there was no reaction.

"He's gone, Reed."

"He's as unpredictable as he is warped."

Reed had them wait about ten more minutes, then they made their way slowly out of the thickets, rocks in hand. The darkness had deepened to pitch beneath overcast that likely covered the whole L.A. basin. Reed peered up the firebreak again, then turned his head to listen.

As Reed stared uphill, Rudy was looking the other way and saw a beam of light wobbling below. "Reed, that's Earl."

Reed didn't answer.

What's with him? "Reed, all that shit was on Garret. Earl refused to help him."

"I see what's coming next." Reed faced Rudy. "Look, he's a big boy, and he has my flashlight and a pack, probably with provisions. He's a hell of a lot better equipped than we are."

"He could be hurt—look how unsteady the light is. I want to wait for him."

Reed released a long sigh. "Alright, dammit."

What the hell? As soon as Earl approached, Rudy dropped his rocks and walked several feet down to him. "Earl, are you okay?"

"Just a little woozy; my head hit the ground."

"Yeah, I think you were almost out cold." Reed came down, stopping well behind Rudy.

"Maybe. I already forgot your name." He shined the light on Rudy, then Reed.

"I'm Rudy, and he's Reed. He ran Garret off again with rocks."

"Kill that light, now," Reed snapped at Earl as he came closer.

Earl complied, then faced Reed. "So, Rudy was right. You did come back."

"I'll take my flashlight," Reed told him.

Earl handed it over, then reached down into his pack and handed Rudy two dollar bills and some other papers. "Sorry, I couldn't find all of it."

"It's okay, Earl. Thanks."

"Yeah," he answered, shivering a little. "Where's Garret now?"

Rudy took off his flannel and shook it. "He's gone. You're cold, take this." Mild pain emerged in Rudy's forehead as he handed the shirt to Earl.

Reed turned on the light to check Rudy's face, revealing a half-moon-shaped bluish-purple contusion on his upper right cheek. Reed turned off the light. "Damn, that's ugly, and it's close enough to your eye for a shiner." His voice was still muted. "Let's get outta' here."

"What about your ankle? Do you think it's worse than a sprain?"

"It's not broken; that's what matters." Reed turned on the flashlight but obscured the beam with his fingers. He aimed it straight down, then led them uphill, limping badly.

Earl was behind Rudy, who turned and saw him sway a little. "You okay, Earl?"

"I'll be all right."

Rudy had Earl take his shoulder. "Hang on, Earl."

Like war refugees on the evening news, they struggled along uphill with their various infirmities, the flashlight still aimed at the ground. It took them about half an hour to trudge up the firebreak, almost to the trail junction. "Wait here a sec," Reed told them. He hunched over and picked up some rocks, then crept ahead about fifteen feet. He cast the flashlight beam all around, then stood up straight.

Rudy nearly caught up to him. "God's sake, Reed, he's gone—" A burst of snapping brush cut Rudy off. Before Reed could move, Garret had started a full swing with a branch as thick as a baseball bat. He struck Reed in the solar plexus; he folded to the ground.

"Ha! Told you I'd get you back, faggot!" Reed tried to get up, then Garret stabbed him in the groin with the end of the branch. Reed groaned, then lay silent, squirming. Rudy went to him.

Garret hissed out a laugh. "Good, it's fat-ass. I have another shot for both of you."

Earl had slowly approached Garret. "Leave them alone, or I tell the old man. He's sick of your bullshit."

"Probably too stoned to care. Your little friends are lucky I don't mess 'em up good. Find your own damn way home." Garret followed his penlight to one of the main trails and was gone. Earl picked up the flashlight and gave it to Rudy along with a small canteen from his pack.

Rudy touched Reed's shoulder. "Are you going to be okay?" He offered the canteen.

Reed stood up slowly as Earl walked unsteadily away toward some nearby underbrush.

"Use the water on your face," Reed told Rudy. "The prick only knocked the wind out of me. He poked me mostly on my leg, or I'd be down for the count. Which way did he go?"

Rudy aimed the flashlight. "That trail."

"Then well go back the way we came—I just need another minute or two." He leaned back on his elbows and released a long breath. "Rudy, what in hell do you plan to do about Earl? None of this is any of our damn business."

"We take him home." Rudy directed the light toward Earl, who had started walking slowly back to them with his pack. "Earl, do you think Garret will go to your place?"

Earl sat on the ground. "Yeah, since the old man will be asleep. I'll go to my mom's."

Earl picked up the canteen and splashed water on his head, then combed his fingers through his dishelveled hair. He picked up his pack. "I feel better—not so dizzy."

Reed stood and took the flashlight. "Okay, let's go." He led them to the deer path, then it took a half-hour or so to slowly descend to the wide spot. Rudy saw the bright panorama was replaced by puffs of light in the overcast, making the city appear otherworldly.

After they entered the thick bramble again, Rudy tried to ignore his various injuries and the headache, hoping to save his dwindling supply of aspirin. It seemed to him that Reed was somehow revital-ized. He had found some of their earlier bushwhacking and made the descent go easier than Rudy expected. As Reed shoved and forced his way down, Rudy and Earl struggled to help and keep up until they all finally made it down to the aged elderberry.

Rudy faced Earl. "That was the worst of it."

"Yeah, I can just walk it from here. My mom lives just off Vermont."

"No, we're taking you."

They scuffled along silently for another half-hour on the good trail and the dirt road, until Reed stopped. He hadn't spoken since they left the trail junction. "Alright, we're only a couple hundred feet away. Take the flashlight, Rudy. I'll check for that asshole, then be right back." Reed turned to Earl. "Did you come in a Dodge Dart?"

"Yeah, that's right."

Rudy watched Reed try to jog away, but he came up lame and limped into the dark. Rudy shined the light toward Earl, who put his pack down and sat right on it, frowning.

"Doing okay, Earl?"

"You guys really helped me, but I lied about something. Garret works; he loads trucks. We have enough money; this is just what he likes to do. Nobody else knows he does this shit."

Jesus. "So, you take care of your dad and try to keep Garret out of trouble."

"Yeah, something like that."

Not ten minutes later, Reed made his way back to them using a sturdy branch for a hiking stick. "The bastard's gone. Let's go." Reed took the flashlight and led them slowly to the Citroen, then he shined the light on his shattered driver's-side window. Rudy peered in at a three- or four-pound rock on the seat, shards all around. Reed leaned his hiking stick on the car, opened the door, removed the rock from the seat, then dropped it.

Earl had moved closer to look in the window. "Garret."

"You think so, Earl? Get out of the way." After he gave the flashlight to Rudy, Reed pulled the driver's door wide open and punched out the remnants of the window with the branch.

Rudy turned the light on Earl, now walking unsteadily down the road. *Why is he so hell-bent to get there on his own?* As Reed brushed off the driver's seat with an oil rag, Rudy came over to him. "So, maybe we should go to the cops about Garret."

Reed turned, shaking his head. "We? You got a mouse in your pocket? Shit, Rudy, if you go to the cops, don't expect me to come, and don't give them my damn name."

"Okay, okay. Maybe I'll just talk to Earl's mother."

"Your funeral."

Why is he still pissed? Rudy sighed. "What about your window?"

"Those guys I know will fix it." He saw Earl on the road. "Let's get this over with." Reed inhaled fully, then forced out a breath as if blowing out a candle. He tossed away the stick, took off his flannel, and covered as much of the driver's seat as possible. He sat down gradually on the prickly seat, then started the car. "In back, Rudy."

Reed turned on the headlights. Rudy sat with most of his weight on his right thigh. Reed drove up the road and stopped by Earl, who turned to Rudy. "I'll be okay. You guys didn't deserve all that bullshit. You helped me enough."

Rudy pointed to the other back door. "C'mon, Earl; you might get dizzy and fall."

He got in, brushed off a piece of glass, then Reed drove out the dirt road to turn right on Vermont. Earl was checking out the inside of the Citroen. "Never been in one of these," to Rudy.

"Join the club. Okay, Earl, your mother lives right on Vermont?"

"A block off, but way the hell down there. You can just drop me at City College."

Reed stopped for a red light, shaking his head as he dusted off his business shirt with a clean rag, then clipped on the tie. He sighed. "What the hell—in for a penny, in for a pound."

Part II:
WHO WOULD STEAL A CITROEN IN KANSAS?

CHAPTER 11
The Fountain

Reed drove in very light traffic straight down Vermont, the cool air rushing in through the broken window's space. After a few blocks, they came to an all-night gas station, awash in a circumference of harsh light.

Damn. "Reed, I gotta' go."

Reed turned in and parked by the bathrooms. The attendant, an older Asian man, was nodding off inside a glass booth.

"Right back." Rudy got out and brushed the worst of the grime off his clothes. Inside, he patted cold water gently on his cheek, then the lump on his head. *At least that thing doesn't hurt much.* When he returned after a couple more minutes, Reed was filling a tire with air.

"Reed, why don't you use some of Helen's gift for some good tires?"

"These'll last a while." He returned to his task.

Rudy got in back again with Earl. "Rudy, why is Reed so pissed at me?"

"He's pissed at me, Earl. He's getting over it." Rudy winced from a headache, the first bad one since dealing with Garret. He fished the tin out of his pocket and swallowed a whole aspirin, leaving only a half. Reed got in, and they continued down Vermont.

You do the talking, I guess. "How far is it, Earl?"

"Past the college and under the freeway, then a ways after that."

"So, what will I be looking for?" Reed asked, his eyes straight ahead.

"You turn right at Taco Macho, then a block to a pink apartment building."

Reed peered out at a bank clock. "It's three-thirty. Stay awake, Earl, in case I miss it." Earl nodded solemnly, then looked out.

At least Reed's talking. Rudy was surprised that some houses between the clumps of closed businesses still had their lights on. Neon signs from a few fast-food joints and convenience stores lit up some of the street corners. After they passed a residential area, Rudy inadvertently fixated on the steady streetlights and began to sense the same vacuous state that he had experienced so often.

Reed looked at him in the rear-view mirror and broke the silence. "Snap out of it, Rudy; I don't want you to miss out on all the fun."

"I wasn't sleeping."

"Yeah, I know."

Maybe he's right. Do I really need to talk to Earl's mother? "How far, Earl?"

"We're over halfway. We passed Sunset; we're coming to City College."

"You ever take any classes there?"

"No, maybe I'll study there for the high school test someday."

"That's good, Earl." *He just might.* Watching the light traffic, Rudy wondered about the motives of people who drove around the city at four a.m. A mile or two after Reed drove under the Hollywood Freeway, Rudy saw that this part of Vermont was mostly businesses, the side streets residential. Three blocks after a main intersection, Reed came to the taco joint, which was dark and surrounded by temporary security fencing. Two young Black men stood there, eyeing the improbable Citroen with a chauffeur at the wheel. Reed turned right and drove one block.

"Right there," Earl muttered.

A weak spotlight showed *THE   ALMS APARTMENTS*—its letters fastened to salmon-colored stucco; not even an outline remained of the missing *P*. There were no functioning security lights for the two-story building, although a few windows provided some dull illumination from 24-hour TV and living room lights.

Reed found an open space and parked in front of a desiccated palm tree. He glared up at the dead fronds. "Okay, Earl."

"Thanks." Earl removed Rudy's shirt. "You don't need to come in, Rudy. Thanks—"

"I'll just come to the door for a minute to be sure you don't get blamed for anything."

Reed looked into the rear view. "I suggest you listen to him, Rudy."

Can't hurt to go along. "Back in a minute."

Rudy and Earl got out and walked through an opening in the chain-link. The remains of a wrought-iron front gate leaned against a pole that once supported it. They entered the horseshoe-shaped complex that surrounded a derelict, fenced-in swimming pool. The apartments had alternating green and orange doors, part of the original tropical motif along with a few bent, pink metal flamingos and another palm, this one with green fronds. Reed got out and started picking glass from the other front seat.

Rudy followed Earl to a first-floor apartment, where they stepped up to the door. Earl knocked; they waited a while. "You sure she's here, Earl?"

"Yeah," he said, his round face gloomy.

Rudy watched the door open halfway and a gaunt woman in shorts and a t-shirt appeared in the breach. Her cigarette glowing, Rudy hardly spoke to her before the lady bawled out, "Get the hell outta' here!" Earl went in; his mom slammed the door in Rudy's face.

Rudy stumbled once on the way back to the Citroen, where Reed had stopped picking at the upholstery. "Rudy, get your shirt. I got most of the glass out."

He reached for his shirt and covered the seat. "Don't you want to hear what happened?"

"I heard the last part. Tell me when you want to." He paused. "Rudy, I'm sorry."

He sat on the front seat, mostly on his upper thigh again. "For what?"

"I got pissed back up there; acted like a jerk."

"It's all right, you got over it."

"I should've tried harder to warn you about coming here. I was pretty sure of what you were getting into."

"I didn't think of that."

"Doesn't matter now." He paused. "Okay, this ride might be a little rough on our butts, especially yours," he said with a grin. Reed started the car, drove back to Vermont, turned left, then settled in the right lane below the speed limit. The first few stoplights were flashing yellow.

The stark city reminded Rudy of old sci-fi movies that used filtered shots of Los Angeles at four a.m. to create apocalyptic daytime scenes. *Tell him about Earl's mom.* Instead, Rudy began with what Earl had shared about Garret and their father.

Reed responded after Rudy finished a few sentences. "Earl probably lied at first because he's ashamed of the old man."

"And his mother too, I'd guess. When she came to the door, I think she was wasted on something besides booze. All I got out before she freaked was that Garret was getting Earl in trouble. That's all—you heard her sincere goodbye."

"Yeah, anything could've set her off; I'd bet that Garret was once her little darling."

"Before we got to the door, Earl said he was just going to get some things and go to his aunt's place. At least he has a refuge. Does his family remind you of yours?" *Shit.* "Sorry, I—"

"Different, but equally fucked up. The old man probably beat all of them."

"God." Rudy became lost in his reflections about Earl until Reed came to a main intersection and had to brake for a red light, jostling Rudy to attention.

"Looks like you're not ready to let it go, Rudy."

"I was just wondering what will happen to Earl. He's trapped and vulnerable, but he doesn't seem very motivated to get out of it."

"I'm not so sure. He's smarter than Garret; I think he'll find a way. Somehow, Earl's a good guy, and you wanted to help him. It's who you are now, which I admire, even if it's not my thing. What I am sure of is that if you get more involved with that family, it will jump up and bite you in the ass again."

Rudy sighed at the sight of a dreary block lit up only by street lights.

"You still there?" Reed turned to see Rudy nod. "The problem is people who say they want to help others are not always who they seem to be. My guess is that Earl's mother would be suspicious of anything you'd say."

"Why?"

"She probably had you pegged for a do-gooder, just walking up all superior and normal, pre-judging that the family deserved its problems. Or a different kind of do-gooder who's just nosey; titillated by seeing misery up close. Then, my personal favorite—a missionary sent out to do *good works*—the sanctimonious. They want a transaction— their help in exchange for your soul, the same deal their devil offers. Worst of all, the predators—maybe a scout leader, clergy, teacher, social worker—could be anyone in an advantageous position who's supposedly helping. My therapist calls himself a professional, but he's actually a degenerate lecher who hides it well. Since the court forces me to go, I've considered it my obligation to drive him nuts or drive him out. I was getting close."

Was? Rudy watched the forlorn gas station where they had stopped earlier. "Reed, don't you think there are people without ulterior motives who help others?"

"Sure, but they're exceptional. As for you, acting on empathy is something pretty recent, although you haven't really hurt anyone, except maybe yourself." Reed paused. "You're not even overtly hostile to Si, although he disgusts you and all that."

"So I've heard." Rudy felt a pain like a pinprick in his back, and dull aches were creeping into his cheek, head, and rear end. *Damn, it better hold off—half an aspirin left.*

Reed grinned slightly. "Tell me more about this growing idealism of yours."

"I don't know if it's idealism, but I've been thinking about it a lot. Look at how much shit Artie's had to take; he shrugs it off as childish, but I know it hurts him. It's not only racial; I see hostility toward anyone who's different, whatever *different* means. Like you, I guess."

"And maybe *you*," he said with a smirk.

"I guess." He told Reed about incidents with Noah, Jonny, and Wayne. "...with Harry, at least it's obvious, not the subtle bullshit I see every day from teachers like Leon, Parker, and—"

"You sound so surprised," Reed interrupted, along with a loud, sibilant exhale. "Remember the nurse in junior high who only signed up free-lunch kids for her lice check?"

"Yeah, some guy I know made sure she was busted."

They chuckled as Reed stopped for a red light behind two cars in the right-turn lane for Los Feliz Boulevard. "Yeah, it's a challenge to undermine mindless authority, and if it helps somebody—all the better. Teachers like those you mentioned aren't rare, and neither is the abuse and brutality you saw today—a world behind the curtains of Oz."

"I get what you're saying, but just remember that *you* helped Earl and me tonight."

"I plead guilty, but if you weren't part of that mess, I would've taken off." Reed made the turn. Yawning occasionally, they didn't speak for a few blocks before the car approached the Mulholland Fountain at the bottom of a hill.

"Rudy, I need to wake up before we go back. If it's okay, let's walk over to the fountain."

At five a.m.? "Sure." *Another first.* "What about your ankle?"

"Yeah, what about your cheek and your butt cheeks?"

"Funny, but isn't your ankle pretty bad?"

"It's just sore. If I can make it down that trail, I can do this."

Reed parked by a two-story apartment building a half-block before the landmark. They got out, peeled their shirts off the seats, shook out residual bits of glass, then put them on.

"Good news, ladies and gentlemen," Reed called out to the apartments, his arms wide open, "besides the latest in air-conditioning, there's no need to lock this fine French automobile!"

Rudy snickered. "That was nuts."

"Must be why it felt so good." Laughing, they both started limping downhill.

"What about cops, Reed?"

Reed pocketed the keys. "This late, I've only seen them around here once. I told them the truth—couldn't sleep, out for a walk. They told me to go home, then left. White boys' privilege, I guess. You don't look all that sleepy, Rudy."

"Actually, I'm kind of buzzing."

"Your body thinks it's time to get up—for a little while anyway."

They crossed a side street, then came to a sidewalk that led them to the floodlights that surrounded Mulholland Fountain. As if they hadn't been there numerous times, Reed and Rudy took a couple of minutes to watch the lights dance in the cascading water.

Reed scoffed. "Gram told me about Mulholland. She said he and the city of L.A. finagled water rights from some people up north who farmed confiscated Indian land. So-called anarchists dynamited Mulholland's aqueduct, but he fixed it, then built dams. Get this: One shoddy dam breached, and hundreds drowned—farmers, dam workers, but mostly farmworkers, some who were never found—expendable, it seems. Somebody took Mulholland and the city to court, they got off, and *voilà*, here we have L.A.'s homage to Mulholland and his lawns in the desert."

Rudy glowered at the fountain. "Genuinely disturbing—and gone missing in history."

"At school anyway. Rudy, let's get closer to the water."

"Okay." They meandered over to the shallow pool. A breeze skimmed enough cool air off the gurgle and splash of the fountain to make Rudy button his shirt. *What is he doing?* Reed had stopped to sit on the edge of the fountain; he was taking off his left sneaker.

"What's going on, Reed?"

"My ankle stiffened up." He pulled off the sock and felt his ankle. "Swollen, not bad."

He rolled up his pantleg a couple feet, swiveled on his rear, then inserted his foot into the water. "Colder than I thought. Good."

Who else would do this? Rudy remained standing nearby, smiling. "Does it feel better?"

"It will. It would help to do this where that lunatic hit me with the branch. I should just jump in." Reed released a sigh. "Man, Rudy, busy day for you." He paused. "You confronted some of the shit that has bothered you for a long time."

Maybe. "I did okay in the dark because I was with you, but I guess I feel a little more confident." His shoulders rose with an exhale. "It was you and Artie who had the guts."

"Bullcrap," Reed stated. "I was scared tonight, just like Artie was. Like you said, Garret and Harry are psychopaths—it'll be jail or a straight-jacket for them. Rudy, you began to deal with your fears, helping both Artie and me. Don't dismiss or discount what you did."

"I'll think about that, but—"

"Rudy," Reed broke in, "there's something else I want to say to you. First, some good stuff." He extracted his foot for a few seconds then put it back in the water. He sighed again. "Rudy, I've always admired your family because you have flaws and just hang in there—"

"Yeah, barely. Just don't confuse us with the *Cleavers*."

"No chance," with a grin, then he turned somber again. "Rudy, you're probably the closest to a brother I ever had. We even get pissed off like brothers once in a while."

He means it. "I, um—"

"It's okay, Rudy—best friends." He put the sore ankle up on the edge.

"Yeah, best friends for sure."

"Not only that, I also won't forget you when I'm famous."

"No, I don't think you would." The damp air chilled Rudy again.

"You still don't believe it'll happen, but that's okay." Reed dunked his foot again.

"Reed, I believe you'll do something unique with your talent, and you'll do it well. Most of the teachers and kids never had a damn clue about you. Next week, it will be like you were never there—out of sight, out of mind."

"Screw them all, the long, the short, and the tall."

"Yeah, so what's the bad stuff you wanted to say?"

"It's not so bad. Gram asked me to discuss something about Si. Will you hear me out?"

Great. A headache had checked in along with some dull abdominal pain. "I'm listening."

"Give me a sec." He took his foot out and started to pull the sock over his wrinkled skin.

"How's the ankle feeling?"

"Good enough." He put his shoe on. "Okay, Rudy, it's another fear—unique to you."

What? "You think I'm afraid of Si?"

"No, Gram believes that for years you have feared being *like* Si. I think she's right."

"Okay, explain."

Reed stood up by Rudy and they slowly shuffled away. "Gram says you were disgusted by Si when you were a kid and afraid you might become like him. You never got completely over it, and I don't think you're aware of how many things you still do that are the opposite of Si: diets, manners, cooked vegetables, clothes—trivial shit like that, anything *not* to be like him."

"Okay, okay, I get it. I'll think about it." His temple had started beating. *But not now.*

"Are you okay, Rudy?" They stopped under one of the bright lights. Reed recoiled from Rudy's pale, injured face. "Man, you look like hell."

"I just need aspirin—last one." He took the remaining half.

"Okay, let's get going."

When they came to the hill, Reed rested his left hand on Rudy's shoulder to reduce the pressure on the ankle. They made their way slowly up the block to the Citroen, opened the front doors, and spread out their shirts. Rudy sat, trying to lean on his thigh again.

"Rudy, let's rest another minute."

Fine with me. "Are you okay to drive with that ankle? I can do it."

Reed grinned. "Sure you can, but let's keep it to one juvenile delinquent per car. I'll be fine." He put the seat back and stretched out his legs.

Rudy watched the sparse traffic until an old Hudson beater, belching smoke, stopped over at the park entrance, then turned around. *Si would drive a piece of crap like that. Yeah, so what?* "Okay, Reed, what else about Si?"

"You sure? We can just wait until you feel better."

"No, go ahead."

"All right." He sighed. "Your disgust for Si and your fear of becoming like him has gradually become something different over the last few years."

*Yeah, plain old shame. God forbid that somebody might **see** me with him.* "I think I know what you mean." His head jackhammered; Rudy cringed and turned away.

"Must be one hell of a headache. Should I stop and get aspirin?"

"I'll make it back. Thanks." Something rubbed against his side. He found Helen's book. He swept it off with his shirt sleeve, then blew off some reflecting slivers of glass.

On the ride home, Rudy made himself watch the traffic, not the lights; his headache moderated, but his stomach roiled. By the time they arrived at Ontario Place, the streetlights on the dormant block were just flickering off. Reed parked at the curb in front of Helen's.

Through the windshield, Rudy watched the first tinge of light to the east. "What a night."

Reed shut off the motor. "Yeah. Feeling better?"

No. "I'm okay. You?"

"Fine. Will you be in trouble for getting in this late?"

"I'm not worried about it." He blew on the book again.

"I'm glad we got out tonight, but I need to get started with this window. This is when those guys work. I doubt they can find the right window, but they'll figure out something for the kind of bread I can pay them now."

What's the big hurry? He looked at the hood. "What about those dents?"

"Cosmetic. I just want it to run okay and with no wind in my face."

"Reed, I'm not going to tell my parents about Garret." He touched his throbbing bruise. "Guess I'll just invent something about my face."

"That's up to you, Rudy. If you want, you can tell Gram the truth about the Citroen, or I'll do it in a couple of days."

I'll be damned. "That's a crappy way to handle it. I probably won't see Helen until after school tomorrow. That gives you time to tell her yourself." *Shit.* Rudy got out with the book, walked around the car, then stepped up to the parkway, several feet from Reed. He calmed down and watched the ethereal grey and yellow stratus clouds surrounding Mt. Wilson.

Reed turned to Rudy from the window. "Look, don't worry about telling Gram about the car, but talk to her about Si when you can."

"Yeah, I'll tell her I'm ashamed of my own uncle," his tone self-deprecating.

Reed waited a few seconds. "That's right, but you're too rough on yourself again."

"So, all is well—except we're both liars."

"Shit, Rudy. When did we become perfect? I've gotta' get money and gas."

At dawn? "What the hell, Reed—you're going to stay up all night fixing this thing?"

"Yeah, I guess so." Reed started the car and drove off.

CHAPTER 12

The TV-Tray Massacre

After the long night in Griffith Park, Rudy finally made it to his room. *I shouldn't have gotten pissed at Reed.* Rudy removed his filthy clothes and took a quick shower; his sore face reminded him to check in the mirror. There wasn't much swelling, but the bruise, turning the color of fox grapes, nearly touched his eye. Rudy checked his tooth; it wasn't as loose; no bleeding. He had an ordinary headache, but he still took two aspirins, got into light pajamas, and went to bed. *What will you do about Reed? What **can** you do?*

Sleeping on his side, he woke about two hours later, before the alarm. *What? I still have an hour.* Expecting to go back to sleep, he started looking around his cluttered but neat room. It dawned on him that the bedroom itself was a journal of his childhood. *Rudy's crappy museum.*

In one corner, his bat, spikes, and glove waited, unused since eighth grade. Above his gear, he had taped a poster of Alex Johnson, the 1970 American League batting champion, the only one in Angels history. A tall bookcase, his childhood desk, and a chest of drawers—all dusted regularly by Rudy—covered his only long wall. The top of the bookcase was home to three faded paper mâché school projects—a once-gay *piñata,* a stegosaurus, and a large model of a heart and its arteries. Rudy also kept his old Royal typewriter up there, a hand-me-down from his mother.

On the top shelf, next to a baseball signed by an obscure Angels catcher, three discarded Dewey Decimal drawers held his baseball cards. The rest of the shelf was neatly piled with his comic collection, generally abandoned after sixth grade. Mostly paperback books, neatly arranged, filled the next shelf down. They included some duplicates from Helen's library, gifts, purchases, and a few hardbacks that his grandmother used to read to him—like *The Sneetches* from when he was little, and *The Christmas Carol* a few years later.

He kept his writing materials on the third shelf down: a dog-eared collegiate dictionary, a thesaurus given to him by Helen, an old atlas, then a stack of spiral notebooks—the ones on top for his observations and stories—his old poems on the bottom. He kept a pile of his high school essays, a majority of them *B+* or better, the rest *C* or worse. The bottom shelf held a crisp set of 1974 Britannica encyclopedias—a gift from Mildred before Rudy started high school.

Rudy got up and took a few steps to get his notebook of observations. He lay on the bed again and read his short narrative about the flattened hubcap. *Pretty strange.* Sighing, he put the notebook down. Rudy felt a little pressure near his feet; it was Helen's book. *Lucky it didn't get ruined.* He yanked on the blanket to keep the book from falling, but the tug had the opposite effect; the novel flipped, then clunked onto the floor. *Damn.*

"Rudy, you're up?" his mother asked from out in the hallway.

May as well stay up. "Yeah." *Get your story straight.*

Katie came in wearing her grey sweats; she picked up the book and put it on Rudy's shelf. She glanced at his dirty clothes, then saw Rudy's face as he sat up. "What in goddam hell happened to you?"

Sobriety confirmed. "I ran into something—not as bad as it looks." A grating headache rolled along the top of his brow.

"Ran into what?"

A fist. "Take it easy, Mom; it was just a big branch."

"A branch? Where did that happen?"

"Griffith Park—Reed and I were hiking, and I didn't see it coming. Took a shot right there." *Not bad.*

"Mmm," suspiciously. "How late were you up there?"

"We got back a couple hours after midnight." *Close enough.* "Reed has a car now."

"His own car? Jesus wept. Hold on, I'm getting ice. You have more explaining to do."

Crap. She walked out and around the corner; Rudy heard her rummaging around in the freezer. He fixed the alarm button so it wouldn't go off later, then lay back down.

Katie came back with two green and yellow bags of frozen vegetables. "One for your cheek and one for your eye." She gently wiped the bruise with a damp washrag, then put a clean one there, and another over his eye. She applied a frozen package to each washrag.

"Does it feel better?

No. "Not much."

"Give it a few minutes. Are you going to stay home from school?"

"No, I'm going."

"Alright, tell me. Did Reed get you beer or something?"

"For god's sake, Mom, no."

"Okay, sorry. You know I empathize with what Reed's been through. It's just that he—"

"I don't want to hear it."

"Fine. So, what happened? Including why in hell you went up there on a Thursday night."

The bare minimum. "I celebrated with Helen and Reed; he passed his GED." After that, Rudy only told her about the hike, the view, and Greek Theater. "That's it."

"I didn't think you were even interested in doing something like that. Do me a favor and don't go up there after dark anymore. Your father and I will have more questions later."

Like Dad will ask anything. After she left, Rudy removed the ice from his eye, then put it on the lump above his ear. A few minutes later, he got up to the bureau and put on his clothes. Rudy lay on the bed for a while with a compress on his face and eye.

When he got up again, Katie was waiting for him at his bathroom door. "What's your hurry? You're way early."

"Maybe I'll walk today." He looked past her into the mirror, not surprised that the bruise was gruesome, but his eye was worse than expected, as if painted with black Halloween makeup. "Is there any way to cover these just for today? It should be okay by Tuesday."

"Tuesday?"

"No school Monday. Teachers' workshops."

"Oh. Shar has every cover-up and foundation they make; I'll be right back. Wash your face." She touched his nearly smooth cheek. "And shave," she said with some sarcasm.

Very funny. Rudy relieved himself, then shaved in a minute or two with Larry's hand-me-down electric razor. He washed and dried his face, spotting his aspirin tin on the sink.

Katie soon came in with a plastic bag full of small containers, tubes, a powder puff, and more. "Glory, Rudy, aren't you sick of this bathroom and that cave you sleep in? It's time you moved into the empty bedroom."

"And have all that to clean? I don't think so."

She picked up the aspirin tin and casually flicked it open. "Empty," she said, suspicious again. "You took all of them?"

"There were only a few—must have spilled them in the dark."

She pointed to a new aspirin bottle by the sink. "I left that for you. Rudy, you have to see Grampa about these headaches. What's this lump on your head, for God's sake?"

"The branch got me there too; doesn't hurt. I put that ice on it for a while."

Katie cleaned the wound, then applied some medicine she had brought. She wrapped an old beach towel around his neck and over his shoulders, then she started to work. "Okay, I'll try to cover both of them. Hold still, dammit. Hm, Shar's coloring is about the same as yours..."

Rudy ignored her nattering, then catnapped. He woke up when Katie dabbed a powder puff on his face. The mirror reflected his well-disguised injuries, but his face emitted a sickly pallor. *A damn mannequin.* "Are we finished, Mom?"

"Yes, regardless of you squirming in your sleep." She handed him his cap. "With your hat on, nobody should notice much. No sweating or touching, or you'll be a mess. Don't forget—you and Si tonight, and the anniversary party on Sunday."

A real doubleheader. You'll live. "Yeah, got it. Thanks."

Katie followed him back into his bedroom to get the dirty clothes, then she left as Larry came in the kitchen door. Rudy's face itched while he was putting on his sneakers. He reached for his cheek as he entered the kitchen, where Katie had earlier set out cold cereal, muffins, and orange juice. His parents were drinking coffee.

"Don't touch your face," Katie nagged.

"Forgot." *Man, how does anyone stand this crap?* "Hi, Dad."

"Morning." Larry, in his overalls, was focused on his coffee.

Rudy sat and poured some juice. "Mom, did you invite Reed to the party on Sunday?"

"Just Helen. I didn't think you'd want your friends there."

You thought wrong. "I'll invite him."

"Okay, and your other friends?"

"Maybe Artie can come."

Katie put her cup down. "What about Noah and Jonny?"

He checked the kitchen clock. "Not if I can help it."

"Why, Rudy?" she asked

"Because they're jerks; I don't want to talk about it."

"Fine." She paused and watched Larry sip his coffee. "I haven't had a chance to tell your father about your excursion with Reed."

He glanced at the clock. "Okay, I have to go." Rudy drank his juice and took a muffin.

"Just so you know, Rudy," Katie jeered, "we're also going to discuss Reed's, um, influence on you."

Bullshit. "You always assume the worst about him." He pointed to his cheek. "You help me with this crap, which I appreciate, and then you say something like that."

Larry stood. "I have to go too." He walked away, then out the door.

Rudy saw her pouting. He returned to his bathroom, handled basic hygiene, then filled the aspirin tin after taking one. He found his books, then pulled down the brim of his cap and went outside with the muffin. Rudy was careful not to work up a sweat as he hurried by two plumbing vans, the T-bird, and Katie's Beetle. Out in front, he passed by Si's Studebaker. *No Citroen—damn.*

To avoid eating in front of the kids on the bus, he quickly ate the muffin. Brushing off crumbs, Rudy came to La Plata Avenue where the half-full high school bus was at the end of its usual five-minute wait. He climbed the steps and sat reticently on the first open bench seat instead of in the back where the four of them always sat. Jonny had recently begun to pick up Noah, and Artie was preparing for track season, jogging to school on Monday, Wednesday, and Friday.

Unlike students on the afternoon bus that Rudy rarely used, the morning riders were, as usual, gloomy or in some stage of sleep. The bus merged into light traffic. Rudy pulled his brim down even lower and grimaced when the side of his cap touched the knot on his head.

He opened his notebook and checked homework assignments. *English—finished. Algebra—Artie will help. No biology. History—finish the report later. So, español it is.* He started on his assignment. *Good—no damn verbs to conjugate.* Despite a mild headache, he finished quickly, then closed his eyes, pulling the brim of his hat all the way down.

He was nearly sound asleep when he felt the bus sway, then pull up in front of the high school. Rudy pushed the brim up halfway and watched hundreds of students milling around. Influenced by styles from the late '60s, many boys wore bell-bottom pants, thick-heeled shoes, and colorful shirts. Most girls were in showy colorful tops and short skirts. The increasingly popular neon-colored backpacks were sprinkled throughout the throng.

Like many of the older Los Angeles schools, Truman had a large grove of eucalyptus trees. To get there after he got off the bus, Rudy walked around a two-story grey classroom building to where he and his friends, except Reed, met on most mornings.

Looking ahead at their bench in the dappled shade, Rudy eyed Jonny and Noah, madly copying the Spanish homework from Artie, who was between them. *Same ol' shit.* Rudy approached, kicking some fallen eucalyptus pods. He pulled down on his brim again, but not so much as to draw attention. *Don't take any crap from Noah.*

Eyes on his copying, Noah spoke as if they hadn't bickered over the phone. "Rood, we can start on my report in a minute." Artie raised his brows to Rudy and shrugged.

"Do you want to copy this?" Jonny said to Rudy, holding up the Spanish homework.

Dumb ass. "No, I did it on the bus—it was easy."

"Sure," Noah said, his head still down. "Hey, Rudy, did you go see your pal next door?"

"Yeah, Reed's finished with this fine institution of learning."

Noah erased something on his paper. "He quit again, or they finally expelled him?"

"No, he passed his GED."

"Bullshit." Noah searched for something in his notebook. "You done, Jonny?"

"Yeah."

"Here's the math. I got it from Fineman." Noah exchanged papers, then carelessly bumped Artie on the head with an elbow. "Watch out, midget."

Rudy glowered at him. "*You* watch out, beanpole."

"Shove it, Rudolph." He stopped copying. "Is that makeup? Covering zits for the girls, Rudy?" Noah smirked. "So, how was your date with Reed?"

Jonny laughed. "Yeah, did you and Mucholoco read poems?"

"Screw you guys—we had graduation dinner with his gramma."

"You expect us to believe that GED bullshit?" Noah ogled a girl walking by.

"Believe what you want. Reed passed it." *No need for them to know about his car.*

Jonny finally looked up at Rudy. "No way—he can't do that. It wouldn't be fair that we have to stay in school."

Rudy scoff-chuckled at Jonny. "I've seen Reed's GED materials; you couldn't pass one of the tests, genius."

"And you could?" Noah scowled.

"Maybe four of them; Artie could pass all five."

"Right, if they're written in Mexican." Noah guffawed; Jonny joined in—so loud that kids fifty feet away turned to them. Noah pulled Jonny closer. "I saw some pro basketball players do this on TV. Raise your hand." Noah had to sit down to execute a *high-five* with runty Jonny.

"That is *so* cool." Jonny raised his hand again to repeat the gesture with Noah.

Artie and Rudy had moved a few feet away to the end of the bench. "That is like a celebration, Rudy? Of what?"

"His pitiful joke about you."

"They think the test is too difficult for Mexicans?"

Afraid so. "Um—"

Noah had come closer and heard Artie's question. "Can't take a little joke, Artie?"

"It's not a little joke," he answered coolly. "I pay attention so I can do my assignments. You can't copy them anymore."

"What about Rudy copying your math?"

"It is not the same class. I explain if he has questions. Rudy does the work."

"Hey, wait, don't be like that," Jonny whined. "We'll fail Spanish."

Artie looked askance at Jonny. "*¡Qué lástima!* Such a pity."

"Artie, take it easy—we're sorry." Noah acted as if he were nobly interceding. "Here." Noah returned the homework paper. "You'll get over it, right? Let's just drop it." He turned to Rudy. "Rood, I'm finished. We can work on my report now."

Rood, is it? What was it Reed said? "We? You got a mouse in your pocket?"

"What's that supposed to mean?"

"It means you're on your own." *Asshole.*

"What?" Noah sniveled. "You said you'd help me."

"I'm just following your dad's new rule." *Damn, another headache.* Noah had set his jaw. "Screw you, Rudy."

"You don't scare me, dipshit." *That doesn't even feel like a bluff.*

Noah scoffed passively. The bell rang; Jonny headed for his homeroom in the wood shop. Artie and Rudy started across the grounds toward the main building, then Noah came up from behind. "While you fags are watching *Star Wars* again, I'll be making out." He ran ahead, then turned back. "Rudy," he cat-called, "maybe you can take Uncle Slob to the movie."

Artie turned to Rudy. "What is he talking about?" They stopped.

"He and Jonny aren't coming tomorrow. They're going out with Walt and some girls to see that disco movie."

"But we are still going to *Star Wars?*"

"Sure. We planned on it." Rudy stopped walking.

Artie waited for a boy to pass by. "He said, *Uncle Slob*. He means Si?"

"Yes, he's visiting again."

"The meaning of *slob* is not clear to me."

"It's someone who's dirty, spills food on…" He finished as they came to the doors. They entered, then stepped off to the side of the spic-and-span hallway, soon to be messed up again.

"In Spanish, such a person is *bruto*, a very disrespectful thing to say. But *brute* in English isn't the same as *slob*, right?"

"Yes, *brute* is more like a mean beast—like Harry."

"So, *slob* is another terrible insult." They walked on. "Your uncle is kind to me."

God, if Artie knew what I think about Si.

In homeroom, their assigned seats were far from Noah, who was trying to schmooze Libby in the next aisle while glancing at Rudy. *He isn't **too** obvious. At least she didn't stop doing her homework.*

"Your uncle's visiting alone, Rudy?"

What? "Yeah, Artie, he's not the marrying kind."

"Maybe we *should* invite him to the movie."

Damn. "He probably wouldn't want to go." *Sure, Rudy, he hates outer space shows.*

"Oh. But ask him, okay?"

"We'll see what's going on at the house. Artie, my doctor's appointment after school is canceled; I can walk to Freddy's."

"Good. So, Noah and Jonny won't be coming?"

A bonus. "They'll probably use Jonny's car to get haircuts. I'm finished with those two anyway, but you don't have to be."

"Noah doesn't respect me anymore and Jonny never did. Why did Noah change?"

"He wants to fit in with rich kids and the basketball players. I've heard him repeat crap they say like it's the absolute truth—doesn't even sound like him."

Artie pointed to himself. "But we are still friends."

"Of course, Artie."

Because of his makeup, Rudy shied away from everybody all day. He used one of Reed's forged library passes to skip P.E. and work on his history report, but he kept nodding off until his sore butt woke him up for good. On the walk after school, Rudy was mostly silent and kept closing his eyes for two or three seconds while Artie talked about *Star Wars* and Reed's GED test until they were almost to Freddy's Freeze.

"Rudy, when you see Reed, tell him I said congratulations on the test."

"Sure." Rudy yawned. "But I might not see him for a while. He has a car now."

"He does?"

"We took it for a ride last night. I'll tell you about it tomorrow." Rudy yawned again.

"Okay. You look really tired, Rudy."

"Yeah, not much sleep." Skipping Freddy's, they walked to the corner. "Artie, since our plans changed, why don't we go to the matinee instead of the six o'clock show?"

"Good idea—and it's cheaper. I work in the morning, but I can make it."

Before splitting up, they planned to meet at eleven-thirty the next day at the Italian grocery, which was on a bus route to the movie theaters in Glendale. Although his head, face, and rear end ached, Rudy tried to walk at a normal pace, but he had to stop twice to lean back on a telephone pole and close his eyes. Shuffling on, he finally passed the market, his old school, then Jonny's. His eyelids heavy, he dallied along to the corner of Ontario Place and La Plata Avenue. *Still no Citroen—damn.* Rudy pressed on up to Helen's door and knocked. *God, maybe Reed already called and told her the truth.*

Helen came to the door in denim attire and a blue paisley bonnet—one of her gardening outfits. "Hello, Rudy. Come in. You look exhausted."

"Yeah. Thanks, Helen." He left his books on her porch bench. They entered, she sat at her desk; Rudy remained standing. "Any word from Reed?"

"No. Just after dawn, I heard him come in and out of his room. He was very quiet, trying not to wake me, so I started back to sleep, then heard the car leave out front."

Rudy sat on the edge of a hard, wooden chair, winced slightly, then stood up. "I think I can explain that. We got back really late—"

"Excuse me, Rudy, is that makeup on your face?"

"Yes, it's covering a bruise. We had, um, an incident last night with some guys."

"Is Reed also hurt?"

"He has a sore ankle, but he's okay." *I guess.* "Some punk broke his window—long story. I think he's getting it fixed." Rudy yawned without opening his mouth, trembling a little. "Helen, can we talk tomorrow about three-thirty or four?"

"That's fine. You don't look well, Rudy. Is someone at home?"

"Yes." *Probably just Si.* "I'll get going then. Please call if you hear from Reed."

"Yes, get some sleep, Rudy."

"Thanks, Helen; I'll see you tomorrow."

Rudy went out, picked up his books, and passed by Si's car. He walked up the driveway and saw that Larry's T-bird wasn't there. *Good, they're gone; so is Charlotte.* Stew's gate from the pen to the yard was open; he was digging in the soil near the far fence. Rudy entered the kitchen and heard distant TV gibberish. *The human being I'm so damned ashamed of is in the den. He sure as hell isn't ashamed of me.* **Yeah, give him a break.** *Easy to say, Reed.* **At least try something he**

likes to do. *TV, I guess. Then, I gotta' sleep.*

He put his books on the kitchen table, then checked out the food Katie left in the refrigerator for them. Rudy walked through the dining room into the parlor, where Si was sitting on the sofa in his customary place, right next to the end table. Not cognizant that he was mining into one of his nostrils with a baby finger, Si was fixated on the window. *Make the food, or talk to him? He won't care that I look like shit.* Rudy walked closer. "How's it going, Si?"

Lowering his hand, Si turned slowly from the window. "Hi, Rudy."

The only difference in Si's appearance from the previous day was a large stain on the same light-brown shirt. The blotch resembled a map of Alaska with the mainland under his chin, then the archipelago dotting the shirt all the way down to his belt.

So what? Rudy nodded to the den. "Watching TV, Si?"

"Katie turned it on, but it switched to a talk show."

"Maybe we'll eat dinner in there on the TV trays. Katie left us a lot of picnic food for dinner—sound good?" *So sweet, Rudy.*

"Yes."

"I think we can even use disposable plates—no dishes to wash."

Si had been looking out again. "Okay."

"What kind of sandwich do you want? There's sliced turkey, cheese, peanut butter and jelly, and, um, summer sausage."

"I'll have the same as you."

"I'm having peanut butter and jelly. Would you like two of them?"

"Yes."

Jelly everywhere. God, stop it. "Alright, and we have potato chips and raw vegetables—watermelon for dessert. It'll take me a little while; let's find you a TV show."

"Okay."

*You're not **too** condescending. Crap, like he knows that.*

They entered the den, sat on the long couch, then Rudy reached for the remote control on the card table, yawned, then repeated the demonstration of how to use the device. After Si showed again that he could flip through the channels, Rudy got up. "Okay, Si, find something you like."

"What if I break it?"

"You won't." He watched Si stay with the same channel, a soap opera. Rudy pointed to the old TV trays on the wall rack. "While

I'm gone, would you set up two TV trays?" Rudy acted like he didn't notice that Si was wiping something on his pant leg. Rudy headed for the kitchen. *Well, I didn't get totally grossed out.*

He came to the refrigerator, took out a loaf of bread, and dealt six slices like playing cards onto the chopping board. *Funny. At least you're more alert.* Rudy assembled the sandwiches and put them on Styrofoam plates with potato chips, celery sticks, peeled carrots, and napkins.

I know—try a joke. He returned to the den and put the plate with one sandwich on Si's tray. As Rudy placed the two-sandwich meal on his tray, he saw that Si was engrossed in the soap opera. "I thought you were going to change the channel."

"No," his eyes still on the TV.

"How about if I try to find something else?"

"Okay." Si took a glimpse of the food.

The third channel Rudy switched to was showing *Gunga Din,* a scene with Cary Grant in full British uniform talking to the title character played by a black-faced Sam Jaffe. Rudy had watched the old movie two or three times over the years.

Perfect. "Have you seen this, Si?"

Si was already riveted to the screen. "Yes, but I like it." He turned briefly to Rudy. "Do you want to watch?" His attention returned right back to the movie.

This was your idea, Rudy. "Okay, I'll get some drinks." Rudy walked over to the blue and yellow refrigerator, opened it, then called back to Si. "What'll it be? Let's see, we have orange juice, ginger ale, diet cola, and root beer." Si didn't drink beer, so Rudy didn't offer it. "Si?"

"Hm?" hardly breaking his concentration.

Damn. "Beer, mineral water, prune juice, or root beer?"

"Root beer."

Bad, Rudy. He came over to the sofa and put the bottle of soda on Si's tray. Recently allowed one beer at home, Rudy put the can on his tray in front of a soft recliner. He let his rear end descend normally, then sighed in relief. *Not too bad.* "Keep it on *Gunga Din,* Si?"

"Yes, I like the old rifles."

Naturally. "Si, after this, I'll be going to bed early. Will you be okay?"

"Yes."

"Good, let's eat."

Si reluctantly turned from the movie and was about to pick up the sandwich.

"Wait, Si, you said you wanted two sandwiches." Rudy stood, then switched the plates. "I was playing a little joke on you."

"Oh."

Just friggin' hilarious. Crap—no harm done. Rudy sat, took a couple of celery sticks from his plate, and started to munch on them and watch the movie. He peeked at Si, who already had jelly on his chin. *Don't look until he's finished.* Rudy took a sip of beer and started on the sandwich, his eyelids getting heavy again.

Rudy had a minor epiphany as he ate and watched *Gunga Din. I guess this was intended to be historical. When?* He put down his sandwich and closed his eyes. *Okay, so the Indians in turbans are with the Brits, but who's this army of beggars they're after? Why do they call them **thugs**? And why didn't I notice any of this before?*

When the battle ensued, and the water-carrier-turned-hero was saving the day against the inscrutable Thuggee cult, the increased racket brought Rudy out of his catnap. *What the hell?* He saw Si glued to the battle on the screen. Rudy and Si watched the movie draw to a close at Din's grave. Melodramatically, an officer finished Kipling's poem aloud: "…you're a better man than I, Gunga Din." *Corny, but true.*

He yawned through the credits, then turned to Si, who was watching a commercial for tanning lotion. His food was gone, just a smear of peanut butter on the tray and faint streaks of red jelly on his plate. *Used his finger to lick it clean. You don't know that, and so what if he did?* Potato chip crumbs and jelly had congealed on Si's shirt, and a carrot nub was on the floor by his foot. *Not so bad—when you don't watch.*

Rudy took a full gulp of his beer. "Ready for some watermelon, Si?"

"I gotta' go—now." Si got up, passed gas, then urgently limped toward the bathroom under the archway to the parlor.

Some sulfurous air reached Rudy. *Gross.* Si went in, then cut loose with a loud rumble of gas that seemed to last for seconds. *Double gross. Damn, if ya' gotta' go—*

Rudy began to clean up, then stopped for a moment when his eyes drooped again. *Shit, wake up.* He wiped off his tray, then walked over to hang it on the rack, surface side out.

He's still in there. "You okay, Si?" he called.

"Yes," a deep guttural response.

"Take your time." *No crapping accidents, please.* He went back to Si's tray, wiped off the smears, then started to take it to the rack but accidentally bumped the card table. Si's tray fell to the floor, logo-side face-down. *Damn it.* Rudy reached down to pick it up but stopped when he noticed scores of minute green, grey, and brown flecks stuck to the tray's bottom like tiny dark stalagmites. He touched one; it was brittle and cracked right off, but another one was softer and glossy. Rudy reflexively wiped his hand on the rag. *Boogers? Si's goddamn boogers?*

He shuddered with revulsion, then carried Si's tray over to the wall and dropped it flat on the floor by the rack. *Shit, check your tray.* His head thumping, Rudy removed the tray he had used, opened it, then dropped it face-down onto the floor, revealing years of dried mucus on its underside. *Shit!* "Shit, shit, shit!" Each of his expletives was more intense than the last. *I'll be damned if anyone ever uses these again.*

His drowsiness gone, Rudy didn't bother to check the other two trays; he grabbed all four by the connecting rails, carried two in each hand, extending them away from his body as if Si's mucus might touch him. He stopped for gloves in Larry's fishing closet, then hauled the trays out of the den and through the house to the kitchen until his arms fatigued. With an excruciating headache, he put the trays down and took two aspirins at the sink. He forced air through his lips. *Get it done!*

As soon as he was outside, Rudy slammed the trays onto the steps, cracking one of the connecting rails. *Good, now finish it off.* He rushed into the shop, switched on its lights and the outside floodlight, then found Larry's chopping maul and a couple of two-by-fours about five feet long. Rudy returned, put one end of each two-by-four on the bottom step, and laid the tray across. He struck it with the hammer side of the maul; the rail split easily. He struck it again, then again, and saw Stew watching him, his head cocked sideways. *Yeah, Stew, crazy shit. I'll bust 'em all.*

Rudy resumed annihilating the tray, his hat falling off. On another blow, the wood shattered like a baseball bat and sent a small splinter up into his black eye. *Damn it.* His remedy was to keep the eye shut while he worked, hardly noticing the discomfort. Now accustomed to the task, it seemed to Rudy that clobbering and chopping the second and third trays into kindling took no time at all. *Another tray bites the dust.* He rested for several seconds and noticed bizarre angular shadows formed by the floodlight's beam passing through the jumble of sticks and wood chunks below. *Shit, finish it!*

The bottom of the fourth tray had no smears or pieces of snot. He vigorously destroyed it anyway. *That sure as hell wasn't being like Si.* He glowered at the wood scraps for several seconds. *The opposite of Si. So? Doesn't matter.* His headache was milder but still constant.

He took a long breath, carelessly kicked the wood, then spotted mucus specks on the underside of a small triangular scrap of TV tray. He flipped it with another kick.

A better attitude toward Si? Who do you think you're kidding?

CHAPTER 13

Star Wars

Rudy went through the kitchen to his bathroom. His steady headache, lack of sleep, and adrenaline withdrawal were catching up to him. He shook his head to clear his mind, then washed his hands and examined his eye in the bathroom mirror. *Ugly, but the splinter's gone.* He had worked up enough sweat outside that the makeup resembled drooping skin. As he cleaned off his face with warm water, soap, and the scouring side of a sponge, his reddish-purple cheek smarted, his eye not so much. *Damn, how do I explain the trays?*

He went into the kitchen and took the watermelon wedges out of the refrigerator. *No way I can watch him eat this.* Rudy put three slices of melon in a cereal bowl near the sink and left the kitchen. *Now to the scene of the friggin' crime.* Rudy walked down to the den. *Don't look at him.* Si was on the sofa, watching whatever came on after the movie. Rudy approached him from behind, then stopped a few feet away to inhale. *Just B.O.* "Si."

"Hi, Rudy. It's a quiz show." Si didn't turn around. "Sometimes I know the answer."

"Si, your watermelon is in the kitchen. Eat it over the sink, okay?"

"Yes. Can I wait for a commercial?" his eyes on the screen.

"Whenever you want. I'll be in my room; probably in bed."

"I know this one—marsupial."

Rudy eyed the empty rack on the wall, then trod wearily through the house, his headache relentless but not all that severe. *So, what the hell are you going to do?* He stopped in the kitchen near Si's watermelon. *Maybe hide all the wood in back—give you time to think. Right, they'll still see the empty rack. What do you tell them? I saw how old and scarred the trays were getting, and I—Who's gonna' swallow that?*

He took a package of peas from the freezer, then stopped in his bathroom again for an aspirin. Rudy entered his room, turned on the light, and sat on the bed. *Teen angst turns violent—more at eleven. Smart-ass, think. You sure as hell can't tell Mom the truth.* Rudy lay back and applied the compress to his face. *Finally, a good use for peas.* He held still.

Damn, what about Reed? Helen will call if she hears from him. Get some sleep. Rudy pulled off his clothes, let them fall to the floor, then got under the covers on his side, moaning a little. He brainstormed excuses about the trays, but they seemed implausible, even comical. It was well after midnight before he fell into a fitful sleep.

Near the end of his agitated slumber, Rudy was watching a dream that seemed like an Italian avant-garde film he once saw on TV. He was chopping up the TV trays, but the last one turned whole again. He smashed the new one, but it was immediately replaced by another, then another. Rudy watched the pile of broken wood grow faster than he could wreck the trays.

"Wake up, snot!" Charlotte shouted to the back of his head, then moved a few feet away.

What? Rudy opened his eyes. "What do *you* want?"

Charlotte laughed. "You're really in deep caca this time—even Dad is mad." She pointed toward the driveway.

God, the real trays. Dumb dream. He turned to her.

Her eyes widened. "Jesus, what did you do to your face?"

"What did you do to yours?"

"Typical high school punk answer. No chance you gave the guy much of a fight, Gramma's boy."

Yeah, no chance. "That's the best you can do?"

"Gramma's *baby* would be better, but that's Si."

Crap. Rudy sat up under the covers. Charlotte was wearing pastel-green cotton pajamas and the forest-green Christmas slippers she had taken good care of since she was twelve. "Boys and girls, it's Wacky Elf, and just in time for Halloween."

"Shut up," she said, pointing to the driveway again. "So, why in hell did you bust up all the trays?"

None of your business. "To kill the termites." He checked his clock. *Just after eight.*

"What?" She paused. "You finally went all-the-way bat-shit crazy."

She moved to the door. "The royal snot is awake," she called across the kitchen.

Katie came to the doorway in her pink terry-cloth robe; Larry was behind her in a work shirt. Katie regarded Rudy, then glowered at Charlotte. "Shar, leave us, please."

"No way, I gotta' hear this."

"He can tell you later. Go." When Charlotte didn't move, Katie turned to Larry, who gently touched his daughter's arm.

"What are you doing?" Charlotte spouted at her father. "You're taking his side too?" She stormed off into the kitchen.

Larry perched on the small stool; Katie sat on the end of Rudy's bed. "Well?" she said.

Boogers, boogers everywhere. "It was Si's fault," Rudy said, straight-faced.

Katie's cheeks blanched. "What did you say?"

"Joking. I did it."

"That's one lousy excuse for a joke."

"Yeah, you're right. I'll clean up the wood and save up to buy new trays."

Katie bridled, drawing in her chin. "Damn right, but that's not the point."

Rudy saw that his father had barely moved. *But he's listening.*

Larry made eye contact. "Just tell us why, Rudy."

"It's hard to explain." *No, it isn't.*

"Well, give it a try," Katie jeered.

She couldn't handle the truth. Stalling, he reached for his clothes on the floor. "Okay, I was pissed."

"You don't say," she bristled. "Were you fighting with one of your friends?"

Yes! Thanks, Mom—good one. "Yeah." He pulled up his jeans, not tucking in the shirt.

"Was it Reed?"

What? "I'll be goddammed. You ever see me that pissed off with Reed?"

"Rudy, don't speak to your mother like that," Larry said impassively.

A golden oldie. Rudy faced Katie. "Yeah, sorry. Okay, Noah and I were fighting on the phone." *Good—totally believable.* "You'll be glad to hear that a girl was involved." *Well-played.* "He was making fun of a girl I like."

"Oh?" Katie fought off a grin with pursed lips. "You were angry enough to break those trays? Must be some girl."

He shrugged. *I hardly know her.* Rudy had stepped into his low-top yard sneakers; he started to tie them.

"Fine. Where was Si during the argument with Noah?"

Camped on the toilet. "Watching TV."

"Good. You know how arguing upsets him a little."

"I made the call in your office." *This lying is getting easy.*

Katie frowned. "When we got back, Si was alone. You said you'd keep him company."

Never said that. "I went to bed. He's a big boy."

Charlotte arrived at the door in one of her skimpy white tennis outfits, a racquet case over her shoulder. She scowled at her mother. "I don't really give a shit why Rudy did it. In case I get any calls, here's Mona's number in Palm Springs." Charlotte handed over a piece of scrap paper, then started into the kitchen. "I'm in a tournament, but I'll be back for the party on Sunday. Oh, and after that, I'm out of here as soon as I can swing it. You're *all* crazy." Moments later, the screen door in the kitchen slammed.

Rudy stood. "Are we finished, Mom?"

"No, we're not."

"Okay—I'll be in the bathroom for a minute." He walked in, urinated, then washed up a little and checked the raw bruise on his face. His parents had stayed in his room and were speaking just loudly enough that he could overhear them.

"Did you know about the tournament, Larry?"

"Yes."

"And she told you not to tell me?"

"Yes. She thinks she can win and improve her chances for a scholarship. I told her to go for it."

"She only started playing again a couple of weeks ago."

"More like six weeks, but that's what she said you'd say."

"Jesus wept. She's of age, Larry, and she knows where the goddamn door is."

"Sounds like that's her plan."

"She's all talk."

"Maybe you could just try to support her, Katie."

"Don't spout Seth's crap to me."

Jesus, that's how they talk now? Rudy flushed the toilet, then walked in to sit on his bed.

Katie peered at his raw face. "You scrubbed that makeup too hard." Katie exhaled audibly through her nostrils. "Okay, what are your plans today?"

"First, the wood."

"Just put it with my other wood scraps," Larry said. "You can help me make new trays out in the shop next week."

"If Monday's good, there's no school."

"The shop's booked those two days; let's start Wednesday afternoon."

"All right." Rudy faced Katie. "Artie's expecting me to meet him to go to a matinee."

She eyed him. "We haven't resolved anything about your, um, outburst."

Want to hear about all the little surprises your brother left under the TV trays?

"Rudy?"

"Like I said, Noah really pissed me off—I got carried away."

She sighed. "Then I expect you to talk to Seth about your anger."

Oh, so it isn't Seth's crap anymore?

"He'll be here tomorrow morning to help set up; you can meet with him then."

"I thought you wanted me to help out."

"You can help after you talk to him. Go to your damn movie."

"Yeah, after the wood." Rudy went out to the remnants of the trays. *The pile is so small—stupid dream.* It took about a half-hour until he was sweeping the smaller bits into a dustpan. He rolled the wheelbarrow back to Larry's scrap pile and dumped it.

Maybe Reed called. Rudy came back to the porch and went into the kitchen to call Helen; she didn't answer. *You'll see her after the movie—almost two hours until you meet Artie.* He returned to his room and stretched out sideways on his bed. Rudy spotted Helen's book over on the desk. *It's short and probably good.* He shuffled over to pick it up, blew on it again, then came back to lie on the bed. *What lessons in morality this time?* He turned to the title page:

OF MICE AND MEN
John Steinbeck

Jonny used to love those cartoons that made fun of this. The old movie was good, but I don't remember most of it. Rudy began reading. *A few miles south of Soledad…Not Mexico, like the other book.* He read the next few pages… *the Salinas River…Yeah, here, but up north.*

After a description of the dusty ranch country east of the coastal range and west of the Gabilan Mountains, Rudy read several more pages that mostly introduced the two central characters—massive Lennie and slight George. He stopped reading again. *Starting to remember, but when is it taking place? Boxcar hobos, canned beans with ketchup. A threshing machine. The Depression, I guess—before Pearl Harbor.*

One thing for sure—Helen thinks it's pertinent to me. Is it Lennie and Si? Maybe, but Lennie's much simpler and more talkative. George protects him and has to cuss him out when he's in trouble. This could be more about George than Lennie.

Rudy finished another chapter, then checked the clock. *Get moving.* He flipped through the slender novel and found it only had six chapters. *Oh yeah, the girl messes with Lennie; he hurts her by accident. Then off into the ol' sunset? Can't be that corny. Helen roped me in again.*

He got up, showered quickly, then put on fresh clothes—nearly new jeans and a loose navy-blue polo. Rudy combed his hair in the bathroom and found his newer cap before walking over to the kitchen telephone. He dialed Artie's number.

"*Bueno,*" a female voice answered.

"Hi, Mrs. Mata. This is Rudy."

"Yes. *Hola, Rodulfo.*"

I can see that smile of hers. "How are you?"

"Good, thank you. *Arturo* is coming."

"Thank you, Mrs. Mata."

"Welcome. Say hello to the family. *Momentito.*"

Rudy waited, then heard the Mata's phone clank. Artie said something to himself that didn't sound like Spanish. "What did you just say, Artie?

"A *Zapoteco* word—like *oops* in English, I think. Rudy, I just came home from work. I'm in the bath now, then I'll leave."

In the bath now? You know what he means. "No hurry, we have forty-five minutes."

"Yes, at the market."

"Okay, see you." They hung up.

Rudy munched on a raw blueberry toaster tart as he went out to check Stew's water. He noticed that it was going to be warmer than predicted, probably about eighty. He ruffled the dog's ears and tossed the ball a few times. Remembering that he was going to find some makeup, he hurried back to the kitchen, then to his bathroom mirror. Katie had only left him a lipstick-type tube of cover-up. *Not enough for my cheek—it would melt anyway.* Rudy applied makeup to the skin around his eye, then put his Angels cap back on. *That'll have to do.*

He walked out past Larry's T-bird, one of the vans, then Si's car. *Still no Citroen. Maybe they haven't finished his window. Or maybe—maybe what? You need to tell Artie about all this.*

Rudy started down La Plata Avenue, then eyed a shrub where several bees seemed to be agitated by some fall blossoms. *They aren't bothering you.* Rudy still quickened his pace, turning back to check on them. After that, he slowed down so he wouldn't be too early.

When he approached the small store, Rudy saw Artie, about a block away, jogging effortlessly up La Plata Avenue. Rudy checked the small neon clock above the market's entrance; they were almost ten minutes early. Rudy crossed the street to the bus stop and waited a few seconds in the shade for Artie. He was practically in his Sunday best—black slacks, shined brown shoes, and a short-sleeved white dress shirt, its collar open.

"Artie, we still have a few minutes. You didn't have to run."

"Just in case." He saw Rudy's bruise. "*Híjole*, that's a bad one."

"Actually, it's better. It was covered up yesterday; I still have makeup around my eye."

"And a black eye? What happened?"

"We tried out Reed's car on Thursday night; he was helping me…" Artie asked a couple questions as Rudy described the hike, mostly Garret's assault, then Reed and Rudy's retaliation.

"*Ay*, so you got it twice in one day. How are you now?"

"My butt still hurts the most. And you?"

"Stiff neck." Artie smiled. "I'm glad you helped Reed."

"I was still scared, but I think our deal with Harry helped me. Anyway, we took the other guy to his mother's…" Rudy told him what happened there and a little more about Earl's family.

"He has no way out, I think."

"Maybe not, but it's Reed I'm worried about now—haven't seen him since that night."

"He went somewhere in his car?"

"All I know for sure is that he's getting the window fixed." Rudy checked the clock again. "The bus is late."

Artie looked over his shoulder. "Yes, but here it comes."

The white and brown city bus cleared the intersection, then pulled into the stop. They got on, the driver lackadaisically punched their passes, then Artie and Rudy sat together several rows back in the empty bus. "We leave in two minutes," the driver said without looking at them.

"Rudy, your uncle couldn't come?"

"No." *Lying to Artie sucks. No way I can tell him about the TV trays—wait for a better time. Yeah, when would that be?* Two elderly women got on the bus and sat a few rows ahead. "Artie, your mom's English is even better. How did she learn more than your dad?"

Artie hesitated. "They grew up very far from each other, which isn't common for a couple in Mexico." He had lowered his voice by the end of the sentence. "She grew up in Juarez on the border and met my father in El Paso. They moved to his village in Oaxaca, where I was born. We moved later back to Juarez, then here. I'm talking too much."

"Maybe I was too nosey."

Artie held his answer as two more people entered the bus, then the driver started off. "It's okay," he said, just above a whisper. "My father doesn't want us to tell anybody this, but I know I can tell you. My father and I have false papers; my mom, sister, and brothers are U.S. citizens. My parents won't separate us, so they always worry about all of us being deported."

"For god's sake," Rudy murmured, "they can do that?"

"For my uncle, it was one ticket. They arrested him and might have let him go with a fine, but he told the judge he wasn't speeding. We know it was the truth—we always joke about his slow driving. *La migra* took him and my aunt—also my two cousins who are citizens—they are all back in Juarez now. We have to lie in order to work—a difficult lesson for my family."

"To not stand up for your rights?" He kept his tone of indignation down.

"*La gente* don't have rights unless you have a lot of money. It's similar in Mexico."

"Artie, everything you said is safe with me."

"I know; I should have told you before."

"How will the immigration rules affect going to college and med school?"

"I don't know yet, but I'll find a way. Probably junior college to start. I'll take the hardest science and math courses and try to be the best student in every class. My cousin did that, and now she has papers and is a teacher near San Diego."

"So, the standards are different; you have to completely excel in order to have a chance."

"Yes, and that's what I'll do," his tone intrepid.

"I believe it." *Jesus, he told you everything. Tell him today about the trays.*

After stopping a few times for passengers, the bus rumbled across the train tracks into Glendale on Brand Boulevard, known in La Plata as *the strip* because of its four theaters. The venues were a block or two apart, starting with the cheapest—their favorite as kids. Its marquee now boasted: SCI-FI DOUBLE FEATURE & 10 CARTOONS. Each succeeding theater was more expensive; the fourth one always had the latest blockbuster—this time, *Saturday Night Fever*.

Rudy and Artie got out at the bus stop past the third theater's marquee: HELD OVER! STAR WARS! The ticket booth was already open, but Rudy and Artie passed it because the line went around the corner ahead. They jogged up there, but people were queued for the entire block, so they turned onto another block and found the end of the line. About half of the moviegoers were kids, nattering excitedly. Some boys and early teens brandished toy light sabers; a few others wore Darth Vader or storm-trooper masks. Most of the high school and college-age youth tried to act as nonchalant as the scattering of adults in the line.

"This movie has been here a long time," Artie said, "and still the long lines."

"Yeah, we might not even get in." Rudy turned around and saw about a dozen customers already waiting behind them. "I'd say it's about fifty-fifty."

"What did you like best the first time we watched it?"

They talked about Obe Wan and R-2 D-2 until the line began to move very slowly. A guy nearby with a transistor radio groaned. "The damn Dodgers lost. Down three games to one."

Good. "Hear that, Artie?"

Artie pointed ahead. "Yes, but look, somebody's coming." A hefty, squarish woman, about five-seven, had turned the last corner and was strutting toward them, counting off people with her walkie-talkie. She wore a tiny pill-box hat and an old-time usher suit with crimson stripes down the sides of tan slacks. Not far from her, a short guy stumbled out of line.

God, it's Jonny. Rudy pointed. "Look, Artie." Some guy, not much taller than Jonny, shouted at him. Noah left the line; he towered over the other guy, but the usher stood in Noah's way. Artie and Rudy watched Noah argue with her before he and Jonny got back in line.

Rudy shook his head. "Dickheads. I guess their movie sold out."

Noah had spotted Rudy and Artie. He said something back to the others, then left the line with his date.

I'll be damned—it's Libby.

Rudy saw Libby release her hand repeatedly from Noah's grip, then he finally didn't try again. *Smart girl.* The usher was chatting with people as they moved slowly along.

As they approached, Rudy saw that Noah was neater than usual in his one pair of good slacks and a pressed short-sleeve white shirt. Libby's rust-colored hair was pinned up in back; she wore a white top and a loose dark-blue skirt that nearly hid her ample hips. About five-six, she wasn't tall enough to keep a few people from gaping at them as the long-and-short-of-it.

"Rudy," Artie murmured, "Libby's with Noah."

"Yeah." *And she looks good.* "She doesn't seem too happy about it." He turned the bruised side of his face away from them as they came closer.

"Ru-dy, Ru-dy, Ru-dy!" Noah crowed from a few feet away.

Screw you. He tried to look bored with Noah's exuberance and nodded shyly to Libby; she returned a tentative smile. *She's wondering what's going on. Yeah, me too. A plan, Rudy.*

Noah moved in so his back was to Artie. "Rudolph, remember Libby from homeroom?"

Prick. "Yes, and so does Artie." Rudy saw Libby furrow her brow.

Artie stepped right around Noah. "Hi, Libby."

"Hi, Artie." She gave him a full smile. "Did you figure out that trig problem we have?"

"It's tough, but I think I got it."

"Me too; we'll go over it before class."

"Sure." Artie glanced at Rudy.

She's in Honors Math? He saw her reject Noah's hand. *Libby scores again.* "So, Noah, what happened to Disco Duck?" he asked, delighted when Libby chuckled.

"Real funny—sold out. What happened to you?" pointing at the bruise.

"Harry nailed me after you ran away."

Artie stepped forward. "After you left, Rudy and I got Harry back."

Noah hesitated. "I bet," he grumbled. "And I didn't run away, liars."

"*You* are the liar, Noah," Artie blustered.

"It's okay, Artie." Rudy faced Noah. "So, what just happened up there with Jonny?"

"He said something loud about chinks; some oriental guy yelled at him. I tried to—"

"Sounds like Jonny deserved it," Rudy interrupted.

Noah ignored Rudy and turned to Libby. "We call *Ar-too-row* here the Flytown midget." Noah's peal of laughter stopped some nearby conversations; Libby glared at him.

"You're so full of it, Noah," Rudy said calmly. "Nobody says that, except you."

Noah laughed. "The fat-ass and the midget—you're both askin' for it." Some junior high boys got out of line to see if a fight was brewing. Noah took a half-step forward and squared off, all knees and elbows, sniggering. Libby scowled and walked away from him.

Artie stepped up next to Rudy. "So you want both of us?" he dared Noah.

The usher's almost here. "You look like a deranged giraffe, Noah. Bend your neck all the way down here." His snide remark evoked titters from the small crowd.

His face turning red, Noah took another step, then balked when Rudy and Artie held their ground. The usher approached, and Noah straightened from his awkward stance.

Artie pointed to Noah and spoke to the usher. "*He* came over here looking for trouble."

The usher snarled at Noah. "You've had your warning."

He smirked at her. "Who asked you, Princess Leia?" The junior high kids giggled.

The usher's jaw stiffened toward them. "I think you kids might make it into the movie if you get back in line." She turned to a small group of adults. "Anybody see this differently?" When they shook their heads, the usher faced Noah again. "Okay, I'm authorized to ask you to leave—should've done it before. You're not welcome here today."

"Shit, you can't do that."

The usher pointed her walkie-talkie at him. "Please leave, sir, or I call security now."

Libby took a step toward Noah. "You're an embarrassment. I'm going back to Trish—don't you dare follow me." She faced Rudy and Artie. "I'll see you guys at school." She left.

A basket-plus-one for Libby.

Noah glared at Rudy. "This isn't over for you or the wetback."

The usher turned on the walkie-talkie and put it up to her ear.

Noah took the hint and started to walk away. "You're still a chicken-shit, Rudy—all talk."

Wincing from a headache, Rudy watched him go. "Another good bluff, Artie."

"No, Reed would approve of your plan. It bothered Noah when we didn't back away."

"Yeah, I was counting on you."

"Any time, *amigo*, but Noah is the one who is all talk, not you."

Sure. "Thanks, Artie." Rudy exhaled deeply as they got back in line, then tried to speak privately. "Artie, I didn't know Libby was in your math class."

"And I didn't know you liked her until we walked by her house the other day. She's also my friend—just my friend. Isn't she in your advanced English class?"

"The other one, I guess." Rudy inhaled deeply then exhaled slowly. "Man, I like how she handled Noah." He paused. "After all that, I'm worried she thinks we're punks."

"I told you; she's my friend—my smart friend. She knew what was going on."

"Artie, I think I'd like to know her better."

"What's wrong with that?" Artie still kept his voice subdued as they inched ahead.

"I don't think I could talk to her alone."

"Yes, it's hard. *Fíjate*, two years ago, I saw this pretty girl in our village, but I was scared to talk to her. My mother explained she was *Carolina*, my friend from *primaria*. Just days before we left, I found the courage. We started writing; I'll see her again soon at Christmas."

"Good for you, Artie."

"Your chance will come, *amigo*. Maybe it already has." He smiled.

"I don't know, Artie." *Ask what he knows about her? No, bad idea.* They walked silently up to the ticket booth.

After the movie, Rudy and Artie got on the bus and talked about details from *Star Wars* that they missed the first time. The bus soon turned onto Palm Street, the Italian market just a few blocks ahead.

"Rudy, *Star Wars* reminds me of my father's story of an ancient hero in our village."

"But no light sabers." He grinned. "How long ago?"

"Many hundreds of years, when our people were the Maya."

"The Maya? Can you tell me some of the story?"

"It would be better to hear it from my father. In time, I think he will be pleased that you are interested."

The bus came to the grocery store, stopped, and they stepped down.

"Artie, we're having a party tomorrow afternoon at two for my grandparents—lots of food and bad music. We could also shoot pool or do something else."

"Thank you, but after mass tomorrow, my parents have a picnic with family and some friends. Good food *and* good music." He smiled. "I'll invite you next time."

"Thanks, Artie. No school Monday, you want to come over in the afternoon?"

"Yes, that's a good day. Maybe Reed will be around."

I doubt it. "If he is, we can play some poker. I'll give you a call."

CHAPTER 14

Passions

Mildred Krenshaw married Seth Grant in 1947, about fifteen years before Rudy was born. Seth was now called *Grampa* by Katie and Cami, but Charlotte, Rudy, and their uncles and aunts on Mildred's side, including Si, continued to refer to him as Doc Grant or Seth. Over the years, Seth advocated for Si as much as Mildred—a foundation of their thirty-year marriage.

Physically, the decades had been kind to Mildred. Trim but not thin, she had benefitted from no further pregnancies and from healthy and sufficient nourishment after years of often depriving herself for her children. Notwithstanding facial stress lines and grey tones to her long, auburn hair, Mildred, at seventy, was sometimes mistaken for a woman in her late fifties.

During her years of working as receptionist and assistant for Seth's practice, Mildred became adept at switching between "standard" English and her colloquial speech. In recent years, her mental acuity had diminished some, but her practical approach to life had blossomed into a broad appreciation for the natural world that Seth had shared with her. Mildred's dedication to Si's well-being and her dotage on Rudy had grown even stronger.

Unlike Mildred, Seth seemed to show every bit of his seventy-five years. He was completely bald now, his often-sunburned face had crumbled a little with a few dark spots and small cancer scars. His previously cavalier attitude toward his own skin motivated him to admonish patients to learn from his poor example. His athletic body had been slowed by arthritis, and a minor slouch took away a modicum of his height. Nevertheless, Seth kept up with bi-weekly tennis for seniors and rarely missed his Sunday nature hike.

Years before, Seth came to believe that he helped his patients most by listening to them; he gradually began to prescribe less medicine. After researching cognitive therapy for years, Seth had started to unofficially use what he considered the most sensible of those techniques, usually with patients from families he had known for more than one generation. With all of that, he hadn't seriously considered retirement but did reduce his hours by half.

After watching Artie jog down La Plata Avenue from the bus stop, Rudy ambled off in the opposite direction. *He runs like a machine.* Rudy passively walked by Noah's house. *Artie won't let anything hold him back. Epidemiology, for god's sake. He'll find a vaccine or something to help those villages—a passion, like Reed. What does that feel like?*

Rudy passed Jonny's without so much as a glimpse and soon came to his corner. *No Citroen. Tell Helen about Reed's lies?* He approached her place and saw Seth's scrupulously maintained antique Packard in the Lanier driveway. *Thought they were coming in the morning.*

He approached Helen's place, then knocked. Holding her cane this time, she opened the door in an apron printed with colorful fall leaves. "Hi, Helen. New apron?"

"No, an old-timer. Since I was expecting you, I resurrected my unremarkable culinary skills and made a pecan pie this morning."

"Sounds great." He entered and followed Helen slowly as she used the cane to hobble into the kitchen. "No word, I assume, from Reed?"

"No, not yet. How was the movie?"

"*Star Wars*, second time. It's worth discussing—another day." Rudy sat on one of the breakfast nook pillows facing the dark-brown pie, a spatula, two dessert plates, forks, and napkins. "Looks good."

"It's a bit overdone, but edible, I believe. I'm having coffee; milk for you, Rudy?"

"Yes, please. I'll get it." He walked out to her ice-box. *Toaster-tart, popcorn, and pecan pie. Diet of champions.* He brought the quart of milk and a glass to the table. Helen was using the spatula to cut half of the pie into three unequal portions. She gave the largest wedge to Rudy, the smallest to herself.

"Thanks." Regardless of his queasy stomach, Rudy started right in on the dessert.

"While we enjoy our treat, perhaps you can finish your account of the hike."

"Okay. It was Reed's idea to help me with my fear of the dark…" Around bites of the rich dessert, he repeated his abridged story again, finishing with a non-graphic description of the incidents related to Earl and Garret. "…I admire how Reed handled that creep." He drank some milk and took another mouthful of pie.

With her fork, Helen cut off the very apex of her wedge of pie. "That's the one saving grace from spending part of his youth around Will McCool and his vile friends. Reed quickly learned how to manipulate and outsmart them." She ate the morsel.

"Yeah, this Garret guy didn't know what hit him—literally." Rudy's pie was down to crust and a bite or two of the sticky filling.

She grinned. "I take it the pie is okay." Helen hadn't lifted her fork a second time.

"Yes, it's very good." *Inhaled it.* Rudy finished his narrative, telling her about Earl and his mother, then Reed's speech about do-gooders.

"So, Reed spent the night helping, then warned you to be wary of the kind offices of man," Helen said as Rudy finished his pie. "He is not, of course, as cold-hearted as he says."

In certain ways… "Reed and I also discussed our friendship…" Still a bit soured by his last talk with Reed, Rudy understated the fealty they had expressed for each other.

Helen formed one of her genial half-smiles. "Your friendship is based on loyalty and honesty—a rare achievement these days."

He nodded and took a drink of milk. *What about honesty with Helen? Tell her about the car now? No, Reed will call—hopefully.* Around a sigh, he wiped his mouth with a napkin. "We also talked about Si a lot, including what you asked Reed to discuss with me."

"I hope that doesn't seem nosey. I could have spoken to you about it myself, but I thought Reed would be a more appropriate messenger."

"It wasn't nosey. I promised him we would talk about it."

"Of course." She frowned at her wedge of pie. "Nervous stomach, I guess. More pie, Rudy?"

"No thanks." He looked away from his empty plate, then back at her. "Helen, I want you to know that Seth is going to have a shot at me in the morning." Rudy scoffed. "I'm a community project."

She smiled again. "Well, Seth and I have both studied therapy with more than passing interest but talks like this are just informal private discussions. Seth can, however, refer anyone to a certified therapist, which he did for a lady in my elderly group."

"Has he ever had one of his talks with Reed?"

"Reed is down on therapists and doctors—nothing personal toward Seth. Reed and Amity have had some good providers, of course, but the counselor Reed is required to see seems to be lacking in more ways than one. I can't even imagine those sessions."

"He told me about that guy." Rudy finished his drink. "Fortunately, he has you."

"And you. Reed trusts us—our true qualifications." She sipped her coffee. "Rudy, will our talk about Si overlap too much with your discussion with Seth?"

"I don't think so. Mom wants me to talk to him about my anger. She knew I was angry with Noah and Jonny, then she saw the results of my, um, meltdown."

Her brow furled. "Your meltdown?"

"Afraid so. After I left here on Friday, I was supposed to get dinner for Si and me. Reed and Artie have chipped away at my attitude toward Si; I decided to at least try to do better."

"Good, Rudy."

"You won't say that after you hear this." He told her the main details of the tray incident.

Helen didn't respond right away. "Okay, so finding Si's mucous under the trays obviously set you off. What were you thinking about after you broke them?"

Rudy pursed his lips, then exhaled loudly. "I realized my anger was just the opposite of Si, like Reed explained." Rudy's chin touched his chest, then he spoke in a low, contrite tone. "There's more to it than fear of being like him. I admitted to Reed that I've become ashamed of Si. I don't despise him, but maybe I'll always be ashamed." He raised his chin.

"And maybe not—especially since you've learned that most of this is about you, not Si. I'm not sure you can isolate your shame for Si from your anger. It looks to me like there *is* going to be some overlap when you talk to Seth."

Not if I can help it.

She frowned slightly. "Rudy?"

"I can talk to Seth about Noah and Jonny, but not about why I busted up those damn trays. Seth has been a father to Si all these years; I couldn't say that to him or Gramma."

"As you know, Seth is very understanding. You could still be truthful by telling him you aren't ready right now to explain your anger and the trays. As for Noah and Jonny—tell the truth, and then consider Seth's advice." Helen checked her clock. "Rudy, let's talk more about Si after you've had a chance to mull over everything."

"Okay. Thanks, Helen."

"You're welcome. It's getting late, but I wanted to ask if you started *Of Mice and Men.*"

She's still on Si—Si and Lennie. "Finished half of it, maybe."

"Good. As short as it is, it's not a book to be read fast. What do you think so far?"

"I saw the movie a long time ago, but I don't remember much. Anyway, like the other book, the characters are intense. I'm not sold on George yet. I'm not sure I get his angle on helping Lennie, but I'll give it some time."

"That's the beginning of a thoughtful review. We'll have an interesting discussion."

He nodded. "I assume you see something in this book that might be relevant to me."

"Yes, but how relevant—that will be up to you. If not, just enjoy the book."

"Okay, tonight might be a good time to finish it."

They said goodnight; Rudy crossed the front yard and walked up the driveway to the kitchen stairs. Inside, Katie was preparing salad to go with dinner. "Hi, Mom," he said blandly.

"How was the movie?" she asked, not looking at him.

"Fine."

"That's good." Katie finished peeling a carrot and reached for her highball, a ritual she had recently added to dinner preparation. She took a sip from the nearly finished drink.

Since Gramma's here, she'll keep it to one or two—works for me. He noticed the two turkeys for the party still thawing in the sink. "Why are

Gramma and Seth here already?"

"Mom's going to help me with these birds. They decided to stay the night." Katie started to wash some lettuce. "They're on a walk to the store for me—you can have your meeting with Seth after dinner, instead of tomorrow."

"Okay." *After a nap.*

"Rudy, I told him about the TV trays and the problems with your friends."

Great. "All right. What about the decorating tomorrow?"

She went on with her chore. "Gramma rounded up a few of your cousins and their friends; they're having an actual rumpus out there. Larry is sort of supervising."

"Mom, have you noticed that Dad's a little more, um, gregarious?"

Again, she didn't face him. "I suppose."

"Seth is still trying to help him, right?"

"Yes, he helps because Larry's too damn stubborn to go to the V.A."

What the hell? "Don't you think Dad might have good reasons?"

"Not really." She put down the lettuce, turned around, then scrutinized Rudy's face. "I see you didn't try to cover the bruise, but it looks better—even if you don't. Didn't you sleep?"

"Not great. I think I'll read and take a short nap."

"Yes, do that."

That was relatively easy. He took a glass of water with him, then entered his room and swallowed an aspirin. He picked up *Of Mice and Men* and lay on the bed, favoring his rear.

So, what's up with Lennie and George? Rudy took out his bookmark and found where he had left off...*swell time I could have without you. George doesn't mean it; he's into the pipe dream too—live off the fatta the lan' and watch out for each other—Lennie tends the rabbits.*

Rudy finished the chapter, then drifted off. Near the end of his long nap, he watched George and Lennie walking down a dirt road. His dream self caught up to them, only to see Rudy and Si face him. *Predictable dumb dream.* Rudy opened his eyes to the clock. *Damn, get up, you slept through dinner.*

He got dressed in clean jeans and a blue summer shirt. Rudy grabbed his newer Angels cap and entered the kitchen. His mother was washing the dishes in a loose housedress that hid her moderate middle-age rolls even better than her sweats did. *Which Katie awaits us now?*

"Almost seven, sleeping beauty." Katie pointed to a stack of leftovers in plastic containers on the counter. "There's some food, if you want it."

Cold sober. "Thanks, not hungry. Where is everybody?"

"The kids are gone," not turning to him. "Your father let them make a mess of it out there; he can just fix it up in the morning."

"So, who's still here?"

"They're in the parlor; Seth is waiting for you."

"Okay." *Thanks for the nice chat.* A sour trace of the rich pie repeated in his throat.

Si entered the kitchen with a dessert plate and fork, then put them in the sink—one of the ingrained manners that had survived his childhood. "Hi, Rudy."

"Si." Rudy followed him into the dining room where Si helped himself to a brownie from a platter, then went on. Rudy saw that about two-thirds of Mildred's revered four-layer maple cake remained. *Oh, man. No, chubs.* He entered the parlor, where Si had joined Mildred on the sofa. He was next to the end table again, eating the brownie, its crumbs falling to the rug. *How many boogers under that table? Don't even think about it.* Larry, standing in work clothes, spoke quietly with Seth, who was sitting casually in one of the antique chairs, a dessert plate on his lap.

"Rudolph!" Mildred had risen and opened her arms, prompting Rudy to go to her.

They hugged, then he held both of her hands, chuckling. "You know, Gramma, I *was* over there less than a week ago. Today's the actual day, right? Happy thirtieth to you and Seth."

As they released each other, her eyes were riveted on his injuries. "Um, much obliged, dear, but what in kingdom-come took after your face?"

"Just an accident—it's getting better."

Her frown slowly morphed into a smile. "How'd ya' know today's our real day?"

"Your number-one grandkid is supposed to know these things."

Larry groaned in fun. "On that note, I have some work in the shop." He left.

"Ol' granny's just gonna' steal another hug." She embraced

Rudy again.

"Mildred, give the boy some air." Seth chuckled as she let go. "Rudolph, it should be warm enough to have our chat on the patio." Seth tapped Si on the shoulder. "Simon, I think your mom is going to be with Catherine for a while. Rudolph and I will be talking out back."

"Oh." Si picked up his puzzle magazine.

Rudy, Mildred, and Seth returned to the kitchen, where Katie was wiping off the kitchen table. Seth put the dessert plates he had gathered on the sink; he and Rudy started washing them.

Mildred smiled at Rudy. "Rudolph, I'm reheatin' some supper on low—all things you like. It'll be ready whenever you want." She moved closer to him and lowered her voice. "If ya' eat dessert first, it won't matter. Take along some maple cake?"

"It looks great, Gramma—later for sure." Rudy saw Katie roll her eyes. *Pissed at Gramma or me? Probably both.*

Seth and Rudy finished up and went out to the driveway. Walking toward Larry's shop, they could hear grinding in progress. The yard was well-lit by floodlights near the shop, patio, and pool—all of them attracting flying insects, large and small. They stopped at the patio and started to sit on the Adirondack chairs, but Rudy got right up and led him over to sit on the plastic-covered patio couch. "This is more comfortable." *For me anyway.*

Seth's face was momentarily curious. "So, the Yanks are ahead three games to one."

"Yeah, too bad they can't both lose."

"Still don't like the home team?"

Rudy touched the brim of his Angels cap. "No, I still do." He glared up at the bugs.

"Your loyalty is admirable." Seth looked up through the limbs of the walnut tree to the drab sky. "Not such a bad evening, Rudy." Since they were alone and in an informal session, Seth used Rudy's everyday first name.

Rudy looked up, and then back down. "I hear that somewhere up there are stars and planets."

"Let's hope so," Seth uttered quietly. "Okay, Rudy, your mother wants me to talk with you about your anger. The question is, do *you* want to?"

"I'll talk about Noah and Jonny."

"Good. Remember, this is private, just as when we speak in my office."

"Right. Can I ask you something first?"

"Sure, go ahead."

"Mom said that Dad works with you because he won't go to the V.A. What's that about?"

"Larry has never trusted the V.A. You can ask him if you want to know why."

Confidential. "Okay. So, Noah and Jonny…" He gave examples of their treatment of Artie and Reed. "…and we're not friends anymore, whether they understand it or not."

"Any regrets?"

"No."

"What close friendships do you still have outside of the family?"

"Reed, Helen, and Artie." *And Libby. You wish.*

"Any other conflicts at school or anywhere else?"

"Just a bully or two."

"How have you handled that?"

Rudy looked down at the concrete, then straightened up to point at his bruise. "I wasn't hit by a branch like I told Mom. Some creep who Reed and I ran into in the park slugged me, then I helped Reed run him off, but the guy had the last laugh—broke the window of Reed's car."

"I assume you were angry."

"Sure, I was angry." *And scared.* "But I learned strategies from Reed to help me deal with jerks like that. Reed thinks there's a better chance to outsmart a bully than to fight one."

"I agree, unless you turn to a different form of violence."

Rudy grinned, nearly straight-faced. "Does throwing rocks or dirt count?"

"That's for you to decide."

Garret got off easy. Rudy flinched when a huge insect floated just above them, making a *clacking* noise before it fluttered to the ground nearby. Rudy shuddered briefly. "Damn things are still around."

"Arizona Mantis." Seth got up slowly and took a few steps to check out the insect.

Gross, he's touching it. Si would do that, and probably Reed.

Seth returned to Rudy. "Fine specimen, unharmed. The largest

North American species of mantis. Very beneficial. I noticed your discomfort when it was landing."

"Insects bug me—pun intended, as Helen says."

A cursory grin on his face, Seth waited a few moments. "Rudy, I know that you and Reed have been close friends for most of your lives, but Catherine, as you know, doesn't approve."

"That's too bad. She heard gossip that he has a mental diagnosis. He does, but it's none of her business." Rudy sighed. "Reed never thinks of me as a spoiled fat kid, and I try to give him the benefit of the doubt when he has one of his, um, unique ideas." *Not this time, I didn't.* **When did we become perfect, Rudy?**

"Rudy, are you okay?"

"What?" *Damn.* "Sorry, I'm fine."

"Rudy, are you as close with Artie as you are with Reed?"

"Yes, but it's not the same. Artie was just a quiet kid who asked me questions about English, then he started hanging around with us. Now, Artie and I can confide in each other about most anything, and he's also good friends with Reed." He glowered at the floodlights again, where one praying mantis after another attacked the squadrons of smaller insects swarming to the lights. *Yeah, they're beneficial alright.*

"Rudy, was it actually Noah and Jonny who brought on the anger to break the TV trays?"

"No, I lied to Mom."

"So, can you tell me what set off your anger?"

Boogers. "No, I can't. It relates to someone in the family; I'll explain eventually." Rudy saw that Seth was momentarily nonplussed.

"Rudy, you have no obligation to tell me, but I'll listen when or if you want me to."

"Thanks."

"Of course." Seth paused again. "I have another question. Will the end of those two friendships make you wary of new relationships?"

"Maybe. I want to meet people who feel a purpose, a passion for something, even if I don't. Reed has his passions for art and acting, but Artie keeps his passion to himself. He's dedicated to doing medical research to help his people."

"Yes, he and I have talked medicine a couple of times—he's a very impressive young man. Besides Noah and Jonny, are Artie and Reed ridiculed much at school?"

"Yes. Talk about anger, *that's* something that really pisses me off."

"A passion, but not the kind you were just talking about."

"Right." Rudy and Seth turned to see Larry leave the shop and hurry through the shadows to take the stairs in two leaps. "They must have finally had a reason to buzz Dad from the kitchen. He put that gizmo together in one day. I guess he hopes to save time for his carving."

"Yes, wood is like clay for him." Seth raised his brows and waited for Rudy's reaction.

Okay, I get it. "Yeah, his carving is a passion—never occurred to me. Dad should make more time for it; he can afford another plumber."

"I agree." They watched Larry jog back to the shop.

Is Dad considering that? "Seth, I think you're passionate about your work too."

Seth was briefly speechless. "There's no finer compliment. Thank you, Rudy."

"It's just the truth. I don't know if I'll ever find that."

Seth waited a few seconds. "Well, you won't get the sixteen-and-no-goals speech from me. Your Aunt Camilla drove her school counselor crazy when she turned down a prestigious university to volunteer with refugees right here in Los Angeles. After that and college, she found a career she loves. Sooner or later, you'll find your way—uncertain as it all seems now."

"I didn't know all that about Aunt Cami. It does seem reassuring."

"Good. You might think about writing to her in Ethiopia. She would gladly discuss it with you. Speaking of writing, thank you for letting Helen share some of your work with me. It's very good; very real, Rudy."

He's just being nice. "Thanks." *My English teacher doth protest.*

Seth had waited to see if Rudy had more to say. "So, from what I've heard tonight, Rudy, I think anger has been a troubling but inevitable part of your life, as it is for most of us. Let's celebrate what gives us joy, but how we handle anger, fear, and loss is also part of the bargain."

I'm cheating that side of the bargain.

"Rudy?"

"Just thinking about what you said. What can I do about my anger?"

"As with any emotional challenge, there's no magic formula. There are anger management techniques we can try, but for right now, be very conscious of your anger and try not to act on it until you talk to someone you trust. If that includes me, I'd be honored. If you do act impulsively, you risk harming yourself or others."

"Or TV trays," wryly. "You'd be someone I'd talk to."

"You also have Reed, Artie, and Helen—perhaps even your dad someday. Rudy, I don't think Catherine realizes you and Helen have serious talks sometimes."

"Which is how I want it. She's so unreasonable about Helen and Reed." He bit the nail of his pinkie. "I don't even think of Mom as one person anymore—more like five. Ironically, if she's just had a couple of drinks, that's when we get along okay."

"Interesting. We are encouraging her to give A.A. another try, but she tells us she isn't as bad off as the people at the meetings, and that it's too *churchy.*"

"I didn't know she quit. At least she isn't violent like Uncle Nick."

He nodded. "So far, neither of them will consider professional therapy."

"Is there anything I can do about Mom, besides feel useless?"

"Since you asked, when something comes up between you and Charlotte, try to ask yourselves if it's just small stuff you two can handle on your own. It might cut down on the tension a little, but Catherine also has other sources of anxiety."

Including Dad, I guess.

"Rudy?"

"Sorry, um, I'll try if Shar will."

"Good. Perhaps you two could talk."

"Okay." *Maybe she knows more about Mom and Dad.* He saw his father leave the shop for the house again.

"Last thing, Rudy. Your mother is worried about your headaches and heartburn."

Worried? "I won't mention any of that around her anymore—small stuff."

"Fine, but it wouldn't hurt to drop by my office for a quick check-up."

Not now. "Okay, if it gets any worse."

Seth and Rudy started to go in, then came to the kitchen steps as Larry was on his way down. He stopped in front of Rudy, who grinned. "Dad, maybe Morse Code would help."

"Yeah, guess I'll spring for an extension. Phone call for you—Helen."

"Thanks." *She heard from Reed, or maybe he showed up.*

CHAPTER 15

Broadway or Bust

Rudy and Seth entered the kitchen. Katie, looking cross, held her hand over the receiver.

"What's wrong?" Rudy asked her.

"It's awful late for her to be calling."

Crap. "Please tell her I'll pick up in your office." Rudy rushed down to the parlor, passed the pre-occupied Si, then ran-walked through the den and rumpus room to pick up Katie's phone.

"Hi, Helen."

"Sorry about calling so late," her voice weak. "It must be busy with the party coming."

"Don't worry about that. Did Reed call?"

"No, I'm sorry if I got your hopes up." The kitchen extension clicked.

"That's okay. What's going on?"

"Normally, I wouldn't be worried about one of Reed's jaunts, but it's more than two days now. It finally occurred to me that having a car widens his parameters considerably. I was snoopy and took a look at his things; he packed his essentials and some clothes. When he first brought the car over the other day, did he say anything about taking a trip of some kind?"

"No." *Wait, what about during the hike?*

"Not to me, either. It gets more troubling. I wanted to see if his father knew anything, but Will is in jail again. I was finally allowed to speak to him a little while ago. He was livid when I told him Reed has the car. He said Reed probably lied to me about the court and his license."

Damn. Rudy closed his eyes for a moment. *Tell her.* "Helen, he's right. Reed told me he hated lying to you. He said I could tell you the truth, but I told him he should do it; we got a little pissed at each other. He was going to call and apologize to you. He hasn't, obviously; I shouldn't have waited so long to tell you. I'm sorry."

"It's all right, Rudy. You were giving him a chance to reconsider." She sighed quietly. "I am disappointed that he felt he couldn't tell me. You know how brutally honest he can be, but also rash when he perceives that something or someone is in his way." She *tsked.* "Perhaps the car and the money made one of his plans more feasible."

"Helen, I thought of something from the other night. During the hike, Reed talked about taking classes to polish his skills, and then he would find work in Hollywood or Vegas, eventually Broadway. I told him taking it a step at a time and getting more experience made a lot of sense, then he said it sounded too conventional." *Damn, what have I done?*

"Oh, dear." She was silent for a few moments. "I suspect he feels as free as the proverbial bird—thinking about going straight for the top."

"I got the feeling later that he'd made up his mind, but he wouldn't tell me anything specific. It's possible he's still getting the car fixed, or maybe driving somewhere to pick up the window or, um, something else." *Grasping at straws.* "Helen, I can come over there if you want to talk more, and I could bring Seth—"

"For now, only you, please. Thank you, Rudy."

"Sure. What should I tell them here?"

"Reed leaving for a couple of days shouldn't surprise anyone. Your family has been good to him; I don't want to upset them since we don't know very much. I also don't want to detract from the party tomorrow."

"Okay, Helen. I'll see you in a few minutes."

Rudy left the rumpus room, then went around to the kitchen, where Mildred and Katie were brewing what they called their *evening weak coffee.*

"Rudolph, is everything okay with Helen?"

"She's a little upset, Gramma. Reed took off without telling her; she wanted to ask me some things."

"That boy will be the end of her." Katie spoke more to Mildred than Rudy.

Shit. "I should get over there."

"Rudolph, please remind Helen we have drivers an' cars if she needs a ride anywhere."

"Right, Gramma." He hurried down the driveway and over to Helen's; she was waiting at her door, not visibly upset.

"Rudy, let's go into the kitchen." She started away with her cane. He followed her, entered the kitchen, and sat on a pillow in the nook.

Helen was opening a cupboard; she took out two tall glasses. "I have apple juice, milk, or water. Oh, and leftover pie."

"Apple juice is fine, thanks." Rudy looked at his distorted reflection in the old toaster. *I really screwed up.* Helen returned from the porch and prepared the drinks. Rudy went to the kitchen counter to get two full glasses of iced carbonated juice that resembled cream soda.

"See if you like that, Rudy." She put a paper napkin beside each drink, then sat down. "Real juice plus soda water makes homemade soda pop, no added sugar."

I don't care. He took a swallow. *Lighten up, for god's sake.* "It's good, Helen. Gramma said to remind you that we have transportation if you need it."

"Thank you. I don't think I will, but I'll give her a call soon."

"Do you think Reed's father will report the Citroen?"

"No, he won't want to involve the police. What Will wanted was to sell the car."

Prick. "What do you want to do if this drags on?"

"I'm not sure," with a plaintive sigh. "Reed's a survivor, but I'm still concerned. He would be furious if I sent the police after him. I still expect him to reflect on all this and call."

"I hope so. I shouldn't have told him that his original plan made such good sense."

"No, Rudy. We don't know for sure what he's doing. Even if he does something rash, there's no blame involved." She made another glum sigh, tenting her hands again. "If he did take off, at least he has that money to keep him off the streets."

The telephone rang in the living room. *Reed?* "Would you like me to answer it?"

"Please. I'll join you in a minute. I need to move my joints."

Rudy was already on his feet, walking across the kitchen to the black telephone on her desk in the living room. He picked up the receiver and remained standing. "Hello?"

"Is this Mrs. Crowley's residence?"

"Yes, excuse me for one second." Rudy watched Helen come back and sit in the padded armchair and leave the cane across her lap. She exhaled fully, closing her eyes.

"She's resting now," softly. "Who's calling, please?"

"This is Officer Crandall, Keller Police Department in West Kansas."

Kansas? Can't be about Reed—unless he drove straight through.

"Sir? I'm sorry to disturb her, but I must speak to Mrs. Crowley or, um, Mrs. McCool."

"One moment, please." He covered the receiver, his hand trembling a little as he handed it over to her. "A cop from Kansas. They probably stopped him for a red light or something."

"Yes, probably so. Get on my extension, Rudy. Unplug it when you're finished, please."

Rudy went into her bedroom, plugged the line into her telephone jack, picked up the receiver, and sat on her bed. *Damn, it must be his license and all that.*

Without interruption from Helen or Rudy, the officer informed them that a Citroen once registered to Amity McCool was on a two-lane side road around dusk, its speed estimated at about fifty. A tire apparently lost physical integrity and burst, sending strips of rubber in all directions before the car went off the road into a bar ditch. Somberly, the officer explained that the car rolled over and caught fire; they found the driver burned beyond recognition.

Wait, they don't actually know who it was.

Officer Crandall apologetically asked Helen for a dental contact so they could request records. They had called the license plate number into the California Highway Patrol and found the title and expired registration, and also the record of Reed's learner's permit. Officer Crandall said they would be in touch soon, then he respectfully expressed his condolences. He gave Helen his number before they finished the call.

Rudy returned to the living room. *None of that proves anything.* Rudy had never seen Helen cry, but she began sobbing quietly after the call. He consoled her as best he could for half an hour or so before she asked him to unplug her desk phone.

"Sure, Helen. Can I get someone, maybe Mildred, to stay with you tonight?"

"That's very sweet, Rudy, but I'll be okay. Thank you for being here. You're taking it better than I am."

Because it isn't over.

Helen told him she would be taking the bus to visit Reed's mother in the morning; Rudy agreed to come over in case of any phone calls. He unplugged her phone, said goodnight, then plodded home, staring at the ground. He found Katie alone in the kitchen and told her about the call from Kansas, and that they had assumed Reed was dead.

"I'm sorry, Rudy." Katie gave him a cursory hug. "What do you mean by *assumed?*"

Rudy related a couple of details, then his mother's eyes opened wide, and she interrupted him. "My god, we can't have the party tomorrow with this going on. We'll have to postpone." Katie paused. "Mom and I need to put together a list of calls to make first thing in the morning. I'll get her; she's probably reading." She scooted in her slippers across the kitchen, heading for the hallway to the newer bedrooms.

Rudy was already on his way to his room. *She really doesn't give a shit.*

Rudy slept in on Sunday morning, then spotted a medium-sized spider on the wall. He shuddered once, then smacked it with the flyswatter he kept by his bed. *Another life, cut off. It's a damn spider, Rudy—and Reed isn't dead.* The clock showed it was ten before ten. *Damn, I told Helen I'd be there by now.*

He dressed, stole through the vacant kitchen, then over to Helen's. Rudy knocked on her door, but she was gone, as expected. He found Reed's hidden key and opened the door, then put it back under the painted clay mushroom in a side garden. *Reed will still need it.*

After entering, he plugged in the phone. Helen had left a note to tell Rudy that after she visited Amity, she needed to contact Reed's father. Lastly, the note told Rudy to help himself to the leftover pie or anything else she had. She thanked him for minding the phone.

Rudy scooted her chair with a pillow to the desk, sat back, and focused on the bright colors in a polished geode on her desk. He reflected on the call from Kansas. *Anybody could have stolen that damn car. Sure, who would steal a Citroen in Kansas? No, there's still a chance.*

Rudy called home and was relieved when Mildred answered. He informed her that he would be at Helen's indefinitely. He asked Mildred to tell Katie that nobody should come over yet. After the call, Rudy didn't move from the phone except to pet Agatha, go to the bathroom, or get water. The only caller was an obituary editor from a newspaper in Kansas. Rudy took the number and told her he would pass it on to Helen.

By early afternoon, his growling stomach led him to eat a wedge of pie, which brought on heartburn again along with an annoying but moderate headache in his upper forehead. He began to pencil meaningless doodles on a scratch pad, darkening them over and over again before his gluteus protested the long sit. He moved to Helen's stuffed chair to read a *National Geographic* before realizing he had been on the same page for several minutes. He eyed a picture of Reed on one of Helen's nearby end tables. *Doesn't even look like him. I don't think Helen would mind if I called Kansas; see if there's anything new.* He returned to the desk and found the number on top.

"Keller Police," a lady answered with confident jack-of-all-trades efficiency in her tone.

"This is Rudy Lanier. May I speak with Officer Crandall, please?"

"Oh, yes, Mister Lanier," sympathy in her voice. "Just one moment, please."

The line switched to instrumental cowboy music. *Ya-hoo, Dodge City. Crap, Rudy—they've been helpful.*

"Mister Lanier, I was about to call you."

"Afternoon, Officer Crandall."

"Yes, I hope you and Mrs. Crowley are doing as well as could be expected." He paused. "I need to inform you the case was taken over by the Highway Patrol this morning. They should be calling soon. They investigated the crash site and found some evidence we missed."

Evidence of what? "What could they find that wasn't incinerated?"

"They kept it all hush-hush—didn't tell us. I'm sorry, sir. Please call again if we can be of any help. Also, folks around here send their prayers to Mrs. Crowley and you."

Great. He muffled a sigh. "Thank you, officer, I'll tell her." They hung up. He sat back in the chair and closed his eyes, willing his mind to be still. *Call Artie.* He dialed; Artie answered.

"Hi, Artie—can't do anything tomorrow. Something happened," he said gravely.

"You sound upset. Is it something you want to tell me?"

"Yeah. It looks like Reed might have been in a roll-over accident."

"By himself? Where?"

"Kansas. He took off in his car two days ago." *Spit it out.* "They claim Reed, um, died."

Artie was quiet for a few seconds. "I'm sorry, Rudy." He paused. "Why did you say *they claim*?"

"The driver burned to death, but they can't prove it was Reed." He heard the front door rattle. "Artie, I'm at Reed's; Helen just came in. I'll call you when I know more."

"Okay, let me know if I can help."

"Thanks, Artie."

Helen came in, panting. "Those three blocks from the Los Feliz bus stop are becoming a challenge." In sweater, blouse, and sturdy trousers, she left her cane by the door.

She must be boiling. "Hi, Helen." He stood.

"Hello, Rudy. Thank you so much for doing this."

"Of course."

"Who was just on the phone?" She removed her sweater and draped it over a chair.

"I called Artie and told him what we know so far." He picked up the note from the desk.

"I'm glad you thought of that." She took the note, read the message, and placed it and her small purse by the phone. "Rudy, what about the party?"

"Mom postponed or canceled it—not sure which."

"That's a shame. I hope they reschedule it." She shuffled over to the rocker, sat on its flat pillow, and leaned back against the pad.

"Helen, how did it go with Amity?"

"Not well." Agatha reliably jumped up to settle on her lap. Helen stroked the cat. "It turned out to be an inopportune time to see her. She had a difficult week, but a nurse took me in for a brief visit. Amity didn't speak or seem to know me, so I told the nurse about Reed. Her supervisor said I would have to arrange a time with the doctor to tell Amity the news."

Rudy noticed that one of Helen's cheeks was moist. "Can I get you something?"

She sniffled, nodding to her small purse. "Seeing Amity breached my dam a bit." He handed her the pocketbook. She dabbed her eyes and face with a handkerchief, then worked up a self-effacing, tearful smile. "It has to come out eventually."

He waited a few seconds. "Helen, how did Reed's father react?"

"All Will could say was something to the effect of *that's too bad*, then he was angry about the car again. He ranted that Reed was always messing up, except he didn't say *messing*." She massaged the cat's ears. "He said he didn't want anything to do with the whole business."

Good. "That's good, right?" She nodded, then they were silent for a few moments.

"Helen, I called the Kansas officer a while ago. I hope you don't mind."

"Not at all." She dabbed one cheek. "What did he say?"

Rudy explained how the Kansas Highway Patrol had taken over the case from Keller.

"They found evidence? Of what?"

"They didn't even tell the Keller police."

Frowning, she cleared her throat. "We'll see what they come up with."

"I still think it's possible that somebody stole the car from him. Do you think I'm crazy to want more proof?"

"No, Rudy, of course not. I think you need to have it."

"Why don't you?"

"I reviewed the information and believe that Reed is dead."

No. "I don't see it. Can't see him all—" *Jesus, shut up.* "Sorry."

"It's okay." She paused. "Has anyone spoken to Si about Reed?"

"Mildred or Seth, I'd guess."

"Perhaps you could talk to him for a minute?"

What good would it do? "Okay, soon as I can." They sat for a short while with their thoughts. The phone rang; Rudy picked up the receiver. "Yes."

"This is lieutenant Mark Nielson, Kansas Highway Patrol," his voice formal. "Is this the residence of Mrs. Helen Crowley?"

"She's resting, lieutenant. How can I help you?"

"This concerns Reed McCool, her grandson. I spoke with his father, Will McCool. You must be Rudy Lanier. Mister McCool said he didn't know why you were involved with this. In fact, his words were, 'It's none of his business.'"

I'll be damned. "Just a moment." He pressed the phone into his thigh and relayed to Helen what the lieutenant said and what Will told them, including his comment about Rudy.

Helen pointed to herself, then her bedroom. Without her cane, she moved haltingly toward the hallway.

"Are you there, Mister Lanier?"

Hold your damn horses, cowboy. "I'm here. She'll be on in a moment. Lieutenant, do you know that Reed's father has convictions for domestic abuse?" Rudy heard Helen's phone click.

The trooper was silent for a few seconds. "Yes, and we know he's incarcerated now on different charges."

Give him more shit, Rudy. *Damn right.* "Wouldn't it be appropriate to ask *me* why I'm involved instead of taking the word of a repeated felon?"

"Lieutenant, this is Helen Crowley on the other line. Please understand that Mister Lanier serves as my personal assistant, and he was Reed's closest friend. I wouldn't be able to handle all of this without him."

"Yes, ma'am." He muffled the receiver and spoke aside to someone. *What happened to 'Sorry for your loss.'?*

"Ma'am, are you aware that we have taken over the investigation of the incident?"

"Yes."

"Mister McCool maintains that the car was stolen from behind his property."

"I assume that Officer Crandall informed you that my daughter, Reed's mother, recently signed the papers to transfer the car from her to Reed. He can hardly steal his own car. As for Will McCool, the truth is that he doesn't care, and this is none of *his* business. *I* am Reed's guardian."

"Nevertheless, the boy drove off without a driver's license in an unregistered vehicle."

"Yes, he shouldn't have been driving, but what troubles me, Lieutenant, is that my grandson is deceased—the rest is trivial. So, if you don't have anything else—"

"Excuse me, Mrs. Crowley, our investigation is centered around suspicion that your grandson was involved in drug trafficking. We found a stack of singed fifty-dollar bills and an amount of marijuana hidden in a warped metal box under the seat. We estimate the cash to be more than seven thousand dollars.

No wonder they took over—idiots. **Go on, Rudy.** "How much marijuana, officer?"

"I am not at liberty to say."

A joint or two. "You know what, maybe you should find Reed and ask *him* about it."

"What are you saying, Mister Lanier?"

"You heard me. You can't prove Reed was the driver—so maybe he's out there."

"Sir, I suggest you be more cooperative. There is no question that Mister McCool was the driver. The confirming forensics will take a while, but we have additional evidence. We found one of those souvenir metal coins in his remains. Enough of it is legible that we know what it says on one side—*REED THESPIS McCOOL.*"

No. Tears burgeoned in his eyes; he inhaled deeply. *Shit, you've been fooling yourself.*

"Mister Lanier? I need to continue with Mrs. Crowley," dismissively.

Wait. "I suggest you ask her about the money before you call in the FBI and Columbo."

There was silence again for several moments. "Ma'am?"

"Yes, the eight thousand dollars was a recent graduation gift from me."

"One moment, please." The lieutenant spoke aside again. "Mister Lanier, do you know where the deceased obtained the marijuana?"

Cold-blooded jerk. Don't let him haul Reed through the mud.

"Mister Lanier?"

"So, your supposition is that he was using his grandmother's gift for running drugs because you found the money, a couple joints, and his lucky coin?" Rudy's fervor increased with each clause. "Reed probably got the joints at school or from one of his father's scumbag friends," he flared. "Don't you have criminals to chase in goddam Kan—?"

"Lieutenant," Helen broke in, "I have a Western Union receipt for the money right here."

"Just a moment, ma'am."

Shit! Rudy slammed a fist on the desk.

"Mrs. Crowley, I hope you understand that we're just doing our job. The serial numbers are still readable on most of the bills; we can arrange to have most or all of the value replaced, but it takes a while. A copy of that receipt will help verify the owner."

"That's fine, lieutenant. After we hire a funeral home, I presume they need to call you."

"No, when forensics is finished, we'll have Officer Randle in Keller contact the morgue to arrange for the release of the remains."

Is that beneath you? "Don't you mean Officer *Crandall?*" Rudy goaded, more pressure mounting around his eyes.

"We don't appreciate your attitude, sir. Ma'am, here's our address…"

Rudy dropped the receiver carelessly on the phone's base. When Helen came back into the room, she found him with his head and arms on her desk like a punished grade-school kid. As Rudy tried to sort out what had just happened, a ramming pain struck his head and interfered with his thoughts. He began to sob quietly.

"Reed is a terrible loss for you, Rudy; you can't internalize it anymore. Just let it go," she said through her own tears, patting his shoulder.

His arms sticking to the desk, Rudy sobbed. He began to recall a montage of old events: He saw Reed jumping from a half-story window in the gym, then sprinting away from a vice-principal. Rudy watched him scale the fence to ruin Otis's "go-out-for-a-long-pass" trick, then Reed lobbed a heavy rock onto the firebreak to scare Garret. Rudy chuckled at the image of Reed shouting up at the apartments near the fountain.

You have something to take care of. Now. He sat up, wiping his face on a sleeve.

"How are you, Rudy?" Helen asked from her rocker, petting Agatha again.

He released a deep exhale. "Sorry I got so mad. That cop really pissed me off."

"Yes, he was unnecessarily terse, but you weren't very agreeable either."

"I don't care. It's all wrong. Reed was the one with the talent and creativity. So-called normal people treated him like shit. I hate that; I'll always hate it."

"Rudy, anger is to be expected now, but you can't let it get ahold of you."

Seth's echo. "I'll remember that." *After I get them.* "Helen, I need to go out for a while."

"Do you mind telling me where?"

"Just walking to clear my head. I won't be of much help to you anyway."

"You've already been a big help. If something comes up, I think

Mildred and Seth would give me a hand."

"Yes, or my dad. I'll tell them before I go." Another headache rolled over his brow.

"Are you sure you're feeling okay, Rudy?"

"I'm fine. He mustered a seam of a smile and left. Beginning to plan his retribution, Rudy left Helen's, then hurried over to his driveway. *Who's first?*

He checked Stew's water out of habit. The dog came over as Rudy topped off the bowl. Stew took a short, sloppy drink as if to show appreciation. Rudy distractedly rubbed Stew's ears…*their Sabbath was yesterday; they'll be watching the Series…*

The headache escalated as he took the steps up into the kitchen, where Katie and Mildred had dismantled the two turkey carcasses and were filling plastic bags for leftovers.

"They know for sure now," Rudy mumbled to them.

Katie turned. "Who? What do they know?"

"That Reed is dead."

"Well, of course he is. What are you talking about?"

"No matter," Mildred said in her calming voice. "Rudolph, y'r peaked. Feelin' sick?"

"No, Gramma, I'm fine. I'm sorry about your party."

"Pay no mind, we're jus' feelin' so bad about Reed—an' you. How's Helen?"

"She's okay." He turned to Katie. "But she's *not* ready for casseroles and all that crap."

"That's what we told people," as blunt as Rudy. "You aren't getting enough rest."

He exhaled noticeably. "Maybe you can stop nagging me about it."

Mildred spoke softly. "Rudolph, Catherine is just concerned."

Concerned about Katie. "I'm going to take a walk. Gramma, could you be available in case something comes up and Helen calls?"

"Yes, Rudolph, we'll be here."

"Thanks." He started for his room but turned back when Charlotte burst into the kitchen with a trophy and a smug face. She placed it firmly on the table in front of her mother.

"There, Mom," her eyes as sharp as glass shards. "Third place. I barely lost to a girl from Cal State who won first. You think I'll get that scholarship now?"

"Congratulations." She paused. "Shar, we need to tell you—"

"Figures—congratulations, then blah-blah-blah." She saw Rudy in the hallway. "What are *you* doing?" He didn't answer; Charlotte faced Katie and Mildred again. "Where is everybody? Why are you putting the turkey into freezer bags?"

His head drumming, Rudy winced. "Shar, she actually does have something to tell you."

"Charlotte," Katie used her most authoritative voice, "listen to—"

"Whatever it is, I don't want to hear it."

Katie took a step in Mildred's direction and pointed to a chair. "Alright, don't listen to me, but sit down, dammit, and listen to Gramma."

Charlotte looked puzzled and finally sat. Rudy went to his room and heard Mildred patiently begin to explain what had happened to Reed.

Just a short rest. He took an aspirin, then lay down long enough to slow the headache. *Sounds pretty still out there.* **Now get those bastards.** He got up, entered the bathroom, and splashed cold water on his face. The skin around his eye was still a sallow dark grey; the bruise on his cheek had retreated slightly toward the now plum-colored point of impact.

Hoping not to see anyone, Rudy walked through to the parlor, then stopped when he saw Si in the den. *You promised Helen.*

Rudy stepped down from the parlor. Si was sitting in his favorite spot on the couch. *Booger alert. Enough, Rudy.* He checked the TV. "Si, how are Matt and Festus doing?"

Si continued to watch. "Matt just slugged some guy who bothered Miss Kitty."

"Yeah, nobody fools with Matt Dillon." *Forgot to call Artie.* "I'll see you in a minute."

"Okay."

Rudy went out, then into the rumpus room and the office. He dialed; Artie answered.

"Hi, Artie." A long sigh. "Reed's, um, gone."

Artie briefly mumbled a prayer in Latin. "I'm sorry, Rudy. I am not sure what to say."

"Nothing to say," his tone bitter. *It's Artie—don't be a jerk.*

"Rudy, how are you handling all of this?"

"I'm pissed, mainly at Noah and Jonny."

"They disrespected Reed too much, but you can't do anything about that."

The hell I can't. "Artie, can you catch the morning bus tomorrow? Then we can talk about all this on the way in."

"We don't have classes tomorrow."

Crap. "Yeah, I forgot. Can you do it on Tuesday?

"Yes, I take the bus that day anyway."

"Good, see you then."

"Take care, Rudy."

Strategizing for his mission, Rudy returned to the den. "Si, I need to mute the TV a sec."

"*Gunsmoke*'s done."

As Rudy muted a commercial, Charlotte stepped down from the parlor, came closer, then looked right at him. "Rudy, I'm sorry about Reed."

Rudy thought her voice was stark, but outwardly, she didn't show emotion. Charlotte went out to the backyard. *God, I think she meant it. Or maybe it was just Gramma's suggestion.*

Si turned from the TV to Rudy. "Rudy, you were at Helen's."

"Yes, that's right."

"I like Helen." He looked back and forth between the TV screen and Rudy.

He's asking about her. "She's doing okay, Si."

"Good. Reed was my friend too," he said to a silent commercial. "We played Scrabble sometimes. He'd give me fifty points."

"Yes, he always liked you." *A lot more than I have.*

"In the army, you see what dead really is."

Jesus—didn't expect that. "Must have been hard."

"I didn't like it."

"I wouldn't either."

Si faced Rudy. "Are you my friend, Rudy?"

Damn, what do I say? "Um, you and Danny are my favorite uncles, Si."

"Good." Si faced the TV. "Here's another *Gunsmoke*. Want to watch?"

Gotta' go. Rudy tapped the mute button, then sighed. *Crap, a couple minutes won't kill you.* "Si, I can only watch for a few minutes, then I have to go somewhere."

"Okay, Rudy."

Rudy thought that Si watched the show's opening like it was his first time, mesmerized by Matt Dillon eternally outdrawing the bad guy on the main street of old Dodge City.

CHAPTER 16
Figments

*G*unsmoke didn't register at all for Rudy; he told Si he would see him later. Rudy crossed through the house, leaving his books in the dining room, then sat on the end of his bed. *Some quick research.* He got up and found a used but blank spiral notebook, then scooted the small stool up to his dog-eared Webster's and the nearly new encyclopedia. While reading, he wrote down several terms with brief definitions. He studied the information for a few minutes, then grabbed his cap and hurried into the kitchen with the notebook. *Almost two—get those pricks.*

Seth was the only one there, drying dishes. Stew had come in and was asleep on his blanket. "Rudy, I see you're in a hurry. Could we discuss something when you—"

"Sure, is after dinner okay? I'll be back before we eat," he said, already near the door.

Rudy rushed through the backyard, then ran determinedly down his dark shortcut between houses. He came out front, passed Helen's, then arrived at the corner in what seemed like seconds. He started south on La Plata Avenue on the straight shot down to Noah's.

He felt like he was sprinting on the sidewalk as fast as Reed could. With each tree that was close enough, Rudy jumped to smack a branch with his thin notebook. With each blow, his eyes clouded with more tears; his head drummed harder and harder.

Rudy came to Jonny's place, where he crossed the street, racewalking. *I'll be back for you, pissant.* Between the elementary school and the Italian market, he wiped his face and slowed to an ordinary pace. *Pull yourself together.* Rudy came to the first of the palm trees and slowed even more a half-block before the Korman's. He stopped at their front gate.

What is this, Rudy? *It's for you. Good god, talking to a figment.* He could see activity inside through their front window.

He opened the gate, went up the walk, then the three familiar steps to the small, screened porch. He entered, then knocked on the inside screen door, positive that Mrs. Korman would answer—part of his plan. She soon came to the door, and Rudy removed his cap. A medium-sized woman, Mrs. Korman wore an ordinary white blouse and a dark skirt. She had light-brown hair and was fairer than most Jews he had met.

"Why, Rudy, it has been a while since we've seen you." She didn't gawk at his injured face. "Please come in; I'll find Noah."

"Thank you, ma'am, but may I speak with Mister Korman out here, please?"

"Oh? Certainly. I will get him."

"Thank you, Mrs. Korman." As she left, Rudy could hear the stadium organ on TV as the Dodgers and Yankees played game five of the Series.

Rudy knew that Mr. Korman was well-educated but had chosen to persevere with his tailor shop out of loyalty to his grandfather's dream of a successful enterprise in America. He came to the door and opened it. About six-two and not as thin as Noah, he was in tailored heavy trousers and a short-sleeved white business shirt under black suspenders. Rudy observed that Mr. Korman, who sometimes wore a *yarmulke*, was not using one this time. He had neat dark hair, a thin beard, and wasn't as fair as his spouse. Mr. Korman's face maintained a sober demeanor, his dark brows slanting downward. Like Mrs. Korman, his eyes didn't dwell on Rudy's injuries.

"Hello, Rudy."

"Afternoon, Mister Korman." They remained at the doorway.

"Mrs. Korman said you prefer to talk out here. Let's sit and enjoy the breeze—if there is any." He came out, and Rudy put his hat back on.

"Still the Angels? I must inform you the game is about over—the Dodgers are far ahead."

"The Yankees will be tough back in the Bronx."

"Indeed. Well, I'm sure you didn't come to talk baseball."

They sat on two unpainted wooden chairs. It was late enough that the two palm trees out front gave them a little dappled shade.

"What can I do for you, Rudy?"

Rudy opened his notebook. *Here goes.* "Sir, I'm working on a cultural project for my World History class." *Not bad.* "I have a series of questions which are similar for parents of Jews, Muslims, and others—mostly about how their children adapt to predominantly Christian culture." He checked his notes. "In your case, the questions would concern the challenges of passing down Judaic religion and customs. Your answers would be anonymous, of course."

"Interesting. I know what a good student you are, Rudy. I want you to know how impressed I am with how you have just presented yourself. Please go on."

"Thank you, sir." Rudy tried not to glare at Noah's silhouette on the other side of the screen door. *Listen to this, asshole.* He turned back to Mr. Korman. "Sir, my first question relates to your Sabbath. Saturday, correct?"

"Not quite. *Shabbat* is from sunset on Friday to nightfall on Saturday."

Blew that one. He scribbled on the page. "Sorry, my mistake. And during that time children must follow the Commandments from the Torah?"

"They must follow them all the time. However, there are 613 Commandments; some not related to life here, like the protocols for shearing wool." He allowed himself a slit of a smile.

So far, so good. Rudy nodded to Mr. Korman's light humor, then jotted again. "What are the more common transgressions to the Commandments by some Jewish youth?"

Mr. Korman's face turned dour, then he spoke deliberately. "Anger, hatred, greed, self-centeredness, disloyalty, dishonesty, irreverence, and revenge—these and many more."

He's suspicious. "So, if a Jewish boy started a fight—"

"That would be a disgrace to his family."

"And if a Jewish boy took a non-Jewish girl to a movie?"

"We have to be flexible in the modern world, but the boy would need to describe the movie and get permission." Mr. Korman glanced at the screen door. "In this household, such a boy would be discouraged but not prohibited to go out with a girl who is not Jewish."

Yeah, he knows I'm up to something—get in one more. "And what if that boy chided another boy because of his race?"

"Shameful, of course." He frowned. "Rudy, I believe I have an idea of what you are doing here."

"Sir?" *I didn't even get to his cheating.*

Mr. Korman turned to the door. "Noah, you will come out here, now."

"Papa, look at his face. He's been fighting somebody." He opened the screen door.

Mr. Korman stood. "Rudy, is this true?"

"I was actually assaulted, sir."

"Was Noah involved?"

"No, sir."

Mr. Korman pointed to his chair. "Sit here, Noah."

In his patched weekend jeans and white t-shirt, Noah sat, glowering at Rudy.

Ignoring Noah, Rudy tried not to be intimidated by Mr. Korman, who peered down at the two of them.

"You have both been lying, which undermines the harmony of our homes and families. Rudy, you lied to me in order to make me aware of Noah's transgressions."

"Yes, sir." *And I'm not sorry.*

"Did you take me for a fool, Rudy?" he asked in an even tone.

Be honest. "No, sir. I thought you would see right through it."

Mr. Korman sighed, then glared at Noah before speaking to Rudy again. "So, my guess is that Noah threatened you."

"And Artie."

"I know Artie." He faced Noah. "So, he was the victim of your disgraceful prejudice?"

"I was just fooling around."

"Yes, as is your wont."

"What does that mean?"

"Ask Rudy. He is a student, regardless of what he did here today."

His face bleak, Rudy shook his head. "Sir, I lied to get revenge."

Mr. Korman sneered at Noah, then turned back to Rudy. "For threatening you?"

"No, sir. Noah treated my friend, Reed, disrespectfully because he was, um, different."

Noah chuffled at Rudy. "Different? Papa, Reed is completely nuts!"

Rudy shook his head solemnly. "No, Reed is dead."

Noah scoffed, then turned to his father. "Papa, Rudy's still fooling you—"

Mr. Korman pointed at his son. "Not another word." His face even more morose, he turned to Rudy. "I don't believe you would joke about such a—"

"Papa—"

"Silence." Mr. Korman eyed Rudy. "Reed was your close friend?"

"Yes, sir. He lived with his grandmother next door."

"I am sorry for your loss." He paused, his face grim. "Wasn't he the narrator of *The Little Matchgirl* in your final year of junior high?"

"Yes, he was in every play."

Mr. Korman turned to his pouting son. "I recall asking you for his name, Noah."

"Yes, sir."

"He was remarkable, far beyond his years. Rudy, is this why Reed was shunned?"

"That's part of it, sir."

"Ignorance, at its worst. If I may ask, how did he pass on?" Mr. Korman closed his eyes before Rudy began his answer.

He exhaled audibly. "Reed took his mother's car, drove off, and made it only to Kansas." Rudy paused when he felt pressure around his eyes again. "A tire blew out…"

After Rudy finished, Mr. Korman opened his eyes. "And where was he going, Rudy?"

"New York—Broadway, I think," sniffling a little.

Ashen, Mr. Korman turned to Noah. "Although you played no part in this horrible accident, you have dishonored yourself and our family." He paused. "You will now be studying the Torah at synagogue on both Wednesdays and Saturdays, and I will test you. You will do *all* of your homework here, and I will test you. No extra school activities for now; you will take the bus both ways, and I will monitor you. You will not speak to Rudy or Artie unless they speak to you first. Go inside now and accurately report everything that has transpired here to your mother."

"Yes, sir," Noah left, trying not to cry.

Mr. Korman waited for him to go. "Rudy, as you are obviously in mourning, I have decided not to bother your parents. I know this is not typical behavior for you, but I hope you examine your unfortunate decisions. Retribution will not serve you well in the long run."

"Yes, sir." *But he knows Noah deserved it. One down, one to go.*

"Do you have someone you can talk to about this?"

"I do, sir." Rudy stood.

"Good. One last thing, unrelated." Mister Korman left a longer pause. "Rudy, where did you pick up words like *Torah* and *Judaic*?"

"Just a little research."

"Of course." He paused again. "My best to the boy's grandmother."

"Thank you, sir." Rudy walked out the front gate and started for Jonny's house. **Isn't that enough, Rudy?** *No, it isn't.* He began to run again; there were only palm trees on this block, so he smacked his leg with the notebook as he ran, fueling his anger again. He slowed down at the Italian market; their clock showed it was just after four. *It's not too late—just right.* He disposed of the notebook in a trash can outside of the grocery. All of the exercise was catching up to him, so he jogged, then walked, ruminating over his plan for Jonny.

Rudy knew that Jonny's mother went regularly to some sort of club meeting on Sunday afternoons, then returned for dinner. Jonny would probably be watching TV. Rudy jogged past the school, resting on and off until he came to Jonny's park-like yard in about ten minutes. As Rudy expected, his mother's car was not in the garage.

Activating his simple plan, Rudy entered and crossed the yard, then skipped stairs up to a screened front porch at least three times larger than the Korman's. Crowded with a wet bar, two leather couches, three stuffed chairs, and a porch swing, it was all covered with heavy plastic for the imminent cooler months.

Rudy pressed the doorbell and waited. Instead of the Danish woman who had been there for years, a middle-aged Mexican woman in an apron came to the door.

"How I can help you, sir?" with a negligible accent.

Beware of these people, lady. "Hi, I'm a friend of Jonny's. May I see him, please?"

"Yes, I call him."

Rudy glared at their superfluous cherub doorknocker, then he heard someone approaching the door from inside. *Here's the little prick.*

Jonny came to the door in ironed Bermuda shorts, a new summer shirt, and deck shoes without socks. His hair was greased flat on his scalp. *Like he's ten and his mother dressed him.*

"What's up, Jonny?"

"I'm watching *The Snowball Express*. Want to watch?"

Disney lives on. "No, I don't think so."

"All you like is *M*A*S*H* and *Twilight Zone*. I can't stand either one."

You don't say. "Yeah. I thought you might want to play some golf or croquet."

"Okay, croquet; I'm pretty good at that."

No, you suck. "I'll wait in back." Rudy went out past the mature, beginning-to-yellow weeping willow that Mr. Jojima always left with a precise upside-down bowl cut. He came to the expansive lawn where Jonny's father once put in a short three-par hole, occasionally used now by guys who patronized Jonny in order to play.

Rudy pulled the croquet box from a shed and took out the green-striped mallet. *When he comes out, piss him off with this. Then you—*

Then you what, Rudy?

He hated you. I'll kick his ass.

Like Harry would?

Moisture welled up in Rudy's eyes. *Okay, okay.* He heard the Wilsons' rear screen door shut. As in a track-and-field hammer-throw, Rudy circled the mallet in the air. Then, grunting out loud as if it were heavy, he launched it over the back garden wall into the alley. Through his tears, he saw Jonny halfway across the lawn. Rudy wiped his eyes with a forearm.

"What do you think you're doing, Rudy?"

"Subverting this tedious diversion."

"Don't talk like that. If you mean you don't want to play—it was your idea. You crying?"

Rudy yanked the yellow mallet from the box.

"Don't do it again, Rudy. Go home, or I'll get the housekeeper."

Grimacing from a stabbing headache, Rudy wiped his face with his shirttail.

"Go away, Rudy. You're acting crazy. I'm calling my mom."

Rudy threw the mallet, but this time it cracked against the wall. "Crazy like Mucholoco?" Rudy pulled out the red mallet. "You and Noah will never call him that again."

"We will if we want to," Jonny said, more whiny than defiant.

Rudy approached him, gripping the mallet over his shoulder like a baseball player ready to swing.

Jonny cowered, an open hand straight out. "Okay, okay. I won't call him that."

"I know you won't." He flung the mallet away. "Reed is dead."

"What? This is one of your dumb tricks—that's fake crying."

"He was in a car accident; it caught fire. He's dead."

"I don't believe you."

Yes, you do. "All that's left of Reed is black cinders and bone fragments." *Jesus, Rudy.*

"Stop it! You're lying," between sobs. "I'm telling my mom," he blubbered, then ran for the house.

Rudy started out to the front yard; his headache was worse. *Reed?* He kept walking while he waited for an answer. *Well?* He waited again. *You can't make a figment talk, idiot.* He went out the front gate and turned up La Plata Avenue.

Reed would say what I did to Jonny was sick. He'd say those two had nothing to do with it. Rudy walked faster, starting to cry again. *I'm the one who could've convinced him to get rid of those crappy tires.* His face wet with tears, Rudy covered two more blocks. *If I'd kept my mouth shut about his plan, maybe he'd be signing up for a class now.* Rudy inhaled and exhaled deeply. *He would've eventually pulled off at least one of his dreams. If you don't believe that, then you're just another asshole who thought he was a freak.*

The closer Rudy came to his house, the more his head throbbed in sync with his heart. At the corner of Ontario Place and La Plata, Rudy realized that he would be in time for dinner. *Don't want to see any of them. Check on Helen.*

Rudy sniffled, wiped his face again, then walked up to Helen's and knocked. She came to the door. "Rudy, you look exhausted again. Have you been crying?" They went in but Helen made no move to sit down, and neither did Rudy.

"I'm okay. Did you have to call my house for anything?"

"No, everything's fine." Agatha circled her legs.

"Good. I was, uh, taking care of a couple things," shrinking away from her.

"What does that mean, Rudy?"

She knows I screwed up. "Nobody got hurt."

"Was your anger involved?"

"Yes," his face downcast.

"Do you think this is the time to talk about it?"

"No, I just wanted to see if you were okay."

"I appreciate that. We can talk tomorrow."

"I'll be over after I get up if it's okay. We don't have school—teachers' workshops."

"Fine, Rudy—see you in the morning. Get a good sleep."

He left Helen's for his house and, for once, walked in the front door. *Can't handle them all at the same time.* From the parlor, Rudy noticed Si in the den, but Si didn't see him. *The Talking Heads* weren't blasting from Charlotte's room, so he thought she was gone. Rudy came to the kitchen, where Seth and Larry were eating their dinner while Katie stared at her plate listlessly. To Rudy, the table was a nightmarish collage of repulsive food: turkey casserole, succotash, scalloped potatoes, and some sort of dark bread. Katie had a fresh highball in her hand.

How far gone? "I was at Helen's." He stood behind a chair, ready to leave. Katie tried to zero in on Rudy, but she couldn't maintain her gaze. She rested her other hand on a Manila folder near her plate. Seth and Larry picked at their dinner, occasionally taking a glimpse of Rudy.

Katie tried again to focus on Rudy. "The fridge'z stuffed wi' turkey," she slurred. "Make y'rself a sandwich or eat with us. All y'r favorites. Ha!"

He shook his head. *At least four sheets—no wonder Gramma's gone.*

Katie sipped her drink. "Jonny's mother called. What'd ya' do to 'im?"

Seth and Larry sat still, waiting on Rudy.

"What did his mother say?"

"That ya' terrified her li'l brat." This time Katie took a full swallow of her drink.

Rudy sat on the edge of a chair. "Yeah, I guess that's what I did," cringing at the succotash right in front of him.

"Godssake, Rudy." Katie pushed away her untouched dinner.

"He and Noah treated Reed like a freak," he said in a matter-of-fact tone.

"Ya' went ta' Noah's too?"

Rudy nodded. "Let's just say I helped Noah get into some trouble with his dad, but Mister Korman said he won't be calling you."

"Good. So, how'd ya' upset Jonny?" Katie's eyelids sagged. Seth waited for Rudy's reply; Larry stared blankly at his plate.

"I was ready to beat the crap out of him, but I remembered something Reed said."

"So, what'n hell'd ya' do?" Katie took another drink.

"I didn't touch Jonny, but I pissed him off, then I made up a gory description of Reed's remains. He started bawling."

Seth calmly put his fork down. "So, you still hurt Jonny," he stated.

"Yes." *And myself—I get it, Seth.*

Katie put down her glass. "Anyway, Mizzus Wilson wants a 'pology, but her head's up her snooty a—" Katie stopped. "Since ya' didn't actually hurt 'im, ya' don't hafta' 'pologize."

Rudy shook his head. "No, it was like scaring some little kid. I can't stand Jonny, but I'll apologize to him."

Katie frowned; her shoulders briefly shuddered. "An' Noah?"

"No, I might have done that jerk a favor."

"Y'r not makin' any sense. Maybe talk to Seth s'more."

Rudy faced Seth. "No disrespect, but I'll be talking to Helen about this."

Katie had picked up her drink again. "Jus' a damn minute, she's not—"

"Catherine," Seth interrupted, "Rudy's right. If they want to involve somebody else, they know I'm available."

Katie shrugged and took another swallow. "I don't like it."

Larry got up. "Excuse me." He took his plate to the sink, then went out the kitchen door.

"Pissed again—too damn bad," Katie said, opened the folder, then took out a sheet of paper. She flicked it with a finger. "Helen's gonna need a mortician for whatever's left of him."

"Jesus, Mom, that's as bad as what I said to Jonny."

"I didn't say nothin'. These'r numbers for every boneyard not two hunnerd miles from Killer, Kansas," she boasted, then gave the paper to Rudy.

He walked away with it. *Thanks for nothing.*

CHAPTER 17

Rudy's Fan

Rudy retreated to his room and stayed up Sunday night reading *Of Mice and Men*, but the story kept deflecting him to his relationship with Si. It was nearly two a.m. when he came to the book's fatal conclusion. *Jesus,* ***that*** *was in the movie?* He fell into an uneasy sleep, then a dream. Si was staring out of the parlor's picture window. Rudy, like George, sneaked up close with a pistol aimed at Si's head. Dream-Rudy looked at his weapon. *Like a stupid western—always put the horse out of its misery—he can't do it. God, now he's aiming at Garret...* The alarm had been buzzing before Rudy finally poked the button. *Enough of that crap.*

He dozed in and out, then got up before eight-thirty and put on school clothes although it was a day off. A little dizzy, he lay on the bed again, focusing on the light, its plain fixture opaque like the city streetlights. He felt a nuance of the void he had experienced so many times.

Rudy sat right up, his head pulsing. He found Katie's mortuary list in the covers and began to read: *Pioneers Eternal Haven; Prairie Angels Rest—awful.* He stuffed the paper carelessly into a pocket. *First thing—talk to Helen.*

He walked into his bathroom, took care of essentials, then checked his black eye. It had faded a little more, but the bruise on his cheek was about the same. *To hell with the makeup.* He smelled bacon frying, then entered the kitchen, where his mother and grandmother had served an "old-fashioned breakfast to soothe the soul," one of Mildred's family institutions. Larry, Si, and Seth had started in on the bacon, eggs, hash-browns, orange juice, and coffee while Katie and Mildred still fussed with the stove and oven. Charlotte was gone.

"Morning," Rudy mumbled. Larry and Seth quietly returned the greeting. *They think Mom and I will go at it again. Not if I can help it.* Rudy took the chair next to his father. Si, preoccupied with his full plate of food, was seated on Larry's other side. *Why hasn't Si left?*

Katie sat at the table. "Nice of you to join us, Rudy. Since you don't have school, Mom wanted to hold up breakfast for a while—now maybe you'll eat something."

Cold-sober—watch out. "Haven't been very hungry."

"Heartburn again?" Katie glanced at Seth, took a sip of coffee, then got up to go to the stove. She returned right away to put the gravy boat in the middle of the table. Katie sat down as Mildred placed a ceramic mixing bowl in front of Rudy; it was full of hot biscuits, the two on top thicker and larger than the rest.

Mildred had stayed near Rudy. "Rudolph, even with all that's been goin' on, I never imagined the day when you'd pass up one a' my biscuits." She moved over to sit by Katie.

Good ol' Gramma. "I don't think that day's here yet, Gramma." Rudy took one of the two extra-large biscuits, sliced it to work like a sandwich, then he spread on margarine and homemade strawberry jam. He put the halves together and chomped out a cartoonish half-moon bite. "Real good, Gramma." *Pass them.* "Sorry, who wants a biscuit?"

Rudy picked up the heavy bowl and held it toward Larry. "Dad?" His father declined with a slight headshake and passed the bowl. Rudy watched Si take the other large biscuit. He got up to hand the bowl across the table, revealing the red cloth napkin on his chest—a finger-painting of yolk and juice. *Soon to be mixed with crumbs and brown gravy. Stop, Rudy.*

Other than snippets of praise for the food, there was scant conversation as Rudy served himself some bacon, potatoes, and juice. He was eating when the phone rang.

Katie got up and answered. "We're fine, Helen." Pause. "You?" Pause. "That's good. Rudy's up and eating breakfast. He'll be over when he's finished." Pause. "You're welcome."

How cordial. Already standing, Rudy pushed in the chair, drank the juice, then took the rest of the biscuit from his plate. "I'll be going. Thanks." He carried his dishes to the sink.

Katie had been watching him. "Rudy, you didn't eat."

He showed her the biscuit. "Dessert." Rudy went out into the drab sunlight of another smog-obscured day. The biscuit was nearly eaten by the time he knocked on Helen's door.

"Good morning, Rudy. So, you didn't have time to finish your breakfast?"

He popped in the last hunk of biscuit. "Just finished." He entered behind her.

"You still look pretty tired, Rudy."

"I got some sleep."

"Okay. I'm going to refresh my coffee." She picked up her cup and started slowly for the kitchen. "Something for you?"

"I'll get myself some water." He went in to the sink. As he filled a glass, Helen faced him. "Rudy, I've made some decisions on how to proceed with Reed's remains, but I need your advice on one issue."

"Sure." *What advice could she need from me?*

They went back in and placed their beverages on her cork coffee-table coasters. She sat in her rocker, Rudy on the settee, holding an aspirin from his tin. He took it with the water.

Helen sipped some coffee. "Headache, Rudy?"

And ass-ache. "Not bad, barely worth an aspirin."

Agatha jumped onto Helen's lap. "Rudy, here's where we are with arrangements, nothing cast in stone—hm, an unfortunate image." She told him that she called the nurse about Amity; she hadn't improved. Helen had decided that Reed would consider any formal service or burial as foolishness, and she would mostly follow her own end-of-life instructions. She told him that Reed's remains would be cremated, and there would be no formal service. Helen explained that she couldn't abide the presence of shirttail relatives offering hypocritical sympathy, and Will McCool wouldn't come anyway.

She certainly didn't need my two cents on that. Give her Mom's list. He took out the wrinkled paper and handed it over. "From my mom—a list of, um, mortuaries back there."

"Please thank Katie for me. I spoke with Sergeant Crandall—such a kind man. He's going to arrange things with the morgue as soon as I give him the name of the mortuary. He offered a couple of suggestions, including the only one in Keller." She skimmed the typed information on the crumpled page. "My, these places sound so pretentious."

"And probably expensive." He drank some water.

"I think I'll stay with Keller Mortuary. It's not on Katie's list. Will she be upset?"

None of her business. "If she asks, I'll tell her you already made your choice." He paused. "It must be difficult for you to decide all this."

"I suppose, but it keeps me from being too idle. Rudy, I was cavalier with the truth yesterday in order to get that state patrol officer to come to the point. I don't expect you to sit over here all the time like a secretary."

Tactful—things are handled. "Okay, whenever you need me, Helen." He cleared his throat. "I think I should tell you about yesterday afternoon—if you feel up to it."

"Of course. I've been concerned about you." She reached for her coffee again.

"I'm doing okay." He sighed, then summed up his revenge for Noah and the interactions with Mr. Korman. "…and he gave me some advice about retribution. He sent his regards to you."

"That's very nice of him." She paused. "That wasn't so bad; it sounds like you learned something."

Maybe. "But then I went to Jonny's…Reed kept me from harming him, although I still scared Jonny intentionally…finally, the obvious dawned on me—those two had nothing to do with Reed's death." A couple of tears on his face, he lowered his head, wiping his eyes with a forearm. "Sorry, Helen. I know I disappointed you."

Helen got up and held his shoulder for a few moments. "No, Rudy. Dealing with death is always a live-and-learn situation." She sat again. "Do you feel up to answering a question?"

"Yeah." Rudy sniffled and drank more water.

"You said Reed kept you from physically harming Jonny. What did you mean by that?"

"At first, it was like hearing his voice, but I was just recalling his advice, like a conscience. Sounds nuts, but it felt real."

"I don't think it's nuts when you remember good advice."

"Last night, I tried to clear my mind by finishing the Steinbeck book. Didn't work."

"I've had second thoughts about recommending it because of the violence at the end—simultaneous with Reed's horrid death."

"No, it's okay." Rudy sighed. "I compared George's treatment of Lennie with how I treat Si, which I think you expected."

She nodded. "Do you think you would be ashamed of Lennie?"

"No, I'd probably want to help him."

"But not Si?"

"How? He doesn't know or care that he's stuck back in time. Si does what he does; he knows what he knows, which is a lot, but he doesn't learn anything new. I've tried."

"I don't believe all of that is completely true. We know how much he values friendships; as for the rest of it, there might be more going on with him than meets the eye. Rudy, we can try to accept Si and his faults as unconditionally as he accepts ours."

"Do you think he does that consciously?"

"I don't know, but does it matter?"

"I guess not. I've been avoiding him again. I can give it another try."

"Good, Rudy." The antique clock chimed once. "Ten-thirty; I didn't think we had been talking so long. If you wish, we can pick up where we left off later." Helen covered a chuckle with one hand. "You can also tell me if it seems like I have been spouting a lot of claptrap."

"Of course not." *Wait, she wanted to ask me something.* "Helen, you said there was a decision you still had to make, and you wanted to talk to me about it."

"My goodness, thank you for reminding me—Reed's ashes. When I speak to the mortuary today, I'll ask if their cremation services include shipping—what a blunt way to put it. I thought you might have an idea about dispersing his ashes, not that Reed would necessarily care. If you're willing, I'd like you to be in charge. Nothing formal at all, just a few people who actually knew him—if they want to come."

Rudy didn't answer right away. *Yeah, I know just the place.* "I have an idea, but I should think about it. Could we discuss it tomorrow?"

"That's fine; I know you'll think of something appropriate."

"Helen, you've done all this more than once, haven't you?" *Damn, Rudy.* "Sorry, I don't know why I said that."

"Don't worry, dear. By the time you're my age, this sort of thing is old hat, but I don't believe the falderal ever has much to do with the person you've lost. When it comes right down to it, it's between you and how you remember him or her, warts and all."

Man. Rudy inhaled and exhaled heavily. "Yeah, I'll remember how he was before we dealt with Earl's brother the other night." Rudy sniffled a little. "Reed was so excited about his work and his plans, and he told me about a concept he learned from you—mindfulness. He was always mindful of everything around us."

"Bless his heart." Her eyes moistened a little; Agatha jumped down.

"When I told Reed some things he didn't know about Si, he got all enthused about the three of us collaborating on a memoir about Si in Korea. He persisted, but I didn't want anything to do with it—crappy thing to do. If I had shown interest, maybe he would've thought twice—"

"No, Rudy."

Another tear coursed down his face. "I also could have talked him out of—"

"Rudy," she interrupted again. "If you blame yourself for Reed's death, you're distorting the truth. It *wasn't* your fault."

"It doesn't seem that simple." He wiped his face on his sleeve. "I'll think about it some more." His headache throbbed in time with his pulse again. "I guess I'll take off. Just call if you need anything. Thanks, Helen."

"Of course, I'll see you tomorrow."

After his departure, Rudy stopped outside. *Can't go home like this. Need a break from all of it anyway.* He walked from La Plata all the way past Parkview to El Rancho, more than two miles away. From a corner, he saw the Krenshaws' old place, more dilapidated than ever, like much of the neighborhood. His Uncle Nick was working out front on an old car, his torso deep into the engine. *Shit, he'll see me.* Rudy turned around and started back for La Plata, distracting himself by watching what kids were up to on their bonus day off.

Rudy came to Ontario Place but stopped before his house. *Not yet.* He took an aspirin dry, then watched a Steller's blue jay pilfer a peanut-in-the-shell from a bowl Helen always left on her porch. *Helen's old pal. Just go.*

He ambled up the driveway, saw that Charlotte's car was still gone, then Rudy petted Stew and took care of his water. In the kitchen, he looked at the clock; it was almost noon. Katie was washing the breakfast dishes, her hands immersed in the left basin; her highball glass was down to ice. Dirty pots and pans were stacked next to the sink; she put a glass in the drying rack.

"Hi, Mom."

"Hi. After that late breakfast, I told them it's make-your-own turkey sandwich for lunch—I'm behind on my accounts again. Get a dishtowel and dry, except the pots."

Two sheets? He grabbed a towel. "Mom, even Gramma uses the dishwasher."

"I can do them faster by hand."

Keep it light. He had already started on the glasses. "Where is everyone?"

"I told Mom and Seth to take a rest, your dad's on a service call, and Shar's off at five. She took a minimum-wage job scooping ice cream."

"Really." He dried the last cup, then started on the dishes and bowls.

"By the way," she said casually, "Si took two vacation days in case there's something for Reed soon. I told him probably not—that he should save the days, but he's still here."

"Right, it might be a week. Helen asked me to be in charge of spreading Reed's ashes."

She bunched some rinsed utensils and put them in the drying rack. "So, no funeral. Well, it *is* Helen, after all."

Jesus. After he dried the last plate, he started on the silverware.

His mother was scouring a pot. "Anyway, Si will be disappointed."

"Yeah." *Maybe he won't have to be.* He finished the spoons as she rinsed a frying pan.

"Lots of sandwich makings." She pointed at the fridge.

"I'm okay. I'll go talk to Si." He dropped the towel onto a small pile of wash.

"See how fast that was?" Katie turned to him. "Cheer up, Rudy."

*Crap, **you** cheer up.* He walked out, then through the dining room. *Si sure as hell won't tell me to cheer up.* Rudy stepped down from the parlor into the den, where Si was in his regular spot on the couch, watching TV. *Ignore whatever slop is on him.* Rudy sat in a recliner. "Hi, Si."

"Hi, Rudy." Si was slicked-up to his maximum, as if daring any dirty object to defile his outfit. His face was closely shaved, he had tucked a short-sleeve pastel-yellow business shirt into dark slacks; his old black loafers had a military spit-shine. He was watching a *Bonanza* rerun.

"Look at you, Si; you have a date?" *Don't be a jerk.*

"I'm ready for the funeral, just in case." He kept his eyes on Little Joe.

"Si, there's not going to be a funeral, exactly."

"Oh. Katie didn't know."

"Some of us will get together later to disperse his ashes."

Si faced Rudy. "If it's tomorrow, I have another vacation day."

"It might be a week or so from now. Si, I can try to arrange it for a weekend so you can be here when we spread the ashes."

"You could call me, and I could drive back?"

"Sure, that's how we'll do it. Maybe next weekend."

"Okay. I can drive home after lunch today and work my shift tomorrow morning."

"Right, and I'll call you during the week."

"Okay." Si watched Little Joe flirting with a woman, but a bank commercial came on. "Rudy, I read your story." Si picked up the thin manuscript and gave it to Rudy.

"Already?" *Don't sound so surprised.*

"I had to look up some words, but I liked it."

"I'm glad, Si."

"Can I read the next chapter?"

"It was a story, Si, not a chapter."

"Oh. I wanted to read more about Bobtail, but can I read another story?"

"Sure, Si, I'll get one before you leave."

"Thanks. I think you'll be a writer, Rudy."

"I doubt it, Si. I just like to write sometimes."

Si turned to the TV. "It's back on. Want to watch?"

"Sure."

"Rudy, can you get the story for me in case I don't see you later on?"

Brother. "Okay, how about one that happens in L.A.?"

"Yes, that one."

"Okay, I'll get it."

Rudy went to his room, switched manuscripts, and brought the story to Si. Rudy paid attention to Hoss for a few minutes, then considered his tentative plans for Reed's ashes.

Part III:
THE VOID

CHAPTER 18
Libby

Rudy called Helen on Monday evening to arrange a short visit before he caught the bus on Tuesday morning. Wearing his windbreaker for the unusually damp and chilly morning, Rudy knocked at Helen's door. He took an aspirin as she called back to him.

He went in with his books, then they sat at the breakfast nook. Rudy explained his proposal for a night hike in Griffith Park to disperse Reed's ashes.

"That sounds very appropriate to me, Rudy. When would it be?"

"Maybe next Sunday evening. We need some time to contact people and make sure Sunday works. I also want to set it up around Si's availability—he really wants to go."

She sipped some tea. "Very considerate, Rudy."

Yeah, always looking out for Si. "What about the ashes getting here?"

"Yes, Sergeant Crandall called this morning. The forensics came out as expected."

It's official. "Man." He pursed his lips.

"Yes, the finality of it is a bit stunning." Her fingers formed a tent again as she released a long breath. "The mortuary has permission to send the ashes and a few personal effects by priority mail; the package is supposed to arrive by Thursday—Friday at the latest."

"That works." *Not so fast.* "Helen, there's a drawback to my brilliant plan. This hike won't be a casual walk. It would exclude—"

"The ol' grey mare?" she asked with a grin. "Why not have everyone meet here before the hike for coffee or cocoa?"

"Yes." Rudy brightened. "That would make you part of the whole thing."

"What about Seth and Mildred?"

"I'll be lucky to keep up with Seth on the hike. Gramma only does level walks—"

"I think she will prefer to help me here anyway. I'll call her."

Is this fair to them? "Helen, we could just do this somewhere else. Maybe drive out to—"

"No, no, no; I think it's perfect. Don't fret, Rudy. Perhaps you could write the whole experience into a story for Mildred and me."

Oh sure. "Maybe so."

"Who else do you think might come besides you, Seth, and Si?"

"Dad, I hope, and probably Artie and Mister Collison. Maybe a couple more, but less than ten is probably about right."

"I agree. I did think of someone last night who would probably want to be included—Reed's friend, Diana—such a fascinating person."

"I'm sure she is. Reed was planning to have me meet her."

"I should have told her sooner about Reed's death. I'll make the contact right away; I know the receptionist at their clinic."

"That's, um, about seven people. Should we go ahead then, maybe six-thirty?"

"Yes, I have plenty of room for a group that size—it's becoming a small wake. Maybe we can cheer it up a little with Halloween dessert."

"Okay, sounds good." *And a bit dark. No, Reed would think it was great.* "I guess we can just tell them what we're doing, the time and place. If that works for most of them, we'll let people know after it's more settled, and tell them what to bring." *Damn headache is hanging on.*

"Preparing for Sunday will be a welcome project for me, and you be sure to ask for help when you need it."

"Okay, if you promise to do the same."

After he left Helen's, Rudy got on the high school bus five minutes early. There were about a dozen or so students there, mostly morning-subdued tenth-graders; he again sat in an empty seat about halfway back. Their regular driver, Mrs. Daley, a gaunt middle-aged woman who always wore a floppy denim hat from the '60s, had returned from surgery. After picking up about ten more students at the Italian market, she drove down La Plata to the stop at Freddy's Freeze.

Rudy looked out to see a small crowd, including Noah in a Truman Toros lettermen's jacket, its red and black colors washed out, and its varsity *T* missing. The coat was too short and loose, as if its previous owner was a squat, 230-pound lineman. *He'll take shit for that.* Noah was also violating other varsity norms: waiting at a bus stop instead of driving or riding to school, wearing his game sneakers with slacks that rippled in the light breeze, and most egregious of all, he was talking to Artie. There were several more Mexican students in a group nearby, not far from a larger gathering of mostly White kids. Two of them scuffled around, squealing and grab-assing as they likely did back in seventh grade.

The bus stopped; Rudy saw Noah pointing at Artie, who turned away with a smirk. Noah followed the crowd to the bus; Artie was four kids behind him in line. The students walked in sedately; a few tried to sleep. Noah took an aisle seat five rows behind the driver as Artie came to the top of the stairs. Noah stretched one of his spindly legs across the aisle, but Artie moved right through it, twisting Noah's knee a little.

"That hurt, beaner." Noah turned to the driver. "You see that?"

"I saw and heard *you*, Korman." Most of her riders paid no attention.

Artie sat with Rudy, their books between them on the seat. "He's really angry, Rudy."

"Yeah, I got him in trouble with his father."

Noah got up, started back, then took the open seat right ahead of Rudy and Artie. No books in hand, Noah sat, facing front. He turned to Artie when the bus started off. "Dodgers tie it up today," he said, as if Artie cared about the game and was sitting alone.

Rudy spoke toward his window. "Headline—Reggie creams Dodgers. Yankees in six."

Noah checked Mrs. Daley, then sneered at Rudy. "You don't know crap, Rudolph."

Prick. "You're not supposed to talk to us."

"Shit, I'll do more than that," keeping his voice down.

Rudy puffed out his scorn for Noah. "So, where's your little chauffeur and his mommy's car?" His words were still muted. "Oh, and nice coat. What will the varsity think?"

"Shut up. I got news for you," jeering. "Jonny's mother said your crazy pal wasn't in an accident, that he probably killed himself," with a smug chuckle.

Bastard. Easy, Rudy. "First, Jonny's mother doesn't know shit from Shinola," he said evenly. "And you can shut the hell up about Reed," gritting his teeth. *Calm—assess.*

"You can scare Jonny, gramma's boy, but I'm going to kick your fat ass." Noah turned to Artie. "You too, wetback, just for the hell of it—before homeroom at the bench."

"You forgot I'm not afraid of you, *cabrón?*" Artie was just loud enough for Noah to hear.

"Shit, you wussies won't even show up." Noah turned forward, sulking.

Mrs. Daley was checking Noah on and off as Rudy began murmuring to Artie.

Noah heard them, then turned back after a few more seconds. "Say it to *me*, chicken-shits," he dared over the background chatter on the bus.

"Alright, that's your warning, Korman," Daley scolded through her rearview mirror.

"Yeah, you better contain your cavernous oral cavity." Rudy's voice was still low.

Noah seethed. "That bullshit again?" he said out of the side of his mouth.

Rudy looked at Artie. "He didn't understand because his English sucks. Maybe his Spanish has improved."

"I doubt it. *Noah, si su boca gorda está cerrada, no entran las moscas.*" He spoke deliberately, pantomiming some of the words.

"Monkey," Noah snarled, "speak English."

"*Sí, chango.* If your fat mouth is closed, the flies won't go in."

Noah pivoted around, his knees on the seat. "Faggots!" He cocked his lanky right arm and tried to deliver a punch, but Artie and Rudy together deflected his fist and pushed it away.

Mrs. Daley's eyes daggered at Noah in the rearview mirror. "Okay, Korman, that's it—right here behind me." She always reserved the four spots in the first row for rowdy students, mostly for her routes with younger kids.

"I was just joking around," Noah whined. He walked forward, razzed by some kids who were awake, which roused a few more to join in the fun as Noah sat down.

"Knock it off, or you join him," Daley said tersely; they gradually settled.

Rudy turned to Artie. "He'll be on report; his dad will come unglued." Rudy tried to ignore a steady headache that had begun during the scuffle. He leaned his head on the window and stared at the mostly idle shops and homes on Garner Drive. *Each store, each house, each car, and in here—all separate worlds. Death will change all of them. Jesus, Rudy.* He straightened up.

"Artie, we decided what to do for Reed." Rudy began a hushed explanation of the hike.

Artie listened, then spoke quietly. "So, it's a service with his ashes?"

"In a way, but not really a service." Rudy revealed more of the plan. "…I'll let you know later if there's anything else you need to bring."

"Sunday night could be a problem; I don't know if my father will let me go."

"It wouldn't be right without you. Your mom knew Reed; see if she can help."

"Yes, I'll ask her."

"One more thing. Instead of walking home on Thursday, could we take the bus? I'd like you to help me with something before it gets dark."

"Why not tomorrow?"

The damn trays. "I'm helping my dad."

"Thursday is better anyway. What do you need help with?"

Rudy glanced at a guy two seats behind them. "I'd rather not talk about it now."

Artie raised his brows. "Okay, Thursday, then. Meet at your house?"

"No, at the field. If it's okay, ride your bike over as soon as you get home."

"Are you going to walk over there?"

"More or less. Thanks, Artie."

Rudy and Artie got off the bus and smirked when they saw Mrs. Daley and a vice-principal, squabbling with Noah at the curb. The boys started off for homeroom, and when they approached the entrance, Rudy saw that Libby was there in a seasonal pastel-orange blouse that highlighted her red hair. *Man, she looks great. She's looking right at us. What's going on?*

As they came closer, she smiled at both of them. "Artie, can I talk to Rudy for a second?"

"Sure, Libby. See you in math." Artie grinned slightly at Rudy, then went in.

Funny, Artie. Rudy moved to the side of the hallway with her.

Her fair, pleasant countenance turned grave. "Rudy, I heard about Reed. All I can say is that I'm very sorry. You two were close."

How does she know that? "Um, thanks, Libby. So was Artie."

"Yes, I know. Rudy, I was in all the junior high plays with Reed. He always carried the rest of us, even here with those sets he designed."

C'mon, talk. "You were both always good," impassive to the kids jostling by.

"Thank you. If I didn't love voice training, drama would probably be my thing."

"I've heard you in the school choir; you're very good at that too." She shied away a little. *Damn, Rudy—you're embarrassing both of us.*

"Um, Reed mentioned your writing once. Do you still write?"

He did? "I try." *Now what do I say? I'm so terrible at this.*

"That's good." She left a long, awkward pause. "Rudy, I wanted to know if there will be a funeral for Reed. We weren't close friends, but we talked in Art sometimes."

Really? "Um, no funeral, just an informal spreading of his ashes."

"May I attend?"

"You're welcome to come, of course, but it will be Sunday night in Griffith Park."

She sighed. "My mother won't go for that."

The wake, dummy. "Libby, before the hike, we're having sort of a wake around six-thirty at his grandma's place next door to us. Could you come to that?"

"Sunday at six-thirty. Yes, I'm sure I can. May I contribute some cookies?"

"Sure. Um, thanks. Can I call you with the address?" *Whoa, you could just tell her.*

"Please." She ripped a piece of paper from her notebook, jotted the number, then handed it to him. "Well, I need to go in and do some homework."

"Yeah, me too." The first bell rang.

They walked into homeroom together. "Thank you, Rudy."

"You're welcome." Heading for their assigned seats, Rudy saw Libby sit. Noah's desk across the aisle from her was empty. *Ha! I wonder why.* Rudy looked down at the scrap of paper in his hand. She had written *Elizabeth* and her number in flowing, clear longhand.

She didn't have to give me this. Doesn't mean anything, but at least now you know her a little.

Charlotte was working that evening, Si had left for Orange County, so Rudy had dinner with his parents. The house was still, and his mother had not been drinking. He explained the basics of what he and Helen had planned. Katie groaned at the idea; Larry listened but didn't respond.

Katie put down her coffee. "So, the mortuaries I sent weren't good enough, and now you'll just stomp around in the trees. How respectful. I thought Helen had more class than that."

Larry shoved his plate and stood up. "For god's sake, Katie—*class?* Damn, listen to yourself." Larry silently took his plate to the sink.

"Go play in your damn shop," she said, but Larry was already opening the back door.

Don't say anything; he said it all. Rudy moved past her with his plate. Neither of them spoke, then Katie left. Rudy rinsed all of the dishes and put them in the washer. *Are you going to call Libby or not? There's time, first talk to Dad about the hike.* He went out to the shop and noticed that the carving closet was open.

Larry stood below the fluorescent lights, scrounging in a drawer before he saw Rudy. "I'm sorry you had to see that, Rudy."

"It's okay." *She deserved it.* "I'm glad to see you carving again." He paused in case Larry might answer him. "Can I talk to you about next Sunday?"

"Yes, I'd like to come along."

"I was hoping you'd say that. Do you mind helping us?"

"Sure, what can I do?"

"I didn't bother to explain all of it at the table." Rudy described the hike's terrain, then the details of spreading Reed's ashes. "There will be some of us who are not experienced at messing around in the woods after dark."

"But you have been on this hike at night with Reed. Right?"

"Once. It's more bushwhacking than hiking." Rudy grinned. "We need experienced outdoorsmen like you and Seth to lead us into the wilds of Los Angeles."

"That would be Seth," Larry stated. "The business with the tree—how tough of a climb?"

Man, an actual conversation. "Um, Reed said it was easy—lots of limbs—but it seemed pretty tall to me."

"I'll bring ropes, just in case."

"Dad, could you call Seth? Maybe you two could suggest what people should bring. There will probably be seven to ten of us."

"Okay, after I talk to him, I'll leave a list by the phone for you."

"Thanks. Last thing. If we do have ten people, I'm not sure how many will be willing to drive on that dirt road up there."

"One of the vans can be refitted to take four passengers and the driver."

"Thanks, that should take care of it. How can I help?"

"Well, you can drive the van that night. I think you've mastered parking lots." Larry stared at Rudy for a moment. "It's a tough time for you right now, so if you don't feel like—"

"No, I'll do it."

"Good. The automatic will be easy after Katie's Bug. You're sixteen next week, right?"

"Yeah, but I'm not ready for the driving part of the test, especially parallel parking."

"I think you can do it before Thanksgiving. First things first. Instead of starting those TV trays tomorrow, you could help me put the bench seat in the van after school. You can also tell me more about all this bushwhacking."

"Sure, that'll be good."

"Maybe on Friday or Saturday we'll get you some driving practice."

"Great. Thanks, Dad." *Especially for the talk. Damn, what about Libby? It's probably too late to call. Chickened your way out of that one. Take the address to school, I guess.*

Walking to homeroom in a crowd of students on Wednesday morning, Artie told Rudy that he had permission to go on Sunday night and could also meet him at the field the next day.

"Thanks, Artie." Rudy summoned his courage. "Um, I need to wait out here a second."

Artie smiled. "I wonder why?" He turned toward the building.

"Wise guy. Maybe you can help me with my math in a minute." Rudy watched him enter, wondering if Libby had gone in early. Noah walked by with a basketball player, acting as if he didn't see Rudy.

Fine with me. He turned back. *Man, here she is.* "Hi, Libby."

"Hi, Rudy."

"Um, here's the address and directions for the wake. Are you all set to be there?" He handed her the paper.

"Yes." She read the paper in a couple of seconds. "Thanks, Rudy." She waited for the first bell to stop ringing. "I thought you were going to call."

So did I. "I was, but something came up with my family. Sorry." *Pathetic.*

"It's okay." She looked askance at some giggling girls rushing by. "Rudy, I need a few minutes to talk to you about something without all this, um, noise. Call me tonight about eight?"

What? C'mon, Rudy. "Sure, talk to you then."

"Good. We'd better get inside."

Before dinner that night, Rudy helped his dad with the van, and they discussed the list of hiking necessities. Just before eight, Rudy walked out to Katie's office and sat, staring at the phone. *What could she need to talk about? C'mon, do it.* He examined her name on the scrap of paper. *Only a teacher would use her real name. Stalling again.* He finally called.

"Good evening."

Her mother. "Hello, Mrs. Kerry. This is Rudy Lanier. May I speak with Libby, please?"

"Is Elizabeth expecting your call?"

Libby is. "I believe so, ma'am."

"She's right here," she said abruptly. "One moment."

Only a few seconds passed. "Hi, Rudy."

Man. Talk, fool. "Hi, Libby. Did I say something wrong to your mom?"

"Rudy, I'm going to switch to my extension. Be right back."

Damn, I already put my foot in it. He eyed Katie's wet cigarette butt in a highball glass.

"I'm back, Rudy. Sorry, my mom is suspicious of anyone new who asks for Libby."

"Do you prefer Elizabeth?"

"Only family and a few friends say it. *Libby* is fine."

"My grandparents always call me Rudolph, but almost nobody else does. Thank god."

Libby laughed. "Sorry, I'm not laughing at you." She paused. "It just struck me funny how both of our families make such a big deal out of our names."

It is funny. "Yeah." *Laugh all she wants—it's infectious.*

"Rudy, it's like what Juliet said, 'What's in a name?'"

"Right." *I guess. What's this all about?*

"You're not upset with me for laughing?"

"Of course not." *Elizabeth.* He took a deep breath.

"Rudy, I'm, um, feeling sort of tongue-tied. Excuse me, but I need a second, please."

"Sure." *Yeah, me too, but why is **she** nervous?*

"I'm back. Here goes." She left a long pause. "Rudy, our community choir is performing a holiday concert with selections derived from the classics and from traditional folk. I have a solo in 'What Child is This?'" She sighed. "You don't have to answer right away, but if that doesn't sound too boring, would you like to come?"

Really? "Sure, Libby." *God, I'm not **too** eager.*

"Good. There's something else. To be honest, I think my parents and girlfriends are burnt out with my concerts. It's embarrassing to say, but I decided to make a list of boys whom I thought might enjoy something like this. It had you, Reed, a boy in school choir, and Artie, who's a good friend; I guess he's probably your best friend." She sighed again. "So my big idea was to get tickets for as many of you who wanted to go. The guy from choir laughed, so now it's you and Artie. There, I said it."

What? How would that work?

"Rudy? Are you thinking it's a dumb idea?"

"No, Libby. Reed would've gone for sure." *I think.*

"Thank you for saying that, Rudy."

"Sure. Did you ask Artie yet?"

"I wanted to see what you thought. Maybe the three of us can go out and eat afterwards."

Why not? "When is it, Libby?"

"The Saturday after Thanksgiving."

"Sounds like fun." *And I might have my license!*

"Okay, I'll talk to Artie in homeroom." She paused. "Well, homework is calling; I'll see you tomorrow. Thank you, Rudy."

*Thank **me**?* "Sure. Thank you."

After they hung up, he exhaled through his teeth. *Brilliant.*

CHAPTER 19
A Bike Lesson

After the call with Libby, Rudy called Helen to arrange a short visit. He went right over, then told her that Si was all set for Sunday. Helen said that Diana was coming and had invited her therapist, who couldn't come. She added that Diana had seemed a little upset because Reed's therapist volunteered to take his colleague's place. Rudy showed her the list of what everyone needed to bring, then they checked the guests' names to decide who still needed a call.

"Who's Libby, Rudy?"

"She was in school plays with Reed. She'll be here, but not for the hike."

"I probably saw her on stage. I'll enjoy meeting her."

They divided up the calls, then Rudy left. Before bed, he went to the shop to check Charlotte's old bicycle, now used only by Katie on an infrequent whim. He had to inflate one of the old balloon tires for the next day.

Before school on Thursday, Rudy didn't mention the concert to Artie. During homeroom, Artie came back to his seat after talking to Libby. "The concert," he said quietly to Rudy, "are you sure you want me to go? If it interferes with you getting to know her, I won't go."

Rudy took a glimpse of two guys nearby, then whispered back. "No, Artie, I want you to come for sure."

"*Está bien.*" The next bell rang; Artie got up and walked toward Libby. At noon, Artie told him that Libby was glad they were both coming.

After school, they got on the afternoon bus and spoke quietly to each other.

"And you're still not going to tell me why we're meeting at the field?" Artie asked.

Not with all these kids around. "Let's just keep it a mystery." Rudy smiled.

"Okay," Artie said, his face puzzled. The bus came to Freddy's, Artie got out, then Rudy rode up La Plata Avenue to the bus stop just before Ontario Place. He jogged from there to his house. Rudy changed into old clothes, then went out to take care of Stew. After an abbreviated game of fetch, he went into the shop and discovered that the same tire on the bicycle was low again. *Piece of crap.* He inflated it, strapped the hand-pump back onto the frame, then walked the bike down the driveway.

Loping alongside, Rudy pushed the bike toward the park. *Anybody sees me, they'll just think I have a flat.* He blamed the hectic day for his low-key but constant headache, hoping it would back off when he was with Artie. Rudy crossed the bridges over the river and the freeway, then came to the Griffith public pool, closed for the cooler months.

Unlike where Rudy and Reed had hiked in the chaparral, this side of the immense park was flatter and more developed, including many hundreds of square acres for picnicking, baseball, golf, a full-sized carousel, pony rides, a miniature train, and the city zoo. Most of the amusements were separated by expanses of lawn or a short ride down the road. According to local lore, the area was part of Walt Disney's inspiration to create the "happiest place on earth."

The field, a vast strip of level ground not far from the pool, always seemed to have a recently mowed mat of soft grass, perfect for pick-up football over the years, even in the semi-darkness thanks to the fountain's floodlights. Artie was waiting for him, sitting on a boys' five-speed bike, a secondhand purchase with his greenhouse earnings.

Artie coasted up to him. "Rudy, what's with the bike?"

"I'm going to ride the damn thing—it's my sister's old bike."

"Now? I thought you were scared of heights or something."

"No, scared of breaking my neck. I would appreciate any advice you can give me." He took a deep breath. "I'm ready."

"Fine, but why couldn't you tell me about this before?"

"Sorry. I'm ashamed that it still scares me."

"So, this is another first step for you. Rudy, all of us have fears that are not logical. When my brothers and I misbehaved, my father scared us with stories of spirits like *La Llorona.* I don't believe any of that now, but if I'm alone at night I have to convince myself."

Really? "But you'll be okay on Sunday?"

"With people around, I probably won't even think about it." Artie glanced at the yellow bicycle. "Okay, riding a bike isn't like swimming; you don't have to keep taking lessons. You just practice. Also, everyone falls a couple times, so you picked a good place."

Great. "Yeah, nobody around."

"Alright, let's go." He turned his bike around to move it side-by-side with Rudy's. "That old fat seat shouldn't bother your butt much. Okay, get on—feet on the ground, like this.

"Right now?"

Artie just looked at him, expressionless, until Rudy got on. "Alright, the basic concept is simple: forward momentum defies gravity. I think you should start over there." Artie pointed to a gently sloping berm at the edge of the field.

What? "Start from the top?"

"Yes. We will go up there, then you sit like you are now. That bike has plenty of room for your full skirt."

"Hilarious." Rudy smiled. "How did you become such a joker?"

"A good teacher. Okay, you push off with your feet, rest them on the pedals, and off you go. Keep the front wheel straight, then before the bike slows down, you need to pedal to keep momentum. If you start to fall, put your feet down and try to stay up. Just remember how much we fell here playing football—that's about the worst that could happen on a bike like that."

Sure, no sweat. "And that's all I need to know?"

"For now. I'll show you the brakes after you glide down once. You probably won't need them."

Probably?

They walked their bikes together to the top of the berm. Artie repeated his instructions, then coasted down to the level ground below, where he turned to watch.

Rudy made a full exhale. *Here goes nothing.* His eyes riveted on the slope, it appeared to be much steeper than it did from below. His heart started thumping. *You can't just sit here, and you can't walk away. Damn it, go.* He closed his eyes and pushed off. *Open your damn eyes!* The bike had started rolling down the grade at a good clip. *Jesus, feet on the pedals and front wheel straight. You're still up; it's not so bad.* "Piece a' cake, Artie!"

"*¡Sí, pan comido!*" Artie's enthusiasm waned when Rudy came to the bottom. "Start pedaling, Rudy!"

He tried, but the bike was already wobbling. *Shit.* He removed his feet from the pedals, but it was too late to keep himself and the bike from falling.

Artie had already ridden over to him. "You okay?"

He stood up. "We did it, Artie!"

"I guess. Now, if you can just remember to pedal."

"I will." After Artie demonstrated the old bike's manual brakes, Rudy coasted down several times with only two crashes. After he gained confidence with pedaling, he was riding all over the field, turns and all. It was almost dark when they rode back to the foot of the berm.

"Pretty good, right, Artie?"

"Yes, you are 'the pro from Dover,'" one of their favorite *M*A*S*H* references. "You think you can ride it back to your house?"

"Sure, after I give my butt a rest."

Artie chuckled. "Okay, last lesson. When you ride on the street, some drivers will act like you don't exist; a few of them even get mad for no reason." They laid the bikes down on the grass and sat on the berm, watching the headlights pass by.

Rudy lay back on his elbows, fixated on the fountain across the street. *Just a week ago, right there with Reed—eccentric, gifted, so tuned in. Damn, I miss him.* "Artie, was it hard to get your dad's permission for Sunday?"

"He called it a pagan ritual. My mom told him how some Catholics say the same about his old ceremonies. She said it's my obligation to honor my friend." Artie also leaned back.

"Your mom is something else, Artie. I hope I'll get along with your dad eventually."

"You will. He's just very careful about everything. He doesn't dislike you."

"If you say so." He paused. "Artie, you remember on the city bus when you told me about your family and all the immigration problems?" Rudy watched him nod seriously. "Well, you trusted me, so I need to explain something to you about Si."

"I think I know. That same day on the bus, you said Si couldn't go to the movie, but I don't think you even asked him. I guess you are ashamed that you think he's, uh, *un bruto*."

Man. "Nothing gets by you, Artie." Rudy sighed. "Reed and Helen said my shame comes from a fear that I would become like him. I've tried not to be mean to him, but then he would gross me out and I'd stay away from him. Just a few days ago, I…" Rudy told him about the boogers under the TV trays, then his anger. He stared down at the grass with tears in his eyes.

"And now you feel ashamed of yourself."

Rudy sniffled. "Yeah. I promised Helen I would try harder with Si. Reed always told me to give him a break, but I didn't. You're always good to Si, Artie. Thank you."

"*Claro que sí.*" Artie glanced at the bikes. "Rudy, why the sudden need to ride a bike?"

"I wanted to try before Sunday. Like your mom said, to honor our friend."

"Yes, I see." He exhaled deeply.

"Artie, on the hike with Reed, I told him about Harry, and how you used Reed's strategies for bullies. He was proud of you."

Artie extended his lower lip, shook his head slowly, and wiped one eye. *He's choking up?* "You okay, Artie?"

"When Reed taught me about bullies, I promised to teach him some boxing. I never did."

"Artie, you know how busy he always was with his projects. I know this much for sure—he didn't have many friends, but you were one of them. He really admired you."

Artie smiled, then made a rare sigh. "I won't forget the boxing lessons for you." They both lay all the way back, watching the fountain for a couple of minutes.

Rudy got to his feet. "My damn butt is aching again."

Artie stood and pointed to the old bike. "Also, your back tire is soft."

After they inflated it, Artie promised to show him how to repair the tire. They started off on the bikes and soon came to a narrow path, where Artie went first.

"Artie, my dad wants me to drive part of the way on Sunday." Rudy practically shouted because Artie was at least ten feet ahead and getting closer to the noisy traffic.

"In your mom's Volkswagen?" Artie called back.

His bike clunking and rattling, Rudy rode up closer to Artie. "One of the vans," he said, not as loud. "He's letting me practice this week. It's an automatic—easy, like a Driver's Ed. car."

"*Híjole*—you ride a bike for the first time, but you're not afraid of driving a van in traffic? Rudy, that *is* something to be afraid of!" he blared, although Rudy was not far behind.

What? "Why, Artie?"

"Driving scares the crap out of me, like you say. I never drove anything larger than a bike. My father says I can't drive until I practice in the fields in Mexico at Christmas."

"Will you have time?" he said, a tease in his tone. "What was her name? Carolina?"

"*Kah-ro-lean-ah*," he corrected. "I'll find time for both."

"That's not so far off, I can show you some basics like starting the car, learning the gears—that kind of thing. Then it won't seem so strange when you begin."

"I think that will help. Thanks."

"Sure."

Artie turned his bike away from the traffic onto some dirt where they rode together. "Rudy, Libby is very happy you are coming to the concert."

What does that even mean? "C'mon, Artie. You're exaggerating."

"I don't exaggerate in English—not on purpose anyway."

"Okay." Back onto a wider sidewalk, they rode for a few minutes before Rudy realized he was staring at the monotonous streetlights. *No, dammit.* The bike hit a bump, then swerved, but he took control. *Pay attention, for god's sake.*

"You okay?"

"Yeah, still getting used to it."

"You're doing great." They came to the bridge over the freeway. "Rudy?"

"Yeah?"

"I believe Reed knows you did this tonight. You don't agree, right?"

"Right, but it still felt good."

Artie glanced at the traffic. "Um, I never asked why you don't go to church."

"I've been a few times. To me, religions are based on elaborate stories that help people not to fear death. And that's fine, but I can't buy into it."

Artie crossed himself as they started over the second bridge. "Rudy, you know I'm Catholic and also want to be a scientist." He paused.

"The *contradicción*, um, contradiction is something I think about a lot, but I have made no conclusions. I can't talk about such things with my parents. It would be sacrilegious to them."

"Well, you can always discuss it with me, but it would probably be better with someone who has considered it much more than I have, like Helen or Seth. You'd hear all sides."

"Yes, I could learn much from them. Thank you, Rudy; I think you helped me tonight more than I helped you."

That'll be the day.

CHAPTER 20

The Wake

Friday afternoon, Rudy and Larry took the van out for Rudy to practice. Rudy and Helen tied up loose ends on Saturday, including a shopping trip with Larry to buy some items for the wake and the hike, then Rudy and his dad went out after dinner for some night driving.

On Sunday evening, after six, Rudy and Larry left for Artie's place in the temporarily converted van. Rudy brought along some notes in a folder that he put down between the seats. He wore a flannel, old jeans, and his Angels yard hat; his father was in boots, a military field cap, sweatshirt, jeans, and a leather belt with a silver buckle.

Larry patted his slight paunch and looked over at Rudy in the front passenger seat. "Nothing better than spaghetti and garlic bread before hiking."

"Yeah." *With heartburn.* "Dad, I'm surprised Si isn't here yet."

Larry turned onto La Plata. "He'll make it." He drove on silently, block after block.

Rudy was watching the streetlights. *Damn, don't stare at them.*

Larry glanced at Rudy's bruise. "How are you feeling, Rudy?"

The question startled him a little. *Just a small headache.* "I'm fine, even my butt."

Larry chuckled, then was silent for a few seconds. "I want you to know I'm impressed by the help you've given Helen—and dealing with Reed's death at the same time."

Talking again—good. "Thanks, but we couldn't pull this off tonight without your help."

"Oh, I think you would've found a way."

Maybe. Rudy looked out above the streetlights at Venus and a couple of stars. "It's more or less clear up there, like they said. Do you think it will stay like that?"

"Hard to say." Larry paused. "You seem pretty nervous."

"I guess so—until it all comes together."

"So far, so good."

"Except Si. He really wants to be here."

"I know for a fact that he will."

How could he know? "Okay."

"Rudy, a little bird told me you have a new friend coming tonight." He cracked a rare, full smile. "Could that be part of your nervousness?"

"That little bird has big ears. Libby was in plays with Reed."

"Oh," with a slight smirk.

Rudy turned to Larry's frame pack behind; it contained basic hiking necessities, an attached rope, and the urn. "Any more questions about this deal, Dad?"

"Not yet." He left a long pause. "Pretty soon you're going to make *me* nervous," with a grin. Larry passed the elementary school and came to the stop sign at the Italian grocery, where he waited for one car before crossing.

"Dad, is Mom coming to Helen's tonight?" *And in what shape?*

"She said so—can't be sure."

Right. "She never much liked Reed anyway."

Larry, mum again, looked up at the palm trees as they passed Noah's house.

Rudy checked the dashboard. "It's almost six-thirty. We should've left earlier."

Larry came down to the Garner Drive stop sign, waited for a few cars, then crossed.

"You remember which house, Dad?"

"A La Plata classic. Right up there."

The Matas' Pre-World War II, square, stick-built home with chain-link all around seemed small at first glance until you noticed the windows of their full basement.

"Have you met Artie's parents?"

"Yes, we met at junior high graduation, and we've spoken a couple of times since. Artie's from good people." Larry pulled up to the curb and left the motor running.

As he got out, Rudy felt a brief rush of pride for both his dad and Artie. He opened the gate and hurried up their walkway to the front porch. Some cut-outs of skeletons seemed incidental to an artistic arrangement of cornstalks, Indian corn, lit candles, and squash of varied size, shape, and color—all of it on and around a bale of straw. Rudy wondered about a small plate of Mexican candy near a framed photo of an indigenous man in white clothes.

The porch light came on before Rudy could knock. Mrs. Mata came to the door with her usual welcoming smile, wearing a white apron over a colorful shift. A bit taller than her eldest son and moderately overweight, her complexion was much lighter than Artie's. "Hello, *Rodulfo. Arturo* is finding a light." She looked past him. "You can come in for coffee?"

"Thank you, Mrs. Mata, but people are waiting for us. Next time, I hope."

"*Ojalá que sí.*"

Artie approached her from behind. "*Mamá,* in English you say, *I hope so.*"

"*Está bien, maestro. Tengan cuidado*—I hope so."

Rudy and Artie smiled at her before they left the porch. Artie wore jeans, a dark-red stocking cap, and a blue sweatshirt; he held a plastic flashlight and well-used work gloves.

"She called you teacher, Artie." Rudy quickened their pace.

"Yeah, she always wants me to teach her English. She cracks me up."

New expression. "You crack *me* up."

"Well, some *gabacho* told me idioms don't stick unless you use them." They came to the driver's-side window of the van. "Hi, Mister Lanier. Thanks for helping us."

"You bet, Artie. You guys can go ahead and sit in back."

Rudy opened the sliding door, and they sat on the bench seat before Larry drove off. Artie and Rudy reviewed the whole plan, especially Artie's role at the end of the hike. Rudy groaned when Larry hit a long red light at Glendale Boulevard. Finally, the van slowed in front of Helen's. Seth's Model A and three other cars were out front. *No Studebaker, damn.*

Larry parked in the Lanier driveway; they got out and Rudy hurried off. At the duplex, Rudy simultaneously knocked and entered, Artie and Larry not far behind. Rudy saw that the few guests included a woman Rudy didn't know, likely Diana, who was perusing books far away from a man whom Rudy assumed was Reed's therapist. Rudy saw his mother speaking boisterously to Rob Collison and Libby in the middle of the small living room. Those two glance-smiled at the new arrivals. *They're trapped. Mom's going to embarrass the hell out of me.*

Larry had walked off toward Katie; Artie turned to Rudy. "There's Libby."

"Yeah." *Not yet.* They started over to Seth, who wore mostly khaki and was chatting with Katie's sisters, Margie and Candy, standing behind two side-by-side card tables covered with a black tablecloth. Rudy's aunts were in Halloween aprons and in charge of the hot drinks, apple juice, wine, a case of water in plastic bottles, and a huge bowl of apples, tangerines, and bananas. Relish trays filled with candy corn were placed around platters of baked treats, including ghostly sugar cookies, Halloween muffins, and a crisp batch of flat, overbaked chocolate chip cookies.

Rudy and Artie greeted everyone at the table as Helen entered from the kitchen in a brown pullover with a bright overflowing cornucopia on front. She ambled slowly to the table, then reached out and took both of Artie's hands. "Artie, so good to see you again."

"Nice to see you, Mrs. Crowley."

"*Helen*, dear." She smiled. "I want you both to meet someone." Rudy left his folder under the fruit bowl, Helen took his arm, then they walked over to the woman who Rudy had presumed was Diana. About five-six and apparently stocky under her green-and-black mackinaw, she was prepared for the hike in jeans, work boots, and a longshoreman's navy-blue stocking cap. Her long, dark-brown hair was braided into a single pigtail that hung behind. She carried a small rucksack in one hand. Examining an indigenous *olla* on a shelf, she turned to them. In her mid-to-late thirties, Diana's plain, jowly face had no makeup behind her thin-rimmed granny glasses.

"Diana, these two young men are Reed's good friends—Rudy and Artie."

"Hello, Artie; Rudy," she said shyly. She put her hand out to Rudy, her wrist adorned with a pewter bracelet set with a rough turquoise stone—her only jewelry.

Rudy hardly touched her fingers when she teared up; they spontaneously but briefly hugged. *Damn, Rudy.* "Sorry, Diana, I feel like I know you."

"Yes, I feel the same." Her hushed words were precisely spoken, adult to adult, no hint of condescension to a teen. She and Artie shook hands affably.

Her face beaming, Helen shuffled away, then stopped at the hallway entrance and called out, "Everyone, our one and only loo is down here; the line forms after yours truly. Any tobacco users are welcome to use the front yard to smoke." She left amidst some light laughter.

Rudy saw Reed's therapist look askance at Artie, then at him. In a thin tan sweater, brown corduroy pants, and deck sneakers, he was about thirty, five-ten, thin and pale, with short brown hair and a pre-cisely-trimmed nascent beard. His raised brows gave him a cocky mien.

Diana led them to the therapist. "Rudy, Artie—Martin Scofield; he worked with Reed." A cold nod was Martin's only attempt to greet them; Rudy and Artie said his first name courteously before Scofield walked off. Artie began to chat quietly with Diana.

Rudy watched Martin, now standing by himself, holding one of Helen's books, shaking his head judgmentally. He had an unlit pipe in his mouth. *Like the pretentious shrink he yearns to be.* Rudy took a step back to Diana and Artie.

Diana bridled momentarily toward Scofield. "Technically," she said, her voice low, "Martin assisted my therapist, Rose, with our group meetings." She brightened a bit. "Rudy, Rose sends her regrets for not being able to make it tonight. She valued Reed in so many ways."

"Thank you, Diana." Rudy looked at the guests, conversing with refreshments in hand. *Damn, still no Si.* It had not turned out to be a women-one-way-men-the-other sort of group. Helen and Seth were talking with Libby at the tables. *Thank her for coming, for god's sake.*

Katie was at the refreshment table while Larry still chatted with Rob Collison, who exchanged passing waves with Rudy. A daypack by his feet, the school counselor wore a yellow END APARTHEID button that Rudy had seen at school. In his late thirties to early forties, Collison stood about six-four, not counting a modest afro under his Giants baseball cap. His dark eyes and almond-brown face alternated between serious and jovial expressions. A thick beard grew down below his chin and brushed against the grey woolen poncho he wore over a brawny frame.

Rudy wondered if his father would care that Collison was a Vietnam veteran who had protested the war. Holding a bottle of water, Larry's eyes grew heavy. *Back in his shell.* Rudy saw Larry head for the front porch while Katie raised her glass, spilling wine and gushing unintelligibly toward her sisters. *Four sheets or worse—damn.*

He watched Martin slither past the others and cross the room to the table, where he barged in on Helen and Libby. *Jerk.* Libby nodded courteously to Martin, then her brow furrowed in response to whatever he said next. *Good for her.* Libby spoke to Helen, then walked toward the bathroom; Martin returned to the books.

Rudy followed Artie and Diana to the tables, where Helen spoke aside to him. "Libby is charming; such a talented and bright young woman."

Nodding, he half-smiled. *Yeah, everyone has spoken to her except me.*

"It's such a wonderful gathering, Rudy; thank you so much."

"Of course, Helen." *But where's Si?* "You did most of the work."

"Hardly." Seth came from the kitchen with napkins as Helen turned and called out, "Please have some goodies, everybody." She retreated to a corner to talk to Diana.

Rudy and Artie came to Seth. "Hi, Doctor Grant," Artie said.

"It's Seth, Artie." They shook hands, smiling, then Seth faced Rudy. "So, it seems that most came prepared."

"Yeah, assuming gloves and flashlights are in the cars." He saw Libby chatting with Collison again. *Okay. Now go over there.* "Excuse me," Rudy said, then started toward Libby, but he stopped when his father came in from the porch and waved to Helen. Now with her cane, she walked to the door. Rudy watched her hug someone before he or she could enter.

Helen turned and took a step or two toward the gathering with her arm around Si. "For those who don't know him," in her loudest voice, "this is Katie's brother, Si—or Simon—Krenshaw." Si was expressionless in his faded army-green patrol cap.

God, that same yellow business shirt. Dad knew he was coming alright. Rudy caught Larry's eye; he grinned back.

"Yup, Simon Krenshaw," Katie garbled over everyone, "my big, big brother."

Good god. Rudy saw Helen turn back to the front door.

"Come on in, dear, indulge an old lady." Helen led Charlotte in, then turned to the group. "And Si's chauffeur tonight, Charlotte Lanier." Charlotte came in and stopped; she was in jeans and a white blouse. "After Si's car broke down," Helen announced, "Charlotte drove down to Orange County to get him." A light round of applause followed; Charlotte backed up a half-step.

My, my, aren't we shy?

Helen directed Si to the refreshment table. He came over and greeted his sisters, then turned to Rudy.

"Hi, Si. So, you made it."

"Yes, Rudy. Charlotte got me."

"Right. Si, you remember Artie."

"Hi, Si." Artie extended his arm; they shook hands casually.

"Reed was my friend, Artie."

"Me too, Si." Artie patted his arm.

Si looked around, then turned to Rudy. "This is a party."

"More like a wake, then we're going out to release the ashes."

"Oh. Rudy, I'm in my jeans, and my flashlight's outside with my gloves."

"That's good, Si." *Maybe Helen has a shirt for him.*

Helen had joined them and started to offer a platter of ghost cookies to Si, but he reached for the table. "Chocolate macaroons. They look like my mom's." He started to eat one.

Don't watch. He turned to Helen to ask quietly if she had an old shirt that Si could wear.

"I'll find something." She finished mixing hot chocolate for Si, who was now in a two-way conversation with Artie.

Who but Artie could talk to him like that? And about what? Si already had crumbs on his shirt, and a chocolate streak on his yellow sleeve.

Rudy noticed his sister in a corner with their dad. She stopped talking and signaled for Rudy to come over. Larry headed for Katie, who was working on another glass of wine.

To what do I owe this sincere invitation? "Helen, I'm going to talk to Charlotte for a minute. Maybe we can get this deal on the road when I get back."

She grinned then turned serious. "Certainly. Rudy, please give Shar a chance."

For what? Artie had taken Si over to meet Libby and Collison. *Good god, Libby now gets the whole Si experience. She must be pissed at me by now.*

Rudy crossed the room to his sister. "Shar. Thanks for getting Si," he stated.

"Yeah," her face was staid but not glum. Her casual ponytail flopped over her left ear.

Is this a stunt? "Well?"

"Shit, Rood, give me a second."

That's more like it.

"Your friend over there is cute, and she handles her, um, heftiness well."

How nice. "She was Reed's friend."

"Oh." She paused. "So Dad's all shy again, and Mom's blasted."

"That's about the size of it. Is that what you wanted to talk about?"

"Wait, damn it." She heaved a sigh. "Rudy, since Reed died, I've been thinking," she said, a trace of a tear on her face. "I talked to Helen; even to Seth and Dad a little." Charlotte sniffled. "Helen really listens to me but also calls BS—in her way. But you know that."

"Yeah." *How long has she been talking with Helen?*

"It's no big deal—same ol' Shar. Anyway, you didn't know it, but I started to admire Reed, especially after Helen asked him to show me some of his art a couple months ago. I've always liked hearing about his pranks, pulling them on somebody who deserved it, but not pissed about it." She took a deep breath. "I'm the opposite—pissed all the time, and all I know how to do is play tennis and squawk on a clarinet. Anyway, I told Helen I was surprised by how upset I was when Reed died. I didn't take him very seriously before; I feel like a fool."

"Okay." *Where's this going?* "Too bad you didn't tell Reed some of this."

"Yes, but what I want to say is that you liked him when nobody else did; that took guts."

Not really. "Thanks, Shar. Um, Helen and I have to get this moving."

"Rood, can I be part of the rest of it?"

"You mean the hike?"

"Yes, and I have a little more to talk to you about—up there, maybe."

Yeah, maybe. "You'll need a hat, flashlight, and…"

She listened to the list. "Okay, be right back. Thanks." She hurried out the front door.

"There gozh my li'l girl, tennish champ!" Katie gushed. Larry was there to steady her.

Damn it. Rudy returned to the table, where Helen handed him a sweatshirt and two flannels. "These were too large for Reed—been in a Goodwill box for years. The extras are just in case. Are we ready to start, Rudy?"

"If my mother shuts up." He started to mix some cocoa. "Helen, please go first."

"Rudy, did Charlotte leave because she was upset?"

"No, she's going with us."

"Wonderful." Moving over in front of the food, she turned to the group. "Everyone!" she said boisterously, then waited a few moments. "To quote my good friend, Rudy Lanier, we need to get this deal on the road—literally," she said to a few chuckles. "First, my thanks to Mildred Grant for her superb Halloween baking. She has a bit of a cold and didn't want to spread germs.

"And thanks to all of you for coming. Reed would be surprised and honored by your presence—or he might call it foolishness, depending on his mood." She paused. "I have a few words, as does Rudy, then anyone feel free to say something—or not." She took a few moments to gather herself, then Charlotte entered in a white bucket hat and Katie's blue yard jacket. She stayed away from her mother and stood near Martin.

The scumbag's leering at her. Rudy retrieved his folder from under the fruit bowl.

Helen smiled to her guests; the room became still. "Like all of us, Reed was an imperfect human being." Helen glanced at Rudy. "Amity, my daughter and Reed's mother, did her best as a parent before her mental illness took over. She used to say that she raised Reed to be a Renaissance Man; as a result, he had early opportunities to explore and practice his many talents. He was an artist and an individualist, the latter sometimes clashing with convention. Reed perished on his way to Broadway, where he would have pursued the next steps of his dream. Finally, Reed loved his mother and his gram, and we loved him," she said proudly, not a tear on her face. "Thank you for remembering him tonight."

After some sympathetic murmurs from the group, Helen turned to Rudy. He stepped forward with his folder, briefly wiping a tear with the back of his hand. *Come on, or you'll never get through this.* "Thank you, Helen." He exhaled deeply. "I have a paragraph that is representative of my close friend, Reed McCool." He opened the folder. "This paraphrases a few things Reed told me not long ago." Rudy released another long sigh.

"Okay." Rudy paused again. "'Sure, I'm judged and prejudged for being different, but that's who I am and that's how I will end. Everybody prejudges whether they admit it or not. In my case, I try not to judge old people, but their rampant conformity drives me nuts—from Buicks to Lawrence Welk. If I grow old and turn that narrow, please pull the plug. But I know there must be more like Gram, who is untouched by the status quo because hers is a life well-lived, and on her own terms. She has always been my inspiration.'"

The small audience was somber up to the last line, then most turned fondly to Helen. She was holding back tears this time, taking some steps toward the kitchen. Seth gently took her arm, mumbled something to her, and they stayed.

"Anyone else?" Rudy asked the silent group.

There was no response until Si uttered, "Reed was my friend."

Artie nodded. "Yes, and mine too, Si."

Rudy saw Martin smirk. Rob Collison stepped forward to shake Rudy's hand, then whispered, "I'll never forget how you stood by Reed." Collison faced the others, stalling his emotions. "You probably don't know that Reed finished his **GED** recently. For him, it was a concession to conformity and also a chance to escape from it. I will remember Reed as an artist and performer with a complicated mind. I am proud to have been his teacher and confidant."

Rudy nodded to Rob, then waited. "Thanks, Mister Collison, and to all of you for being here. We'll go over the plan for tonight in a couple of minutes. Meanwhile," pointing to the table, "there are paper bags and plenty of water and provisions for the hike; please help yourselves." *God's sake, Rudy, go over to Libby.* He took a sip of his lukewarm cocoa and started for her.

"We'll missh that boy!" Katie spouted from the middle of the room. "But geez-us wept, he was a queer kid. Never could figure 'im out, an' he—"

Rudy watched her stumble, but Larry was there to catch her. Charlotte hurried over and took her other arm and urged, "C'mon, Mom," but Katie had passed out.

How could she pull this shit tonight? He walked on over to them.

Helen was already there. "Charlotte," Helen said, "you and your father take her to my bedroom; I'll watch over her until she sleeps it off."

"Thanks, Helen," Larry said calmly. "Rudy, we've got it handled. Keep this going."

Right. Hey, everybody, don't pay any mind to my plastered mother.

Helen led the way for Larry and Charlotte; they had draped Katie's arms over their shoulders as they hauled her off, toes dragging on the floor like a stunned boxer. Seth followed them, but most of the others had migrated to the table, trying not to stare at Katie's exit.

"Jesus Christ," Rudy said to himself, then sat on a chair, bent over, a palm to his head, which was now pounding. He looked up to see Martin gawping at him—a posh tourist to a street beggar. *Screw you, Martin.* Rudy got up, went to the kitchen and splashed cold water on his face. "Shit," he grumbled, then sensed someone in his peripheral vision.

Seth came to him. "I'm sorry, Rudy. Katie's fine. Maybe this is a wake-up call for her."

Fat chance. He dried his face with a dishcloth. *Damn, this is not about her.*

"Rudy, everyone out there is with you and still expecting to go."

"That's good." *Pull yourself together.* "Thanks, Seth."

"Of course." He paused. "And Libby is waiting to talk to you."

She hasn't left? "Thanks." Rudy went out to the table and saw Margie and Candy heading for the door. Si and Artie were selecting items for their sacks while Libby cleared bits of trash from the tables for Helen. Rudy hadn't noticed earlier that she was wearing a dark-grey jacket with matching slacks, an outfit that complimented her full figure. *Man, she looks twenty.*

She moved a few feet away to discard empty packets and some plastic spoons. He approached her as she turned toward the table. "Libby, I'm sorry. I didn't mean to ignore you."

"I know, Rudy. I saw you trying to come over."

She's not mad. "I'm also sorry you had to see my mother do her thing."

"It's okay, we have a similar situation in my family. It's hard." They moved away from the table. "Rudy, you and Helen handled this so well; you both made such heartfelt remarks."

"Thanks."

She sighed quietly, then perked up a little. "Artie told me a little about your uncle's challenges. I think Si is very sweet."

My god. "Yeah, that's Uncle Si," he said, not intending sarcasm.

"Rudy, I'm sorry about my hard cookies." She rolled her eyes and smiled. "Awful."

"No, I doubt they'll survive the evening," with a grin.

She nodded, then an awkward silence came between them. The others still milled around; some looked expectantly at Rudy.

They can wait a second. Talk to her. "Well, it was a good turnout." *Brilliant.*

"Yes." She inhaled deeply. "This is not a good time, but I was wondering if you've changed your mind about the concert. If you have, I'll understand."

Can't blame her for wondering. "No, Libby, Artie and I are both looking forward to it."

"Good." She paused. "I wish I could go up there with you, um, all of you, tonight—I'll keep Reed in my thoughts."

"I really appreciate that."

She smiled. "It's after seven; my dad will be out there."

Ask her. "Is it okay if I call you Elizabeth?"

"Of course, Rudolph," wryly. "Just joking, Rudy."

"What's in a name? Right?"

"Exactly."

"Good night, Libby. Thanks for coming."

"Good night, Rudy." She turned and started for the door.

Man-oh-man. A fist over his mouth, he disguised another deep sigh. *C'mon, switch gears.* He turned to the group and took a step forward. *Apologize for my mother?* "Okay, everybody, the beat goes on." *That's good enough.* He nodded to Helen. "Thanks to Helen for all of her work and hospitality. She told me that she and my gramma will be with us vicariously tonight."

Rudy pointed to the table. "I hope you all got your water and snacks. I see those macaroons all found homes." He waited for chuckles. "If you ended up with too much to carry, Seth and my Dad have extra room in their packs. Okay, we'll meet first at the fountain on Los Feliz." He counted heads. "So, Mister Collison lives near Vermont and will just be going one way. We can fit one more in the van; I think that leaves three people—one more vehicle should do it." Charlotte raised her hand. "Shar, do you want the last spot in the van?"

She snickered. "As much as I hate to miss a ride in one of our plumbing vans, I think I can fit all the rest in my car."

Martin cleared his throat to get everyone's attention. "Perhaps

she's had enough driving for one day," his words intentionally mag-
nanimous. "I have plenty of room."

"Is that okay?" Rudy asked his sister, expecting her to decline.

"Sure, I'll go with Martin."

Martin, is it? He's a creep, Charlotte.

CHAPTER 21
Ashes

After bathroom visits and paying respects to Helen, the nine of them left Ontario Place in their curious little convoy: Larry's plumbing van, Martin's new Mercury, and Rob Collison's old Volvo wagon. After Larry turned in at the fountain, he switched to the passenger seat, and Rudy drove up to Vermont and turned right, the other two vehicles not far behind. He arrived at the turn-off, made the left, and stopped.

They waited a few moments for Rob and Martin, then Rudy proceeded on the dirt road, the van rattling and clunking. Larry turned to Rudy. "This road's even worse than it used to be."

"Yeah." Rudy glanced at Artie in the rear-view mirror. "How's it going back there?"

Artie smiled and made the sign of the cross with his hand.

"Funny, Artie. How about you, Si?"

"Good."

Rudy lowered his eyes from the mirror. "Dad, will you explain to everyone when we get there how to handle the bushwhacking?"

"Sure, with Seth's help, but you're running this show. Are you still ninety percent sure of your markers?"

"Maybe eighty-two-point-five."

Larry grinned. "More challenging that way." Rudy came to the trailhead turnout in a couple of minutes. They all parked near the mature oak and got out. Rudy didn't detect any sign of the night's crescent moon, so it was even darker than when he was there with Reed. The weather forecast seemed accurate so far—no clouds, just haze with fog expected later.

The hikers gathered near the tree, facing Rudy and Larry. Most of them had already turned on their flashlights, making it reasonably easy to see each other. They all put on gloves, except Martin, whose pale hands stood out in the dark.

Crap. "Martin, do you have gloves?" he asked as politely as he could.

"In my coat, of course."

"That coat will likely get ripped. Helen sent extra shirts if you'd like one."

Martin didn't answer, but Collison did. "If you have a fairly big shirt, I think I'll leave my poncho—it's not quite right for out here."

"Good idea." Rudy pointed to the van. "The shirts are up front." *Martin can learn the hard way.* Collison retrieved the sweatshirt, then started back, spotlighted by the group. He struggled to pull the one-size-too-small garment down over his burly physique.

Familiar with Collison's minor predicament, Rudy drew attention away from him. "Okay, everybody," his tone conversational, "when I was here with Reed, he valued relative quiet when possible. Let's try to observe that. Also, we're fortunate to have the old Army Ranger with us." He turned to Larry, who rolled his eyes. "He has all the essentials in his frame-pack, and, of course, we even have Doc Grant and his first-aid kit, just in case."

Seth nodded. "Okay, please remember it's pack-it-in and pack-it-out. My pack is also for empty bottles and sacks; there's a plastic bag in there for peels, apple cores, and such. Rudy?"

"Thanks, Seth. Instead of the old Scout trail…" Rudy quickly described the terrain, the bushwhacking, and the trails. "I hope this will be fun and interesting—Reed would approve. When we're finished, you're on your own to get back down here." He feigned surprise at some nervous buzz in the small group. "Okay, not so funny."

After last-minute adjustments and a chance at the outhouse, they gathered at the hitching post, started off, then soon circled the gate. They continued on the gradually uphill dirt road, some of them mumbling with excitement. Most didn't bother to aim their lights ahead because Larry's hand-lantern was so strong. They gradually broke into smaller groups, not very far apart, except for Martin, Charlotte, and Diana, who had moved about twenty feet away from the rest. Rudy walked with his father up front; Artie was just behind with Si, who kept up well with the moderate pace. Seth and Rob were last, carrying on a steady, low conversation.

Rudy couldn't help but glower over at Charlotte, walking and talking with Martin, neither of them using their lights. Diana was about ten feet behind them, shining her light near their feet as if she were chaperoning.

Get closer to them. "Dad, I think Si would enjoy being up front for a while."

"Sure."

Rudy turned and cast his light on Si's flannel shirt. "Si, how are you two doing?"

"Good, Rudy. It's like the army."

"Except no M-1's." Artie grinned. "Rudy, Si knows the M-1's real name."

Artie turned to Si, who said, "M-1 Garand semi-automatic rifle."

"I bet only a few people know that anymore, Si. You want to take point for a while?"

"Yes. Me and Artie."

Like old pals. They came forward; Larry exchanged his lantern for Si's flashlight. Si shined the strong beam ahead and walked with Artie, a bit faster than Rudy expected.

When Charlotte groaned like she always did at bad jokes, Larry and Rudy turned to her.

"Dad, over here." Rudy led him several feet closer to Charlotte and Martin, who were still about fifteen feet away; Diana remained behind them.

After a few more minutes, they came to the section where a grader or tractor had scraped the road, revealing hardpan as well as large rocks embedded in the ground. They heard Martin teasing Charlotte; Diana's light moved closer to them.

"You goddam prick!" Charlotte blurted in her signature outrage.

Larry had his pack halfway off; Rudy ran toward his sister. Diana was already between Martin and Charlotte.

Rudy heard Martin grumble at Diana. "Mind your own business. She's not your type."

"What's going on?" Rudy moved in next to Diana, Larry just a few feet behind.

Martin sneered. "Your sister is hysterical. She assumed I did something I didn't do. Then she slapped me."

"Bullshit." Charlotte pointed her light at Martin "You groped me, pervert."

Larry came up almost face-to-face with Martin. "And you say you didn't touch her?"

"Completely unintentional. I held her arm when we came to those rocks. I stumbled and apparently touched her in, uh, an unfortunate location."

"There was no stumble," Diana stated.

Charlotte folded her arms. "Not only did the scumbag touch my tit, he rubbed it."

"That's an absurd lie," Martin jeered. The others came closer, led by Collison.

His head now thumping, Rudy cast his light on Martin. "Reed told me about you, creep."

"Easy, Rudy." Larry turned to Diana. "What's the story with this guy?"

"The clinic has an unofficial policy that he doesn't work one-on-one with women or girls. With the shortage of therapists, the director doesn't take complaints about him very seriously."

"He's going to take one now." Larry shined Si's flashlight in Martin's face.

Martin tried to block the beam with his hand. "She's lying and exaggerating."

Larry seethed. "You look at Charlotte now and apologize for touching her."

"I'll do no such thing," his tone haughty. "I didn't do anything wrong."

Larry stepped even closer to him; Collison was now alongside, glowering at Martin.

Martin turned in Charlotte's general direction. "Okay, I apologize for touching you."

"I should've used my fist," Charlotte snarled. "Now apologize to Diana."

"To *her*? For what?"

"The way you spoke to her—and do it *right* now."

Martin looked past Larry to Diana. "I apologize for how I spoke to you."

Diana huffed. "Don't make me laugh."

Larry directed the light at Si. "Let's switch again, Si." He brought the lantern right over, and Larry aimed its beam on the plastic mini-flashlight in Martin's hand. "Okay, I guess we'll let you keep that; now get the hell out of here. It's not even a mile back to your car."

"Alone? You can't just be judge and jury," Martin whined.

"Take me to court. Everybody, turn off your lights." Larry kept his light on Martin. "By the way, it's well-known that at least one mountain lion roams Griffith Park. Better be careful."

Martin scoffed weakly, then hurried away with Larry's strong beam trained on his back.

Their lights still off, the group came together, chatting quietly. When his lantern showed Martin beginning to run, Larry turned to them. "If there *was* a big cat around, he just did the worst thing he could do." He lowered his light. "Okay, he's gone. If he breaks an ankle, we'll scrape him up on the way out."

They turned on their flashlights, aiming them toward Rudy and Larry. Seth was at the front of the group. "Huzzahs to everyone for the way you handled that."

Charlotte laughed. "Is *huzzah* a good thing, Seth?"

Rudy waited for the chortles. "One small problem. Three of you came with Martin; I suppose we'll squeeze you into the van later."

"Rudy," Collison said, "I'll drive back to Helen's—it's not all that far out of the way."

"Thanks, that works great. So, let's resume our *quiet* little hike."

Not as spread out as before, they trekked on silently until the dirt road narrowed. Larry and Rudy hiked together in front of the others until Charlotte came up from behind. "You two were pretty brave with Collison next to you."

"Funny," Rudy said. "Martin already met his match with you and Diana."

She puffed at him dismissively. "Rudy, can we finish our talk?"

I guess. "Dad, we'll catch up after everyone goes by."

"Okay, just don't let us pass the marker."

"You can't miss it—taller and wider than all the other bushes." As soon as everyone was well ahead, Rudy and Charlotte began walking. He watched the clipped-toenail of a crescent moon just clearing the foothills, leaving a dim horizon.

"Rudy, this isn't easy," Charlotte said, her voice muted, "So, I'll just spit it out. I've been a shit to you more than you have to me." She cleared her throat. "I want us to start getting along better before I leave home—nothing phony, just getting along."

Fair enough. "Can't hurt to give it a try. Did Seth mention this to you?"

"Helen, but I was already thinking about it."

"Starting now?"

"Yes, but I might slip," with a grin.

"Yeah, me too." He sighed. "Shar, do you think Mom and Dad are having problems?"

"God, Rudy, it's been years since hearts and flowers." They slowed down after they started to catch up to the others.

"How do you know for sure?"

"It's obvious."

"Not to me, I guess."

"Man, where've you been?" She looked away. "Sorry, that was mean—I didn't last very long. Anyway, at least we can try not to be a pain in the ass while Seth tries to help her."

"Yeah, I agree. Can we talk about Mom and Dad more when we have time?"

"Okay. Dad's waving at you anyway."

"I see him." *Okay, focus on the hike.*

Charlotte joined Rob, Diana, and Larry, who was facing the enormous bush. "Biggest damn elderberry I've ever seen," remembering to speak quietly.

"Must be tapping into water somehow," Seth added.

"That's the one alright," Rudy said, his voice also hushed. "Ready, everybody?" They all came closer to Rudy, some of them sipping water. "Okay, we start by climbing up and around this bush—meet on the other side."

Larry picked up his heavy frame pack and hefted it onto his back. He and Seth followed Rudy past the elderberry and up the embankment to the edge of the high chaparral. They stopped; Larry scanned the terrain with his light. "Okay, Rudy, we're ready for the next marker."

He looked up. *Shit, where's that damn tree? There it is—relax.* "It's that oak way up there." He pointed up at the tree's distant, pale silhouette, formed by the waning moon with light from the city. The rest of the party had joined them. "Okay, from that tree," Rudy moved his arm to the right, "Reed said ninety degrees." Rudy pointed. "I think we took off about there." They cast their lights into a thick, five-foot-tall entanglement of scrub and saplings. *That's not it.*

Artie stepped forward hesitantly and pointed more to the right. "Rudy, maybe that way?" Larry shined his lantern into some other tall bramble with more gaps in the growth.

"Yeah, that's it." *My crappy geometry.* "I pointed forty-five—right, Artie?"

"About that, I guess."

Seth checked his compass and said, "Okay, that's north-northeast."

Rudy turned to his father. "What do you think?"

"That scrub isn't too bad, but I'm sure we'll find some that's too thick to get through. Then we go around, and Seth's compass can keep us on the general bearing."

"Right," Seth agreed. "Also, it shouldn't be necessary to destroy plants. We just clear dead material and push away the rest. When you let go of a branch, be careful of those behind."

"Okay," Rudy said, "about halfway up to the path, we'll see the oak up there again at an opening in the brush. It's also a good resting place. Dad, how do you suggest we approach this?"

"We just need to make it through, not make a road. Let's try three at point, one with my lantern, then another three, and the last two get a break and provide more light for the ones ahead. After a while, we can adjust or change places."

Listen to him—he and Seth are in their element. "Dad, maybe I'll go with the first three since I've been here before."

"Show the way, Rudy; I won't be much help up front with this pack."

"Okay." *He could do it, eyes closed. He **wants** me to do it.*

"Since I'm a Lanier," Charlotte said, "I get to be bossy too. My rule is biggest one clears first; that's you, counselor." Rob raised his brows amidst hushed snickers.

Si had come up to Larry. "Can I be in front again?" Si put on his gloves.

"Sure, Si." They exchanged lights again.

Rob stepped up, grinning. "Reporting as assigned by Ms. Lanier." Collison got on one side of Si, Rudy on the other, followed by Larry, Diana, and Artie.

"Charlotte and I are rear guard," Seth said quietly.

They started up into near-pitch darkness, slowly bushwhacking and adjusting before they forged more efficiently through the thick bramble and gradually became two interchanging groups of four, the one behind providing light for the other.

On a subsequent rotation up front, Seth, Si, and Artie followed Rudy around some thick, tangled scrub oak. "When I was with Reed, he spotted an owl around here; there was a bat and some other small animals." *Real small, like a spider.* Rudy held the lantern for Si and Artie, who were moving a hefty, dead limb out of the way.

Seth aimed his light into the dark. "We must sound like a stampede to the animals." He touched some desiccated coyote brush, then the branches of a half-smashed sage. "It looks like people have been through here several times. Hopefully, we're the last ones for a while."

"Why not make it into a real trail?" Rudy asked as Si and Artie rejoined them.

Seth frowned slightly. "Well, this park is one of the last relatively wild bastions against human sprawl in L.A. County. I'd say there are more than enough trails."

Rudy expected Seth to continue talking. Instead, he was checking the hikers behind with his light. "Rudy, we probably need a break pretty soon."

"Right, I think we're getting close to the spot where we can see the marker."

It took a bit longer than Rudy expected until they finally came to the rocky area. Rudy pointed his light to the break in the vegetation. "Dad, I think that's it." Larry and Seth released their packs and went over to check the spot while everyone else waited.

Rudy turned to Artie. "How's it going so far?" *He isn't even breathing hard.*

"Good. Si's making it easy for me. What about you?"

"Just pooped." *And a damn headache.*

Larry and Seth came back to them. "It's up there alright, Rudy," Seth told him. "We just need a direction."

Not at all sure about this one. "Okay." Rudy turned his light on the others and spoke quietly. "Let's take our break."

"Hold on everybody," Larry said, "if nature calls, let's have pointers go that direction, um, and squatters, that way. I also have toilet paper and a camp shovel—if you use them, please take your own direction. The packs will be right there." He and Seth put their packs near a small boulder. Some of them gathered around to get their lunch bags and water. Larry, Seth, and Artie started toward the opening.

Rudy's stomach growled. "I'll be right there." He reached into his shirt pocket, then took a bite of one of Libby's cookies he had felt obligated to try. *Dry as a cracker. So what? She gave it a shot.* Rudy took a bottle of water from Seth's pack, drank half of it, then jogged over to catch up with the others. He pushed aside the branches, then they all switched off their lights to view the outline of the tree.

Larry turned to Rudy. "Doesn't seem much closer, son."

Son, *my god.* "I know, but now we head almost straight for it until we get to the trail." He faced Artie and Seth. "Reed said to the right of the tree about thirty degrees." *I think.* Seth and Artie agreed on the heading, then chatted in the language of arcane geometry.

With the onset of sour acid in his throat, Rudy regretted having eaten anything. Heading back to the others, he noticed their flashlight beams refracting in the plastic water bottles. Rudy finished his water, went to Seth's pack to dispose of the bottle, but he didn't take his lunch sack. *Any more food and you'd be spitting fire.* Charlotte, Diana, and Rob were sitting several feet away, chatting quietly while eating their snacks. Si was alone near them with a half-eaten Halloween muffin in one hand, water in the other.

Taken for granted like furniture. Rudy sighed. *It's okay, Seth will come back and sit with him.* He saw a flashlight back at the opening in the thickets. *Probably Seth. C'mon, Rudy, it won't kill you.* He walked over to his uncle, who had sticks and dry leaves all over his shoulders.

"Hi, Si. You helped us through a lot tonight."

"They had machetes in the army."

"Man, that had to be dangerous."

"I don't know."

"Some of the trail is still on you; I'll brush it off." Si stood, then Rudy used his sweat-stained Angels cap to sweep off most of the debris. They sat a few feet from each other. "What do you like about the hike, Si?"

"Mm, I like—all the hike," his mouth full of muffin. "That rhymes."

"Sure does." Rudy watched Larry come out of the pointers' bushes, sit by his pack, and lean back on it, chomping on an apple. Larry craned his neck and looked up at the few stars or planets that emitted enough light to pierce the atmosphere. Artie emerged from the undergrowth to sit near Rudy and Si, who was peeling a banana.

Rudy waited for Si to peel and eat the fruit, then bolt down a macaroon. "Well, Si, maybe we should get going." *Think of another job for him.* Rudy turned to Artie. "Ready?" The three of them walked to Seth, who had returned and was reorganizing his pack. They discarded their refuse, then told the others that they would be waiting over at the gap.

After they all came together, Rudy pointed up at the oak. "We go that way now, a bit to the right. Back into the thick stuff for a while, pretty steep, then the trail." He paused. "Dad?"

"Rudy, maybe you, Seth, and Artie start us off—all that savvy up front," he said drolly.

Right, did I mention this is the hardest part?

Si joined them to stand with Artie. The other four filled in behind, and the group began to filter and force its way through dense dry foliage up the grade. More than half an hour later, Rudy stopped. *Shit.* "Shit." He turned back to his dad.

"What's wrong, Rudy?" Larry asked.

"We're lost," Charlotte said. "Don't worry, Rood, Daniel Boone and Ol' Smokey here will figure it out."

Rudy moaned. "She's right, I don't see anything familiar."

"That's not surprising out here," Larry said, turning to Seth. "What do you think?"

Seth looked up from his compass. "I don't think we're on the wrong tack. Rudy, do you recall if it took you this long with Reed to find the path."

"I don't think it did. Maybe I messed up the angle."

"From how you described the path, I think it's more likely that we missed it."

Now what? "I don't know," Rudy said tentatively, "maybe two or three of us can go ahead with the lantern; the rest wait here for a few minutes." *Brilliant. C'mon, Dad, take charge.*

"I can go up there with Rudy," Si told them.

"Thanks Si," Larry answered. "During the day, it would be a good idea, but we can't split up out here now—somebody could end up more lost than we already are."

"If we follow the compass back," Seth said, "we can look for the trail, then the worst scenario is we return to the rest spot and try again."

"I agree," Larry stated. "Not to frighten anyone, but we weren't kidding Martin about the lion. If we drop the silent treatment and make some racket, then I don't think we need to worry about any big kitties tonight." His half-smile was followed by nervous laughter from the group.

Well, he has our attention now. "Okay, so how do we do it?"

Larry turned to Rudy. "We turn around and fan out eight across, not more than a few feet from the light next to you. Stay close and help each other as we look for the trail." He paused. "Okay, let's go," Larry shouted on purpose. "Let's make some racket and call out if you find it."

They spread out, Seth and Rudy on one end with Artie and Si next to them, then the other four. The line worked its way downhill for a few minutes, everyone intentionally stomping through the briar and speaking loudly to each other. Rudy looked off to his right; the other beams winked through the branches like Christmas lights.

"Are there really mountain lions out here?" Artie called from a few feet away.

"I guess there's proof of a couple of them," Rudy answered.

"Pretty creepy." Artie picked up some twigs, then cracked them over his knee.

"Right, that'll scare 'em."

After about twenty more feet, there was a shout from the other end of the line.

"C'mere!" Everyone scrambled toward Charlotte's voice. "I think I found the damn thing," she said as the others approached. "Is this even a trail, Rudy?" Their lights showed how the path barely cut a break uphill through the scrub.

Way to go, big sister. Rudy's exhale was audible. "Yeah, this is it." He aimed his light straight down at the ground. "Reed called it a deer path. He thought the smaller animals used it like a freeway under the thicket." Most of the group solemnly inspected the faint path.

Looking up the trail, Charlotte broke the silence. "There's still crap to move off the path."

Larry was aiming his lantern uphill. "Charlotte's right, some shrubs off to the sides have branches in the way, but it's better than what we just went through. Right, Rudy?"

Rudy looked up at the tree again. "Yes, and it's not very far, but a little steeper." With the increased proximity, he could now make out the oak's gnarly limbs.

"The tree doesn't look like a problem," Larry whispered to Rudy.

"Good." *Let's go.* He turned. "Si, will you lead us again with my dad's lantern?"

"Yes." He moved right up in front of Larry.

Rudy faced the group. "I'll be behind Si and my dad; please follow us single file."

They started slowly up the grade, occasionally moving branches that crossed the path. After a few minutes, Rudy asked Si to stop. "Okay, Si, you can go on ahead with my dad to help." Before they left, Artie moved to the end of line, per Rudy's previous instructions. Rudy turned to the five behind him. As he expected, the city was blocked by the tall, dense thicket.

"Where's Dad going?" Charlotte asked.

"To get ready for what we came here to do. He won't be far away."

"Oh, okay."

Diana was stargazing; Seth, Rob, and Artie were also fixated on the night sky.

Stall a minute; don't mess this up. "Anything familiar, Diana?"

"Just a hint of the heavens, but you can see the big dipper; we're going north now."

Charlotte moved past Collison. "Then let's *go* north."

"Rudy," Rob grinned, "I think we have our marching orders."

The six of them hiked on and soon came to the wide spot in the path, not fifty feet from the oak. Following Rudy's plan again, Artie aimed his flashlight at the top of the tree. "Is that Larry way up there?" Their flashlights lit up the treetop as Si came down the path with the lantern. Still aiming at the top, Artie said, "I think I saw him move."

Rudy turned and looked over them at the city. *Not bad at all.* "Okay, everybody, we'll see what my dad's up to in a minute. Please turn off your flashlights and close your eyes." Rudy shut his light off. Charlotte groaned a little, then complied as the last of the flashlights blinked off.

"Okay, please keep them off, turn around, open your eyes, be quiet, and listen," Rudy said, his voice subdued. Someone gasped after they faced the city, although the view wasn't as spectacular as when Rudy was there with Reed. On this night, the L.A. basin seemed to be divided roughly in half like a pie. The west side was below dense fog that moved imperceptibly to the east, where the city's lights were nearly as brilliant as before. Harsh manmade sounds from far below mingled with a few natural noises in the chaparral—crickets, a dove's lament, and a coyote squalling at the drab crust of the moon.

After the hikers maintained their silence for half a minute or so, some of them murmured, but nobody turned on a flashlight. *What would Libby think of this? Maybe I'll have the guts to find out.* Rudy walked closer to the others and came first to Si.

"I see Mars, Rudy." He pointed.

"Good, Si." Rudy looked up. "Show me another planet on the way down, okay?"

"Yes. I can find one."

Rudy moved on to Diana. The city lights reflected rivulets of tears on her cheek.

"Rudy, I feel Reed standing here with you—he's enthralled."

Man. He patted her once on the shoulder, wiped his own tear with a sleeve, then faced the group. "Okay, everybody turn on your lights again and aim about two-thirds of the way up the tree—not the top." Si aimed the lantern up there; it revealed Larry's belt buckle glimmering in the branches. They all trained their lights on that spot, then waited only moments before a long wisp of ash fell from the limbs into the beams of light, caught a ripple of breeze, then floated down and away.

Artie turned to watch Rudy walk slowly with Larry's camp shovel up to the oak and bury Reed's lucky coin.

CHAPTER 22
Runners

On the Monday morning after the hike, piercing headaches woke Rudy from dreamless sleep. *Damn—this must be a migraine.* His mother had come in earlier to warn him that he'd be late for school. Now, as soon as Rudy sat up, he was dizzy. *God, lie down.* He lay there, eyes closed, hoping for sleep that didn't come.

He opened his eyes when his door rattled from a double knock. Katie entered wearing her terry bathrobe. She lethargically checked Rudy's clock. Her face wan, a lack of makeup revealed long age lines and what could pass for two black eyes.

"Happy Halloween," Katie said, not happy.

It's Vampira. "Yeah, trick or treat."

"Congratulations, you're late. Why didn't you get up?"

"I was about to—guess I'm sick."

"You guess? Another headache?"

"Yeah." *She probably has one too.*

"Only the headache?"

"Yes. I'm taking a sick day."

"How many have you taken so far?"

For god's sake. "One."

"Alright, I'll get some aspirin."

After Rudy swallowed the two aspirins she brought, it took a while for the headache to subside a little, but his stomach checked in with dull but constant pain before he dozed off.

When Rudy heard Katie come back in, he opened his eyes to 11:35 on the clock, then faced his mother. She had tidied herself and was dressed in black slacks and a white blouse.

This time, she put her palm on his forehead. "Is it better?"

Downright motherly. "Yeah, better."

"No temp. I think you were exhausted."

"You look better too."

"What do you mean by that?"

Nothing. "Earlier, we were both pretty rough."

"Speak for yourself," she stated indifferently.

So much for motherly. "Mom, who's still around?"

"Charlotte's off somewhere; you know where Larry is. Seth and Mom just came; I'm going to show her how to use my old IBM."

Fascinating. "Did I hear Si in the kitchen?"

"Yes, it's Halloween."

"Right, his favorite holiday."

"He had Halloween all pre-arranged with his boss; I guess you'll have to survive another day around him."

Don't let her goad you. "Where is he?"

"He went to the den after breakfast. Probably watching TV."

"Maybe I'll join him."

She sneered. "Don't do us any favors."

Go to hell. In his underwear and bathrobe, Rudy went into the kitchen. He made cereal, ate less than half, then shuffled down to the den. Si was on the couch, working on a crossword and peeking at the TV. Mildred was nearby in the plush chair, knitting while Stew slept at her feet.

Rudy sat on the recliner that had a blanket; he pulled it onto his lap. "Hi, Gramma, Si."

Mildred beamed. "Rudolph, feelin' better?"

No. "Yes, and you?" Stew meandered over to him, and Rudy ruffled his droopy ears.

"False alarm—my little fever broke. Seth said the meetin' for Reed came out jus' fine."

"Yes, it did. Everybody liked your cookies and muffins." She smiled, and Rudy tried to ignore the steady pulsing in his head. He sat partway back. "Si, what's on after all the commercials?"

"I think they said *Beverly Hillbillies.* Are you sick, Rudy?"

"Just a little."

Mildred got to her feet with her knitting. "What can I get you, Rudolph?"

"Nothing, Gramma. I feel better just lying here." *You're* **lying** *alright.*

"That's good." She pulled the blanket up over his chest. "Okay, you two enjoy y'r program. I'll be with Catherine in her office." She left through the sliding back door.

Rudy watched Si fill in a word in his crossword magazine. "Hard puzzle, Si?"

"It has words like *cupid* and *Romeo*. I got those, and *arrow* and, uh, *love birds*." Si looked up to watch a cartoon toucan on TV make a pitch for cereal before the re-run of *The Beverly Hillbillies* began. Si put down his magazine and fixated on the show's opening. "Beverly Hills, that is," he repeated from the theme song.

Yee-haw. Rudy's head was beating harder; he reclined the chair the rest of the way. When the commercials returned, one of them caught Rudy's attention. "Si, did you hear that? They're having a *Hogan's Heroes* Halloween marathon—it goes from four o'clock until nine. Want to watch some of it?" *God, my TV buddy.*

"Doesn't it have Nazis laughing at people?"

What? "Si, it makes fun of Nazis." *He's right. How is a Nazi funny?*

"Oh. You'll watch it with me?"

"Sure, but we can watch something else if you want."

During the episode of *Hillbillies*, Rudy kept nodding off only to be roused by a headache. When the show finished, a talk show took over, and Si went back to his puzzle. *Damn aspirin never really kicked in.* "Si, I'm going to my room. See you and Colonel Hogan at four."

"Okay, Rudy." Si showed the slightest glint of a smile.

Did I really see that? Rudy went to the kitchen; no one was around. *Good.* Stew had followed him and was settling on his dog bed. Rudy took another aspirin, then checked out what the refrigerator offered. *Something sweet. No, nothing here.* He closed the fridge door. *The trick-or-treats? No—maybe something from the baking shelf.*

Rudy searched the cupboard and found a half-full bag of small multicolored spice drops. He opened it, took a red one, and popped it into his mouth. *Hm, stale—better that way. Cinnamon, I guess.* After some laborious chewing, he tried a green one. Rudy took the bag with him to his bedroom; he hardly noticed the mild gnawing that came up in his throat.

He sat on his bed with the bag of candy, then tried to predict their color by their taste until his head throbbed. As if in a trance, he ate a few more candies until they all tasted about the same. *Why the hell am I doing this?*

Rudy got up and went into the kitchen for some water. Seth came in wearing a sport coat with one of his bow ties. "Hey, Rudy." He opened the refrigerator. "How are you doing?"

Good question. He had been swishing water in his mouth; he spat it out. "I'm okay."

"You did a wonderful job yesterday, Rudy."

"Thanks, everybody was great." *After Martin.*

Seth took two apples from the refrigerator and washed them in the sink. "Mildred, Katie, and I are taking in *Annie Hall*. Interested?"

"I promised Si we'd watch *Hogan's Heroes*."

"Good, then he can still give out the candy. Okay, we'll be back after six. Larry's in the shop, and the treats are in the parlor. It's actually raining—won't be many goblins."

"Okay, have a good time." At the sink, Rudy watched the comforting soft rain outside and considered taking a walk, but his headache disabused him of the idea. He took yet another aspirin and returned to his room, where the heartburn rose again. *Damn.* Rudy spotted the remaining spice drops on the shelf over his bed. He grabbed the bag, fired it at the trash can across the room, missed, and watched candies roll around on the floor.

More crazy shit, Rudy. He lay back down and felt the headache turn into something altogether worse. *What the hell? Like brain freeze, non-stop.* Dizzy, he hoped for sleep again, but the abject pain held on for a while and left him in fitful semi-consciousness.

"Rudolph, wake up. Time for supper." Mildred stroked his arm.

Feeling her soft touch, he opened his eyes, pain behind his sockets. "Gramma?"

"Yes, sweetheart."

Rudy checked the clock. *Five-forty. Damn, Si at four.* "Guess I dozed off for a while."

"Somethin' still ailin' you, Rudolph?"

Double feature—heartburn and headache. "Just a little stomachache."

She noticed the empty bag and the candies on the floor. "My, it's no wonder. I'm thinkin' those are from last Christmas."

"Yeah, I'll clean them up."

"Katie and me turned lazy bones an' got us store-bought chicken an' fix-ins for supper."

I don't think so.

"Everybody's waitin'. That'll perk you up a little."

No, it won't. "Okay, Gramma." As she left, he sat up, but left his feet on the floor while he summoned the motivation to move. Rudy finally got up and walked to his bathroom. He did his business on the toilet, barely cognizant when he flushed that his stool was black again. Rudy washed his hands diligently and threw cold water on his face.

Still in his bathrobe, Rudy entered the kitchen. Charlotte and Si weren't there; Mildred was talking very quietly to Seth and Katie. At the far end of the table, his father ate silently. *Not lively Larry today.* The take-out food had been transferred to bowls and platters—fried chicken and the usual side dishes. Rudy smelled cookies baking in the oven. *How can cookies smell that bad?* Katie eyed Rudy as if daring him to speak.

Nothing to say to her. "Dad, where's Si?"

"Don't know." Without eye contact, he continued eating.

Seth responded. "Simon almost missed dinner for *Hogan's Heroes.* He's eating in the dining room so he won't miss any trick-or-treaters."

Mildred beamed. "You an' Simon will be watchin' your program together?"

"Yes." His headache persisted, but not as extreme. Rudy took a drumstick, a small plop of mashed potatoes, and some raw vegetables from a relish tray. There was also a tall glass of clear carbonated liquid near his plate. *Gramma's magic elixir.*

"Rudolph, I let the soda go almost flat."

"Right. Sip until it's all gone. Thanks, Gramma." He took a sip.

Katie finally spoke. "Gramma said you were still not feeling well."

She looks as bad as this morning—wants a drink. "I'm okay." *Show them— eat.* He sipped the soda again, then nibbled some crisp chicken, oozing with oil. *Ack—awful.* Rudy picked at his dinner silently, responding with an occasional nod to small talk from the others.

Seth put his silverware on his plate. "Rudy, your mother and Mildred are going to Helen's at seven for a short visit. Your dad and I will be in the shop."

"Okay." *Mom's so desperate she might drink Helen's sherry.*

Si came in with his plate and took it to the sink. "No trick-or-treaters now. Rudy, I can listen for them from the den."

A hint. "Sorry I slept in, Si. Be there in a minute." Rudy went to the sink, scraped off the leftovers, then rinsed the plate. Wryly, he showed Mildred his glass of soda as he left. When he reached the parlor, a sharp spasm struck his stomach. He put the drink down and rested in a chair until he was sure it had stopped. *Spice drops and greasy chicken—what did you expect?*

He made his way down to the den and sat on the same recliner. Si was on the couch. Rudy put his glass on the floor, then adjusted the chair halfway back.

"Si, what's Colonel Hogan doing to the pathetic Nazis?"

"He wants to meet Colonel Klink's secretary."

Rudy's stomach settled more. "Ah, let me guess. He's bribing Sergeant Schultz with sweets or champagne."

"You saw this one."

"A lucky guess. Do you want to watch something else?"

"No, Sergeant Schultz is funny." The doorbell rang and Si left the den, moving as fast as he did on the hike, then he returned right away to the couch.

Damn, should've taken another aspirin. "How many goblins, Si?"

"Three. Dracula, a pixie, and, uh, they were wet." He watched Colonel Klink again.

Rudy got halfway up to reach down for the blanket. He covered himself and fully reclined. "Okay, Si. I might rest my eyes a little, but I'll be listening to the show."

Those were the last words from either of them for a while. Rudy had been staring at the pine ceiling. The varnish made the dark-blond lines of grain more visible than untreated pine. Rudy saw the lines as roads that circumvented dark, round knots in the wood. *This was all real once—alive.* He tried to zoom in on one of the knots, then follow the grain to see how close he could get to another knot. It barely registered with Rudy that on TV Colonel Klink scolded Schultz with *Dummkopf!*

He watched the roads avoid a knot, then re-form the same pattern on the other side. Some lines were only a few inches long before fading, but others seemed to span the entire ceiling. In some places, they converged, ran adjacently like a racetrack, then they seemed to bend or swerve in order to avoid an oncoming knot.

Go with them. How? A racecar? A runner like Reed or Artie? No, me. In an Angels hat, his runner started its journey on the widest road, right above Rudy's head. He sped onto a straight dark track that unexpectedly narrowed and stopped. His runner jumped to the right into the middle of three parallel beige lanes where an amorphous charcoal-grey runner awaited him. *What the hell is that?* They accelerated side by side. *Are we racing? Why?* They bent to the right on a curve. *Gravity—here? Straight again—good.*

He became aware of a massive oncoming brown knot; its top seemed to protrude inches above the surface. The grey runner started around on the right. Rudy tried to go left, but he couldn't. *I guess I go where it goes—okay with me. At least my damn headache is gone.* Halfway around, a runner of Earl's brother, Garret, appeared at an opening in the knot. *Ha! We're so fast, he couldn't do anything.*

Not cognizant of any pain, Rudy's lanes converged with some others to make six. The grey runner's form was still nebulous while the lanes on both sides widened into the shape of an oblong lake before they merged back next to Rudy. *What now?*

"Rudy, watch the next one?"

What? Crap. Si's voice had released Rudy from the course, but he didn't look down from the ceiling. "Sure, Si, let them keep going."

"I know about World War II—this is not right."

Okay, okay. "Yes, but to get the jokes, you have to forget the real war. Do you want to watch something else?"

"No, this is okay."

Good. Rudy heard footfalls approach from behind. *Damn.* He lowered his head a little.

"How are my two favorite boys?" Mildred clucked. "I have cookies for your dessert. Halloween butter cookies for you, Simon."

"Thanks, Mom."

"And for you, Rudolph, two plain cookies with pieces of ginger—settles the tummy."

Gross. He turned to her. "Thanks, Gramma." He anxiously eyed the ceiling again.

She set Rudy's plate on the floor near his drink. "Still a tad warm—enjoy 'em while me and Katie visit Helen. Have a good rest, Rudolph." She pulled his blanket up again.

Peripherally, Rudy saw Si pick up a cookie; he heard Mildred's footfalls behind. *You gotta' eat one—for her.* He took a bite of a cookie, vaguely aware of a scene in Hogan's jolly barracks on TV. He slowly finished the gooey snack; a headache had returned. *Get back up there.*

Before he could look up, Rudy regurgitated acrid fumes and sensed the cookie dough in his stomach. *Gut bomb. Lie back; close your eyes.* Rudy dozed, still aware of the pain. He woke up to Garret's runner on the TV screen. "What the hell?"

Si turned from the TV. "Rudy, you were sleeping and groaning."

"Sorry, Si. Didn't you just see that on the screen?"

"See what?"

Shit. "Nothing. Never mind."

"Another episode already started." He faced his nephew. "You're white, Rudy."

What? He means pale. "Si, what's going on in this one?"

"They're playing cards with Sergeant Schulz. I think you're sick, Rudy."

Who says he's oblivious? "I'm okay, Si."

"Good." He gazed at the TV. "Rudy, are Danny and me really your favorite uncles?"

Back in left field. "Yes, Si." He grimaced from the resurging pain.

"He's my favorite brother, Cami's my favorite sister, and you're my favorite nephew."

And so richly deserved. "Um, thank you, Si."

"Colonel Klink just came in."

"They'll trick him somehow." He checked the ceiling again. *Can I still get up there?* He chose a place where ten or so lanes seemed to take a long, straight course. His runner appeared, accelerating down the steady lanes. Rudy's maladies seemed to dissipate again; the grey runner was back at his side. *What does it want? Is Garret up ahead again?*

At the next knot, not only was Garret waiting for him, but also two runners in the forms of Harry and Rudy's P.E. teacher, Otis, both dressed as Kansas Highway Patrolmen. *Shit.* Rudy stopped his runner, lowered the chair, and glared at Klink on the screen. The TV marathon paused for a tardy Halloween commercial.

Go back up there? No headache now, maybe you don't need to go back. Do something else. "Si, isn't Scrabble your favorite board game?"

"Yes."

"Do you want to play?"

"Yes, but first I need to go."

To the can. "Okay, I'll get the game."

Si headed across the den, holding himself in front. Rudy stood, felt dizzy, then made his way through the house, wobbly at times, his stomach roiling again. He came to the utility room shelves and reached for the stack of games. His head ached again as he carried away the reddish-brown game box. *Damn, only one way to stop it.*

Si was back, sitting at the card table below the fluorescent light. Rudy pushed the plush chair over near Si and sat with the Scrabble box. Si opened it and put the gameboard and racks on the table, then he poured the blond wooden tiles into the lid and started flipping those that were showing letters.

"Thanks, Si." Rudy tried to help but had difficulty turning over the tiles. Off to the side, he saw Katie and Mildred approach. *Damn.*

"Startin' a game?" Mildred asked rhetorically. "Feel better, Rudolph?"

No. "Yes, how's Helen?"

Katie shrugged. "I'll say this, she's a tough ol' bird."

Sorry I asked. No sherry, Mom?

Si finished preparing the game and walked back to the TV. Mildred followed him, then returned with Rudy's plate and his drink. "You only ate one, Rudolph."

"They're real good, Gramma, but that was a big dinner."

Katie groaned. "Which you didn't eat."

His head beating, Rudy leaned back and looked up at the ceiling. *Can't see shit around that damn light. Now what? Have they left?* Rudy turned. "Do you want something, Mom?"

"Just checking up on you two—making sure you didn't have girls out here."

Real funny. "We have two each, coming in an hour." His head continued to throb.

"Oh? That'd be good for both of you," Katie said, smug with her retort.

Mildred *tsked.* "Catherine, goodness." She put Rudy's cookie and drink on the card table.

Katie sniggered. "So, Rudy, how's your stomach?"

Killing me. "Okay." *Get lost so I can do something about it.* He heard Mildred walk off.

"So, need a spice drop, Rudy?" Katie needled. "It's obvious you made yourself sick."

You *make me sick. Go make a highball.*

She had started to walk away. "*Ffff,* don't answer me."

To hell with her. "Okay, let's play," he called to Si, who came back from the TV

"You keep score, Rudy."

He's all business. "Okay." Rudy took a tablet and a pencil from the box.

"Reed and Seth always give me fifty points because I don't know all the new words."

"Fifty it is." His hand shaking a little, Rudy wrote the number crookedly on the pad.

"Sometimes it takes five minutes for my turn, Rudy. I pass after that."

Five minutes? That won't work. Rudy took two aspirins from his tin and swallowed them with the flat soda. *How do I get out of this?*

Si shook the lid; they drew for first turn, then chose seven tiles and put them on their racks. It took Si ten seconds, not five minutes, to put down *THORAX*. "That's forty-eight, Rudy."

"Good, Si." *That was quick—thank god.* He wrote down Si's score.

Si finished choosing his six new tiles. "I'm winning now."

No kidding. Go, Rudy. Right away, he spelled *FOXY* across the *X*, but didn't count his points. "Twenty," he guessed, then took some tiles as Si concentrated. *C'mon, Si, take your damn turn.* Rudy clumsily put the tiles on his rack, realizing he had chosen a second blank, which served as any letter. Rudy put them together as Si still mulled over his play. *Wait.* Rudy turned the two blanks over and around several times on the rack until the grain of one combination nearly matched. *These will work! Small, short course, so go slow.* He fixated on the side-by-side blanks, then his runner appeared and started off; the lanes were straight, but instead of being compact, they expanded and seemed endless. *And no knots!*

Si counted down, using his watch. "Rudy, I pass."

No, Si, **now** *take your time.* "Take five more minutes, Si. I was probably bothering you." He focused on the two blanks again.

"That's not the rules."

Damn, lost my runner. "Okay." He checked his rack and saw *H*, *E*, and *M*. His head and gut aching, Rudy thought he played them under a *T*.

"*H-H-E-M?* Is that a new word, Rudy?"

What? "No, I made a mistake. Your turn." *And use all five minutes, please.* Rudy returned to his two blank tiles. His runner and the grey one gradually appeared and began to move. *No bends, no knots, no errors—no headache. There's the edge—we're going under.* He came out the other side back at the beginning again. *Why is the grey thing still here? Forget it, just go—*

Si played *G—ENADE* over an *R*. "Grenade, Rudy. Twenty-six points; that makes me almost to a hundred."

"Uh, good, Si." *Hurry, make a play!* He frantically took a blank off of his rack to use as an "*S*" and held it over the end of Si's word. The thought of *grenades* merged with his exploding headache. *No, you need both blanks to get back to the lanes!* He withdrew his hand and the blank tile, but his elbow knocked over the box lid; the tiles and Rudy fell to the floor.

CHAPTER 23
The Dictionary

Rudy lay still on his side, his head couched in his right elbow; he opened his eyes to the *Q-10* tile a foot or so away. *What the hell? Scrabble, Si, runners, brain freeze, gut bomb. Get up.* He tried to raise his head, but it just inched up his arm to rest near his shoulder; the movement brought on a headache. *Far enough.* Between the floorboards, he saw straight lines extend all the way across the den. *Good, take the closest one!* His runner materialized and Rudy sped away—no pain, no anxiety. The cryptic grey runner joined him and pulled in front. *It's leading me.*

"Rudy, are you still sick?"

Don't bother me, Si. Rudy and the grey runner bolted down the fastest lane ever. *Much better.* He heard someone come in. *Go away, we're busy.* His runner and the other one stopped.

"What's with him?" Katie asked Si. "Don't tell me—he got mad and knocked it all over."

"No." Si turned to her. "I think he's still sick."

She jostled Rudy's leg with the toe of her shoe. "See there, Si?" She laughed. "Eyes open—playing 'possum." Katie leaned down, her face near his.

Go away. Rudy focused on the wood grain. *Get going.* The two runners were on course again. *Straight ahead—yes. This is good, nothing else matters.*

"Damn it, Rudy."

To hell with her. Keep going.

"If you're resting, at least move to the couch." She lifted one of his arms and Rudy let it down normally. Katie got to her feet. "It should've flopped, faker. Listen, Rudy…"

Her words became bland dissonance and didn't detract from his speed on the track.

"…Shar gets home, I'll send *her* to get you up." Katie waited for Rudy to react. "Don't pay any attention to him, Si. He'll be up in a minute."

"No."

"What?"

"He can't get up."

"Si, he just needs a little break." Katie left for the parlor. "Matter of fact, so do I."

Zipping along the course with the specter, Rudy was dimly aware that Katie had left.

Si spoke to him. "Rudy, I'm getting help."

Si's words jumbled. Rudy's runner moved faster and left the grey one behind. *This is where it wanted me to go? Nothing here—another void. Why?* A headache seemed to slam into his brain; he closed his eyes.

Rudy was unaware that minutes had passed before Seth shouted, "Rudy, can you open your eyes?"

What's he yelling about? Gotta' sleep.

"Rudolph?"

There was a gentle touch on his arm. *Just sleeping, Gramma.*

"Rudy," Seth said, much quieter, "whatever's wrong, we'll take care of it. Mildred, please cover him up to his waist, then find a small pillow and another light blanket."

What did he say? As Seth lifted one eyelid, then the other, Rudy saw only blurs of Seth's face. Seth's fingers rested on Rudy's forehead, then moved to his wrist. *Si must've brought him.*

"Rudy, try to take some deep breaths."

Rudy understood this time, but Seth slid in a thermometer before Rudy could react. A stethoscope moved spot to spot on his back and chest before the thermometer was extracted. Rudy felt snug pressure on his upper arm, some poking around on his abdomen and chest; the latter made his now slightly bruised upper torso flinch.

"…and enlarged pupils, slight fever, but sweating and pale," Seth grumbled, then raised his voice. "I've seen enough. Okay, Larry, call an ambulance."

Ambulance? Crap, I'll be okay in a few minutes.

"Rudy," Seth said, "I know you're in there. What hurts?"

He opened his eyes. "Seth, where's Si?"

"Ah, so there you are." Seth's relief escaped in a soundless whistle. "Simon's sitting right there at the table; he's fine. Tell me what hurts most, Rudy."

"My head." He was looking at the floor. *No runners. What's wrong with me?* Rudy heard his mother sobbing; he closed his eyes again. *What's with her?*

Katie sniffled. "Can I help, Grampa?"

Mildred answered her. "Yes, Catherine, take the bedding."

"I know this—you don't move him," Katie said, reverting to her lifeguarding days, "and don't elevate his head, right?"

Barely able to follow their conversation, Rudy felt the blanket slide over the other one, then his eyes seemed to close of their own will.

"Thank you, Catherine," Seth told her. "And raise his feet with the pillow, please."

Rudy felt his feet elevate a little, then his mother's cold hand rested gently on his head.

"They're coming," Larry said, "maybe five more minutes. I'll go out and wait. Want to come out, Si?"

"No thanks. Mom, why are Rudy's eyes closed again?"

"He's restin', sweetheart."

"Simon, he's going to be okay," Seth said.

"Good. Rudy says me and Danny are his favorite uncles."

His eyes still closed, Rudy heard some of the ruckus with the arrival of the medics. They spoke with the family, but their speech didn't connect for him until one guy approached and blurted,

"Rudy! C'mon, bud, let's see those baby blues. Rudy!"

What's with all the shouting? Squinting up into a glare, all Rudy could see of the medic was a skeleton covering his uniform. "Trick-or-treat," Rudy said, closing his eyes.

The medic snickered. "That's right, Rudy. Where you hurtin' most now?"

Probably my ass. He kept his eyes closed. "Head and gut." Rudy felt a gentle poke near his stomach, another, then a third poke, which induced a flinch.

"Bingo. Nobody touch that again. That's not the appendix,

right, doc?"

"Right." Seth frowned. "I completely missed it. His upper chest is also tender."

What? He heard the words, but again they didn't fully register until the medic spoke.

"It's okay, Doc." The medic paused. "Alright, pack 'im up gentle—Kaiser Hollywood."

Seth cleared his throat. "May I go along, please?"

"If his mom or dad don't want the spot."

"Please let Doctor Grant go," Larry said.

Rudy heard the medic announce, "Okay, this is a big boy, all hands on deck."

Rudy felt them carry him gently to the gurney. "Back on my side, please."

"You got it, Bud."

Once outside, Rudy savored a passing breeze, fresh from the recent rain. His eyes still closed, he was jolted by the clunking and slamming as they inserted him into the ambulance. They finally started off, but each crack, bump, or pothole stunned him. Finally, the ambulance settled into a glide as if they had driven onto perfect pavement. Rudy opened his eyes to an IV bag hanging over his head.

"How are you doing, Rudy?" Seth asked from the left side.

"Where are we, Seth?"

"Almost to the Hyperion Bridge. No siren or flashing lights—should be an easy trip. Any change with the pain?"

"Headaches are stronger."

He cupped Rudy's forehead. "You're going to be okay, son. I'll be quiet; now try to rest."

His eyelids grew heavy, but someone turned off the interior lights, accentuating every gleam from the darkness outside. *No, turn them back on!* He saw the city streetlights that lined the bridge at exact intervals. Rudy resisted, but he was drawn to them again. *Steady as a merry-go-round—over and over...*

The beating in his head reverberated like kettle drums. Then, as before, he fell into a stupor. *Everything into nothing. God, somebody say something.* Someone was holding his shoulder. *Talk to me!* The thunderous beat in his head strengthened again. *Too late—this is it. It had to be even worse for Reed—good god.* Rudy's eyes closed over tears for his friend.

Why am I not afraid? Who will take care of Stew?

…another damn rumbling cart…gotta' pee…

"Housekeeping, 408, housekeeping…"

Last thoughts—Reed—then Stew, but at least I'm here.

"Code thirty, Doctor Lee, code thirty…"

Rudy opened his eyes to the objects above him: glaring fluorescent lights, two IV bags, and a black helium-balloon, its white skull-and-crossbones with red eyes. *What?* His lower arm on his right side was out of his sight and ached. Because he was propped on his left side, he barely had to turn his head to follow the wires and a yellow tube from under the covers off to the left. *Pee—great.* Rudy peered down the neck of his hospital gown at sensors taped to his chest.

The activity seemed to revive a mild headache and also a tug on his thin chest hair under the tape. *Ow—damn.* On a muted TV attached to a metal arm, he saw a salesman, his lips flapping as he caressed a Ford Pinto. Rudy heard the door seal rub on the tile. *Somebody's here.*

Seth, in a dress shirt and bow tie, stepped in front of the TV. "Well, look who's awake," he said, his face beaming near the foot of the bed.

"Yeah. Hi, Seth." He paused. "I guess I put the cart before the horse."

Seth came around to Rudy's left to face him. "What do you mean?"

"My first thought was that my last thoughts weren't my final thoughts."

"Indeed." Seth pushed two hard-plastic chairs aside, stood near Rudy, then patted his upper arm. "You've really been through it; I'm glad to see you so chipper, Rudy."

Chipper?

Seth turned more somber. "So, how much pain now?"

"Headaches, but not as bad. My gut is queasy but no sharp pain." Rudy shifted his eyes to the right. "That IV—my arm aches a lot, and it doesn't stop."

"Not unusual, but I'll have them check it. Anything else?"

"The catheter. It feels like I have to pee but never do."

"Uncomfortable, but also not unusual." He peeked down next to the bed. "The bag's a quarter full. Until you can use a bedpan or get up, they won't take it out."

Rudy frowned at his attachments. "Bring on the bedpan."

"Okay, three questions. Who is the Commander-in-Chief of the U.S.? Who is the best pitcher on the Angels, and what day do you think it is?"

Cinch. "Jimmy Carter is president, and Nolan Ryan is the *game's* best pitcher." He turned his head and torso a little to the shaded window off to the left, causing another tug on his chest. *Damn.* "Um, it's not dark. So, I'll guess it's the day after Halloween. Monday, November first."

"Good. This is Kaiser Hospital in Hollywood; it's past noon." He nodded to a wall clock he had been blocking. "Rudolph, your condition is serious but stable. Your doctor had to leave; he asked me to explain your status. Technically, I'm not your doctor while you're here."

"No Seth-oscope?"

"I forgot you used to say that." Seth's grin vanished. "Rudy, you were unconscious or asleep more than twelve hours. Do you have an idea of how long you have been awake?"

"One of those rattling carts woke me up a little while ago, I think; then there was all the other noise. I listened some more, then another damn cart came by, and I opened my eyes."

"Those last thoughts you mentioned—do you remember what they were?"

"Yeah," he paused, "Reed's pain when he died. And who would take care of Stew."

"So, you thought you were dying?"

"Yes. What the hell happened to me, Seth?"

"When you're ready, I'll tell you what we think we know."

What? "I'm ready."

"Interrupt if you have questions. One second." He moved away to glance at the monitors.

Why the damn intrigue?

Seth returned. "Rudy, you apparently have a perforated duodenal ulcer—a bleeding ulcer in your duodenum, below the stomach. Have you had black stools?"

What? "I guess so. Why?"

"That's blood in your feces."

Gross. "Has the bleeding stopped?"

"It's under control." He frowned. "A few more hours and those actually *would* have been your final thoughts. A man around your size has ten or eleven pints of blood—the loss of more than half is potentially fatal. We think you lost at least five pints and eventually went into shock. Now, after hours of treatment, your vitals are closer to normal, and you have a little color back in your cheeks."

"If it's that serious, why did I have more pain in my head than my gut?"

"Bleeding ulcers are sometimes insidious. The symptoms vary and can seem like relatively normal aches and pains until the disease comes to a head." Seth nodded gravely, then moved a table-tray with a water pitcher over Rudy's lap. He poured some crushed ice and water into a plastic cup, then held it for Rudy.

Rudy took two long gulps through the flexible straw. "Thanks, that was good. Can I have an aspirin?"

"No, you can't," his tone blunt. "Listen, you'll be here for a few days. If *anyone* brings aspirin—refuse it nicely and say, 'Doctor Howard's orders.' For you, aspirin is *not* innocuous."

What? "Why is that?"

"Excessive internal bleeding brings on the headaches, then you take aspirin, which aggravates the ulcer—a vicious cycle. Fortunately, we do have a pain medication that doesn't aggravate the digestive tract."

"So, all that time, the aspirin was making it worse."

"Yes. You'll have a barium x-ray this afternoon to confirm the diagnosis, then surgery is possible, but I don't think it will come to that. You'll automatically get a bland diet, but it includes dairy products, which often exacerbate stomach acid, notwithstanding medical and public lore about milk and ulcers—just ask for apple juice instead of milk. The rest of the bland diet will be fine for you, albeit unappetizing." He pulled up a chair and sat nearby.

"You don't sound very enthused about what they're doing."

"Well, I've probably treated hundreds of ulcers in my time, and I have never agreed with some of the accepted protocols."

"Seth, you must have been the boy who told the emperor he was naked."

Seth kept his serious demeanor. "Put it this way, young Doctor Howard is one of few physicians around here who doesn't consider me a crank. I called in a favor to get him for you. Okay, enough about my rabble-rousing."

"Seth, I'm surprised I'm on my side."

"You were groaning about your rear end; the night nurse checked and found those two black bruises. She resettled you, then also found faded bruises on your face and chest. I told her I would ask you about it."

"Why?"

"It's procedure in case of abuse. I assume they're from the bully you told me about."

"The ones on my butt are from a different bully—steel-toed boots." *And a little extra.*

"Do you want to talk about this later?"

"Maybe, but I'm doing okay for now."

"Okay, Mildred and your parents are waiting out there with Helen. Mildred called your aunts and uncles, including Camilla; they all send their best." Seth filled him in on family who planned to visit. "That's a lot of commotion, and your top priority is rest; try not to overdo it."

While Seth checked the monitors again, Rudy turned his head slightly to scan the small, standardly equipped, private room; his Angels cap and some flowers were on a table by the window. He turned back to the muted TV. A movie showed a man and a woman swimming together under water. *What the hell, I'm going to do that someday.*

"Daniel and Sharon sent the flowers." Seth pushed a button, raising Rudy higher.

"Seth, I feel different than I did before this happened, but I can't explain it."

"That's understandable. Your body and mind have had quite a shock—literally."

"Yeah." *That's not what I mean. What **do** you mean? Talk to Helen.* Rudy looked up at the balloon. "Who do I thank for the ghoulish balloon?"

"Charlotte left it for you." Seth sat again.

"I should've guessed. Actually, it's pretty funny. Is Si here?"

"No, he had to go back to work or lose a day, but he wouldn't leave until I told him you would be okay. Charlotte drove him early this morning. Oh, I forgot to mention she'll be by tonight with Rob, Artie, and your new friend."

"You mean Libby?" *Man, she'll think I'm a basket case.*

Seth nodded with a crease of a grin. "Do you know who got us moving last night?"

"Had to be Si." *He saved my ass.* "Sorry I missed him. Seth, can I talk to him today?"

"I think we can arrange that—might take a little while."

"Okay. Thanks."

A tall nurse strutted into the room in a crisp white uniform, but no silly nurse's hat.

"Uh-oh, shift change," Seth bantered, "here comes trouble."

"Sergeant Grant, we know who the troublemaker is around here." The slim, middle-aged nurse had a sepia-brown complexion and angular features except for her moderately wide nose. Belaying her stern countenance, the nurse's face transformed into a full smile for Rudy before she began to read his chart. "Is Mister Lanier your clinic patient, doctor?"

"He's my grandson, Phyllis. Doctor Howard—"

"Let me guess," still reading, "Doctor Howard had to leave and asked you to cover."

"More or less. He asked me to explain to Rudy his condition and treatment."

"And you finagled your grandson onto this floor, right next to the nurse's station."

Seth grinned. "Why, Sarge, I wouldn't—"

"Uh-huh. I'd do the same for mine if I had any pull." After checking the chart again, she looked askance at the pirate balloon, then faced Rudy with a more understated smile, holding his shoulder for a moment. "You're getting some pretty special attention here, young man."

"Yes, ma'am, I know." He spotted her badge: *PHYLLIS BISHOP-RN.*

Seth took a step closer to her. "Rudy said he still has regular headaches—not as severe. Stomach is unsettled, no sharp pain. He has steady pain with the IV and discomfort with the catheter. He thinks he's ready for the bedpan."

"M-hm. When did he come to, doctor?"

"Maybe a half-hour ago. I suggest a 325-milligram increase of acetaminophen."

"Doctor Howard did fill out this chart, you know—none of that nasty ol' aspirin on here." Grinning, the nurse left as suddenly as she came.

Rudy tried to reach his water, but his attachments kept him from moving his arm very far.

"If she's not back in thirty seconds, I'll help you. Otherwise, I'd just end up in the way." He chuckled. "No moss gathers under those shoes."

Before Rudy could respond, Phyllis seemed to float in with a tiny white paper cup. "This should do it for now. Okay, open up." She tossed in the white tablet and gave him water. "You'll be doing that yourself pretty soon." She checked the monitors, the IV needle, lines, and bags, then some of his vitals. "Rudy, do you really claim this character to be your grandfather?"

"Yes, ma'am, I do."

"I'll deny I *ever* said this, but more of these young doctors need to see your grandpa at work." She faced Seth. "Don't go getting a big head now." She checked her watch. "Doctor Grant, you have fifteen minutes left of the twenty I'm giving you. And those visitors out there? No more than two at a time for ten minutes. I'll check on Rudy again after all that."

"Wilco, Master Sergeant."

"And don't you forget it, Sergeant," snickering as she left the room.

"She's great, Seth. I take it you've known her for a while."

"We've teased each other for years. Phyllis is another vet—Korea. She'll take great care of you." Seth inhaled and exhaled noticeably. "You need to know before Catherine visits that she feels very guilty because she assumed you were faking last night." He sighed. "I should have put it all together weeks ago from your symptoms along with all the stress."

"I read somewhere that ulcers are caused by stress."

"And there's the rub. Stress, anger, and depression can irritate ulcers, but I don't agree with the doctrine that says ulcers are usually psychosomatic. If an ulcer patient receives all the latest treatment, including counseling, ulcers are likely to return with time."

Great. "So where does that leave me?"

"I have a plan for you."

What does that mean?

His face solemn, Seth situated himself closer to Rudy. "To be frank, I want to do something that is, um, unofficial," speaking softly. "A few years ago, I had a chronic ulcer patient who I was also treating with antibiotics for another ailment. The course of antibiotics cleared up the infection, and his ulcer symptoms also ceased, then never returned. Since then, I've tried this discreetly with the permission of about a dozen ulcer patients whom I've known for years—who have also presented with an infection.

"All but two recovered permanently from their ulcers, no harm done. I can't prove it scientifically, but I am convinced that many ulcers are caused by a specific bacterium in the digestive tract. It's not even a new idea, but someday it will see the light of day." Seth smiled at a small constellation of pimples on Rudy's forehead. "Who knows, it might even clear up acne."

Rudy laughed a little. "Count me in, but what happens if they catch you doing this?"

"If you and your parents agree to try it, and the treatment is successful, it would be worth it. I want to do it one last time—for you and Mildred. The way I see it, the worst that can happen is I close what's left of my practice, then try to find a researcher who might be interested in the treatment." He perked up with a grin. "And it's about time for the Grants to travel, maybe to see Camilla."

"Right, just don't forget your doctor bag." Rudy's quip gave way to a frown. "I don't know, Seth; I don't want you to get in trouble."

"I don't think I will, and I doubt you or your parents will snitch," he said with an uneasy laugh. "So, do I meet with Larry and Catherine?"

"I guess I don't want ulcers my whole life. Let's go for it. I'll talk to them after you do."

"Good. I'll sit down with them this evening. It's time for the others to come in."

He left, then a minute or so later, Mildred entered in a white sweater and a pastel-green dress. "Rudolph, sweetheart." Losing a tear, she planted a lip-sticky kiss on his cheek.

Rudy started to lift his left arm to hold her hand but thought better of it. "Hi, Gramma. Don't worry, I'm fine. Seth is keeping this place on its toes."

She sat on one of the chairs and scooted up close to his left side. "I hope he's not bein' gruff. He can be a mite cantankerous when he's worried about a patient, even when the prospects is good—like with you. Trust his ideas, Rudolph." Holding his arm, Mildred switched to some light talk about what Rudy might need at the hospital, then the treats she planned for his coming birthday. After a few minutes, she kissed him on the cheek. "See you before we go, Rudolph." She left, waving demonstratively back to him.

Rudy's parents came in, Larry in work overalls and a flannel shirt;

he stood well behind Katie. Disheveled in her flimsy blue jacket over grey sweats, Katie's face was drawn and pallid, her eye sockets dark and recessed again. An unlit cigarette dangled from her fingers.

Katie came to the bed, pushed some tubes aside and tried to embrace him. "God, I'm sorry, Rudy, so goddammed sorry." She turned her head to peck his cheek.

He winced again from the sensor tape; she stood, the cigarette falling to the floor. *No booze or mouthwash—but definitely hungover.* "Mom, you don't have anything to be sorry for. You couldn't have known I was sick." He peered past her distraught face. "Hi, Dad."

"Hi, Rudy. No more ghost costume?"

"Yeah, it helps to have some blood, I guess."

Katie reached for a tissue from Rudy's table. "Listen to you two, joking about this." Katie started talking disconnectedly about Rudy's prognosis. He responded with what he knew, although Seth had probably explained it all to her. He saw Seth return to the doorway.

Katie sniffled. "Rudy, we only called Artie. Are you sure that's what you want?"

"Yes, thanks." *What I want is a minute with Dad.*

"We'll be back after Helen." Halfway to the door, Larry stopped to talk to Seth while Katie left the room, dabbing her face. Rudy raised his brows and bent his neck back a little to beckon Seth, who came right over.

"We placed the call, Rudy. They said Simon has a break coming. He'll call soon."

"Good, thank you. Seth, I didn't get a chance to speak with my dad."

"Right, I'll tell Helen it will be a few more minutes."

Seth went back to Larry, then out. Larry returned to the bed. "Rudy?"

"Yeah, thank you again for all of your help with Reed's deal. It meant a lot to me."

"You're welcome."

Rudy waited a moment. *Withdrawn again—just go on.* "Mom hasn't had a drink today."

"Not since last night."

Go on. "Dad, do you still care about her?"

Larry didn't answer right away. "I care about her getting help," chin to chest.

That's it? "Is there any chance you and Mom can work things out?"

Larry exhaled and looked up. "Just worry about getting better, Rudy." He turned to go.

"Yeah, I'll do that."

On his way out, Larry stopped briefly to talk with Seth, who then came back to Rudy.

"Seth, Dad's all introverted again. Before this happened, I thought he was doing better."

"It's a temporary setback. Don't blame yourself or your illness. He cares about you, Rudy, even when he won't talk." He picked up Katie's cigarette, then left. Using her cane, Helen entered several moments later in her colorful autumn sweater.

"Hi, Helen."

"Well, hello to y—" The phone on the side table rang. "I've got it." She picked up the receiver. "Hello?" She paused. "Yes, Si, it's Helen." Another pause. "Rudy's right here." She stretched out the cord and held the receiver to Rudy's ear.

"Hey, Si."

"Hi, Rudy. I'm at work."

"Yes, I heard Charlotte took you back."

"She's gone now. I bought her a taco this time."

"That's good, Si."

"You were real sick."

"Yes, but I'm going to be okay, thanks to you. You saved me, Si."

"Oh. Remember you said I'm one of your favorite uncles?"

"Sure, I think you're my *most* favorite uncle." *How could he not be?*

"Good. My break is almost over, Rudy."

"Thanks for calling, Si."

"Welcome. I can't come until Thanksgiving. No more vacation time."

"That's only three weeks. Si, have you heard about *Star Wars*?"

"Yes."

"At Thanksgiving, we'll go see it."

"Good, can Artie come? He's my friend."

"Of course he can come."

"I'm going to read your story about the city tonight. I think it will be good."

Geez, my fan. "Thanks, I hope so."

"I'll bring it back at Thanksgiving. Bye, Rudy."

"Bye, um, Uncle Si." *Yeah, that feels right.* Rudy sighed.

As Helen hung up the phone, Rudy saw that she was wiping her face with a handkerchief.

She sniffled. "Excuse me, Rudy, but some tears of joy are very welcome right now." She came closer, sat, then gently held Rudy's arm. "What a couple of weeks for you. You look as well as could be expected for someone who was so close to death's door. Oh, dear." Her eyes and brows rose as she sat in the nearest chair. "Please excuse my blunt, trite metaphor."

He smiled. "Forget it, Helen."

"So, Seth seems pleased with your prognosis."

"Yes, I feel good about it." *Can't tell her why—yet.*

"Wonderful. Oh, Diana said she'll bring me to see you in a couple days."

"Good. I can sure understand how she became Reed's good friend." He paused. "Helen, I'd like to tell you something that might sound kind of strange."

She nodded with one of her wizened smiles. "Of course."

"In the ambulance, I entered a kind of void that has terrified me since I was twelve or so. I've always kept it to myself—never even told Reed." He paused. "I've heard and read about near-death experiences, a white light and all that. I've come close to this void before, but last night, I entered it. The pain was non-stop, and I was sure it was all over, but I wasn't scared somehow. I accepted the void, then all I thought about was Reed's pain at the end of his life—and who would take care of Stew." He sighed. "Now it feels like ordinary fears are trivial. I'm not suddenly courageous, but I know I won't be as afraid of so many things."

Helen waited a few seconds. "As you alluded to, Rudy, many people who face death and survive have had epiphanies. For some, it reinforces their religious faith—like the white light you mentioned. Others who have come back report a rational experience, similar to what you found. And I imagine that for some it is sheer terror."

"I just know what happened and how I feel now."

"I believe you, of course, and I want to hear more after you're home." She smiled, then turned away to nod toward Seth. She turned back. "Rudy, there's a gift here for you."

I've had my gifts.

"Rudy?"

"Um," pointing above with his chin, "it'll be pretty difficult to beat that balloon."

Seth, Mildred, and Larry all came in, Katie behind them. Larry was lugging a cardboard box that he put on the bed by Rudy's feet. Rudy could feel the gift weigh down that corner of the mattress. Katie, her face still moist, held the rail near the box. Larry was a few feet behind Helen.

The nurse returned. "Doctor Grant, you know I didn't approve any parties—and why wasn't I invited? Ten minutes," smiling as she left.

Rudy raised his left arm a foot or so. "Okay, so what's the big surprise?"

Seth opened the box and took out a rectangular store-wrapped silver gift larger than a footstool. Mildred cleared off the patient table and Seth placed the present there.

"Well, since I already have a balloon and flowers, this must be candy—lots of candy—just what I need. Right, Doctor Grant?"

Mildred moved closer to Rudy. "Rudolph, the gift's from Simon." *What?*

She held Rudy's arm. "Simon drove me to the mall the other day. He left the gift with me for your birthday, but this mornin' he said to give it to you when you woke up. So, it's early happy birthday from Simon!" Mildred, Helen, and Larry lightly applauded. Seth had his arm reassuringly around Katie.

Mildred broke a brief silence. "C'mon, like the nurse said, it's a party." She helped Rudy slip off the shiny ribbon and remove the loose silver paper to reveal a *Merriam-Webster's* similar to the stationary dictionaries you see on a stand in the library.

The tubes and wires only allowed Rudy to touch the great dictionary. *Man, what was he thinking? Maybe a week's pay.*

Mildred pursed her lips. "Somethin' wrong, Rudolph?"

"No, Gramma, this is amazing, but Si can't afford this."

"Simon Peter believes he can; bless his heart. You need to see what's inside the cover."

She opened it, then Rudy read the inscription silently. *My god.* Tears welled in the corners of his eyes.

Mildred spoke to him softly. "Rudolph, read it so all of 'em can hear."

"Okay, Gramma."

"To a bright young guy with a story in his eye, from your Uncle Si."

ACKNOWLEDGEMENTS

This is the 48th publication by Legacy Book Press, LLC, specialists in personal fiction and stirring memoirs. Author, founder, and president of **LBP,** Jodie Toohey, is an author's editor: supportive, patient, knowledgeable, and dedicated to her chosen projects, striving for readers who will be moved by the authors' stories.

To Carlos Prado (Yakima, WA. artist), who created the authentic painting of Western Yellowjackets, which was incorporated into the striking cover design by LBP designer/graphic artist, Kaitlea Toohey. See an image of the original art by Carlos on his Instagram: unlimited_art_chp

To Kathleen Winet, Micah Winetsky, and Latke Winetsky, who provided comfort, time, humor, silence, and other support when it was most needed. Micah also supplied regular technical assistance.

Most influential in the development of the manuscript was editor and novelist, Peter Gelfan (*Monkey Temple*). Robert Sarg (sic) Winet's encouragement and his recollections of 1946 Los Angeles were vital to the story. To Melinda Winet, who provided steady support for the novel, its publicity, and the author. Content advisor and very first reader was Ona Maria Winet. Dr. Ryan Craft and Dr. William Cox reviewed for accuracy the medical material in After the Wasps, particularly those practices portrayed in1946 and 1977. Other supporters and first or regular readers: Eyva Dawn Winet, Kevin McNew, Joy Colleen Winet, Gene Gade (Author, *The Fearing Time*), Esperanza Lemos, Michael Price, Catherine Long, Miguel L. García, Jim Moon, Randy and Ryan Winet, Jeff Kokita, and the Penells, Duke, and Kimberly.

In memorium: Sol and Mary Winet, Anna, George, and Guy Thomas. Joe and Dora Winetsky, Ona Jackson, Jesús Lemos and Jesús Lemos Jr., Marvin Paul Nelson, Carl Kleinschmitt (*M*A*S*H*), Barbara Prout Dixon, Julia Wheaton, Cliff Claycomb, Clifford Winet, Macho, Fiera, and Ernie Winet.

Terry

AFTER THE WASPS ATTRIBUTIONS

Flood in the Desert – Documentary. *American Experience*, PBS, 2022.

Greek Theater History, (lagreektheater.com, 2022).

In Over Their Heads, article by Hadley Mears, *Curbed* Los Angeles (lacurbed.com), 2019.

Neuritis Occurring After Insect Stings, N.P. Goldstein, et al, 1960, JAMA.

Of Mice and Men, John Steinbeck, novella, ©1937, Covict/Friede. Bantam Edition, 1977 (Use of brief references and three very short phrases.).

The History of Atwater Village, article, 1995, Atwater Village Chamber of Commerce (atwatervillagechamber.com).

The Infamous Detention Facility in Griffith Park, article, 7/9/21. Friends of Griffith Park (friendsofgriffithpark.org).

The Warmth of Other Suns. Elizabeth Wilkerson. Vintage Books, 2010.

Timeline of Peptic Ulcer Disease and H-Pylori, Wikipedia, 2022.

Vision or Villainy - Origins of the Owens Valley…Water Controversy. Abraham Hoffman. Texas A&M University Press, 1981.

World Book Encyclopedia, 1980, World Book, Inc.

World Series, 1977. Information Please Almanac, 1978.

ABOUT THE AUTHOR

Born in Los Angeles, Terry Winetsky took his B.A. in Speech Arts at The University of Arizona, then an M. Ed in Language Arts from the University of Washington. He is a life-long learner who taught English and/or Spanish to students of all ages in Los Angeles, Mexico, the Southwest, Washington State, Puerto Rico, and Alaska. He authored several funded proposals for federal grants in Migrant, Bilingual, and Special Education. His five novels are literary fiction, all with historical overtones. He is a retired Bilingual Education specialist in Yakima, Washington, where he now volunteers for adult farmworkers. Terry and his spouse have four adult offspring. *After the Wasps* is a clean break from the educational settings of his first four novels, which were published separately, then re-published into *The American Teachers Series*. The four books, including e-books, have sold about 4,500 copies over fifteen years—mostly face-to-face, about 10% online. Information on the stand-alone novels or the series can be found at his website, www. tlwinetsky.com, Amazon, or Pen-L.com.

ALSO BY T. LLOYD WINETSKY

Historical Fiction:

-GREY PINE (Chaos in the 1980 downwind ashfall from Mt. St. Helens)

*-LOS ANGELES, 1968, HAPPY RANCH TO WATTS (A fledgling
teacher takes on histories and volatile events in his school.)*

Personal Fiction:

*-MARIA JUANA'S GIFT (In 1976, a teaching couple fights to save their
baby from malpractice on the U.S./Mexico border. A fictionalized memoir.)*

Young Adult Fiction:

-BELAGANA-BELAZANA, An Outsider's Quest in the Navajo Nation

*The four stand-alone novels above (The American Teachers Series) are
available, one or all, from www.Pen-L.com, www.tlwinetsky.com, and
Amazon.*

www.ingramcontent.com/pod-product-compliance
Lightning Source LLC
Chambersburg PA
CBHW020123310726
48970CB00006B/1702